OLDEST KIND
OF MAGIC

ANN MACELA

Jewel Imprint: Amethyst
Medallion Press, Inc.
Florida, USA

Dedication:

To Paul, my husband, inspiration, and real-life soul mate. We met at a Halloween party as a witch and a wizard and somebody's spell worked.

Published 2005 by Medallion Press, Inc.
225 Seabreeze Ave.
Palm Beach, FL 33480

The MEDALLION PRESS LOGO
is a registered tradmark of Medallion Press, Inc.

If you purchased this book without a cover, you should be aware that this book is stolen property. It was reported as "unsold and destroyed" to the publisher, and neither the author nor the publisher has received any payment from this "stripped book."

Copyright © 2005 by Ann Macela
Cover Illustration by James Tampa

All rights reserved. No part of this book may be reproduced or transmitted in any form or by any electronic or mechanical means, including photocopying, recording, or by any information storage and retrieval system, without written permission of the publisher, except where permitted by law.

Printed in the United States of America

Library of Congress Cataloging-in-Publication Data

Macela, Ann.
 The oldest kind of magic / Ann Macela.
  p. cm.
 ISBN 1-932815-43-0
 I. Title.
 PS3613.A2718O43 2005
 813'.6--dc22

2005019793

ACKNOWLEDGEMENTS:

Many thanks to my critique group, Mary Jane, Victoria, Laura, Sherry, Rita, Noirin, and Jan; to Paula, always ready to read a troublesome scene; to Helen, my friend since we were four years old and who has read my stories from the beginning; to Connie, Laraine, Elaine, and Barb, my sisters-in-law, and nieces Megan and Caryn, all of whom were kind enough to read it at various stages of creation and without whom, this would not be as good as it is. And to Windy City Romance Writers for all of their support.

Prologue

Black. Windless. Soundless. Odorless. Empty.

Not cold, not hot. Not hard, not soft.

Definitely not "just right."

Where was she?

In a cave? A huge building without any windows? Another plane of existence?

Apprehension stiffened her backbone as a wave of malevolence swept over her.

Someone or something threatened. Was she in danger? Was someone else?

Who threatened? Where was it?

She'd cast *lux*, that's what she'd do. A ball of light would be of great benefit in this situation.

"*Lux!*" she said, clapping her hands.

Nothing happened.

"*Lux!*" This time she snapped her fingers.

Same result.

What was the matter with her? Why couldn't she cast a simple spell?

Oh, that's right. She had never been able to spell anything except herself.

What was she going to do? The threat grew stronger.

The blackness around her faded to a pale monochromatic hue.

She could see! She could see . . .

Nothing—just a dim grayness.

She brought her hands up in front of her eyes. At least she could see her fingers wiggling.

She looked forward, then back. The expanse yawned in all directions. She still couldn't make out any walls, any edges to the space.

She revolved in a slow arc.

As she reached the three-quarter point in her revolution, a long elevated stage materialized in the middle distance, and she walked toward it over a gray stone floor. She knew she was walking, she could feel her muscles moving and her feet striking the surface, but her footsteps were silent.

As she got closer to the structure, some human figures appeared on the stage. A ramp grew out of the raised platform and the people walked down it toward her.

She felt the menace intensify as the figures came closer. Cold fear washed through her body, tried to overcome her. She refused to give into it. She could defend herself.

Someone appeared at her side. A man. Tall with blue eyes, he looked down at her and smiled. He was not there to hurt her, she knew, she felt it in her bones. He was there to help.

The intimidating figures changed from human to monsters and were almost upon them. She could see their gleaming fangs and scent their noxious, dead-fish odor.

She had to do something. Who did these creatures think they were, fooling around with her? Hot anger drove out the fear; she gathered every little bit of magic in her and cast the most powerful spells she could devise.

Lightning cracked, thunder rolled, fire flashed. A roar vibrated the air, and the ground shook.

Nothing changed.

The creatures still advanced, clawed hands now reaching for her and her companion.

She cast again and again, until she was exhausted.

It did no good.

The blue-eyed man beside her did nothing. Evidently, he was having the same problems she was.

The beasts were upon them. She could see their crazed yellow eyes, smell their foul breath, sense their vile hatred.

She could feel their sharp claws, and she jerked away from them, frantically fighting the amorphous shroud they had thrown over her.

"No, no!" she screamed, but her voice sounded only like a whimper.

She opened her eyes and stared straight into a yellow-eyed face with long sharp fangs.

"Mrrrow?" her male cat asked as he pushed at her arm with his paw. His claw was caught in her nightshirt.

"Yaahh?" asked the female from her other side.

"Oh, for heaven's sake," Daria groaned as the tension drained from her body and her muscles went limp with relief. After a long moment to let her heartbeat return to normal, she stirred. "Okay, I'm awake," she told the cats, disentangling herself from the sheet and the claw.

She reclined on her pillow for a moment. What a dream.

Threatening monsters, a black cave, a man, and she couldn't cast a spell to save them. She ran her hands through her hair and rubbed her scalp.

Where had all that come from? What was going on in her subconscious to cause such a dream?

The job, probably. Something about this last client was bothering her and appearing in her dreams. Only a few more days and it would be over. Thank God. Did she ever need a vacation.

"Come on," she told the cats as she climbed out of bed. "Let's get some breakfast."

By the time she reached the kitchen, she was in control of herself again and couldn't for the life of her remember what the dream had been about. But the memory of the blue, blue eyes of the man who had stood beside her lingered for a much longer time.

Chapter One

"If you have a soulmate, you won't be a virgin anymore."

"Mother!" Daria Morgan felt her face flush. Her virgin state was none of her mother's business. "What does that have to do with anything?"

Had she missed something in their conversation? Over cups of dark oolong tea in the kitchen at the family herb farm and plant nursery in central Texas, she and her mother had been talking about Daria's recent consulting jobs and how tired she was from all the spells she'd been casting. Then her mother had brought up Daria's "casting difficulty" and made that outrageous statement. With a gnawing feeling of vague trepidation, she stared at her mother across the table.

"Daria, dear, you know I love all my children equally, but I've always held a special place in my heart for you," Antonia said. "When your father and I first thought you couldn't cast a single spell, we were so worried. When we discovered you couldn't even spell a family member for healing or defense, something every other practitioner can do, we almost panicked. We were so happy and relieved when we learned you were able to cast spells on yourself."

"I know, Mother. I was too, but I still don't get the connection." Daria took a sip of tea. Usually her mother came right to the point. What was the deal today? And what was with her altogether too-satisfied smile?

"When you find your soulmate, your 'first mating' will probably enhance your magic talents. When we mated, your father and I both became able to reach higher levels. You may be able to cast the most basic spells like *lux* and *flamma*. You might even gain the ability to enchant people or things. Think how wonderful that would be." With a look on her face like she had just imparted a secret of the universe, Antonia picked up the rose-covered teapot and poured more tea into Daria's favorite mug, the one with pink-flowered ginger plants on it.

Daria's thoughts whirled just as her spoon did while she stirred honey into the brew. She didn't comprehend this "first mating" business, so she addressed the subject she understood. "Mother, I don't have a problem," she protested. "Why do I need to cast a ball of light or to ignite a candle with a spell? There's nothing wrong with a flashlight if I need to see in the dark.

"Besides, once I discovered other people perceived me according to the enchantment I put on myself, I certainly found a way to make my talents work to my advantage. I'll admit, a little more power would be helpful for my casting stamina, but what do you mean about this 'soulmate' and what does my virginity have to do with it?"

With a distinct expression of resignation, Antonia took a sip of tea and gazed at Daria. "I should have known you wouldn't remember about soulmates. Your sister didn't either when I talked with her last week. After all, we told all three of you about them years ago, when you became teenagers, and none of you listened to us, you least of all. You were always concentrated on your studies and didn't pay any attention to boys. I know some of that was typical virgin witch behavior, but you never did any of the normal teenage daydreaming about boys or your wedding or the man you would marry."

Daria frowned and searched her memories. What *had* her mother said when she delivered the talk about being a practitioner woman to her and Glori? Her brain contained only hazy impressions. "I remember the term, but I thought the idea was just a lot of hocus-pocus legend or a happily-ever-after fairy tale. I still do. What brought this up now?"

"Mother Higgins came by last week and mentioned she had had some dreams lately about you and Gloriana and Clay. She thinks all of you will find your soulmates soon, you especially," Antonia answered with a pleased look on her face.

Daria closed her eyes, trying to think. All three of them? Her brother and sister too? Mother Higgins had been busy. Daria had always liked the venerable witch, even if some thought she was bossy and hard to take. Daria opened her eyes to gaze directly at her mother. "What could she be talking about? And what is a hundred-and-two-year-old woman like her doing meddling in my business? For that matter, what are *you* doing?"

"Now, Daria. She's only ninety-eight, and going strong. She's not meddling, she just wants y'all to be prepared. And so do I. I know this is embarrassing to you and I wouldn't ordinarily interfere, but it needs to be said. You know your father and I just want you to be happy, don't you?"

Daria nodded and sighed. "I know, Mother. I guess you'd better explain again. I don't remember anything about gaining powers, just something along the lines of 'someday my prince will come,' and I shouldn't get 'mixed up' with any boy or man until then. I thought it was the usual 'stay away from the opposite sex' talk that all parents gave teenagers."

"We weren't worried about you and Gloriana and boys. The soulmate imperative determines our destiny and our spouses."

"Wait a minute, Mother. '*Imperative?*' I know you didn't use the word 'imperative.' I'd have remembered that."

"I think I said 'phenomenon.' It's the usual term. Some experts thought if you said 'imperative' to a young woman, she would automatically disbelieve you, or go right out and do the opposite. And for a female practitioner to ignore the imperative would be a disaster."

Daria waved aside the idea of catastrophe as she concentrated on the business about destiny. "Okay, so it's an imperative. This whatever-you-call-it gives us soulmates."

"Nobody knows exactly how it does that, but we do find each other. Look at your father and me. Look at your aunts and uncles. I did expect you to find your mate before now, however. You're thirty, you know."

"What does that have to do with anything? I'm getting confused. Let's go back to your original statement about ability enhancement. Why does it take a soulmate? If the key to gaining ability is losing my virginity, suppose I just take a man to bed and have done with it?"

"It doesn't work like that," her mother answered matter-of-factly. "The imperative won't let you even look at another man, much less get close to him. That's why you've never had a steady boyfriend. That's why you're still a virgin.

"Your first mating *will be* and *must be* with your soulmate. That's the *imperative* part of the phenomenon. The fact that the mating enhances powers and might, in your specific case, solve your casting problems is simply a marvelous side effect." She smiled as though she was bestowing a wonderful gift.

"My soulmate." Daria struggled to speak the words in a flat tone while she really felt like spitting them out like a nasty-tasting medicine. She glanced around the cheerful kitchen, noting the budding hanging plants, baskets of fragrant dried herbs, maple-topped counters, and white, glass-doored cabinets. The apple pie baking in the oven added its own tantalizing smells to the atmosphere. Everything seemed normal, but she felt like her mother's comments had transported her to an alternate universe. Well, she wasn't going to tolerate this nonsense. She didn't have the time or the inclination.

"Look, Mother," she said. "This is the twenty-first century. I'm a grown woman. Don't I get any say in this? I'm happy with my life just the way it is."

She scowled at the notion. "*Imperative*? Talk about a loaded word! It reeks of coercion. Well, I don't give into threats or intimidation. I haven't in my consulting work and I won't in this. I refuse to hand over control of my life to some ancient whatever. The whole thing sounds so . . . so . . . primitive, so medieval. Or like an arranged marriage. Or out of an old legend. Or a really bad movie. Where is the element of free will? Are we both trapped? Do I have any say at all in this decision of a mate?"

Her mother shook her head. "I should have known you'd resist the idea. You've always been so thoroughly modern, so totally independent. But you're worrying over nothing. You'll see." Antonia patted her hand again and gave her a big smile. "And think how much fun it will be to have children."

"Great," Daria muttered. She hadn't even met the man and she was already having kids. She studied her mother carefully. She must be undergoing some sort of menopausal fit, Daria decided. An urge to have grandchildren had suddenly turned her into a lunatic.

"So, let me see if I have this straight." She raised her hand to count off the points on her fingers. "I'm to find this mysterious 'soulmate,' jump into bed with him to lose my virginity in the hopes of enhancing my power to cast spells, marry—before or after the virginity thing—and live happily ever after, having oodles of children, with this perfect stranger who is somewhere in the world right now, blissfully ignorant of all these plans but who will materialize at any moment, at least according to Mother Higgins?" She ran out of air by the end of the sentence and had to inhale deeply as she waited for her mother's reply.

"Just be on the lookout," Antonia said with a definite complacent tone.

Daria shook her head and, put her elbows on the table, ran her hands through her hair, and then massaged her temples. She could feel a doozy of a headache coming on. "Mother, I can't handle this right now. All I feel is trapped in an extremely weird situation. How am I supposed to rest with all this soulmate stuff storming around in my brain? It'll be a wonder if I get any sleep at all."

"You'll do fine, dear," Antonia answered. "Let me put a couple of extra spices and herbs in your hot chocolate before bedtime. I'll have a little peaceful sleep spell ready too."

"Yes, Mother." What else could she say?

Bent, you need that woman, John Benthausen thought silently to himself as he focused on the financials laid out on the mahogany conference table in his Galleria-area office in Houston on Thursday afternoon. He stacked several pages together and frowned across the table at the head of his Finance Department. "Theo, expenses are still not coming down as they should. Joe Glennell sent me down here eight weeks ago with the strict instruction to contain costs, and we should have seen more improvement by now."

"I had all my managers scouring the books, Bent," Theo Wall assured him. The Finance vice president was a fiftyish, thin, average-sized, balding man with heavy black-rimmed glasses resting on his angular nose. Bent thought he looked like the quintessential bean counter. Theo pushed the glasses up and fiddled with his pencil. "None of them can find any other expenses to cut. Revenues will pick up, but it will take a while. What do you want to do in the meantime, sell some of the former president's paintings for some quick cash?"

"Yeah, the man certainly didn't care about overhead, did he?" Bent glanced around his overly plush office. The southwestern landscapes on the wall weren't bad art; they had simply cost too much, especially for a company oozing red ink from its ledgers. "But no sale. Any money we'd realize would be just a drop in the bucket. And you're right about the difficulty of cutting more. We've already reformed our manufacturing procedures and streamlined or reorganized our departments. The new projects to reduce inventory and overhaul the product line are well underway."

"Perhaps we should further reduce the workforce," Wall suggested.

"No, we're done with that. I think we cleaned out the deadwood enough for now." Or he hoped they had. Layoffs and firings were always hard on morale, even when you were cutting out the employees clearly incompetent or not needed. Bent rose to gaze out the large windows and contemplated his situation while he rocked back and forth on his heels with his hands in his pockets. The conclusion he had come to minutes before seemed even more relevant now. "I believe we do have some other kind of people problem. It's the only explanation left."

Wall looked confused and opened his mouth to say something, but Bent cut him off. He knew he wasn't going to find any answers with Theo. The man was adequate in the Finance vice president position, but he hadn't shown much vision—not so far, anyhow. "I've looked at all the numbers I want to for today. It's almost six o'clock. I'll see you tomorrow at the staff meeting."

"I'll ask my managers for ideas again. Maybe one of them will have a brainstorm." Theo gathered his papers and left.

Bent remained at the window, staring out at the illuminated downtown skyline. Damn, he had certainly taken over a rat's nest when Joe Glennell sent him down to Texas to assume control of the Glennell Companies' latest possession. Of all the businesses he had turned around for Joe, this one looked like it would be the hardest. Nobody, including the heads of Distribution, Manufacturing and now Finance, had been able to explain why expenses remained so high. That he himself could not discover the problems was infuriating.

All right. Apply logic, he ordered himself. What could he conclude from the evidence? All the reports said the proper procedures were in place. What was left? His employees. They must not be doing their jobs properly or efficiently. He therefore had a personnel problem. But which individuals and why were they not working to capacity? What was the best way to answer the question of staff productivity? He'd initiate a study of how the employees worked and how management operated.

Who was best for the job? Certainly nobody in the

company could be objective. He needed outside help. This consultant Harry Scrowcroft had recommended. Harry had pushed hiring her, even set up a meeting with one of her clients, Stanley Kramer, CEO of BallCorp.

Bent remembered exactly what the stout, gray-haired executive had told him over lunch at a downtown restaurant. "Bent, I gotta tell you, Daria Morgan works magic. I don't know how she does it, she just talks to people, then she takes apart your staff and analyzes their abilities and interactions right down to their toenails. Said one of my managers was as good as 'poisoning' his people. I replaced him and productivity went up five percent in that area in a week. And another five the week after that."

Kramer had squinted and looked around as if to make sure nobody was listening to them. Then he had leaned closer to Bent and whispered, "She was the one who tipped off Mort Rydecker about the embezzlers in his finance department. Don't mention it when you talk to her, though. She's downplaying the whole situation. Said she doesn't want people to think she's always looking for crooks or they won't talk to her in the first place. I'm not suggesting you have that kind of trouble, but you can bet she'll get to the source of your problems."

Now Bent just had to get the woman on the phone. His executive assistant had been trying for three days to reach the consultant, but Ms. Morgan had not returned the messages.

Bent rubbed his hands over his face, then stretched. He should call it a day, head back to the hotel, make use of the health club, have a drink. He needed to start looking for an apartment or condo; if the last eight weeks were any indication, making the old Triangle firm into a Glennell Company would not be quick. Besides, he was tired of living in a hotel.

He needed a place where he could kick back, relax, put his feet up, not have to worry about total strangers, even if they were only from Housekeeping, wandering through his place, his home. Home. He hadn't thought of having one of those for years. Home was wherever he was, wherever the next company needed his expertise.

Turning back to the view, he contemplated the city where he found himself now. When he left it, Chicago had been in the dead of winter. Houston was green, just bursting with spring, and it was only March. Flowers were blooming, especially those . . . what were they? Oh, yeah, azaleas. Spring, he mused, when a young man's fancy . . .

Turned to what? Love? He laughed out loud at the thought.

Man, where had that idea come from? He didn't even believe in such a sappy sentiment. Not anymore. Life had taught him he wasn't a commitment kind of guy, and he'd learned that lesson well. Twice, as a matter of fact.

His body must be telling him it could use some female companionship.

A vague feeling of unease, or maybe just restlessness, or more probably horniness, washed over him. He shook it off impatiently. His body would just have to wait. He didn't have time for that right now. Finding a girlfriend should be the last thing on his mind.

Bent started to gather his papers together when his eye fell on his assistant's note about this Morgan woman's failure to call. He reached for his phone with an urgent sense of anticipation. Maybe he'd have better luck than Janet. What kind of consultant didn't return a call to a prospective client?

Rubbing an itching spot at the end of his breastbone, he punched in the numbers with the hand holding the phone.

Thursday evening Daria walked toward the nursery greenhouses with her sister. It was the first time since her arrival that she and Glori had had the time to get together alone. "How's life as the youngest associate professor in the botany department at the University of Texas?" she asked.

"Fine," Gloriana answered, then laughed. "Since I seem to have this 'magical' ability to win grants, everybody loves me—everybody who is not jealous, of course."

Daria chuckled and glanced over at her sister. Glori may have been two years younger than she, but she was three inches taller. The two of them really did look like their mother: same black hair, same green eyes, same fair complexions. Gloriana's hair was much longer than her own cap of dark curls, and Daria had never understood why her sister put up with the maintenance and hassles it necessitated. But they'd had that discussion before, and neither could ever convince the other to change styles. She followed Glori through a door into a large space filled with potted plants.

The sight of the geraniums, petunias, and azaleas already blooming in profusion, even without the help of any spells, stopped her in admiration. Pink, red, white, purple, and other colors combined with the scent of rich soil and growing plants to stir her memory and give her a feeling of deep peace. A Texas spring was ancient magic and needed little aid from humans, even those with the talents of her mother and sister.

"My goodness," she said. "Every time I come in here and smell the flowers, I'm transported back to childhood when we were all helping Mother with seedlings."

"I remember all too well. You and Clay always liked the specialty herb houses, and Mother and I were all about the flowers," Gloriana replied.

"There was something about all those herbs growing for exotic culinary masterpieces or possibly equally exotic potions."

"Besides, you liked to nibble parsley," Gloriana chided.

"That too." She lifted a delicate red petunia blossom to look into its heart. The flower seemed to have no weight at all. "Glori, did Mother talk to you about . . ."

"Soulmates?" Gloriana nodded her head.

"Please, don't say the word. I can't get the term out of my head."

"When she wants us to remember something, she always repeats it so many times it becomes engraved into our skulls," Glori reminded her. "I'm sick of it too."

Daria groaned. "We have to think of something else to

call it."

"Well, anyway, she told me last week. Isn't it something?"

"I felt like one of the hanging baskets had fallen on my head. I think the whole concept is awful. I, for one, don't need anything like a 'phenomenon' to deal with now."

"Yeah, it's pretty stunning. But it does explain why neither of us has ever had much interest in the opposite sex. All the male practitioners we meet become buddies, and the non-practitioners, well . . ."

"The less said about them the better," Daria agreed. "They either don't see you as a person, or they resent your professional success, or all they want to do is have sex. Once I had to throw a whole battery of revulsion spells on myself to fend off a guy who wouldn't take no for an answer."

"I'd liked to have seen that."

"No, you wouldn't. He threw up. It probably took him days to clean his car."

Gloriana laughed. "You know, as I look back, Mother and Daddy never made a secret of their being 'that term.' Neither did any other older practitioner couples we know. They just didn't talk about it. Took it for granted, I guess. Or maybe the imperative makes us oblivious until the guy shows up."

"I guess. You know, just the name of this 'whatever' rankles, especially the 'imperative' part," Daria said. She couldn't help scowling at an innocent petunia. "It makes me feel helpless, like I'm trapped in the middle of some primitive curse, or like I used to feel when I was trying to spell objects or other people. It was so frustrating, not having the control over my world the way everybody else did."

She stopped and put her fists on her hips. "I just realized why this 'X' makes me so mad. I worked long and hard to find my talent, to feel good about myself, to know I was a bona fide practitioner and not a freak. Not some cuckoo bird left by someone in the Morgan family nest.

"And now to find out having sex with a man might solve all my so-called spell-casting 'problems?' I feel insulted. I refuse to believe all my hard work was for nothing, not needed, of no value. What do I need a man for? I'm just fine as I am."

"Of course you are," Glori agreed. "And so am I."

"Exactly," Daria said with a sharp nod of her head.

They entered another room in the greenhouse, this one full of ferns of all description. To calm herself down, she made herself look around and breathe in the humid air. "I see the rainforest is coming along nicely."

"Tomorrow I'll show you what the search team brought back from the real jungle," Gloriana said. "They found a new species of exquisite orchid."

"Good," Daria said and frowned. Her relaxation technique and the greenhouse atmosphere didn't seem to be working; she'd have to talk this mess out with Glori, the way they'd always done, to get it out of her system. "I guess I assumed I would eventually meet another practitioner, fall in love and marry. Now, if Mother is correct, a warlock will show up and sweep me off my feet. If the imperative holds true, I'll have no defenses whatsoever. I'll be participating in my own seduction."

"Yuck," Gloriana said.

Their wanderings took them into a room of herbs, and Daria ruffled the peppermint plants as she passed by, paused to inhale their heady fragrance, and plucked a leaf to nibble. She'd always found mint a cheerful taste. Not this time, she concluded morosely as the notion of an "X" took control of her mind once again. "Why did this all have to happen now?"

"So what are you going to do about the situation? I'm going to ignore it and deal with it if and when it happens. Otherwise, I'll never get any work done," Gloriana stated.

"Well, if a 'whatever' is to be my fate, and that's a big 'if,' he hasn't shown up yet. I don't know a single warlock to whom I'm attracted. I'm not expecting to meet anybody new, either." Daria paused, considered the situation for a moment, and said, "You know, the more I think about it, I'm not sure I even believe in the thing, as a concept or as fact."

Making the statement out loud seemed to clarify and crystallize her thinking. Several ideas came together in her head, and she turned to Gloriana. "Let's be logical and rational for a minute. We're both highly educated women. Let's see if this theory can be proved or disproved. For all we know, a large number of practitioners in the past were simply very good, or very lucky, at picking compatible spouses. Maybe the ability to perform magic acted as a common bond, maybe not. For whatever reason, happy marriages came to be seen as the norm or, more important, as the desired end. Then, over the centuries, the idea was translated, transmuted, and developed into this legend."

"That sounds exceedingly plausible," Gloriana said, leaning against one of the tables. "If I remember correctly from my sociology classes, myths usually serve to explain the customs and institutions of people. Society was better off if couples were happy, productive, and contributing. If nobody ever talked about unhappy marriages, or simply ignored them—after all, divorce in the modern sense is fairly new—then the notion that all practitioners were happy with their mates became reality in their minds. In addition, the idea of, uh, 'X' sets practitioners apart and gives them something else to be proud of."

Daria felt herself warming to the topic. "Hence, the notion becomes a phenomenon, then dogma, true and indisputable and is given the designation, 'imperative.' " She paused and ran the argument through her mind again. "That makes much more sense to me than the idea this 'thing' exists as an independent entity."

"Thinking like a scientist for a moment," Gloriana added, "the phenomenon doesn't make much mathematical or statistical sense, either. The laws of probability must be standing on their heads at the idea that every practitioner *always* finds his or her 'X.' "

"Then this business of enhanced powers on mating becomes something else entirely, probably part of the maturation process." Daria smiled. She liked the way this discussion was going.

"I don't know..." Gloriana said with a skeptical look on her face. "But you're probably right. In ancient times, people married at a much younger age. Gaining powers could be part of the hormonal changes of puberty, I guess."

"Well, I've had about as much of this whatever-it-is as I can take." Daria put her hands on her hips and assumed a belligerent stance. "I don't think this so-called imperative actually exists. I won't believe it until I see it with my own eyes.

"Furthermore, I refuse to let some ancient witch's tale dictate my life. I'm going ahead with my own plans and I *will* control my own future. My presumed 'person,'" she made a nasty face as she said the word, "can just go jump in the Gulf of Mexico. What do I need him for anyway? It's going to take a very powerful warlock to convince me otherwise.

"Now, having said that," she concluded with a grim smile, "I'm going to take a tip from Scarlett O'Hara and think about it later. Much later."

Gloriana gave her a hug. "Sounds like a good plan to me."

Daria hugged her back and resolutely changed the subject to Glori's argument with some old fuddy-duddy mathematician about the "proper" way to cast spells.

As they walked back to the house, however, she started rubbing the center spot at the end of her breastbone beneath which her magic energy resided. It had developed a small itch.

Chapter Two

Daria returned to Houston the following Saturday and pulled her car into the garage with a feeling of relief. As much as she loved her parents, as much as she needed the rest the farm provided, she had grown used to being on her own and relished the solitude her home provided.

As much solitude you could have with two mouthy cats, she thought as she opened the door to their complaints of her being gone. "Hi, you two," she said and knelt to give them each a rub. "Did Clay take good care of you? I brought back some catnip for you."

"Mrrrow!" and "Yaaahhh!" were her answers.

"Just a minute and we'll play," she told them as she rose and went back to the garage to unload the car—two suitcases, three sacks of fresh herbs and vegetables, and a pot of her mother's chicken soup. She stowed the food and took the suitcases up to her bedroom.

"I don't feel like unpacking now," she told her constant companions as she placed the luggage on her bed. "Let's check our messages. I'll bet there's a bunch of them. Mother wouldn't let me do anything connected with business while I was at the farm."

She went downstairs and into her home office. When she saw the pile of mail on her desk and the answering machine blinking rapidly, she couldn't help groaning. "Might as well get this over with," she muttered, reaching for a pen and paper. She punched the replay button.

It wasn't too bad; only three were from telemarketers. Two former clients wanted to discuss follow-up consultations, and three prospective ones asked her to call. A couple of her friends wanted to get together, including Tom Wisemore.

"Hi, Daria, it's Tom." She could hear the smile in his sexy baritone—or what he probably hoped was a sexy baritone. It had always sounded put-on to her. Daria made a face at the machine. Tom was a perfectly nice man, but perfect for someone else, not her. He wanted to go out, of course. She pushed the delete button. She knew he'd call back, and she'd turn him down again. He wasn't a practitioner and certainly wasn't her "X." She liked him as a person but felt nothing along the lines her mother had described. Hmmmm. Maybe she'd introduce him to a friend of hers. She knew just the woman.

"Oh, Daria, are you reduced to matchmaking?" she asked herself out loud, laughing at the prospect. "Just call me 'Mother Daria!' " she told the cats as they blinked at her from their positions lounging on the sofa. From the looks on their faces, they clearly thought she had gone crazy, and she laughed again, taking time to give them both a scratch behind the ears before playing the next message.

Five calls, in fact one a day, came from the same source.

"Ms. Morgan, this is Janet Adams calling for Mr. Benthausen of the Glennell Companies. He is interested in discussing your consulting services. Because of the situation here at Glennell-Houston, Mr. Benthausen would like to speak with you as soon as possible. Please call him back at . . ." Janet Adams gave the number and said good-bye. There were two more like this.

On Thursday, a different voice, this one a genuinely sexy baritone, came over the line, and a shiver ran down her spine at his first words. "Ms. Morgan, this is John Benthausen of the Glennell Companies. Harry Scrowcroft said you might be able to help us. As you may know, Glennell bought the Triangle firm and I've recently taken over as CEO. Quite frankly, the place is a mess and we could use your kind of expertise. Please call me back as soon as you can." He gave the number again and hung up.

On Friday, there he was again. "Ms. Morgan, this is John Benthausen again. Are you even in town? I really need to talk with you." He sounded more frazzled and a little bit angry. Well, as a species, CEOs were used to having their own way—immediately. This one was just going to have to be disappointed, even if Harry Scrowcroft and his wife were some of her family's dearest friends and Harry happened to be on the Glennell board of directors.

She dialed the number and, when his voice mail answered, said, "Mr. Benthausen, this is Daria Morgan. I have been out of town and unable to return your calls. I am not accepting any clients for the next three months. I appreciate your considering my services, but it is impossible for me to take on a client at this time. If I can help you in three months, please don't hesitate to call. Thank you again for considering me." She hung up and hoped the issue was resolved.

She made a mental note to talk to Harry Scrowcroft about his referral. She hadn't seen him lately, so he probably didn't know she didn't need or want any new business.

As luck would have it, Natalie, Harry's wife, telephoned that evening. "Why don't you come for dinner next Friday evening? Mattie has some new recipes she'd like to try."

"Adventurous eating? You bet I'll come!" The Scrowcroft cook was famous for her innovative and delicious meals, using, of course, Morgan herbs and spices. "I'd love to see you too. We have some catching up to do. How are you and Harry these days? He's certainly mentioning my name to everybody he encounters," she said, thinking about the call from Benthausen.

"You know how he loves to help and wants you to succeed, even though we know he can be a little overzealous. But he means well."

"Yes, and we all love him dearly, even if we could throttle him at times."

Natalie laughed. "Come at 6:30, and we'll have a drink before dinner."

"I'll be there." Daria said good-bye and thought about what she would say to Harry when she saw him. She hated to turn away business, but she had to think of herself once in a while. The Scrowcrofts weren't practitioners, so they wouldn't understand her exhaustion completely, but she thought she could make her point stick by enlisting Natalie's help.

By the next Friday, after a week of quiet visits with her friends, some housecleaning to give her a feeling of accomplishment, and hours more of sleep, Daria found herself looking forward to dinner. Thank goodness Harry and Natalie didn't go in for formality, she thought, putting on a hot-pink-and-white shirtwaist dress and hot pink sandals. She certainly didn't want to wear anything from her business wardrobe. At 6:35, she was walking in the lovely River Oaks garden and happily chatting with Natalie, a thin silver-haired matron.

It was a wonderful spring evening, just cool enough but not so much to require a sweater, and the large estate in one of Houston's most exclusive and elegant neighborhoods seemed an island of calm in a hectic world, far removed from the bustling city around it. The new leaves on the live oaks displayed a vivid chartreuse against the early evening sky, and the azalea bushes proudly exhibited their deep red or brilliantly white flowers. Still almost dormant, the wisteria vines and crape myrtles were beginning to reveal the blooms that would mature in the summer heat. A fountain played over to the side, as a mockingbird came to take a drink and whistle at the women, intruders in his domain.

Daria took a deep breath and a little sip of her white wine and smiled to herself. This was just what she needed—good friends, good food and wine, and no worries.

The first order of business was coming up to date on the five Scrowcroft children, their families, and the various Morgans. Natalie proudly showed off the pictures of the latest addition to the list of grandchildren. Daria made the appropriate, requisite noises.

Harry, who had gone inside to answer the phone, was walking out the veranda door of the Greek Revival-style house to rejoin the women when he stopped in the doorway and turned back. "I hear the doorbell," he called to them. "That's our other guest. We'll be right out to join you."

"I didn't know someone else would be eating with us," Daria remarked to Natalie.

"Didn't I mention it? Harry asked the CEO for one of those companies where Harry's on the board. He said the man was new in town and needed some home cooking. Now, don't look at me that way," she said to Daria's frown. "He knows how you feel about being matched up with someone."

"But he never gives up," Daria muttered under her breath.

Daria could hear him greeting someone and receiving an answer. She watched Harry come out onto the veranda talking with a tall well-built man, casually dressed in nicely tailored slacks and a light plaid sports shirt. The fellow's slim, rangy physique and thick red-brown hair made quite a contrast to his host's rotundity and thinning white top. Somehow the man's voice sounded familiar to Daria, but she knew she had never seen him before.

"Ladies, come over here," Harry called. "I want you to meet someone." When the two women reached the veranda,

Harry said, "This is my wife Natalie." The fellow shook hands with her and turned to Daria. "And this is Daria Morgan. Ladies, this is John Benthausen, and he likes to be called 'Bent.'"

Daria had already put her hand out and Bent held it in his before the name registered with her. Startled, she stared into his eyes and felt herself tumble down a deep blue well. The electric shock that raced through her entire system from his touch didn't help her equilibrium either, but it simultaneously seemed to warm her from the inside out. When he put his other hand on top of the one he was holding, Daria felt every cell in her body twitch, especially a spot just under the end of her breastbone. But swift anger at Harry's machinations allowed her to break the eye lock with Bent, and she swiveled her head to skewer the older man with a look.

"Harry, you know I'm not taking any clients right now. Are you trying to ambush me to do otherwise?" She kept her voice calm and said the words with a smile, somehow, despite what Bent's touch was doing to her. She couldn't let Harry get away with this . . . this matchmaking, even if it was of the corporate variety. Harry needed to learn once and for all that he couldn't go around trying to manipulate her, good intentions or not.

"Now, Daria," Harry said, "this is not a setup, in any manner. We wanted to see you, and Bent didn't even know you would be here. Did you, Bent?" He didn't let the other man answer, but hurried on. "We'll set a rule right now, no talking about business, all right? Neither of us will even mention Glennell. This was just an innocent chance to see an old friend and make a new one, I swear." He made an X over his heart, held up his hand as if he were taking an oath, and looked down at Daria with a hopeful expression on his face.

Daria frowned at Harry, then looked questioningly at Natalie.

"Harry, shame on you!" Natalie said. "You know how tired Daria's been after working so hard with no vacation."

Daria raised her eyes to Bent's and felt the tug of that blue again.

"I didn't know you would be here either," he gently murmured.

"No," Daria sighed and surrendered. "I'll give you the benefit of the doubt this time, Harry," she told the older man somewhat resignedly with a quick teasing glance at him. Shifting her eyes back to Bent's, she said, "I'm pleased to meet you, Mr. Benthausen. May I have my hand back?" She wiggled her fingers, still caught in his grasp.

"Only if you call me Bent," he answered with a grin, releasing her hand.

"Thank you, Bent," she said, proud of herself for calming her breathing. Now if she could just slow down the triphammer of her heart, she wouldn't make a fool of herself. What was the sensation that hit her so hard? Why did she feel like a bolt of lightning had zapped her?

"Come on over to the bar, Bent," Harry said. "We have time for one drink before dinner."

Bent followed his host as he worked on controlling his

reaction to meeting Daria. He almost wished the Scrowcrofts weren't there. He wouldn't mind at all having her to himself and exploring the scorching effects of the fire he'd seen in her green eyes and the surge of, of what—attraction, desire, sheer lust?—that had run through his body at her touch.

Whatever it was had locked his eyes with those emerald green flames and hit his body like a thunderclap. He could understand her consternation at finding him there, especially after the somewhat curt message she had left him. Now that he had met her, however, he wanted to get to know her better—much better, whether or not she went to work for him. He wryly reminded himself of his recent thoughts about womanly companionship. The situation was definitely looking up now. He watched Daria's dark curls bounce as she nodded her head to something Natalie said, and he smiled to himself.

As Harry served the drink, he said in a hoarse whisper, "I'm sorry, Bent. Don't take Daria's reaction personally. She's been working too hard and badly needs this vacation she's on. Just ran herself right into the ground. I didn't know her situation when I recommended her to you. And she has a legitimate gripe against me. I may have tried to manipulate a few things in the past." Shrugging, Harry had the grace to look chagrined, but only slightly.

"Don't worry about it, Harry." Bent sipped his drink as he watched the two women chatting. She was just a little bit of a thing, five-foot-two or -three, a foot shorter than he was. Her exhaustion was no pretense. Now that he looked at her closely, he could see it in her overly pale skin and the faint shadows under her eyes.

Lord knew, he certainly needed some help with what he was trying to do at Glennell, but it didn't matter right now. Daria attracted him immediately, and he felt his body stir as he looked at her. Harry had said she was on vacation. All right. Every vacation needs a fling, and why couldn't he be hers? It would solve his companionship problem for the duration of his stay in Houston, and both of them would have some fun. Of that he was certain.

When the men joined the women, Bent complimented Natalie on the garden and she led them on a tour until Mattie called them to dinner.

The foursome sauntered back to the house and were soon sitting at the dinner table. Light from the crystal chandelier glittered off sterling silver and fine china while savory smells wafted in from the kitchen.

Mattie gave Daria a hug before beginning to serve. "I made some Creole chicken and your favorite dessert tonight," the elderly cook assured her. "Looks like we need to put some meat on your bones." Daria just grinned and hugged her back.

At the table conversation was sporadic at first as everyone gave Mattie's food the attention it deserved. Daria did feel little twinges of something—unease, excitement, anticipation?—when Bent looked at her intently from across the table. Too often and too intently, she thought, wishing it wasn't unladylike to scratch the persistent itch on her breastbone that had started during the garden tour. She ignored it as best she could and concentrated on answering Natalie's questions about her family's latest doings. "Mother and Gloriana are coming next week to put in my new garden. They have a pond and waterfall idea this year."

"This year?" Bent inquired, gazing over his wineglass at her.

"Mother and Gloriana have an herb farm and plant nursery close to LaGrange and Smithville over by Austin. They tear up my yard every other year trying out new hybrids. I'm their experimental urban home for the nursery." She held up her hands in a what-can-I-do way and turned back to Natalie. "They've even coerced Clay into helping this year, and you know how he claims he put in his garden time as a teenager. He'd still spend all his waking hours in front of a computer if he could."

"Wait a minute. Clay Morgan, the computer consultant? He's your brother?" Bent asked. "And that means Alaric is your father?"

"Yes. Do you know either of them?"

"I used Clay's help in the last company we purchased. He's a wizard with those computers. Saved us several million dollars cleaning up some poorly designed and sloppily installed systems. Doesn't your father do something with accounting, financials, audits, and the like?"

"That's right, Bent," Harry interjected. "I forgot to mention the rest of the family. Daria, Clay, and Alaric are all consultants of one sort or another. I believe Alaric is semi-retired these days. What's he up to, Daria?"

"If he's semi-retired, you wouldn't know it. In addition to helping longtime clients and teaching auditing classes for a few accounting firms, he's telling my mother how to run her business and driving her crazy. He wants her to sell over the Internet, but she's resisting." She grinned at Harry. "You know how she is, perfectly happy with a small business. From what she and Gloriana say, however, they're going to have to expand. The demand from customers just keeps on growing."

"Where's your family, Bent?" Natalie asked.

"They're scattered all over, one sister on the West Coast and my brother and other sister on the East. My parents are deceased."

"You're not married?"

"No." Bent took a sip of his wine and shrugged, "I travel too much to settle down."

Daria glanced up at him at his answer and quickly down at her plate again as she felt her analytical consulting skills awaken. The manner in which he had clipped off the end of the "no" and the tone in which he added his comment contradicted the nonchalance of his shrug and the simplicity of his explanation. She had the distinct feeling there was more to this story. But she was not working now, she reminded herself, and the Scrowcroft house was no place to be casting spells to wheedle the truth out of another guest.

Over the rich raspberry-and-chocolate cake dessert, Daria watched him out of the corner of her eye. Once Natalie had finished grilling him, the awkward questioning revolving around "Who are you?" and "Who's your family?" had relaxed into true conversation. Bent had proved to have an easy charm, laughing with Harry about another board member's financial notions, complimenting Natalie on her latest grandchild, teasing Daria about her self-acknowledged cravings for Mattie's desserts.

He was handsome in a rugged sort of way, with his broad shoulders and trim body. The personification of a CEO, straight out of one of the ads for expensive executive gadgets, he certainly had the determined square jaw and piercing gaze of a fictional corporate leader. Not to mention a thick layer of charisma. His smile had probably melted many a woman's heart, and those blue eyes . . . Yes, those blue eyes sent a sensual message impossible to ignore. She told herself she *had* to ignore it, she didn't have time for a man now. Rest, she needed rest.

After coffee and dessert, Daria pleaded exhaustion and made her good-byes, hoping to leave before Bent, but he rose also, offering to escort her to her car. As they went down the walk in the cool spring night, Daria could sense him beside her, feel his warmth, almost smell him, even though he did not crowd or touch her. She sighed, partly from the effect he was having on her and partly from weariness.

"Anything wrong?" Bent asked, as he opened her car door for her.

She turned to him, facing him across the door. "No, not really. Look, I'm truly sorry I can't help you with your company. I'm just . . ."

He interrupted. "No, you have nothing to apologize for. I didn't realize how exhausting the last year has been for you. Even I know the necessity of taking time off and manage to actually do it once in a while."

"There's one thing I can tell you, however," she said somewhat hesitantly. He raised his eyebrows and she continued. "I have to preface this with all sorts of caveats, and it breaks several of my own rules to do it, and I don't know exactly why I'm offering the information . . ." Good grief, she was babbling. What was wrong with her? She never babbled. She certainly never gave away the type of information she was about to tell him. But something inside her made her want to help him, and this was the only way she could. She gripped the car door tightly to steady herself.

"But?"

"Once upon a time, the head of security at one of my clients was comparing his operations to those of some other local companies. He intimated that the security operation at what is now Glennell-Houston is highly questionable, and he came close to accusing its chief of dishonesty outright, but he had no real proof.

"Ordinarily, I would not be repeating this, but I know for a fact, this man has enormous integrity and massive honesty. He wouldn't have said anything if the operation had been fine or even marginal. He talked as though the entire security group was crooked, not just the top people, and said he wouldn't hire any of them himself. You may want to take a closer look if the man in charge has been there for a while and if parts or anything have been mysteriously disappearing. And please, do not take what I've told you as fact or take any action without strong proof. This may be nothing more than petty gossip."

His expression grim, Bent stared at her as he rocked back and forth on his heels with his hands in his pockets. "What rules of your own are you breaking?" he finally asked.

She ticked them off on her fingers. "Never share unsubstantiated gossip and rumors. Never give away information for free. Always come to know the person you are reporting to well enough to trust him or her or turn the job down." She realized she felt uncomfortable standing so close to him and tried to step back slightly, only to be stopped by the car frame.

He leaned on the car door, placing his face at her level and looking her in the eyes. Even under the dim street light, his blue eyes seemed to pull her in. "Do you trust me, Daria?" His voice was low and the deep baritone reverberated inside her.

Almost falling into those indigo pools, she gazed at him for a long moment, trying to use every sense short of a spell to test him. Her magic center tingled slightly, and she took that as an omen. "In this, yes," she said simply, even if she could not have told him precisely why.

"Thank you. I'll guard the source of this information completely. I know just the man to help me prove the possibility of dishonesty, one way or another." He straightened, came around the door to stand even closer. "Let me take you out to dinner tomorrow as thanks for the information."

"Thank you, but no." She smiled to lessen the rejection and was surprised at her own regret at the refusal.

"How about Sunday?"

"No, Bent, when I said I was going to rest, I meant it. Besides, I don't need thanks. Consider it a welcome-to-Houston gift." She smiled again and sat in the driver's seat of her car, swinging her legs under the steering wheel. She started the engine, then rolled down her window.

He shut the door for her and, bending down to her level, said through the open window, "I'm not going to give up, you know. Both corporately and socially, I'm coming after you."

She wasn't about to respond to his comment, so she said only, "Good night, Bent."

"Good night, Daria."

She gave him one last look and drove away with his statement about coming after her ringing in her ears. She felt both exhilarated and fearful. And slightly frustrated. She had a faint recollection of having seen his eyes before, but where?

Idly rubbing the itch in the middle of his chest, Bent watched her drive away, and he walked to his own car as he plotted his campaign on two levels, personal and business.

First, he had enough experience with women to know she was attracted to him also. Her slight nervousness, the sidelong looks when she thought he wasn't looking were clear indications. Chemistry between a man and a woman was great, and who was he to ignore it? For once a stay in this strange town might be fun.

He'd wanted to touch her tonight, but had managed to keep his hands off. It was too soon. They'd just met. But, man, it had been difficult to put his hands back in his pockets when they were literally itching to feel if her skin was as soft as it looked.

How would she taste? She had looked good enough to eat in her hot pink and white dress, like a raspberry sundae, sweet and tart and creamy all at the same time, her dark hair like a tantalizing chocolate accent. She'd smelled good too, sort of spicy, kind of tasty. He couldn't help licking his lips in anticipation.

He'd give her some time to rest and then make a move. Personally, he wanted her in his bed. More on first sight, he realized suddenly, than any other woman he had ever met. He didn't think there was another man in her life, or Harry would have included him in the dinner or said something. His way to her was clear.

Second was his corporate campaign. What she had told him about his security was prime, disturbing information. Problems in that department could explain the alarming parts inventory numbers and the dollars spent on equipment maintenance. If what she said were true, she had just saved him untold amounts of time and money.

As for luring her into his corporate clutches, clearing up the security matter would give him an excuse to talk to her again, not that he needed one, but she had to be curious about the outcome of her tale. He had not been totally surprised to hear the news as it fit in with his own theories, especially with his idea that he had a people problem, not a procedural one. Now it appeared Glennell-Houston was in much worse shape than he or any of the corporate bigwigs back at national headquarters thought.

He'd call Dan Roth in New York about the matter tomorrow after he looked at his local security manager's personnel file. For once his standard request for the personnel files of all senior managers was paying off for something besides general background; he could study it without alerting anyone to his intentions.

At the same time, however, he sure would like some help assessing his senior and mid-level managers—help of the kind Daria could provide. Maybe he could convince her to work with him by explaining what he had found and challenging her on a professional basis. Maybe he could talk her into something part time. He'd have to think about that, he decided as he turned into the parking garage at his hotel.

Daria drove home down Kirby Road and found herself at her house off Sunset Boulevard by Rice University before she knew it. As she punched the button to open the garage door, she realized she had been on automatic pilot, her mind . . . her mind was right on a pair of vivid blue eyes, a ruggedly handsome face, and a sheer force of personality that was staggering.

A strange little sense of recognition, of having known him from somewhere nibbled at her brain although she knew she had never met him in her life. Neither had she ever before felt such attraction to a man. It's just all that intensity and masculinity in one gorgeous package. Charisma, self-confidence, leadership, and purpose. No wonder Harry had said Bent was known as the man who could turn even the worst company around.

He hadn't touched her again after their handshake, and she wondered what it would be like if he did, or held her in his arms, or . . .

Whoa, woman. Don't go there.

But he did say he was coming after her, didn't he? What did he mean? "Well, what do you think he means, dummy?" she asked aloud as she let herself through the kitchen door and greeted the cats.

For all of her thirty years, she had never let any man get even close to the idea of changing her virginal state. Bent might be different, she mused, and when the memory of him holding her hand tingled in her fingertips, the enormity of her reaction struck her.

Oh, no. Oh, no, no, no. What was she thinking? How was she reacting? Was what Mother Higgins had dreamed coming true? Could this man be her soulmate?

The idea stopped her so suddenly as she walked through the kitchen that both cats almost bumped into her.

Certainly not, she thought, adamantly rejecting the very

idea. Impossible. Old witch's tale. Besides, she'd already decided that soulmates didn't exist, had no validity, were a figment of collective imagination.

Furthermore, this man couldn't be "X." He wasn't a practitioner. True, it wasn't always obvious. Practitioners didn't have a secret handshake or glow in the dark or anything so ridiculous. She'd been surprised both ways in the past, thinking someone was when he wasn't and vice versa. At least it would be simple to find out. She'd just look him up.

She detoured into her office and fired up her computer. Once on the Internet, she went to the practitioner's Web site, typed in her passwords and activated the little "spell program" her brother had installed to allow her to most effortlessly enter the site. She clicked on the "Practitioner Registry" button and typed his name in the query fields.

No "John Benthausen," with or without a middle initial. None. Anywhere in the world. Ever.

Whew. He wasn't a practitioner. Therefore, he couldn't be her, her "whatever." She could relax. She shut down the computer, turned off the lights, and went upstairs.

The legend couldn't and didn't apply to her, despite what Mother Higgins had said, Daria thought as she walked into her bedroom. This must be just a case of lust or overactive hormones as her body reminded her she wasn't getting any younger. Undoubtedly it was the latter, she told herself as she got ready for bed.

"I don't want a soulmate, I don't need a soulmate, I won't be dictated to by the past or some moldy old legend," she told her image in the bathroom mirror as she shook her toothbrush at herself.

"And I won't go looking for a man, even if it means enhanced powers. So, there," she concluded with a sharp nod of her head. She put away her toothbrush and toothpaste and went promptly to bed.

But she didn't sleep very well, especially after Bent and his stunning blue eyes showed up in her dreams. She woke the next morning with a small itch in the middle of her chest and a vague sense of trying to get somewhere, find someone.

Chapter Three

By the following Thursday afternoon, Daria was convinced Bent had forgotten all about her. Since Saturday, she had spent more time than she cared to contemplate wondering if he would call and then telling herself it didn't matter that he hadn't and furthermore, she didn't want him to. He couldn't be her soulmate and she didn't want to deal with a non-practitioner, no matter how attractive.

All her protestations didn't seem to make her any happier, she discovered. But she had enough to worry about without him, including a pesky itch at the end of her sternum driving her crazy.

Although she usually screened her calls, she was standing right by the phone in the kitchen when it rang and she picked it up automatically. She recognized his voice immediately. It was definitely a sexy baritone, and she couldn't stop the shivers running down her.

"I just thought I'd call to see how you were and tell you your warning last Saturday night is turning out to be true," Bent said after identifying himself.

"I'm sorry to hear that. I know it would have been easier for you if the rumors were false." She had to struggle to keep her voice even. Why was she breathless? Why had her heart picked up its beat? She'd been perfectly fine before she answered the phone.

"Are you getting some rest? What's the noise? I can hear heavy machinery."

"I was until yesterday when Mother and Gloriana arrived." She spoke louder to be heard over the whine of the concrete mixer. "They're pouring the base for the pond and waterfall." She looked out the window to distract herself from the effect he was having on her.

"I'd like to see your garden soon," he said.

"That would be nice," she answered and focused her concentration on the workmen in the yard. "Bent, I have to go. The crew is about to take down a dead tree, and I need to be there. Thanks for calling. Bye."

She hung up just as she felt a hard thump vibrate her body. Was it the tree or had her heart just kicked her in the chest?

Saturday, about eleven o'clock in the morning, Bent pulled up to Daria's house. Her "that would be nice" on the phone wasn't exactly an invitation, but it was close enough for him. He climbed out of the car and surveyed Daria's property for a moment.

Large oak trees graced the street and framed the building, a brick two-story set to one side of a double lot. A garden, many of its beds vacant, filled the remainder of the property. The immediate impression was of an established house, one settled comfortably into its neighborhood. It was a home.

But it was also a house with serious protection in the

form of a tall wrought-iron fence. The fence had spikes—very pointy spikes with a weird greenish cast on the tips. When the gate was closed, the fence definitely said, "Keep out." Protecting the garden's privacy, thick, flower-laden azalea bushes lined the fence and a bougainvillea vine climbed along its streetside wall. Today, however, the front gate was wide open in welcome, and the sound of a chainsaw reverberated from the back of the property. He could hear women's voices coming from the garden side of the house.

Bent walked up the front walk and around to the side. The smell of rich earth and green plants permeated the air.

Two women with plant pots and trowels in their hands were talking and waving the implements toward various parts of the planting area, evidently discussing the placement of each item. They turned to Bent as he approached, and the elder one asked, "Can I help you?" just as Daria came around the corner with a flat of petunias in her hands.

"Bent!" she said. Then she frowned. "I didn't expect you."

"Hi, Daria. I was in the neighborhood and came by to see your progress." He was happy to see she looked less exhausted today. Her skin had a healthier glow, and the shadows under her eyes were almost gone. He smiled at her and turned to the other two women who advanced to meet him. The family resemblance of black hair, porcelain skin, and green eyes was striking. "You must be Daria's mother and sister. I'm Bent Benthausen. It's a pleasure to meet you."

"My mother Antonia and sister Gloriana," Daria said as the two pulled off their gloves and shook Bent's hand.

Antonia looked straight into his eyes and smiled a great, big, wonderful smile that charmed him instantaneously. "Welcome to the Morgan experimental garden."

"Oh, good! Fresh blood!" a tall, black-haired man with a chainsaw in his hand exclaimed as he came around the corner, and Bent recognized Daria's brother. "Bent, what are you doing here?" Clay Morgan asked. "How the hell are you? Say, if you're not busy, I could use some help with this tree stump."

"Clay!" Daria scolded. "Bent just dropped by to see how we were doing, not to work."

"I've given myself a day off and have nothing to do," Bent stated with a grin as he shook Clay's hand. He'd been hoping for an opportunity to stay, and Clay had just handed him one. "What do you need? Do you have another pair of gloves?"

"Sure thing. This way." He gestured with the chainsaw and the two men walked around the side of the house.

"But . . ." Daria sputtered as she watched them go. Oh, Lord. Now her mother and sister and brother would get their clutches on him. She had said nothing to the family about Bent. From the look on her mother's face, Daria realized Antonia suspected something was up. Antonia was delighted to meet the man Daria had neglected to mention.

Damn the man! What was he doing here and why had her heartbeat increased dramatically—again? How could he look so good in old, tight jeans and a Chicago Bulls T-shirt that showed off his muscular build? Not muscle-bound, but rangy, with broad shoulders and . . . oh, puh-lease, get hold of yourself. She plastered a smile on her face and turned to meet her mother's and sister's intense interest in the newcomer.

"Daria! Is he the one you met at the Scrowcrofts?" Gloriana said. "What a hunk!"

"How did you know?" She had not mentioned even so much as an additional guest being there, just relayed their best wishes and family news.

"I talked to Natalie," Antonia answered calmly. "We want the petunias over there as a border," she told Daria, pointing to a flower bed.

"Yes, Mother." Daria gave up. It was impossible to have a private life in her family.

Daria had lunch laid out on the kitchen counters when the gardening party entered. The women went toward the powder room. Clay and Bent hurried to wash up at the kitchen sink.

"Help yourselves to the food," Daria said as she filled glasses with ice.

"This looks good," Clay said, as he eyed the spread of lunch meats, sandwich fixings, and potato salad on the counter. He popped a chip into his mouth. "I've really worked up an appetite. What's to drink?"

"Beer, Coke, Diet Coke, iced tea, water, milk," Daria recited. "What's your pleasure?"

"Tea," Bent answered, slapping two pieces of rye bread on a plate.

"Coke," Clay said, building himself a multi-layered Dagwood concoction. "The real stuff, not the diet kind."

Daria served the drinks and everyone brought their

filled plates to the large kitchen table. Nobody talked as they attacked the food. Daria wished they would not talk at all, but she knew her family would use the opportunity to quiz Bent. She frowned at her sandwich as she braced herself for the ordeal.

Bent finished off his potato salad and looked around the large kitchen. Lots of white cabinets, maple butcher-block counters, hanging baskets with flowers and herbs, a working kitchen. He felt completely at home in it.

From the looks they'd been giving him, he also knew Daria's family would not put off their inquisition of him much longer, so he might as well start the conversation. "From what I could see, you all have really been changing the garden layout. When I talked to Daria on Thursday, she said you were just beginning. I didn't expect you to have the waterfall and pond practically finished by now," he said.

"Hard work and a little magic," Clay answered. "Mother, we've almost excavated that old tree trunk and its roots and should have the bed ready before long. Couldn't have done it without Bent. I told you I needed help."

"Bent, we really appreciate your helping," Daria offered.

"I'm glad I dropped by. It's great to be outside on a spring day. I've been cooped up in that office too long."

"How are things going at Glennell-Houston?" Clay asked. "Rumors about Triangle were flying and few of them were good. You must have your work cut out for you."

"I do, but the place is still not running the way I'd like it to. That's one of the reasons I'm trying to get your sister to help us, but so far, no luck." He turned to Daria. "Maybe we can work a deal, a little yard work for some consulting?"

"Sorry, Bent. The cost-benefit ratio is not in my favor."

"I'll have to come up with a better offer, then," he answered with a knowing wink.

Daria shot him an exasperated glance, but did not answer him. Instead she turned to her mother. "What are we going to put in place of the tree?"

"I'm not sure. I need to see the space without the tree. We may have to bring something from the nursery."

"Just how big is your operation?" Bent asked.

"We have about two thousand acres all told, but not all of it is nursery," Antonia said. "We also have a few horses for family use. You'll have to come out to the nursery soon. It sounds like you could use some rest from all these corporate problems and there's no place like it for relaxation."

"Sounds good," Bent said, looking at Daria as he did so. He grinned when he caught her rolling her eyes. "Will you give me a tour when we visit, Daria?"

"Mother is the best one for that," she said, rising to begin clearing the table. "I'll take care of the dishes. Y'all handle the plants."

"Slave driver," Clay said as he rose. "Come on, Bent. No rest for the working man."

Daria watched the two men go out the door before she carried the dishes to the sink. She braced herself as she waited to hear what her mother and sister would have to say about Bent.

"Now, see, dear, that wasn't so bad," Antonia said after

the door closed.

"What do you mean?"

"I told Gloriana that we weren't going to interrogate the man and to keep her questions to herself."

"Thank you."

"But I have to tell you . . ."

"Daria braced for the next words.

"I think that's *him*," Antonia finished.

Despite being prepared, Daria almost dropped the plate she was rinsing. She had not expected those exact words. *Him*? What a leap of conjecture for her mother to make after spending all of thirty minutes with the man. And trust her to bring up the one subject Daria didn't want to discuss. "Him?" she asked, hoping she sounded like she had no idea what her mother was referring to, but knowing fake innocence had never worked in the past.

"What him?" Gloriana asked, glancing from one to the other, her eyebrows raised. Then she nodded. "Oh, *him*!"

"Go plant your posies, Glori," Daria retorted. "Mother, just leave it alone! Please!"

"All right, dear, but I'm here if you want to talk," Antonia said with a pat on Daria's shoulder and followed Glori out the door.

As her confusion, dismay, and undeniable excitement came to the surface, Daria leaned against the counter in front of the sink and closed her eyes.

How could Bent be *him*? He wasn't a practitioner.

But if he wasn't *him*, why was she reacting like such an

idiot? So happy to see the man, she felt like she was glowing from within? So pleased he had come to her house that she could swear she was floating? Something didn't make sense here. She had never in her life acted like such a twit. It had to be her thirty-year-old hormones, her biological clock.

Now, before she could sort out her feelings, here was her mother claiming Bent was her soulmate. How could she be so certain? Didn't she know Bent couldn't be?

The question had barely formed in her mind when she felt a sharp little pain in the middle of her chest, right in her magic center. What did it mean? Was her center trying to tell her something? Was it a yes or a no?

What was she going to do about him? She was still adamantly opposed to the idea of an ancient legend dictating her life, determining how or with whom she lived. Wasn't she?

Bent couldn't possibly be her . . . she didn't even want to think of the dreaded term. She had to curb her response to him. It would be difficult, she acknowledged, because he was so darn attractive, and she felt a little zing in her middle when she simply looked at him. But she had to resist him. What had her mother said, something about disaster befalling a witch who went to a man who wasn't *it*?

Damn! She was so confused. She felt ambushed all of a sudden, and all she could do was fall back on the child's cry: "This is not fair!"

At four o'clock, Bent announced he needed to leave, pleading dinner with a couple of his vice presidents and their wives. After saying good-bye to the family, he turned to Daria. "Come with me while I wash up. I'd like to tell you the results of our last conversation."

She followed him into the kitchen. No matter what he was, she had to know what he had done with her information, and after planting the petunias, she had herself in control again.

"You were right. A large part of the entire security department was crooked in one way or another," he said as he lathered his hands at the kitchen sink. "We marched in with a complete new squad of guards and replaced everyone Friday morning just as the morning shift was starting. When we took over the manager's and his deputies' offices, we found incriminating evidence. They were so confident, they didn't even bother to hide it."

He rinsed off his hands and turned off the water. Drying his hands on the towel Daria handed him, he continued, "It looks like they had a special garbage collection unit also, because at the plants in Baytown and Sugarland cartons of new merchandise and maintenance parts in the trash bins would have been picked up on Saturday. We expect to find people in other departments who took part in the scam. The merchandise had to be pulled out of the warehouses and then placed in the trash, and it couldn't have been done by security men alone."

"I'm sorry my information proved correct. How many

people were involved?"

"About half the security staff, but we have no numbers on the rest. Our corporate security and the police are sorting it out. Some indictments will come out of this."

He finished drying his hands and, putting an arm around her shoulders like he had a right to, began walking them out into the front hall. She couldn't stop the shiver that ran down her spine, but his touch felt so good. She'd make a fool of herself if she jerked away from him; the hall wasn't too long a walk to endure the small embrace—or so she told herself despite an answering sneer, "Yeah, right," in the back of her mind.

"I really do owe you for alerting me to the possible problem," he said. "To thank you properly, let me take you to dinner tomorrow after the family leaves."

They reached the front door and Daria stepped out from under his arm and opened it. "There are no thanks or payment necessary, Bent. I don't operate that way." Despite the extra space between them now, she could still feel his warmth and smell his scent, a mixture of earth, sweat, soap, and himself, and she could feel his pull as though he were a star she was hurtling toward, down his gravity well. Resist him, she ordered herself. He can't be *it*.

He was gazing at her intently again, leaning down toward her, almost in kissing range, and she felt her heartbeat speed up. Surely he wouldn't . . . Did she want him to . . .

Before she could decide what to do, he abruptly straightened up and looked around, into the living room, down the hall, out the door.

"What's the matter?" she asked.

"I just had the funniest feeling we were being watched." Bent continued to search for the source that had sent a prickle of alarm up his backbone. He twisted around again, but found nothing to account for his reaction.

"We are," Daria laughed, waving at the stairs.

Bent looked up and saw on the landing two cats. A slender, dainty, reddish female sat primly upright, tail curled around her feet, looking for all the world like an Egyptian statue. She seemed to be smiling. The coal-black male, a large thick-bodied panther, lounged indolently, arrogantly, flicked the tip of his tail, and stared at Bent with a look in his yellow eyes clearly stating, "Leave my woman alone."

"Zorro and Lolita," Daria said. "My watch-cats." She frowned at Zorro and told him, "Be nice," but he just yawned, displaying an impressive set of long, sharp, white teeth, and resumed his scowl at Bent.

Bent sent his own scowl back at Zorro and threw in a mental "she's mine now" message. He was not about to let a cat, even a blue monster, dictate his actions, especially where Daria was concerned. He took Daria's hand and pulled her out the door and down the walk. "How about dinner anyway?"

They stopped at the gate and Daria shook her head. "Bent, I'm going to be exhausted after they leave tomorrow. I always am, even when I'm not tired to begin with. All I will be capable of is going to sleep. But thank you anyway, and thanks for helping today."

"Okay," he said. "I'll let you get away this time, but I'll call you soon." Before he, or more importantly she, could think about it, he bent down and kissed her lips softly but swiftly. It took all his willpower not to taste her lips again, but he knew he would not want to stop if he did. So he gave her hand a squeeze and, releasing it, walked around his silver Lexus and got in. As he drove away, he could see her in the rear-view mirror watching with a hand on her lips. "That's one for my side," he congratulated himself.

He'd give her a couple of days to rest up and then see what he could do to take her out for dinner. He didn't quite understand her wariness, but there were definite moments when she was nervous. It wasn't just the nervousness women felt when they were attracted to a man, he thought, there was something else. He reviewed the day in his head, but whatever it was eluded him. Maybe she just needed to get used to him. Yeah, he'd give her more opportunities for that.

"That's it," he said aloud. "Just give her time. Don't rush. She'll come to you if you have patience." The words were hardly out of his mouth before he was flooded with an overwhelming sense of surety that this plan was the right one. Absentmindedly rubbing the itch in the middle of his chest, he grinned all the way back to his hotel.

After Daria watched Bent drive off, she returned to the garden with her lips tingling and every nerve in her body jangling. She still felt the warmth spreading from where he had rubbed her wrist with his thumb.

Her family all turned and looked at her expectantly as if

to say, "Well?"

"Not one word!" she stated between gritted teeth, and glared at each in turn. "I don't want to hear one word about Bent from anybody. Is that understood?" They all just grinned merrily at her and went back to work.

Daria spent the remainder of the afternoon ferociously planting geraniums, coleus, Dusty Miller, and marigolds while replaying every word Bent had said to her. If she shut her eyes and concentrated, she could feel, actually feel, his lips on hers. If she ran her tongue over her lips, she could almost taste him. If she . . .

Her thoughts scattered when Gloriana sprayed her with water.

"Oh, sorry," Glori said, "the hose slipped."

"It's all right," Daria said, then muttered to herself, "Probably for the best." Coming back to reality and with eyes wide open, she attacked the next bed so vigorously that her mother noticed and told her to take it easy. Daria took a deep breath and focused on the plants, but every time she let her mind wander, it shot like a boomerang right back to Bent, his eyes bluer than the sky after a Norther, all his thick hair much redder in the Texas sunlight, his muscles playing under his T-shirt, the warmth of his hand.

By day's end, Daria was a certified wreck. Why was she getting so worked up over a man who wasn't a practitioner and therefore couldn't be her supposed soulmate? What had happened to her certainty that the concept was folklore, not fact? Where was her resolve to resist?

This was no way to get any rest, she advised herself. And she had rubbed black soil into her shirt at the end of her breastbone. Why was that spot itching so much?

Chapter Four

That night, after supper, Daria looked at Antonia. "Mother, I need to talk to you. Glori, do me a favor and watch television or something, would you please? I'd really like to talk to Mother alone." Thank goodness Clay had gone to his own home and she didn't have to worry about his curiosity also. She had always been a private person, preferring to mind her own business and expecting others to keep out. It had been difficult to maintain her privacy growing up between an older brother and a younger sister, both of whom delighted in pestering her.

Gloriana grumbled, something about never knowing what was going on, but she went into the family room and turned on the TV.

Antonia sat down at the kitchen table and looked at Daria. "I thought you'd want to talk, dear. How can I help?"

"This whole soulmate situation is giving me grief, Mother."

"You have to relax, Daria. Bent is a very nice man. I really do think he's the one."

"But he's not a practitioner. I looked him up on the registry and he's not there. He can't be my soulmate, if he's not one of us." She paused, suddenly strangely fearful about what her mother would say.

"No, that's not true," Antonia replied with shake of her head, "You misunderstood me. There was a big article years ago in the *Witches and Warlocks Journal* about how more and more of us these days are finding our mates in non-practitioners. It causes absolutely no harm and does not diminish the enhancement mating confers, as far as anybody can tell. Children always inherit magic talents, even if one of their parents isn't a spell-caster, so you don't have anything to worry about in that regard either."

"Oh, great." Daria felt both exhilarated and depressed—not to mention confused—at the revelation. "Why didn't you tell me before? Where does it leave me?"

"I'm sorry, I guess I forgot. But it doesn't matter. The attraction between you and Bent is so obvious, the air almost crackles. It reminds me of your father and me. Did you notice how Bent fit right in with us? That's just like Alaric and I did with our families. And you do like him, don't you? Can't you feel it right here?" She pointed to the bottom of her breastbone.

"That's not the point." Daria rubbed her own sternum, then jerked her hand away when she realized what she was doing. She waved both hands in a negating manner and took a deep breath as she leaned against the counter by the sink. "I still refuse to concede such a thing exists, but all right, let's say for the sake of argument that he is my soulmate. He's not a magic practitioner. He has no idea I'm a witch or that my whole family are practitioners."

"You're right. I hadn't thought of that." Antonia paused, reflected. "It also means none of your spells will work on him as they do on other people. Just like family members, soulmates can't spell each other, except for healing and defense. That's how they know they're soulmates and not under some outside enchantment."

"We have to explain everything to him, Mother. *Everything*." Oh, God, what had she gotten herself into?

"We, *I* have to be honest with this man," she concluded. "I can hear us now. 'Oh, by the way, your new in-laws are all witches and warlocks. Spells 'R Us.' What are my obligations here? When do I tell him? How? If he's oblivious to my spells, I'll have an awful time convincing him on my own. He won't be able to tell I've spelled myself."

She started pacing around the kitchen table, gesturing like mad, pointing to an imaginary Bent, to herself, to the heavens.

"And since he's a non-practitioner, who knows what his reaction will be? He may not like the idea of being my soulmate one bit, of being tied to me without any say of his own. I certainly don't. What if he's one of those men who doesn't want to or can't make a commitment to a woman? Where is free will in this?

"Or once he finds out what we can do with magic, he may think you've spelled him for me! Or we're just a bunch of lunatics! Or all I want is to use him to lose my virginity in the hopes of becoming a more powerful practitioner." She ran her fingers through her hair, massaging her scalp to help herself think.

"What does that make me? The word rhymes with witch! My professional life is built on my integrity and honesty. I'd like to think my personal life is too. If Bent and I are to be together, we have to be honest with each other."

She paused. *If they were to be together?* What was she saying? "But I'm not just accepting this soulmate business, let me tell you," she backtracked.

"Where was I?" Her vehement digression had thrown her askew for a moment. "Oh yes. Anyway, no matter how I feel, I can't just throw myself in his arms, saying 'Take me, I'm yours,' without telling him *something* first. It goes against my grain." She took another turn around the table.

"But what do I tell him? 'Oh, by the way, I'm a witch and if we go to bed, I might be able to light a candle from across the room?' or 'I'm a witch and you're my soulmate and, especially if you take me to bed, we're stuck together for life,' or what?" She stopped and, breathing hard, slumped against a cabinet. "Oh, God, I'm so confused, Mother."

"Sit down, Daria. You're making me dizzy and you're obsessing over nothing," Antonia admonished calmly. Daria sat and put her head in her hands. Antonia reached across and patted her daughter's shoulder. "I agree, you have to tell him, but not necessarily all at once. You like him, don't you?"

"Yes, I guess so," Daria answered hesitantly. She was afraid she did.

"Then take some time, get to know the man and let him get to know you. Some of this will just come naturally."

"Mother, what if he wants to go to bed with me soon? I don't think I'm ready for that, but I swear I can see it in his eyes every time he looks at me." She paused to take a breath and knew she was turning a bright red. "And I have to tell you, although I can't believe I'm saying this to my mother, the attraction is already stronger than for anyone I've ever met, and he's hardly touched me. And it's going to get worse, isn't it? The mating act binds us together, doesn't it? What if I can't resist him? God, I hate this feeling of being out of control."

"Believe me, I know what you're talking about." Antonia had a fond gleam of reminiscence in her eyes. "I remember when I met your father. I had never paid any attention to men either. Then, there he was. Before we knew it, we were in b—." She cleared her throat. "Well, never mind. The point is, my mother gave me the same basic advice I'm giving you."

"But Daddy is a warlock! He knew what to expect."

"Well, yes, of course." She thought for a moment, then brightened. "I know what we'll do. Let me talk to Mother Higgins and a couple of practitioner women in mixed marriages and see what they say about telling their mates. In the meantime, as I said, take your time. Don't rush the relationship. Go out with him, do things together. Get to know each other. It'll be fun," she added with a smile.

"I have faith in your judgment," Antonia continued, "and in your ability to resist temptation, no matter how strong the provocation, until you decide what, when, and how to tell him. But you *will* feel better about this—and about Bent. You're worried over nothing. Things will happen when you're ready, not before." She smiled and patted Daria's hand. "I know this is not what you wanted to hear, but it's the best I can do."

"I understand, Mother. Thanks, I guess." She rubbed her temples to soothe her aching head. She knew intellectually the phenomenon did not, *could not* exist, but here she was, oscillating like a pendulum between two points. First she was acting like it *did* exist and worrying about being "bound together" by the mating act. Then she was denying it and thinking of throwing herself at him, no matter what the consequences. Either way, she knew she had to explain the situation. Either way, she had no control.

What was she going to do? She had no answers when the family left on Sunday, and she had no answers two days later.

Tuesday evening about six o'clock, Daria sat on her patio in one of the double chaise lounges contemplating her garden and watching the sparrows squabble at the feeders. The waterfall provided a soothing backdrop of sound as it gurgled over stones into the pond. Among the newly planted petunias, a fat robin was hunting worms while keeping one eye on the cats who shared the chaise with her. At Daria's bare feet, Lolita was tucked in, and Zorro had his forequarters in her lap and his hindquarters on the lounge pad. The big black cat's purring almost vibrated the couchlike chair. Unfortunately, this tranquility did not extend to her mind as she rehashed the weekend's activities and subsequent conversations—again, for the umpteenth time.

Daria looked around her garden and sighed. Her whirling

mind had managed to come to a few tentative theories or alternative arguments about the situation with Bent. Maybe he wasn't her mate. She was just the first eligible woman he'd met since he came to Houston, and he'd been attracted. In typical CEO fashion, he was going after what he wanted—her. After all, a couple of other men had tried the exact tactics. She'd been able to reject them easily, though. Not so with Bent.

Maybe Bent was one of those men who came on to every unattached women he met. Now there was a disturbing thought she didn't like at all. No, he wasn't a womanizer. She'd have found some evidence of it when she looked him up on the Internet and read press reports of his ability to turn companies around. There'd been no gossip columns mentioning his name, no photos of the dashing Mr. Benthausen and any princesses, corporate or otherwise.

Maybe if she had some patience, he'd simply turn out *not* to be her mate, and this attraction would all blow over. That idea caused a little empty hole to form in her chest, right in the middle next to her magic center—and her heart.

So, what was she going to do? The only course of action she could think of was passive. Sit there and see what happened. She wouldn't rush things. She'd let Bent take the initiative and come after her and hope his company kept him busy. Put off any, any, any . . . what?

Intimacy?

Well, that was certainly one word for it.

She squirmed at the thought and the emptiness in her filled with a distinct feeling of happiness that caused a shiver down her backbone. Zorro grumbled at her movements. "Sorry," she told him and rubbed behind his ears until he purred again.

All she could really do was wait for Bent to act. She certainly wasn't about to call him. What a puny plan, she derided herself, but it was all she could conjure up at the moment.

Conjure? Oh, why did she choose that word? Magic was the last thing she wanted to use, even if she could. And now here it was Tuesday. He hadn't called, and she didn't want to think about how much she hoped he would.

Good grief, she was still so mixed up, holding diametrically opposed notions at the same time. Hope he'd call versus hope he wouldn't. Have nothing to do with him versus get to know him. Adamantly proclaim repugnance with the whole soulmate concept but wish for said prospective mate's notice and company.

She was such a ninny. Why was she resisting? Out of sheer principle? Because she didn't like any nebulous, ancient, mindless compulsion telling her what to do? Or was she afraid of men in general? Certainly not of this one in particular, she scoffed.

Or was she afraid of rejection, once he discovered what she was? Who knew how a non-practitioner would react to the idea of spell-casters, much less to the soulmate news? The notion came a little too close for comfort, and the empty hole behind her breastbone yawned again. Rubbing it didn't help.

She rested her head against the back of the chaise. She'd never come to any conclusions at this rate. Her mental contortions had exhausted her to the point that all she seemed able to do was sit there with her cats, watch the birds, notice how well the plants were doing, and try to relax.

"Mmrrrrow," Zorro said softly and gave her hand a lick with his raspy tongue.

"I know, I have you and Lolita. It helps," she said, rubbing under his throat and running her foot along Lolita's side. Both cats purred. Then Zorro abruptly came alert and stared at the corner of the house.

Around it walked the object of her reflections.

"Hi," Bent said, pulling the other double chaise over beside hers and sitting down. "I came over to see how you and the garden are doing. When nobody answered the doorbell, I thought I'd see for myself."

Daria watched him make himself at home. He had shed his coat and tie and rolled up his sleeves, his thick auburn hair was ruffled like he'd been combing it with his fingers, and he looked absolutely wonderful. She couldn't help but smile and only hoped she didn't have a totally goofy expression on her face.

Despite growing up with her father and her brother in the house, Daria realized she had become unaccustomed to living around men. She seldom invited one to her house alone, preferring to keep her sanctuary to herself. But here was Bent, big as life, looking just as if he belonged there. And damned if part of her didn't agree that he did.

"We're doing fine," she answered and was proud of the steadiness of her voice, a direct opposite to her insides. "The waterfall is working perfectly."

"It's very pleasant back here," Bent said, stretching out. "Great after a hectic day at the office." He looked her up and down and she could have sworn she felt a physical caress. "You look like you've been getting some rest."

"Yes, especially after the family went home. I've done hardly anything but eat, sleep, and read." And try not to think about you, she added mentally.

Lolita stood up, stretched languorously, and hopped over to Bent's chaise. Then she walked up his crossed legs, stood on his chest, and touched noses. "Hello, Lolita," he said with a grin. "Make yourself comfortable."

The dainty cat blinked at him in a sultry manner and proceeded to make herself a home in his lap. He started to pet her and she purred, bending her head and twisting her neck to make sure he hit just the right spots.

"I seem to have made a friend," he grinned at Daria. Zorro was still glaring at him malevolently, and he grinned at the black cat too.

"You should be honored," Daria said. "She usually avoids men like the plague." In fact, Lolita usually dodged anyone who wasn't a practitioner to begin with. Now, wasn't it interesting that Lolita liked him? Daria tried not to watch his hands stroking the reddish fur. Strong, long-fingered, very masculine hands that would excite . . . uh, better to watch the birds instead.

Soulmate or not, he attracted her like crazy. In fact, maybe crazy was the operative word. She had to be going insane. She never thought about sex, and she'd thought more about it in the last few minutes than in the past two years. She had to stop this. Get her mind on other things. Start him talking about work, that was a solution, so she said the first thing that popped into her mind. "How are things at Glennell-Houston?"

Bent glanced around the garden as he spoke. "We're making progress, but slowly. Dan Roth, who's head of corporate security, has come down from New York and has our thievery problem well in hand. We're getting tips from clean employees about the dirty ones, and several have actually come up to Dan and thanked him for getting rid of the crooks. Intimidation had been keeping them quiet. As for the rest, I'm still not sure how much I can trust a couple of the senior staff." He turned to face her. "You know, I really could use your help, Daria."

"I know, Bent, but I'm just not back to one hundred percent yet. I really won't be able to do my best. I'm sorry."

"Don't apologize. I want you healthy. I'm here to make sure you're eating right. Where would you like to go for dinner? The hotel concierge recommended a place called Goode Company."

"Which one?" Either had a certain appeal, now that she thought about it. She didn't realize she had acquiesced to his invitation by her question until the words were out. His expression had implied his reasons for wanting her healthy; he looked like he wanted to make a meal of *her*.

"Which one what?"

"There are three Goode Companies—barbecue, tacqueria, and seafood."

Bent smiled like a man who knew he'd won. He lifted Lolita off his lap and put her on the foot of the chaise, then rose to sit again on the edge of Daria's lounge. Zorro scowled at Bent's intrusion and the big cat slit his yellow eyes threateningly, but Bent ignored him. "Whichever you prefer."

"Well . . ." Her mouth was already watering at the thought of fajitas.

He took her hand in both of his and raised his eyebrows. "Juicy fajitas? Guacamole? With rice and beans and a good cold beer?"

How did he know what she was thinking? Daria was lost and she knew it but she couldn't tell if it was from the effects of a sudden Mexican-food craving or from Bent's big, warm hands holding hers—and rubbing her wrist with his thumb. Her heartbeat had definitely speeded up, and she could feel warmth radiating from his touch.

Oh, what the heck. She *was* hungry, and she'd be following her mother's instructions to get to know him. "All right. I'd like that," she said, smiling.

Bent smiled back, then frowned and looked down at his own leg. Zorro had placed a large black paw on the top of his pant leg and fully extended every long needle-sharp claw. It was a potent threat. "It's just dinner, Zorro," Bent told the jealous cat.

Zorro retracted his claws, withdrew his paw, gave Bent one more glare, muttered the feline equivalent of "Humph!"

and left the chaise to stalk into the garden. The birds at the feeder fled into the trees at his approach.

"Sorry," Daria said with an apologetic smile. "He's a little possessive and very protective. If you'll give me my hand back, I'll get ready to go." She wiggled her fingers.

He released her, but not before raising her hand to his lips and kissing her fingers. Her heart fluttering, Daria quickly fled into the house to change into long jeans and put on some shoes.

Bent watched her go, admiring the swing of her hips. She'd appeared so luscious sitting there in her Houston Festival T-shirt and cutoff jeans that he wished he could scoop her up into his chaise and see if she tasted as good as she looked. She might be small, but her legs were gorgeous and seemed longer than he remembered. He could just imagine them wrapped around him, an image that had him shifting in his seat. His fingers itched as he thought how much he'd like to get them on her nice little butt.

She was still looking at him a bit warily, like she didn't quite trust him or she couldn't figure him out, but he could handle it. The challenge was invigorating. Or maybe the expression in her eyes wasn't mistrust but rather a secret. Yeah, okay, a secret. He would certainly enjoy unraveling *all* her secrets. Damn, he wanted this woman more each time he saw her. Grinning to himself, he sat back in the chaise Daria had vacated. Lolita joined him again and the two of them contemplated the garden companionably.

In a few minutes Daria called him to come through the

house so she could lock up. Bent entered through the kitchen. He hadn't really paid any attention to the house, except for the kitchen, in his previous visit; he hadn't looked into the other rooms as he went down the front hall and out the door. This time he noticed the open airiness, the comfortable furniture, the large rooms with high ceilings. There was none of the air of relentless decoration he had found in the houses and apartments of some of the single women he had known. Neither was it so feminine that a man might be uncomfortable. In fact, he felt right at home here.

Daria told him to open the front door and then she pressed a panel on the wall. It opened to reveal the buttons for a security system. She punched in the code and closed the panel. After shooing him out the door and locking it, she pressed another panel in the outside wall with the same results.

"That's some security system," he remarked.

"Thanks to my brother. Clay loves these things. He installed it, and upgrades it for me. It's a little cumbersome, requiring entry in both panels, but someone figuring out the one might not realize you have to do something to the other too." She also locked the gate behind them.

She directed him to the tacqueria, and, after ordering, they settled at an outside table with cold beers. Bent looked around at the customers eating, the children running around, and the huge, three-tiered fountain spouting water. From the highest tier, a big blackbird opportunistically eyed the tables for scraps to pilfer. "This is perfect. I can feel myself relaxing already." He drank some of his beer and gazed happily at

Daria, who had the wary look in her eyes again and who took a swig of beer like she needed it to cool off. Yeah, so did he in her presence.

Bent's name was called over the loudspeakers, and they picked up their overflowing plates and sat back down. They spent a few moments of silence wrapping flour tortillas around the succulent beef, grilled onions, and assorted fajita fixings.

After swallowing her first good bite of the delicious concoction, Daria asked, "How did you get into the turnaround business anyway? Clay said Glennell uses you to bring all new acquisitions online."

Bent thought for a minute. It had been years since anyone asked him that question, even the women in whom he'd been interested. It seemed right, however, that Daria had, and he replied, "After I received my MBA, I went to work for one of the consulting firms managing leveraged buyouts. It was exhausting work, but it paid well. After a while, though, it seemed all I was doing was moving paper around, buying this company, selling that one, breaking another in pieces, and not contributing one whit of sense to the whole process or producing a single item anybody needed. Companies were being split up, people were losing their jobs, and to what end? Just to make some rich people richer.

"About the time I started thinking about it, my mentor Ben Kasinsky and I had a long talk, and I found he was feeling the same way. When he accepted an offer to be Joe Glennell's second-in-command at Glennell Corporation, he took me with him and gave me the chance. When I turned around my first company—and it was a little bitty thing, I can tell you—I discovered I liked doing it. That's what I've been doing ever since."

"And you enjoy going from company to company, city to city? Not having a real home?" She raised her eyebrows inquiringly as she took another sip of beer.

"Yeah, I do. Each one's different, a challenge, new people, problems, experiences. Each one tests my abilities to the limit and teaches me something as well. And to run a turnaround, well, it's a tremendous high to pull one off. Then it's off to a new place. I've never wanted or needed to settle down in one place. I can't stand ruts." He blinked as the last words came out of his mouth tasting like dried tumbleweeds. He swallowed some beer, but the cold liquid helped only marginally.

Home. The word from her question lingered and ricocheted around his brain. It finally lodged somewhere in his chest, in a little vacant place he hadn't known existed and where it suddenly seemed to belong. He'd never thought about having an established home after those two fiascoes with Kerrie and Susan. His life was fine, with all the excitement of new places, new demands, new obstacles to overcome. Wasn't it?

He glanced at his companion. She was applying herself to her food, but she had a slight frown on her face. She didn't seem to like his answers, which sounded more glib to him with every passing moment. What about her made him question his lifestyle? He knew down deep he wanted this woman, every way he could get her. But did he want a *home* with Daria?

The vacant place, now filled with home, began to warm up. He took another gulp of beer to cool it off. His eyes met hers, but for the life of him, he couldn't think of what to say next.

Daria watched as he turned those dark blue eyes directly on her. What was causing them to gleam that way? He looked confused all of a sudden, but something else lurked in those depths. Whatever it was attracted her so strongly that she was surprised she couldn't see his magnetic force shining like a tractor beam from a spaceship on the science fiction shows. Okay, so she was beginning to believe what her mother had said about attraction. She was drawn to him absurdly, illogically. Inexorably?

She had to look away before he noticed her acute disappointment at his answers to her questions. He liked, even *wanted* to move from city to city. She hated relocating. Her life was here. If his former pattern prevailed, he'd be gone from Houston in six months. Where did that leave her?

Before either could say another word, a man and a woman approached their table. The man was middle-aged, balding, and a little paunchy. The woman had Texas "big hair" of a blond shade known only in a bottle and was about the same age as the man. "Bent, is that you?" the fellow asked.

Bent looked up and Daria heard him swallow a groan. He did not seem happy to see the couple.

"Yes, Dave, it's me. How are you?" Bent asked as he rose.

"Come here, honey. I want you to meet the man who's been working me so hard," the intruder said to the woman. "Bent, this is my wife, Lorene."

Bent shook hands with Lorene and introduced Daria to them. "Dave Grady is my vice president for Human Resources, Daria."

"It's nice to meet you," Daria said, shaking hands.

Grady stroked his chin and regarded her speculatively. "Daria Morgan, Daria Morgan. Aren't you the management consultant? The one who really takes apart a company's management staff? Weren't you the one who found the crooks at Rydecker's?" He encompassed the two of them with a wave. "Does this mean we're going to be seeing you at Glennell-Houston?"

"I am a management consultant, but as to anything else, I wouldn't describe my work in quite those terms," Daria replied, more than a little dismayed by Grady's referral to her "crook-catching" reputation. The last thing she wanted to be known for was catching crooks. "But I have no intention of working for Glennell-Houston in the near future," she tried to reassure him.

"Well, Bent here seems to have caught that bunch in Security, so I'm sure we have nothing to worry about any more," Grady stated confidently, but his eyes moved quickly from Bent to Daria and back again as if he wanted to be certain he was making the right impression. "Bent's doing a good job, you know, converting us to a Glennell company."

"I'm sure he is," Daria replied as she wondered silently

why Grady seemed so nervous.

Grady started to say something else, but his wife interrupted. "Dave, the kids have a table for us. Let these people eat and don't bother them any more. I'm sure Bent sees enough of you at work. It was nice to meet y'all," she said, pulling her husband away.

"Likewise," Bent returned, sitting down.

Daria laughed softly when the twosome was out of hearing range. "I don't know about Dave, but Lorene has my vote."

"I agree." He sighed. "I had hoped not to run into anybody from the company, especially not Grady. What a jackass, and he'll talk your arm off to boot. He's a gossip and everybody will know by noon tomorrow that you and I had dinner. Speculation will run rampant about your coming to work for us. Grady's not one to take a denial for an answer."

She decided to put the Gradys out of her mind. His blabbermouthing wasn't her concern. She had to concentrate on the man beside her. "Well, that doesn't bother me."

"Then it doesn't bother me either. Now, where were we?" he asked, picking up his fajita again. "Oh, yes. What about you? How did you get into your business?"

"Like you, I went the MBA and consulting firm route, doing much the same sort of work on management as I'm doing now. I couldn't stand the regimentation, though, the you-must-think-like-the-firm mentality or the stultifying office politics. I particularly detested the overwhelming ambition of some of my colleagues to work toward partnership, no matter whose back they had to climb over to get it. After one of them tried to claim my work as his, and I began to question the advice my project leaders were giving to clients, I decided to get out. Thanks to Daddy, Clay, and a few friends like Harry Scrowcroft, I had the contacts to go out on my own. I much prefer the independence."

"And it's just you, no helpers?"

"I use a market research company to help create and to tally the questionnaires when I administer full-company surveys, but the rest of it is just me. I conduct all of the face-to-face interviews by myself. My methodology requires a great deal of concentration and energy on my part and, quite frankly, it can be wearing. I shouldn't have taken the last job on the heels of the one before it, and I'm paying for it now."

Bent drank the last of his beer and leaned back. "My intentions are to see you get the rest you deserve. Now, if you're finished, I'll take you home. Much as I hate to cut our evening short, I have a briefcase full of papers to take care of this evening."

"Oh, we can't go home yet. We must have dessert. There's an Italian gelato place right down the road. What do you say to some really good ice cream?" She raised her eyebrows encouragingly.

"Lead on. Why do I think you'll have chocolate?" he teased with a grin.

At the gelato shop, Daria pointed out the liqueurs, cognacs, and coffees that were available in addition to the ice cream and sherbets. They decided that, after the fajitas, the gelato would be enough for both of them. The outside patio was full so they sat at one of the small marble-topped tables inside after they made and received their choices.

After their first bites of the creamy Italian ices, Bent said, "Harry and Natalie asked me to accompany them to a benefit gala on Saturday. I understand you're going with them too."

Just what I need, more matchmakers, Daria thought, but she kept her tone bland. "Yes. Natalie's already told me they invited you. You'll be able to meet a good slice of the business community there. These functions have always been excellent for my contact list, so be sure to bring some business cards. How's your raspberry-and-cognac-liqueur gelato?"

"It's great. Would you like a taste?" He dipped a spoonful of the icy confection and held it out, practically in front of her nose. She had no choice but to take it.

"I suppose you'd like a taste of my amaretto chocolate," she sighed after she swallowed.

He nodded, a playful little smile tweaking his lips.

She scooped up a spoonful and held it out to him. He winked at her as he leaned over and took the spoon in his mouth. She had to smile and roll her eyes, the whole thing was so corny. He rolled his eyes in return. She licked her lips and he did too. She crossed her eyes and he did too. They both started laughing at their own playful antics.

"Want some more?" he asked, tempting her with another spoonful.

"No, thank you," she replied, scraping up the last of her own dishful, then taking a long time to lick the spoon clean. Two could play the teasing game. "I'm done."

Bent's gaze was on her mouth and he had a funny look on his face as she put her dish down. He swallowed his gelato with an audible gulp and held up both hands. "Okay, I surrender," he groaned.

Daria smiled, mimicking Lolita in one of her smug moods, and handed him her cup.

After throwing their cups and spoons in the trash bin, Bent held out his hand. "Come on, let's go home." He held her hand all the way to the car.

When they returned to her house, Bent escorted her up the walk, a hand on the small of her back. She could feel the warmth of him spreading through her body from that single point, and some of her wariness came back. What had she been doing, playing flirty games? Encouraging him, for sure—but it had felt so good. She entered the security codes outside, opened the door, turned on the hall light, and completed the process inside the front hall.

"Would you like a nightcap or a cup of coffee?" She put her purse on the hall table and turned to Bent.

"Thank you, but I have to decline. I have too much work still to do tonight. There is one thing, however . . ." He moved close to her and tipped her chin up with one hand while the other grasped her waist. "A good-night kiss," he finished, lowering his mouth to hers.

Daria went stiff for a moment, but only a moment. His lips were soft, caressing hers. His tongue slowly traced the seam of her lips, asking entrance entreatingly. His hand stole around her neck to its nape and his fingers slid into her dark curls.

He was persuasive, he was enticing, he was expert, he was seductive. She couldn't help it, she had to do it, she opened her mouth and let him in. He used his hand on her neck to tilt her head for his better access and fit his mouth more thoroughly to hers.

She had expected more aggression, but he remained gentle, tantalizingly gentle, entering her mouth to touch her tongue with his and then withdrawing, coaxing hers to follow. Daria followed, she could do no less, and a delicate duel brought them deeper, exploring, tasting, tangling. She melted as his large hand on her waist moved to her back and drew her into him.

"He's so warm," was her first thought as heat tore through her body, spreading from every place he touched her. "He feels so good," was her second as she wrapped one arm around his back and the other around his neck, running her fingers through his thick hair and over his taut back muscles. "More," was her last coherent thought as she molded herself to his hard, lean body. She could feel her breasts swell and her core ache. She whimpered and rolled her hips to press directly onto his hardening erection.

Bent heard the whimper and felt the roll and groaned in response as he spread his legs slightly, lowered his hands to her hips, and pulled her up and even closer. She felt so good, so right in his arms, just where she was supposed to be. A fleeting question formed in his mind: "Why is that?" But he dismissed it to concentrate on the present matter, Daria and their kiss.

Something important was going on here, he knew. The attraction between them was the strongest he had ever felt for a woman. He knew also from the way she kissed him back she felt it as much as he did. There was hunger here, and desire, and a satisfying feeling of being fulfilled, as though they existed just for each other.

By the time they mutually ended the kiss, both were breathing hard. Entwined in each other's arms, they stood there for a moment, foreheads together, catching their breath. Bent finally straightened, hugged her to him, then stepped back and slid his hands down her arms to capture her hands. When she raised her eyes to his, he knew he could see green flames of passion, not anger or regret, blazing in their depths.

"If we don't stop now, I won't be able to," he murmured. "You won't get any rest, and I won't get any work done."

He watched her come back to herself, blinking as if she wasn't sure what had just happened. She licked her lips, took a deep breath, and said softly, "Thank you for a lovely evening." She paused as if listening to herself and shrugged. Her mouth twisted wryly. "That was an inane comment, wasn't it?"

Bent laughed and pulled her back in for another hug. "I'm at a loss for words too, honey." He gave her a quick, hard kiss, released her, and walked to the door. "Lock up. I'll call you tomorrow." He stepped out, closing the door behind him.

"Yes!" he said to himself as he went through the gate. When he was about to climb into the car, he looked back at the house and waved at the figure standing in the window. Daria waved back and he almost turned to go back to her. "Discipline, Benthausen, discipline. Take it easy. Remember your plan. Let her come to you," he admonished himself and grinned. For once, he was looking forward to a stay in a strange town, he thought as he drove away.

"Take it easy," Daria ordered herself as she prepared for bed after trying fruitlessly to read the new fantasy book she'd purchased yesterday. "Remember your plan. Get to know him. Just because the imperative doesn't exist, it doesn't mean you can't enjoy his company. Just you can't let it go too far. And don't even think about what might happen six months from now."

Easy enough to say, but what she was feeling and thinking was more complicated.

Something was going on inside her, she knew. Probably sparked by that kiss. She could practically feel her original conclusions changing. After spending some time with Bent, her denial, doubts, and confusions seemed to be, if not going away, at least diminishing in their intensity. The thought of Bent as her soulmate was becoming . . . what? Normal? Acceptable? Exciting? Inevitable?

No. None of those. She still refused to accept a soulmate as her predetermined destiny. She would be in control of her own life, no matter what. She would decide if Bent was the man for her and her decision would be reasoned, logical, thoroughly thought out.

Assuming, of course, her mind would stop dithering and get down to business. What was wrong with her thought processes that she couldn't put a persuasive argument together or come to a simple conclusion? Was this what desire did to you? Muddled your brain? What would she be like if she were in love?

Love?

Her mother said soulmates loved each other by definition. That sounded so cut-and-dried. Passionless. Whatever this was with Bent, it certainly wasn't passionless. On that note, she fell into a restless sleep, only to dream of blue eyes and sensuous kisses.

Chapter Five

Bent called each night left in the week, sometimes early, sometimes later, depending on his schedule. Mostly he complained about the idiocies, incompetencies, and poor management he was finding. "People just don't listen sometimes, do they?" he asked her on Friday.

Daria told herself at first she was simply talking to him as part of her self-imposed plan to further their acquaintance, but she quickly found what he had to say interested her professionally and personally. She had never been part of a turnaround before, nor had she actually been on-site when her observations and recommendations had been implemented. She was finding Bent's troubles an education in themselves. She might just have to persuade her next client into letting her observe implementation; she could be missing a whole facet of the business, namely change management. "Does this mean you're making suggestions and someone is not picking up on them? Whatever happened to the 'poof syndrome?'" she asked.

"What's the poof syndrome?"

"I've heard too many tales where the new boss comes in, and everybody jumps whenever he says anything at all. For example, there was one new CEO who remarked that the lights in the reception area seemed dim. It happened to be a dreary day outside. No matter. His subordinates had new fixtures installed immediately and the area was as bright as a TV studio when they were finished. So, see, the boss makes an innocuous remark and 'Poof!'—Things happen. I gather this is not the case with you?"

Bent laughed. "Hell, no. It's the opposite. I'm giving flat-out orders and people aren't following them. I spent the day backtracking what the head of Distribution and his senior managers were supposed to be doing and trying to determine why they weren't doing it."

"And? Why weren't they?"

"Damned if I know. A couple are being deliberately obstructive, in a passive-aggressive sort of way. I'm getting rid of the VP next week. He's given me one excuse too many. Maybe a firing will shake up everybody else." He sighed into the phone. "And here it is Friday night, and I'm sitting by myself, drinking a Scotch, and wishing I was with you. So, enough of me. What have you been up to? Are you looking forward to the party tomorrow night?"

The date had been on her calendar for ages. When Natalie had informed her Harry had invited Bent to accompany them, Daria could not back out. What reasonable explanation for doing so could she give the Scrowcrofts? Besides, she rationalized, she was following her mother's instructions. "I haven't been doing much, but yes, I'm looking forward to the party," she replied. "I just hope you're prepared. Texans love these things, you know."

"Oh, I'm ready. I can't wait to hold you in my arms again, even if it is just on a dance floor."

Daria went to sleep that night longing to be in his arms too. This will never do, she thought, turning over—again—on her bed. Lolita, who had been sleeping by her side, meowed in protest. Daria sank her fingers into the soft fur on Lolita's belly and told her, "I can't be besotted by this man, Lolita. I hardly know him." Lolita offered no advice, but purred harder. Daria reminded herself of what had her mother said. Get to know him better. The phrase was becoming her mantra.

On Saturday night, Harry and Natalie picked up Daria and took her to the Galleria hotel where the gala was being held. It happened also to be Bent's hotel, so he met them there.

As he watched them walk across the lobby on the way to the stairs leading to the ballroom, he studied Daria with admiration. Her shimmering midnight-blue silk, halter-top, V-necked dress showed just enough cleavage to make a man want to see more. The slim skirt wrapped around her small waist and the drape allowed a glimpse of leg to just above the knee. At her ears were emerald drops; and an emerald brooch set in silver and gold secured the bottom of the "V" between her breasts.

Bent also noticed the admiring glances from other men as she passed and he growled Zorro-like to himself. "Keep off, guys," he mentally ordered. "She's mine."

"Here I am," he said out loud, walking up to the group.

He greeted Harry and Natalie and then gave Daria a quick kiss and took her hand. Holding even just her hand made him feel great, ready to conquer the world. He dismissed the thought to study her carefully. "Hi, honey, you're looking rested."

Daria noticed the pleased look passing between Harry and Natalie as she answered Bent. "Yes, I'm fine. And Harry, I don't want to hear a word out of you," she told the older man with the speculative gleam in his eye. She surveyed Bent in his tuxedo. Something about a man in evening clothes, especially this man, just took her breath away. She noted his dark blue cummerbund curiously. It matched her dress, but he had never asked her what she was wearing.

"But darlin', I was just going to comment on what a fine-looking couple you and Bent make," the older man said and smiled like a magician who'd just pulled a rabbit out of his hat.

Natalie laughed. "What are we going to do with him, Daria? He's incorrigible. Come on, y'all. Let's find our table."

On the way into the ballroom, they heard Bent's name called. As they turned, a couple approached the foursome. Bent introduced Theo Wall, his vice president of Finance, to Daria and Natalie. Harry knew Wall already. Wall in turn introduced his wife Sylvia.

"I wouldn't have expected to see you here, Theo," Bent said. "I'd imagined you more the type to attend a meeting of accountants."

"Only too true," Wall agreed. "But Sylvia here has been working with this charity for years, and she drags me along for every big event." He turned to Daria. "Aren't you the management consultant I've heard so much about? Can we expect you in our offices soon?"

"I'll admit to being a consultant. And as for the other, I've no plans to work for Glennell," Daria answered with a smile, although she wasn't certain Wall believed her, despite the bland look on his face. Something about the look in his eyes bothered her, but she couldn't quite decide exactly what it was—a nervousness? Anxiety? Lots of people became nervous around their CEO, however, so she put the thought out of her mind during the social chit-chat.

After the Walls departed for their table, Bent grimaced. "Everywhere we go, we seem to run into someone from the company. I don't know if Wall's a gossip, but this will only feed the rumors Grady started. You may have to come to work for us after all."

"I don't think so," Daria replied, laughing. "But I can't help it if people jump to conclusions just because they've seen us together a couple of times."

For dinner they were seated with three other couples: Stanley Kramer from BallCorp and his wife, and a banker and an oil-company CEO and their wives.

Daria was pleased to see her client, and a little surprised Bent knew him, until Harry mentioned having introduced them.

Kramer said he was delighted to see Daria and immediately began singing her praises. "Well," he boomed, "I can't wait for our six-month follow-up meeting to show you what we've done. Best money I've ever spent on a consultant. Your ideas have already impacted the bottom line positively about three percent, and we're not done yet."

His statement perked up the ears of the other executives who immediately asked for her business card.

Daria distributed her cards and said, "I must warn you, I'm not taking any clients for a while."

"What's she doing with you, then, Benthausen?" the banker asked.

"She's on vacation and I'm her fling," Bent answered, grinning.

Daria frowned at his statement and he just grinned wider. For a moment, nobody seemed to know quite what to say.

Then Harry jumped like Natalie had kicked him under the table and started a discussion of consulting in general. The conversation graduated to other topics as they ate dinner. The after-dinner speeches were mercifully short. Then everyone moved into another ballroom for dessert and dancing.

Bent immediately pulled Daria to the dance floor and took her in his arms. "At last," he murmured, fitting her to him and giving her a squeeze.

Daria surrendered to the exquisite delight of being in his embrace, but only until she remembered his previous words. "What was your statement about your being my 'fling?' " she asked, leaning back so she could see his face clearly.

"Everyone needs to have a fling while on vacation. I'm yours. I'm just here to help you have fun." He waggled his eyebrows. "For as long as your vacation lasts, I'm your tour guide." He twirled her through a series of exuberant turns, grinning all the while.

Daria couldn't help smiling back at the man. His mood was electric, infectious. Then she concentrated on dancing and keeping her face straight while her mind whirled ahead of her body. What did he mean? "As long as your vacation lasts?" He was looking at her as a temporary fling only? Did that mean he wasn't her mate?

Well, it wasn't a question she could answer now. She resolutely banished the episode from her thoughts. She might as well enjoy the evening.

They were relaxing at the table with dessert and Bent was feeling pleased with his progress with Daria when a tall, blond, exceedingly handsome middle-aged man came up behind her, put his hands on her shoulders, and began to nibble on her neck, growling in an awful Transylvanian accent and evil laugh, "I'm thirsty and you look like a handy neck."

Bent rose, ready to consign this "vampire" to hell, when Daria turned and gave the fellow a smacking kiss. "Uncle Greg! I didn't know you were back. Where's Aunt Cassie?"

"Right behind me," he said, pulling Daria out of her chair and into a hug.

Daria turned to her aunt for another hug. "I'm surprised to see you. What brought you back from New York so soon?"

"We finished our business early," she answered and then looked Bent up and down. "And who's this?"

Daria introduced her aunt and uncle, Cassandra and Gregor Barca, to Bent. "Aunt Cassie is mother's sister," she explained. Bent could see the family resemblance in the dark hair and beautiful complexion. She had green eyes also.

After visiting a while, Gregor and Cassandra took their leave, but not before Cassandra enticed Bent onto the dance floor. Bent knew he was being checked out and turned on every bit of charm at his command. It seemed to work because he overheard Cassandra whisper to Daria, "I like him. Your mother was right. This is the one." He didn't fully understand the last sentence, but took it as a good omen. Her family must approve of him.

He was dancing with Daria again when he felt a tap on his shoulder. A medium-height, brown-haired man smiled and asked to cut in. Bent could feel Daria tense a little, but she recovered and introduced him to Tom Wisemore, "a friend of hers." He exchanged a short, crisp handshake with the other man.

Bent let her go reluctantly and made his way back to the table where Harry and Natalie were sitting. "Who's Wisemore?" he asked the couple as he sat down.

"He's a stockbroker. Tom's been after Daria for some time, but she hasn't seemed interested in him," Harry answered. "I don't think he's someone for you to be worried about, if that's what you mean," he added with a sly sidelong glance at Bent.

"Personally, I always thought he was after something besides Daria," Natalie contributed and continued when the men looked askance at her. "I think he wants to become her father's stockbroker."

"Ah!" Harry thought about her comment for a moment. "I think you're on to something. Bent, if you're around the Morgans any length of time, you'll find out Alaric handles the family investments, and they're pretty hefty, too. Wisemore's just ambitious enough to think he could have both Daria and the account."

"Over my dead body!" Bent thought as he watched the couple return to the table. He smiled to himself when he saw she did not look particularly happy. He'd take care of this broker if he tried to share anything with Daria again.

"Is anything the matter?" Daria asked as she sat down after Wisemore left.

"Nothing at all. Why?" Bent said with an innocent rise of his eyebrows.

"You just had a strange look on your face while I was dancing. First a ferocious scowl, then a smile that looked like you were plotting something."

Damn. He'd have to remember Daria made her living paying close attention to people. He had no intention, however, of discussing Wisemore or any other man with her. "Nothing's wrong," he answered mildly, pulling her up. "It must have been something I ate. Let's dance."

Finally it grew late enough that Bent thought he could call an end to the evening. He very much wanted to have Daria to himself. Looking around the dance floor, he murmured in her ear, "If you think I've met everybody I need to, why don't we call it a night and I'll take you home?"

"Excellent idea. Let's tell Harry and Natalie we're going,"

Daria said and gave a sigh of relief. This had been her first night out in a long time, especially in high heels. She was exhausted and her feet hurt. She also had to admit she wanted another good-night kiss—all in a spirit of experimentation, she rationalized. Getting to know him, she told herself.

They said good-bye to the Scrowcrofts and left the hotel in Bent's Lexus after he took off his coat and tie and put them in the back seat. He also rolled up his sleeves before getting into the car. "I hate coats and ties," he informed her.

She thought he looked good, no matter what he wore, but she didn't tell him. That would be admitting too much, but more to him than to herself.

They didn't talk much, just some comments on the gala, on the way to Daria's house. When they arrived, Bent waited as she opened the door and then followed her inside as she entered the second code in the security system. The only light came from two low lamps, one on a hall table and the other in the living room.

Daria put her purse on the table by the lamp and turned to him as she had on Tuesday. She couldn't help it, she was trembling a little in anticipation of his kiss, and she licked her dry lips anxiously.

"Daria," Bent said in a low, raspy voice as he closed the distance between them and gathered her into his arms. "I've been waiting all night for this." He lowered his head and took her mouth.

Unlike his kisses after their fajita dinner, there was little gentle or entreating about this one, Daria realized as she opened in response. It—no, *he* was demanding, compelling, and oh, so passionate. He was dominating, sensual, and thoroughly arousing. She trembled again, harder this time, and kissed him back with the overwhelming feelings rushing through her like a juicy rumor through a ravenous office grapevine: need, want, desire, longing.

He deepened the kiss and shifted his stance to draw her in between his spread legs to the cradle of his thighs. His hands began to roam over her back and down to her bottom as he pressed her hips to his erection.

Daria could feel her heart beating wildly against her rib cage, her breasts throbbing as her nipples puckered, her arms becoming almost too heavy to lift, the core of her femininity heating and aching. She felt the hard ridge of his manhood pressing against her mound become harder and larger.

He tasted of coffee, he tasted of dessert. He smelled like soap and starch and fine clothing and himself, and she hadn't realized until now how deliciously intoxicating a man's scent could be. All her reading and the few giggling gossip sessions with girlfriends had not prepared her for the sheer power of desire, of wanting a man so much it hurt. She heard herself moan as she raked her fingers across his back.

Bent felt her nails and grabbed hard on his own self-control. His blood was pounding wildly in his veins, his cock was steel, and his own hands were shaking slightly. He began moving those hands, kneading her bottom, stroking her back, bringing one hand up around to cup one of her breasts. He felt her nipple harden through the dark blue silk, and he rubbed it with his thumb as it turned into a small button.

Daria suddenly gasped, jumped, and jerked backwards, almost out of his arms. He barely managed to keep his other hand on her waist.

Confused, embarrassed, disoriented expressions flitted across her face. She looked up at him in the gray light, her green eyes still flaming with desire but also searching his anxiously. "I'm, I'm sorry," she whispered breathlessly. "I guess I wasn't ready." Her hands restlessly fluttered across his pleated shirt front, and she bowed her head.

Bent struggled for his own control and put his offending hand on top of hers against his chest. He wasn't sure what had happened, but he didn't want her to bolt. "What's the matter, Daria?" he asked softly.

"I don't know. I guess I wasn't expecting you . . . It's so soon . . . I . . . We hardly know each other." She shook her still-bowed head. "Oh, damn. I'm making a mess of this," she wailed.

He nudged her a little closer so she could rest her head on his chest. With his cheek on her hair, he said, "It's okay, honey. I just moved a little fast for you." They stood there for a couple of minutes and he drew her a little closer each minute while he got himself under control and tried to think about what she had said. Thinking wasn't easy when her scent, a combination of subtle perfume and aroused woman, permeated his lungs and made him lightheaded with desire. She had almost panicked and rejected him. It was going to take longer to get her into bed than he had thought, but he couldn't understand why. She had been his for the taking mere moments before.

"All right," he murmured. He wasn't a problem solver for nothing. He could analyze and interpret phenomena. She did want him. She couldn't have returned his kiss like that if she didn't. But she wasn't a tease; she had been extremely embarrassed by her involuntary reaction. The facts were clear. She wasn't very experienced, and he was evidently going too fast for her. Then he latched on to her statement about hardly knowing each other. Okay, he'd start there.

Bending swiftly, he picked her up—she gave a little squeak at his sudden movement—and bore her into the living room. There he settled on the couch so she could lean her back against its high arm. The arrangement had the added benefit of freeing his left hand from her shoulders to play with her hair. He took her left hand with his right and, raising it to his lips, kissed her palm.

"All right, let's get to know each other." He gave her a quick kiss on the lips. "You ask me a question, and we'll take turns." He would be patient, very patient. It might kill him, but he would be patient.

"You're not mad?" she asked in a tiny voice, looking at their joined hands, not into his eyes.

"Surprised, but not angry. You just need more time, that's all, more time to get used to me and the idea of us, right?" He kept his tone straightforward, yet hopefully reassuring at the same time.

Daria raised her eyes up to his. "Thank you, Bent." She

had been absolutely mortified at her reaction, then terrified he'd think she was rejecting him. Now she was in his lap, and evidently, thankfully, he wasn't upset. She kissed him quickly and lightly before she could think about it and relaxed when he smiled in return.

"So, ask me a question." He kissed her back.

His eyes were gleaming with both passion and amusement in the low light, and he looked like he should have feathers sticking out of his mouth, Daria thought. Smug and complacent, like he had her exactly where he wanted her. When he started to nibble on her neck, she pulled her thoughts together. It wasn't easy, but she managed to make her brain work. What did she want to know? "How old are you?"

"Thirty-six." He moved his right hand to her waist. "On November fifth. What about you?"

"Thirty on May tenth. Did . . ."

"Uh-uh. My turn. What were you like as a little girl?" He gave her waist an encouraging squeeze.

"Quiet, studious, beset upon by an older brother and a younger sister."

He chuckled. "Having met both of them, I can understand."

"I'll bet you were a hell-raiser."

"I'm the oldest, played sports, and worked hard to keep my brother and two sisters in line." This was better, Bent thought. She was relaxing. Under the pretext of straightening out her skirt, he ran his hand down her hip and leg to her knee. His other hand lightly massaged her nape and played with her curls.

"Do you have any hobbies?" She looked like she was concentrating hard, but her words came out slightly raspy.

"I haven't had the time in recent years." But my new one will be making love to you, he thought as he outlined her ear with his finger and flipped the emerald bauble dangling from its lobe. "Do you?" She squirmed a little and he gritted his teeth. Hold on, Bent. Friction on your lap would not be advantageous at this point.

"I read, I cook, I get together with friends, if those can be called hobbies."

"You cook?"

"Mother made sure all of us can cook. It was a means of teaching us about her garden."

"Yum. Beautiful, brainy, and you can cook, too." He grinned rather contentedly. What more could he want in a woman? She started to say something else, but he interrupted. "Time for a break." He kissed her, taking his time about it and doing a thorough job.

Daria had enough presence of mind, although she wasn't sure how when his lips and tongue were so beguiling, to spell herself with an I-am-absolutely-repulsive concoction she had used in the past to good effect with would-be amorous men.

Nothing happened.

Nothing at all.

He didn't gag or choke. He didn't vomit as more than one man had done. He simply kept kissing her and paid absolutely no attention to the spell.

She canceled it as she felt his hand slide from her knee back to her hip and slowly squeeze. She tried another, sort of an I-taste-vile and I-feel-like-sandpaper mixture she threw together extemporaneously.

He only deepened the kiss.

He's immune to my spells, just like Mother said he would be, she thought. *He cuts right through them to my real self. So what do I do next?* She bowed her head away from his kiss, and as breathless as she was, he let her end it.

"What about boyfriends?" Bent asked, turning his attention to the tender skin under her ear.

"Not many, very few, in fact." She didn't like telling him that. She didn't want to tell him of her inexperience—not yet.

"Too smart for the jocks and too pretty for the geeks, I imagine."

He was too perceptive. How was she supposed to answer? She decided not to. "I'll bet you had a lot of girlfriends."

"My share, certainly."

"Were you ever married?" She really wanted the answer to this one.

"No." He was silent for a moment, as if he was mulling over his answer. "Came close once, but . . ."

"But?" She held her breath.

He shrugged. "It just didn't work out." He raised his eyes to her hair and played with her curls with his left hand.

"Oh." Daria stared at him for a moment. He wasn't looking into her eyes and his face had taken on a grim cast. He seemed a thousand miles away. She wanted to ask him what had happened, but he spoke before she could.

"It doesn't matter." He brought his gaze back to hers and seemed to snap back from wherever he had been. He gave her a quick kiss. "I've been assuming you've never been married."

"That's correct." She filed his previous words away for later consideration. He obviously didn't want to talk about whatever had happened. Besides, his fingers on her nape were acting as a powerful deterrent to thinking.

"Nobody special?"

She shook her head.

"What about Wisemore?"

"Oh, Tom's a nice man. I'd like to think he could be a friend, but I don't expect his ego would let him since I've turned him down the last times he's asked me out."

"Good. I want your attention totally on me." He captured her lips again, his tongue delving deep, his hands and arms tightening around her.

He was through being leisurely, Daria realized as she gave herself over to sensation. This kiss claimed and possessed while it blew her thoughts to smithereens. She threw her arms around his neck and arched her back in response to his questing hands. This time when he moved his hand to the underside of her breast, then up to cup it, she jumped slightly and tensed, but let herself enjoy the sensation. He seemed to be almost touching her heart.

Bent sucked on her tongue and explored her mouth to distract her, and he felt her relax again, then tense for a reason he knew was not nervousness. Emboldened, he rubbed his thumb across her nipple until it beaded. When she moaned, he exulted, but he shifted his hand to her waist again before ending the kiss. That was probably all she would put up with for one evening. He could afford to be patient, knowing he'd be successful in the end. He could wait. If he didn't explode first.

"Spend the day with me tomorrow," he whispered, kissing his way down her neck.

"Oh, Bent, I can't." When he stopped nuzzling her and leaned back to frown slightly, she hastened to explain. "I'm cohosting a baby shower tomorrow, and those of us giving the shower are going out for dinner after. It's been set up for weeks and I'm committed. I'm sorry."

"There's nothing to be sorry about." He helped her to her feet and rose to stand beside her. "I'll call you tomorrow night. I have to go to the Baytown plant on Monday and don't expect to be back until late. Why don't we have dinner Tuesday night? I'll pick you up at six."

She agreed and they walked to the front door, his arm around her shoulders. Before she opened the door, he kissed her again long and hard. "Lock up behind me. Have fun at your shower," he said, and he let himself out the door.

Bent drove back to his hotel thinking about Daria and what had just happened. Her response to his kisses was all he could hope for and then some. Why the sudden reaction to his caress? It was almost . . . virginal. Nah, impossible. Who ever heard these days of a thirty-year-old virgin?

On the other hand, his experience told him her first

responses had an air of innocence about them, or was it simply wariness? It wasn't fear, he was certain. She just looked at him sometimes like she was trying to figure him out, like she was unsure of his attentions—or his intentions.

He supposed he should have told her about Susan, but that was a long time ago and had no bearing now. He preferred to concentrate on Daria.

She'd said she had few boyfriends. Maybe the jocks and geeks didn't treat her well and she was comparing him to them. Definitely not a flattering thought. He'd just have to show her, make her understand he was not like those idiots in the past. But first, he needed a cold shower to control his raging libido. Maybe the water would stop the itch in his chest too. Bent didn't know if he could take many more nights like this one.

Daria went to bed in a state of euphoria and confusion. She grew warm all over again reliving Bent's kisses and especially his caress on her breast. She had not expected his touch to affect her so strongly, and she felt her muscles tighten and an ache begin between her legs just thinking about it.

Then she shook her head at herself, remembering how she had jerked away from him. When she realized what she had done, she had vigorously wished for a big hole to appear and swallow her. Where was a good spell when she had really needed one? The man must think she was an idiot, or worse, a tease. But he had taken her babbled comments at face value and not reproached her, even though he had obviously meant for the evening to end in another fashion.

What about his comment, "Came close once"? What did that mean? He was, after all, an experienced man as far as women were concerned. Although her research had turned up nothing, it stood to reason he could have been involved in a relationship in the past. It was not, however, another problem for her to face now, she concluded. She had enough to worry about.

This almost overwhelming attraction she was experiencing had to be more than just her long dormant hormones waking up. The whole soulmate situation was turning out to be more powerful than she had expected. Bent was so alluring, his kisses so seductive. She snorted as she realized all her comments to her mother about free will and her own internal decisions to resist the soulmate concept were coming back to haunt her.

The phenomenon was more than just a concept, she decided; it really was an *imperative*, with all the might, force and potency that the word implied. As her mother had warned, resistance was proving to be futile. Her vaunted willpower to withstand temptation, her attempts to circumvent the soulmate command, her determination to resist were all coming to resemble the ability of a low-level spell-caster trying to oppose a twentieth-level master wizard.

She still had her integrity, though. She couldn't, wouldn't succumb to his charms without telling him about herself, magic practitioners, soulmates, and mating. Soon. She didn't know how much longer she would be able to resist him.

Chapter Six

Daria sat at her computer in her study late Tuesday afternoon, catching up on correspondence, when she remembered she had not collected the mail. She decided to do that before changing out of her jeans and T-shirt for dinner with Bent. She walked outside to the box by the gate, took out the letters and magazines, and sat on the front steps to see what they contained.

Zorro came up and demanded some petting first, so she rubbed behind his ears and looked out at the front yard. "Mother's going to be proud of us this year," she told the large black cat. "The hydrangeas are doing well by the steps and the marigolds are growing nicely. We'll have some pretty blooms before long."

"Mmrow," Zorro said and sniffed the air. Daria knew he was just being sociable. He could care less about the flowers, but he was intently watching a mockingbird as it, in turn, eyed him from the top of the gate.

"Let's see what we have in the mail," Daria said as she leafed through the envelopes. "Here's a notice from the vet. Time for your and Lolita's shots."

"Aerow!" Zorro glared at her.

"Don't take that tone with me, fella. We're going and that's final."

Among the advertisements, she found a plain white

envelope with her name and address hand-printed, and no return address. It appeared to contain only one sheet of paper. "What's this? A new way to get your attention with junk mail?" Something about the envelope didn't seem right, she realized, as she scrutinized the printing. The block letters glowed with a weird greenish tinge. She felt suddenly queasy, but she opened it and pulled out the single sheet. Crude printing formed the message:

BITCH!
STAY AWAY FROM GLENNELL OR YOU'LL GET HURT. BAD!

Frigid air washed down her backbone as the malevolence in the message hit her, and she dropped the paper. Zorro sniffed at it and immediately sprang into fighting posture and hissed.

"It's all right, Zorro. I can feel it too, but the thing's not going to hurt us." She picked up the paper and its envelope gingerly by a corner and took them inside to lay them on the hall table. She had never thought she had the talent, but she could definitely feel the evil and anger coming from the paper.

"Zorro?" she called as she went outside again to bring in the rest of the mail. Then she saw the miniature black panther pacing across the front of the yard, clearly on the lookout for trouble. She left him to it and brought the remainder of the envelopes with her to the kitchen. She put the mail down on the counter, reached for the phone and dialed.

"Clay Morgan." Her brother answered on the second

ring and she counted herself lucky he was available.

"Clay, it's me. I just received a threatening letter in the mail, telling me to stay away from Glennell. *I* can feel the evil on it and Zorro almost had a fit." She told him the message.

"Okay. Lock yourself in and set the alarms. I know you probably don't need them at this point, but do it anyway for my peace of mind. I'll call someone I know in the police and see what he thinks. Then I'll come over." He paused. "I didn't think you were doing anything with Bent's company. Did that change?"

"No. But we ran into one of his vice presidents last week at dinner and we were together at the big benefit gala on Saturday and met another one of his executives. Both of them asked if I would be consulting with Glennell, and someone may have jumped to the wrong conclusion, despite my denials." Then she remembered what she had told Bent about the possibility of security problems. She summarized her statements and the subsequent events for Clay. "I don't know how anybody could have found out about my part in it, though."

"I heard about those arrests over at Glennell, but I didn't know you had anything to do with it. In light of the security situation over there, I'm sure the police will definitely be interested in this letter. We have to bring Bent in on this, too."

"As a matter of fact, he'll be here at six to take me to dinner."

"Good. I'll call the cops and be right over." He hung up.

Daria made sure the doors were locked and the alarms

were set, then picked up the letter with kitchen tongs and made some copies on the photocopier in her study. Just as she returned the original and copies to the hall table, Lolita wandered in, sniffed, frizzed up to twice her size, and took off for the kitchen.

"Well, Zorro and I aren't the only ones who react to this thing," Daria said to herself as she looked after the fleeing cat.

Somebody did not want her at Glennell-Houston. Now why would that be? The more she thought about it, the angrier she became. Someone had decided that she was a threat. Bent had cleared out the security manager and his cronies, but there must be more problems, possibly major irregularities or some sort of criminal activities, going on still. In their phone conversations, he'd complained about the trouble he was having making the company run efficiently. Obviously, the state of affairs was worse than he realized.

Okay, what was she going to do? She now had a vested interest in helping Bent get to the bottom of his problems. Whatever the truth about her involvement, and whether she was ready or not, someone had drawn her into the situation. She seriously doubted if "they" would leave her alone, especially if she and Bent continued to see each other.

She was not going to sit and wait for the letter sender to make the next move. She wouldn't be a sitting duck. Conclusion: she was clearly going to have to go to work at Glennell. By herself, she might not be able to discover exactly what the threat maker and his possible cohorts were up to, but she could at least help Bent and his people by pointing them in the right direction.

She smiled a witch's smile to herself in the hall mirror. The villains did not know what they had started. She wasn't as vulnerable or as easily frightened as these guys evidently thought. Her spells could make the Sphinx talk, and her defenses were strong enough to keep her safe. She stood staring at her reflection for a minute as she mentally reviewed some of her stronger, most "persuasive" spells.

"On the other hand," she said aloud, "it never hurts to have a little extra oomph." She walked back into the kitchen, picked up the phone again, and called her mother.

"Mother, it's me. Ask Daddy to pick up on an extension if he's there, will you?" When both parents were on the line, Daria explained what had happened and that she expected Clay, maybe the police, and Bent at any moment. "Would it be possible for you or Gloriana to come down tomorrow to strengthen the house spells and run through a couple of defenses with me? I would just feel better knowing everything was at top strength."

"We'll be down first thing," Antonia said.

"What are you going to do about this, Daria?" Alaric asked, then answered his own question. "You're going to work at Glennell to find out who's behind it, aren't you? Antonia's told me all about Bent, by the way."

"I was sure she did, Daddy. I have to go to Glennell. You can see that. What if it got out all someone has to do was threaten me with a dinky little letter and I'll back off a job? At the very least my conclusions and advice would be in doubt as not being the fairest or strongest or most unbiased I could make. I'd be out of business in a heartbeat. Leaving the possible 'soulmate situation' out of the equation for the moment, do you see any other choice?" Daria countered, pleased she and her father thought alike, as usual.

Alaric heaved a great sigh through the phone. When he spoke, his tone was grim, but resigned. "Damn, honey, I don't like this one bit, but with the letter reeking of evil intent, I don't think you can do anything else. You're the only one who can quickly find the instigators of this, and you've never been one to sit on the sidelines and let others do the work. You know the family will do whatever it can. How will Bent take your investigation?"

"I think I'm going to have to talk him into it, but I hope Clay will help."

"If you do go to work for him, do your father a favor for his peace of mind and have Bent assign security to you at all times. It won't be a definitive wall, but it will help. I don't want you taking unnecessary chances."

"I know, Daddy. I won't, I promise. I'll see you tomorrow." After "I love yous" from both sides, they ended the call.

Clay arrived within minutes and confirmed the letter's evil nature. "I'm like you, you know, not usually able to feel these things, but the aura emanating from this affects me, too. No wonder Zorro went ballistic. He's patrolling the perimeter right now."

"And Lolita ran like the Hound of the Baskervilles was after her. I talked with Mother and Daddy and they agree with my idea that to get to the bottom of this, I should go to work for Bent for real. Daddy wants me guarded, of course. What do you think?"

Clay sighed just like their father had and rubbed his chin. "Yeah, I agree, too. Don't think Bent will like it, though."

"Well, you'll just have to help me convince him." She looked out the window. "Another car is pulling up. Is this the police?"

"Yeah. Bill Childress is a good man. He took the threat seriously. I'll get the door."

Lieutenant Bill Childress was a lean, medium-height, nondescript man with short brown hair, wearing a rumpled brown suit. He was just the sort of fellow people ignored or flat didn't see, but Daria liked his penetrating hazel eyes and firm handshake.

She showed him the letter and its envelope lying on the hall table.

"What are the tongs for?" Childress asked after he read the threat.

"I watch TV, Lieutenant, so I used them to pick it up and put it on the copier. Here are the copies I made. Will you want my fingerprints?" She wondered if she sounded like a blathering idiot to him.

Childress answered with a straight face. "Maybe. If I can trouble you for a plastic bag, I'll use your handy utensils to put them in it."

Daria went for the bag, certain she liked Childress even more for not laughing at her.

After placing the letter and envelope in the bag, they adjourned to the living room. Daria sat on the couch, Childress took a chair, and Clay roamed by the window.

"How do you come to receive such a letter, Ms. Morgan?" Childress asked.

"I'm a management consultant, but I've done no work for Glennell and had no plans to. I have, however, gone out a couple of times with John Benthausen, the new CEO there. Both times we ran into people who work for him, and they recognized my name. Word about our dates must have gotten around the company, and it appears from this note that someone jumped to an erroneous conclusion."

"We'll have to talk to Benthausen," Childress commented. "I've heard of the multiple arrests at the company."

"We were going out to dinner tonight, and I think he just pulled up," Daria said, having noticed another car stopping in front of the house.

Clay let Bent in and introduced him to Bill Childress. "What's going on?" Bent asked, going straight to Daria and taking a seat beside her.

Childress showed him a copy of the letter and said, "Ms. Morgan received this in the mail today. Can you think of anyone who would send it?"

Bent scanned the letter, looked at her and put his arm around her. "Daria? Are you all right?" After she reassured him, Bent returned his attention to the letter and the lieutenant. "No, I can't imagine who would send something like this, but it appears there is more trouble here than I had thought, and I'll do anything I can to help you find the culprit."

Bent's tone was vehement and the look of resolve on his face revealed his determination, but she wasn't going to let him take over. Not when her good name was on the line. Not even when his arm still around her was spreading warmth throughout her body. "Hire me," she said.

He swung around to her and glared at her in disapproval. "What? Now wait a minute! There's no way I'll let you work there if we have a nut running around loose making threats against you."

"Bent, it's the only way we can . . ."

"Whoa, folks," Childress interrupted, raising his hands in a wait-a-minute gesture. "What are we talking about? Let's get back to my original question. How does she come to receive such a letter? How is she a threat to anyone?"

"You've heard about the thefts and fraud at the company?" Bent asked. When Childress nodded, Bent continued. "Daria was the source for my looking into the matter, although I don't think anyone except Dan Roth, head of security for the corporation, knows it. I certainly told no one, and neither did Dan. It appears, however, that we did not root out all of our problems. Given this note and the magnitude of the security mess, I intend to take this threat very seriously." He turned to Daria. "But I don't intend to let you get involved in anything that might hurt you."

"What can you do, Ms. Morgan, to flush out the person who sent this?" Childress asked, waving the note as punctuation. "For that matter, how did you know Glennell had thieves in their Security office?"

Both Clay and Bent opened their mouths to answer, but Daria spoke quickly and firmly. "It's my business. Let me explain it." The two men nodded but didn't look happy.

She told Childress how she made a living and how she had become Bent's source of information. "At two other clients," she went on, "I have found suspicion of wrongdoing and alerted the company CEOs who launched investigations. In the first instance three years ago, several people were fired. In the second the year after that, at a bank, it turned out to be a major embezzlement and four went to jail. Although I asked the police and the company's executives to keep my name out of it if possible, I know the fact I was involved was spread around."

She pointed to the letter. "Here's the evidence somebody heard the rumors and is worried I'll find him. I'm probably the only one who can find out quickly who's out to get me. My regular interview methods will pick up on any hostility. People often reveal more than they realize when they talk to me." She hoped nobody would want her to explain those methods right now.

She looked directly at Bent and spread her hands in query. "What's our alternative? Would you rather just wait until the letter sender tries something else? Or would you want to try to convince the guy somehow that I'm not helping you? There might be a slim chance of it if we stayed completely away from each other."

"The last option is not acceptable," Bent stated.

"Dad suggests having a security man with her at all times," Clay offered. "And he and I agree that using her is the only way to get to the bottom of the situation quickly. Look, bringing in the police to question people at this stage might just force the person making the threat to go underground. We don't have much to go on at the moment, just this note. The methods Daria uses normally result in a truckload of information about a company and its employees. There have to be some clues buried in all of that data. Otherwise we may be waiting forever, and that puts us, especially her, at their mercy."

Bent duplicated Alaric's and Clay's sighs and then turned to Childress. "What do you think, Lieutenant?"

"Given what we have already found at Glennell, I agree we should take the threat seriously and it probably wouldn't do any good to bring us in overtly with nothing more to go on than the letter. But someone is obviously afraid of something. Alert your security people. I can't stop you from putting her to work, Mr. Benthausen. I don't particularly like it, though, and I don't know if you will be able to find out anything, Ms. Morgan." He crossed his arms over his chest.

"If by chance you, or any of you, do discover any evidence, or even have a hard suspicion, I want to know about it immediately." He skewered each of them with a pointed look. "Immediately, is that clear? Don't try to do anything by yourselves. Keep us informed. Do I have your words on that?" He glanced from one to the other as they nodded. The look on his face clearly stated, "God save me from amateurs."

He handed Bent his card. "Have your security manager call me, Mr. Benthausen. We'll communicate through him. I'll let you know if I need your fingerprints, Ms. Morgan." He picked up the plastic bag and took his leave.

When Daria returned from showing Childress out, she found Bent and Clay with their heads together. "All right. What have you two decided? Am I in or out?"

"We're still arguing," Clay said.

The three of them went round and round over the same ground for a few minutes until Daria had had enough. "I can't let someone chase me from a job, Bent," she said. "Where would my business be if anyone could write a letter and scare me away? How would you feel if you were in my shoes? Believe me, we'll find the culprit much more quickly if I'm at Glennell."

"I concur," Clay put in. "I don't like the setup either, but I like the alternative even less. For what it's worth, she never ran from a fight when she was little, either."

Bent glanced from her to Clay and back again. Daria thought she could almost see his mind working.

Finally he threw up his hands. "Okay. We'll try it." He pointed at her. "But you're going to have a security man as your shadow."

"Not *in* my interviews," Daria stated. "I'll never learn anything then."

"All right," he conceded begrudgingly. "We need to thrash out logistics and decide where to start. I don't want to discuss this in a restaurant. Why don't we just call out for pizza?"

"Not for me," Clay said. "I have a date. Daria, I'll be over tomorrow to check out the security system. I have a couple of bells and whistles to add. Bent, I'd think about bringing in some corporate computer people, if you haven't already. If there's more going on than you've been able to find so far, it's only prudent. There may be some clues in e-mail or in what people are deleting."

"Dan Roth thought the same thing, but in connection to the security fraud, and they're coming next week. Roth is head of corporate security, Clay. I told you about him, Daria. I'll call him right now," Bent said.

"If you want some help from the computer angle, let me know," Clay added. "Uncle Gregor and Aunt Cassie's youngest son is in graduate school in computers and would be happy to slog through your data if you want an outsider looking at it instead of a company employee. I can guarantee no one will know we're delving into the files."

"Let me talk to Dan about it. Maybe after we narrow the field of suspects," Bent replied.

Daria gave Clay a kiss and a hug. "Thanks, big brother. I'll see you tomorrow."

Clay let himself out after shaking Bent's hand.

"Now then," Bent said, turning purposefully to Daria.

"Pizza first." Daria scooted into the kitchen.

After she ordered the pizza, Bent called Roth. "Dan, I'm over at Daria Morgan's. We have a situation and I wonder if you'd mind coming over here right now."

"Of course not," Roth replied. "I can be there in about

thirty minutes."

"Ask him if he's eaten," Daria said to Bent.

"Did you hear that? Have you eaten? We just called out for some pizza and you're welcome to join us," Bent relayed to Roth.

Roth said he'd be glad to join them and would be there soon.

Daria called for a second pizza, what with two men to feed. She had skipped lunch and knew she could eat half of what she had originally ordered. She was turning toward the refrigerator to put together a salad when Bent grabbed her.

"We didn't get to the most important thing," he murmured, plastering her to his body and kissing her hungrily.

Daria just melted. She was sure she was going to flow right out of his arms into a puddle on the floor. She hadn't known how much that letter had shaken her until she realized how much safer and more secure she felt in Bent's arms.

Eventually Bent ended the kiss and drew back. "Food," she said. "Food," he agreed.

Daria pointed out where she kept the wine and asked him to open a bottle of Chianti. He could have beer if he liked, but she wanted wine. As she started on the salad, he poured the wine and told her about his day at Glennell. It wasn't too long before the doorbell rang.

"It's Dan," Bent said, looking down the hall and out the windows by the front door, and he went to let Roth in. Daria followed.

Dan Roth was a sleek, wiry man about Bent's age, and

five-foot-ten in height. Contrary to his Germanic name, he obviously had some additional ancestry, Native American or Asian, perhaps, as he had onyx-black hair, bronze skin, and black, slightly slanting eyes. Just the way he entered the house made Daria think of a cougar: alert, elegant, and deadly.

She had no more than shaken his hand after Bent's introduction than Roth raised his head and looked straight at the landing on the stairs. Lolita was doing her Egyptian imitation again, gazing down haughtily.

"Lady," Roth said, inclining his head slightly. Lolita assumed a smug expression and blinked at him slowly.

Then Zorro stalked in from the living room, stopped, and turned his yellow eyes on Roth. Dan bowed to him, the correct bow of a student to a master. Zorro nodded his head royally in response and continued on his way.

By this time, Bent's eyebrows had almost reached his hairline. He looked at Dan, who blandly returned his gaze, and then at Daria.

She had to grin at his expression. Some people were more sensitive to both magical and non-magical nuances. Dan must be one of them.

"Here comes the pizza. Bent, you get the door, and I'll take Dan back to the kitchen," she said, taking Dan's arm and leading him down the hall. "You've just met Zorro and Lolita. Do you want beer or wine with your pizza?"

While they ate, Bent showed Dan the copy of the letter and explained what they had planned for Daria.

"When will you be at the office?" Dan asked. "I'll

coordinate my staff's schedules."

"Not until Thursday, if that's agreeable with y'all. I need tomorrow to get ready here. Bent, before you leave tonight, I'll give you a list of what I need in the way of office space, a computer, phone, and the like," she answered. "I'll come in at eight on Thursday and we'll set up my schedule from there." She wondered how much trouble having bodyguards would be, and she was not enthusiastic about their disruption to her usual interview routine, but she had agreed to the protection, so she couldn't complain.

"One additional problem—I have to go to New York to headquarters on Thursday night. I won't be back until Monday, or more likely late Tuesday," Bent said. "What will my absence do to your activities, Daria?"

"Nothing, I think. If you introduce me to your senior staff on Thursday morning, I can start with Human Resources as I usually do. I like to go over the personnel records first and HR is a good place to pick up gossip." She thought for a moment. "Dan, if you can give me a couple of your people Saturday and maybe Sunday, and get us into the building and into the personnel records, we can read through the records of the critical people and I can make progress more quickly."

"You want my security staff to help with the records?"

"Yes, the people you brought in from headquarters. I'd rather use them than anyone in Personnel. We don't know yet whom we can trust. There's a fair amount of tabulation and general info I need in chart form. It's mostly grunt work, but having a suspicious mind helps a lot."

"I know just the people and I'll be there also. Bent, do you want round-the-clock protection for Daria?"

"Yes," Bent said.

"No," Daria said.

He frowned at her.

"I don't need people around at night when I'm in the house," she said in answer to the frown. "This place has everything from booby-traps to shrieking alarms, thanks to my inventive brother. There's no telling what he will add tomorrow. I'll go with someone for shopping if you think it necessary, but give me a little privacy, will you?" She gazed at the men imploringly and wished she could tell Bent about the spells her mother would renew and supplement. Knowing the place was protected would certainly make him understand her thinking.

Dan and Bent looked at each other with identically sour expressions.

"If you put someone outside, the neighbors will notice and get nervous, but having a house guest will not be conducive to my work either," she continued. "Let everyone get a good night's sleep. Bent, please don't turn me into a prisoner in my own home."

Bent and Dan both sighed and shrugged. "All right," Bent said. "But you have to promise not to move one step from here without one of us, Dan's staff, or Clay with you."

"Cross my heart," she made the gesture and promised, then thought of something else. "Am I going to be escorted everywhere, inside the building, I mean? Do you plan on stationing a guard outside my interviews? Won't people wonder why? Are we going to offer an explanation?" She could always spell herself not to be noticed, but she couldn't tell them that.

"I see your point," Dan said. "How are you about keeping on schedule?"

"Relentless."

"Let me think about it. We might be able to set up a beeper system to call your guard. I'll get you a cell phone, too."

"I have one, but I don't use it much for business. I turn it off during interviews because interruptions are bad for the flow. I'll give you my number."

"Be sure to leave it turned on, too," Dan added as he rose from the table. "Thanks for the pizza. I'd better get back to the office. I was finishing up my report to you on our security personnel needs when you called."

"I'll expect it tomorrow. Let me walk you out," Bent said. "I have a couple of additions for the report. I'll be right back, Daria."

She said good-bye to Dan and began to clear the table. Bent was certain she could see through his flimsy excuse to have a few private words with Dan, but he didn't care. He asked Dan a couple of questions about the report until they reached the gate.

"You know what I want from your people," he said as they stepped onto the sidewalk.

"I'll alert my staff. This letter was not good news. First the security mess, and now this. I thought we'd gone over this company in our usual thorough manner before we bought it. What happened?"

"Damned if I know. I wasn't part of the purchasing process. You and I just get to clean it up. Telling Joe we have even more problems than just the security department is not going to be much fun either. Put out all the feelers you have. I want to get to the bottom of this threat as soon as possible."

"What about Daria? Will she cooperate? Follow our instructions?" Dan asked as he slid into his car.

Bent thought for a minute. Daria had handled the letter business pretty calmly. "I think she'll be all right. She doesn't seem like one of those screwy heroines in the movies who are always running off on their own. She's certainly not scatterbrained." He shook his head. "I still don't like the idea of her being alone in the house with no one around, inside or outside, but we'll let it go for now. I'd rather fight that battle when I know I can win. Watch out for her when I'm gone."

"Sure thing." Dan smiled and drove off.

Chapter Seven

Bent stood looking after Dan's car for a moment, then turned back and studied the house. It seemed secure enough. She had electronic safeguards and the fence. But the letter had sent a fiery blaze of shock down his back when he read it, igniting within him a fierce need to protect her. The fact that he hadn't been here with her when she opened it left him with a feeling of helplessness.

No, his thinking was irrational, he told himself as he pushed open the gate, then closed it after him. He couldn't be with her *all* the time. But he'd protect her, by any means he could. The first order of business was to bring her to the office, where he and Dan could keep their eyes on her. He headed toward the front door as Zorro crossed his path.

The big black cat stopped his sentrylike pacing, looked up at Bent, and sniffed in the direction of the street. "Rrrrrgh," he growled.

"Damn right, Zorro," Bent said. "Nothing's going to happen to Daria."

Blue eyes and yellow eyes met, heads nodded in agreement, and the two resumed their individual tasks—Zorro to patrol and Bent to find Daria.

He entered the house and walked into the kitchen. The room was empty. "Daria! Where are you?" he called.

"Come through the family room straight back," she

called back.

He followed her directions and paused in the doorway at the end of the family room to survey Daria's study and home office.

The space was as large as the family room. One wall was filled with long windows on either side of a small fireplace; the windows looked out into the garden and waterfall. The remaining three walls held floor-to-ceiling bookshelves with some illuminated spaces displaying paintings, small sculptures, and art glass pieces. In one corner sat Daria's desk and computer, with a combination printer, copier, and fax machine on a nearby credenza. Situated so a person could sit and look out into the garden as well as take advantage of the fireplace were a large overstuffed dark-blue chair with ottoman and a burgundy-leather two-seater couch. A highly carved coffee table with a glass top sat between the sofa and the fireplace.

Bent instinctively knew this was where Daria spent most of her time. He also knew in his bones he would love to have a desk of his own in here with hers. It would fit beautifully in the empty area cater-cornered from her desk. He smiled to himself at his thoughts. Where were they coming from? He had never had this reaction to another woman's home. Never automatically inserted himself into one. But it sure felt good—and a little bit odd.

She was printing a document from the computer and looked up as he entered. She watched him study her office and wondered what he was smiling about. She handed him the first pages from the printer. "Here is my usual draft contract. It's for my complete job and therefore my full fee. How do you want to handle this—sign up for a complete consultation and then I bill you for the work actually done or should we write parameters into the contract now? How long will we have to wait for headquarters' approval?"

Bent sat down on the couch to read the contract. "I think we'll handle this just as a normal consultation so it doesn't look like we're after anyone in particular. Legal has to look at it, of course, but we don't need headquarters' approval. I'm authorized as CEO, and anyway, I've discussed your services with Joe Glennell."

"Already?"

"I was determined to have you, remember?" He grinned. "Corporately, I mean. I'll run it through Legal tomorrow morning and send it to you in the afternoon. You'll be all set up when you get there on Thursday. Janet Adams, my executive assistant, will have all your ID work done also. You'll just have to have your picture taken for the badge."

Daria put her hands on her hips and shook her head at him. The man dropped into CEO-mode in the blink of an eye. "You just have me all planned out, don't you?"

"Yep," he smirked.

"Well, Mr. Smarty, you read that and I'll print the list of what I need in the way of office equipment." She handed him the rest of the contract and turned back to the computer. When the list printed, she shut off the machines, laid the paper on the coffee table and sat down beside him.

Bent finished reading the contract and said, "This looks fine to me." He picked up the list of her requirements.

"Let's see now. Organization charts, I'll send those to you tomorrow. Computer with lots of memory, twenty-inch, flatscreen monitor, e-mail, locking file cabinet, no problem. An office with walls and a lock on the door away from the CEO's office. What's the last one mean? Don't you want to be close to me?" He put an arm around her and pulled her against his side.

She felt a little zing from his touch, but managed to keep her tone businesslike. "No. Not in the office. People will tell *me* more if they don't have to get near *you*. I need a little office out of the way somewhere."

"Okay, but I don't have to like it." He laid the list on the coffee table with the contracts, scooped up her legs over his lap and turned her to face him. "But I want you to promise you won't take any chances. Dan or one of his people has to know where you are at all times. We don't know who this joker is or what he might resort to."

"I promise," Daria said. His look was severe and dead serious, but as she watched, his eyes changed from brilliant blue ice to their normal liquid depth to hot, dark, deep, indigo pools as he gazed at her. She could feel that heat spread throughout her body when he smiled. She ran her hands over his chest and up around his neck, and he cuddled her closer, one arm around her shoulders, the other hand stroking up her jean-clad leg to rest on her hip.

"Setting up security and signing a contract is not exactly

the way I planned on spending the evening," Bent said, punctuating his statement with kisses to her lips before progressing to her cheek, earlobe, and throat. She just felt so damn good in his arms. When he came back to her mouth, he took his time about it, delving deep, tasting, exploring, savoring, inviting her to do the same. She tastes so good, he thought, like chocolate. Chocolate? He pulled back and mumbled against her lips, "Why do you taste like chocolate?"

"I sneaked a piece while you were outside," came the answer before he stopped her from talking at all. Her arms went around his neck and her fingers fisted in his hair.

He decided to be bolder this time, and ever so slowly slid his hand from her hip to under her breast, then tweaked the nipple with his thumb. She jumped just slightly, then arched into his hand as he covered the enticing mound and massaged it gently. She whimpered softly when he removed his hand to lift the hem of her loose T-shirt and come up underneath it to the bare skin of her midriff. Her skin felt like warm satin as his fingers traveled upward.

Just as he reached the bottom of her lacy bra, he realized they had both gone still, lips barely touching, breath barely moving, eyes barely open. He cupped her breast and slipped a finger inside her bra to massage the pebbled nipple. She moaned and the sound galvanized him to reach his entire hand into the cup.

Her head went back and she gasped.

"Do you like that, honey?" Bent rasped from a throat gone dry.

"Y-y-esss," she whispered, arching her back again and clutching his shoulders.

With his free hand at her back, Bent tilted her head down again to take her mouth, demanding more, taking more, giving more. Then he joined that hand with the one under her T-shirt and directed its attention to her other breast. When he discovered her bra had a front hook, he grunted in anticipation, unhooked it, and freed her breasts into his hands. For such a small woman, she was more lush than she looked, he realized with delight as he caressed her.

Eventually, reluctantly, Bent ended the kiss. If they went on any longer, he wouldn't want to stop, and from the tension he could feel in her, he just knew he shouldn't rush her, no matter how much he ached to do so.

"Bent?" she whispered.

"Shhh. It's all right. I have too much work to do tonight to stay, as much as I would like to strip you right here and make love on the floor." He rehooked her bra and settled her T-shirt. Daria flushed deep pink. He chuckled at the startled look on her face. "What's the matter, honey?"

"I, I'm, uh, not used to, uh, anyone doing that," she stuttered.

"You will be," he stated. She would if he had anything to do about it. He scooted her around again so she could stand up.

She put the papers in an envelope for him and walked him to the front gate. "I haven't really thanked you for all your help in this," she said as she opened the gate.

"Daria, you have it backwards. I just wish you weren't involved in what is clearly my problem. Now, give me a hug and a kiss and lock up after me. I'll call you tomorrow." He suited his actions to his words, waited until she had locked the gate behind him, and then drove off with a wave.

On the way back to his hotel, Bent grew angry all over again with the joker who was behind this mess. Then he turned the anger at corporate headquarters and J. Merrick Glennell, the CEO and board chairman, for making him waste time reporting in person and for generating the extra work for which he had left Daria.

"Bent, you're too much a workaholic for your own good," he told himself. "You're a fool for leaving her so soon." Thoughts of her response to him drove the anger out of his head and replaced it with sheer unadulterated lust. He shifted uncomfortably on his seat.

Daria certainly wasn't used to a man's attentions, he was sure. The evidence was leading to the conclusion that she had to be a virgin, or at the least, to have had only one lover in the past, and an inept one at that. Well, he would remedy the situation and for a long time to come.

A long time? His mind and his heart took a jump when he realized, contrary to all his previous history and hard-learned no-commitment philosophy, he was thinking more and more in the long term about a woman. But this time didn't feel like the first one and especially not the second. He didn't feel sick at all. None of the excruciating pain in his stomach. Quite the contrary—he felt as healthy as a horse.

Daria was bewitching him, and damned if he didn't like it. He was grinning like an idiot when some fool swerved into his lane on the Southwest Freeway and pulled his attention back to his driving.

After Bent left, Daria puttered around aimlessly, restless, unable to think of anything other than Bent and his kisses and his hands on her breasts. And how good she felt in his arms.

And how warm he made her. Warm, phooey! Hot as blazes! The memory caused her breasts to tingle, her nipples to pucker, and her womanhood to ache.

She had to talk to him, explain magic practitioners and soulmates, give him the opportunity to leave, to refuse to get involved in such a crazy situation.

But more and more she wanted for him to stay. She hugged herself as the possibility of his rejecting her shot such a bolt of pain through her body that she almost doubled over. If this was what having a soulmate did to you, it was a wonder anyone survived.

The reality of a soulmate—of Bent—had thrown most of her questions and all of her objections right out the window. She was coming to embrace the situation—and Bent—without putting up any kind of fight at all. She had been correct; the soulmate bond was not just a concept, it was a indomitable command, a compelling force of nature. Its handmaiden, desire, overwhelmed her ordinary defenses, fogged her mind, and left her aching and aroused. This latest episode illustrated the point. She would have given herself to him then and there on the couch in the study. Or on the floor. Anywhere!

Bent was the one with the willpower here, she thought ruefully. Maybe the imperative didn't act so powerfully on non-practitioners. Maybe it was simply because he was a man and a workaholic to boot. After all, warlocks did not remain virgins—quite the contrary. For her part, her virgin mind had been disconnected from her body, and she wasn't entirely certain she liked it—or becoming such a quivering mess of . . . what? Lust. Sheer lust, that's what this feeling had to be.

She cupped her breasts, mimicking Bent's touch. When her nipples tingled, she realized what she was doing and jerked her hands away. "Oh, get hold of yourself, woman," she told herself sternly, "but not like that!"

Lolita threw her a knowing glance when she passed the cat on the stairs. "A fat lot of help you are," Daria said, but Lolita just smirked at her.

Chapter Eight

On Wednesday Daria's parents and Clay arrived in the late morning. Antonia spent much of the next three hours replenishing spells on the house and grounds—a stronger repel-evil spell, a few powerful curses on anyone with the intent to harm the inhabitants, a few blessings for those within. She and Daria practiced the more personal defense spells as well. Clay and Alaric concentrated on revamping and strengthening the computerized security system.

Except for the time with her mother, Daria spent most of the day preparing to begin work for Glennell.

Bent sent over the contract, organization charts, and some other information he thought she might need, including photos of all the senior staff. He didn't call until around five in the afternoon.

"Hi," he said. "How are you doing?"

At the sound of his voice, she felt a zing skitter through her system and she took a deep breath to calm herself before answering, "Fine. Mother and Daddy came by, and Clay fine-tuned the security system. I've been organizing for tomorrow. How are you?"

"Frustrated as usual, trying to get everything together for our illustrious chairman. I hope you can find out what's going on in this company. The Poof Syndrome doesn't work worth a damn here."

"I'll do my best."

"Dan will come by at seven tomorrow morning to bring you here."

"I'll be there."

"You're sure you want to do this, Daria? I still don't like the idea of it."

"Yes, I'm certain, Bent. It's the best way I know to find out who's threatening me and, by extension, you."

"All right, then. I'll see you tomorrow."

Thursday morning, Daria rose early and dressed carefully. She chose one of her most conservative suits, a navy blue summer-weight wool blend with a white silk blouse. In these days of "office casual," she found it more productive to present herself first in professional armor. The initial impression the clothing made helped her establish and maintain a proper tone for the remainder of her work; she would be taken seriously, even without the help of a few spells.

Dan Roth arrived at Daria's at seven to take her to Glennell. "What's all this?" he asked when he saw several boxes stacked in the front hall.

"Various things I need for the job," she replied, closing her briefcase after making sure that she had extra diskettes and ZIP-drive cartridges.

"A coffeepot? We do have coffee in the office, you know." He smiled at her teasingly.

"Yes, but not my father's special brew. You'll have to drop in one morning for a cup."

"It's a deal. The office coffee is awful." He picked up the boxes and they loaded the car.

At Glennell, Dan took her through the ID-card process, complete with photo. "The code on the card will get you anywhere in the company," he said, showing her how to use the card in the scanner by the door. Commandeering a cart for the boxes, he escorted her to her new office.

"This is just what I wanted," Daria stated, looking around the twelve-by-twelve office, furnished with a plain desk, a computer, and the other items on her list. "How far away is Bent's office?"

"It's on this floor on the other side of the building. You're technically in the Public Relations department here. This was the most private place we could find. PR's out your door to the left. The executive suite is to your right."

He handed her a small list of numbers. "This is the one you call before you leave this office or return if you're on an unscheduled trip. Otherwise, a security officer will be here to escort you to your scheduled appointments. All you have to do is send your schedule every day to this e-mail address. We have also installed a hidden security camera to monitor your door. Privacy is all well and good, but we don't want you isolated."

"Fine," she answered. "Let's go. I'll unpack later."

"This way to Bent's office." After making sure her door was locked, he led her through two doors requiring her card to the other side of the city-block-long building and into much plusher accommodations indeed.

In the CEO's suite, the carpet changed color from serviceable gray to dark maroon, with a lighter pattern woven into it. The chairs and couches were richly upholstered and appeared to be deep enough to trap a small child in them. Western landscape scenes adorned the walls, and glossy green plants separated the seating areas. The executive receptionist was fortified in an oak embattlement that guarded the doors to the inner sanctum.

Dan introduced Daria to the receptionist and when the woman offered to announce them, Dan just said, "No need," and ushered Daria through the doors and into another reception area. She saw the receptionist reaching for the phone as they exited.

They went through another door on the other side of the inner seating area, and a woman rose from behind the desk. Medium-height, conservatively dressed with brown hair in a sleek bun and an efficient way about her, she appeared to be in her early forties. "Ms. Morgan," she smiled, "I'm Janet Adams, Mr. Benthausen's executive assistant. Welcome to Glennell-Houston."

"Thank you, Ms. Adams. Please call me Daria."

"And I'm Janet. Is your office up to your requirements? If there's anything else you need, please let me know immediately. Here's the folder with the information Mr. Benthausen said to give you for the meeting with the senior staff at ten. I also have your computer passwords and the person and number to call if there is a problem with them." She handed Daria a folder and a slip of paper with the information.

"Is Bent here yet?" Dan interrupted.

"Yes, he arrived before me this morning. Shall I announce you?"

"No need," Dan answered and turning, knocked on the door once and opened it, guiding Daria through into the office beyond.

"Thank you, Janet," Daria managed to call before Dan closed the door.

The phone to his ear, Bent waved them in. As they waited for Bent to conclude the call, Daria turned to Dan. "Do you ever let receptionists do their job?"

He grinned. "Not if I can help it. They're slowly getting the idea here."

Daria looked around the office. It was certainly plush, with leather couches on either side of a heavy glass coffee table, a huge conference table, a large executive desk of exotic woods—ebony and mahogany was her guess—and matching chairs. The carpet changed color again, this time to a deep navy. More Southwestern art graced the suede-covered walls.

She raised her eyebrows at Dan. "Very nice accommodations."

"The former president spent a lot on overhead, trying to match his ego," he stated in return.

Bent hung up the phone and came around the desk to give Daria a hug and a kiss. When she frowned at him severely, he laughed. "I know, no hanky-panky in the office.

Are you getting set up?"

"Yes, Dan helped me carry in what I need, and Janet seems to have come up with everything I requested. I'd like some time before the meeting to go over what she gave me and to arrange my office."

"Fine. Come back here about a quarter to ten and we'll go together. Do you want a rundown on the participants before we meet?"

"No, I'd rather meet them on my own."

The intercom buzzed and when Bent answered it, Janet informed him that New York was calling. "Not again," Bent grumbled. "I'll never get any work done if this keeps up."

Dan walked her back and introduced her to the Public Relations staff just down the hall from her office. Everyone was cordial, as you would expect with PR types, she concluded, and wasn't it interesting that the PR manager was presently closeted with the vice president for Media, Public, and Investor Relations? Probably getting ready for the big meeting.

Two hours later Daria watched as the senior staff arrived in the conference room. She tried to look the group over without showing interest in anyone in particular. Thanks to the photos, she recognized most of them. Every vice president and manager was there, the vice presidents around the table with their managers seated behind them. Most were serious, some seemed nervous, and a couple might be belligerent. No one looked happy.

Bent himself was expressionless, and Daria studied him covertly. She had not seen him in a real leadership position before now and she could feel the energy crackling around him. He appeared relaxed, but his serious demeanor implied that he was not to be trifled with and his blue eyes noticed every move of the participants.

At five after ten Bent sat forward and gathered his audience with a quick look around the room. "I called this meeting to introduce our new management consultant, Ms. Daria Morgan. I'm sure some of you have heard of her and of the fine work she's done for other companies. For those of you who are not aware of her, Daria's qualifications are superb." He proceeded to summarize Daria's background and a few of her clients and references. "I'll let her explain what she's going to be doing." He gestured toward her invitingly. "Ms. Morgan."

Just before standing up, Daria threw on a little I-am-important spell to make sure everyone paid attention, an I-am-trustworthy one, and an I-am-not-a-threat spell, the latter two to calm her audience down. She noticed Dan, who stood at the back of the room, blink and look around as if something had happened but he didn't know what. She expected it from him, after his reaction to the cats. Some people were innately sensitive to spells. Bent, of course, was oblivious to her magic; he just sat back and watched. All of the other staff members looked at her attentively, some with hesitant smiles, a few with poker faces, but no one with outright hostility. That would surface later.

"Thank you, Mr. Benthausen," she began, swinging her glance around the room to make eye contact with her audience.

"It's a pleasure to be here. My goal at Glennell-Houston will be to study and generate a report on the productivity, strengths and weaknesses of the staff, specifically upper and middle management. From this study I will form recommendations to enhance efficiency and improve performance. I expect the study to take at least two months.

"To do my job properly, I will need to interview, personally and at length, all vice presidents, managers, and possibly some of the next lower level, depending on the organization and duties of the department. I will be arranging interview times with each of you individually. I will probably talk with some of you several times so as not to take too much of your time in one sitting. I am relentlessly prompt for both the start and the end of interviews. If a manager does not have an office sufficiently private, we can meet in mine, which is located close to the PR department." She stated the location of her office and her phone number and sat down.

"Let me stress," Bent spoke up, "I trust you all will cooperate to the fullest with Ms. Morgan. Her interviews are to take precedence over your normal work. Are there any questions? Please identify yourselves by name and position to help Ms. Morgan get acquainted."

"I'm Stan Morrissey, acting vice president for Distribution," a short, balding man said. "When do these interviews start and what's the order for them? You know we have the physical inventory count coming up. It'll take everybody in the department to do it correctly."

"They will start on Friday and with Human Resources,"

Daria replied. "That is my usual starting point. I'd like the vice president for Human Resources and the HR manager . . ." She referred to her organization chart. "Mr. Grady and Ms. Brill, to remain after the meeting, if they would, to discuss our schedule. What I learn in HR will determine the order for the other departments. I'll send out an e-mail with a tentative schedule after the HR interviews." David Grady and Ellen Brill nodded in acknowledgment.

Theo Wall, Finance vice president, reminded Daria they had already met, pushed his heavy glasses up higher on his nose and asked, "When do we get to see a report?"

"I usually report only to the CEO and at the end of the project. What you see is up to him. We have not discussed any interim reports." That was true, they hadn't, but she knew Bent would both want and get them.

"I'm Merle Wharton, Manufacturing VP," a man with a chunky build and a bushy moustache said, leaning forward somewhat pugnaciously. "What if we don't like your conclusions? Do we get to rebut them?" Daria knew instinctively she would have to work hard on this man to dispel what she surmised was his automatic contentiousness. He was obviously someone who assumed the worst from the outset.

"That you must arrange with Mr. Benthausen," Daria said, smiling as she did so.

"Don't worry, Merle," Bent broke in. "You'll all have your chance at the report and we will thoroughly discuss all recommendations. Anything else?" He paused for a few seconds. No one said a word. "No? Then we're adjourned."

Daria arranged with Grady and Brill to meet them after lunch. Grady was even more nervous than he had been at the restaurant, but Ellen Brill appeared to be made of sterner stuff and cheerfully shook her hand in welcome.

"I'll get together copies of the various HR reports the government requires, if it will help," Ellen offered.

"That would be great," Daria said. "Any breakdowns on the workforce you can give me by sex, age, ethnicity, department, and so on would be most helpful. I'd like to know how long each manager and above has held his current position and what his former position was, if possible." Those tasks should keep HR busy for a while, she thought, while she could get on with more important investigations.

After Grady and Brill exited, Daria went back to Bent's office with him. The question Morrissey had asked came to mind as they walked in the door. "You know, we haven't talked about the sequence in which I'm supposed to take the departments," she said. "Here's my preliminary suggestion. It's based on what I've done in the past."

She handed him a slip of paper that read: HR, Administrative Services, Distribution, Manufacturing, Sales and Marketing, Finance, and Public and Investor Relations.

Bent glanced at it and said, "This looks fine. Since we don't know where the joker is, one order is about as good as another, I guess." He put the list atop the manila folder labeled "Morgan" on his desk, and came around it to put an arm around Daria and lead her to the door. "Let's take an early lunch. Since I'm leaving late this afternoon, it's my only chance to see you."

As they walked out, Bent spoke to his assistant. "Janet, I'll be out about an hour."

"I'll be here through lunch, Mr. Benthausen, and will have these letters ready for your signature when you get back," she replied.

Daria and Bent spent lunch talking about books, music, and movies, part of Bent's answer to Daria's wanting them to get to know each other better. Discovering they shared their likes and dislikes for the most part, Bent seemed pleased that they got along well. Daria sighed to herself, recalling her mother's words about soulmate compatibility. After an all-too-brief time together, Bent went off to his meetings and eventually the airport.

Chapter Nine

That afternoon Daria met first with David Grady, and then with Ellen Brill.

Daria needed no spells to see David Grady was the perfect example of the business "Peter Principle": a person was promoted until he reached the level of his incompetence. He gave general answers to her most pointed questions and when she bore in for specific details about the other departments under his control besides HR (which included Benefits and Training), he became even vaguer. He referred her often to his managers for details. By the time she left him, his continual hand-wringing and other anxious gestures were beginning to get on her nerves. She made a mental note to look into possible darker reasons than incompetence for his anxiety and set an appointment for a more in-depth interview with him for Friday morning.

In contrast, Ellen Brill, a very down-to-earth woman in her late forties, immaculately turned out from the top of her blonde hair to the tips of her fashionable pumps, exuded confidence and competence. In addition to answering all of Daria's questions fully and completely, she had put together a pile of reports and documents about the Glennell workforce—with statistics and budget details to match—that told Daria more than she wanted to know. The HR manager was clearly out to impress the consultant.

Daria was happy to recognize she could use Ellen's ambition and cooperation to glean more information as the study went on. With the help of a few spells to make certain the manager gave affirmative, honest answers, Daria also knew she could trust Ellen to keep whatever was told her confidential.

"I'm going to need to see a number of personnel files. Where do you keep them?" Daria asked as she prepared to leave Brill's office.

"Let me show you," Ellen replied, leading Daria down the hall to a room with a steel door and a vault-like lock. The walled-off area outside the room had a few small tables and chairs. "The personnel files are locked in the cabinets in the file vault behind the door, and the room itself is locked. If someone wants to look at his or her file, they come here, one of the staff pulls the file, and the employee reads it at these tables and chairs. If they want something copied, the staff does it. The only time the files leave the area is when a vice president wants to review the file of someone in their department. Managers and below must come here to review files of their staff members or they request a copy. In your case, we'd bring you the file since we have Mr. Benthausen's authorization."

"What if I don't want anyone to know which files I've requested?"

"You'd have to come here, pull them yourself, and look at them inside the file room. That's the only way we could do it because of our checkout procedures. There's a copier just outside the door if you need it."

Daria arranged to begin her detailed interview with Ellen

Friday afternoon. She took the pile of reports back to her office and studied them until Dan arrived to take her home.

On the way there, Daria asked, "Have you made the arrangements for Saturday?"

"Yes," he answered unequivocally. "How many people do you need?"

"Three or four. I will also need entrance to the Personnel vault. I'd like some of your staff to read the management personnel folders and compile some data, especially with an eye to noting anything slightly fishy. Knowing a staff's individual backgrounds, previous positions and employers, education, scorings on evaluations, and the like often displays patterns or connections that have proven useful. It's amazing to me how much people lie about those items.

"From what Ellen Brill said, Triangle did not have a procedure for checking references before they hired anyone, except for criminal background checks for people handling money. I'll have some forms for our helpers to fill out and a list of the people. I usually do this myself, but since we need the information quickly . . ."

"No problem. I'll make the final arrangements tonight. How long do you think it will take?"

"Four or five hours. We'll send someone out for lunch."

"I'll pick you up at 9:30 Saturday," Dan said as he dropped her off at her house.

Daria spent the evening preparing the forms to be filled out the next day. When Bent called just as she turned off her computer, she explained what she and Dan's staff would be doing, then asked him how things were going in New York.

"Joseph Merrick Glennell is in fine fettle and questions everything, as usual, but he's approving all my recommendations. Joe is most interested in what you're doing and wants to meet you. He's not at all happy about that note you received. In fact, he wants to see the operation in person and meet the staff, something he didn't do before the purchase. So he's coming for a visit, beginning next week on Thursday. I couldn't talk him out of it. Don't mention it to anybody at the office. I'll announce his visit by e-mail on Tuesday before I come home."

"Isn't that really short notice?"

"It's the way Joe does things. He likes to drop in practically unannounced. Claims he sees the real operation, not one that's been spruced up with all the problems hidden. Will his being there cause any problems for you?"

"Well, it's certainly going to put all the vice presidents and managers on edge, having the biggest head honcho of all here, but I'll work around it." She grimaced to herself. The visit would blow her schedule to smithereens, but she could live with the situation. "He won't say anything about the note, will he? Does he expect me to have any results by then?"

"No to both questions. He promises to concentrate on the business, show the Glennell flag, give little pep talks, tour the plants, that sort of thing. He knows your father, by the way."

"Yes, Daddy mentioned it the other day. He likes Joe."

"Joe's wife will be coming with him this trip, and they

want to take us both out to dinner on Friday. He'll fly back on Saturday morning. Did you have any plans for Friday night?"

"Only that I hoped we could be together."

Bent groaned. "Me, too, but not in the way we will. Save Saturday for me. Between Joe's visit and all the work he's piling on, I'll be lucky to have more than five minutes with you before then. In the meantime, you get some rest this weekend. I'll call tomorrow. I miss you, Daria."

"I miss you, too, Bent. Good-bye." She hung up the phone, organized herself for the next day, and went to bed feeling somewhat empty. She was beginning to yearn for him, for his touch, she realized as she tossed restlessly. Was she falling in love with him? Or was it the soulmate bond driving her, irrespective of love? Her mother claimed they went together. She hugged the pillow and pressed it into the ache in the middle of her chest.

The whole situation was so unfair, Daria thought. She was caught up in a whirlwind of attraction without the experience to handle it. If the phenomenon precluded her from gaining any sexual experience by blinding her toward any man except her soulmate, then how could she expect to keep on an even keel when faced with the reality of it, of him?

Oh, get real, she scolded herself, you aren't supposed to keep your wits about you. You're just supposed to fall into his arms. She took little solace in the fact that she had been correct in her first questions: Where was free will? Where was the ability to come to her own conclusions? Was she trapped? Could she do something about it? Did she want to?

This was so confusing. She needed to talk to her mother again. Maybe she had some insights that would help.

Up in New York, after he put down the phone, Bent stood pensively, gazing out of his hotel window at the city lights and absentmindedly rubbing the end of his sternum. Previously, being in the city had excited him, and he had looked forward to the meetings and dinners with longtime friends from his headquarters days.

This time was different. He didn't want to be here. He wanted to be down in Houston with Daria, protecting her, getting to *know* her. The desire, the longing—hell, the sheer lust he felt for this woman—all were stronger, immensely more powerful than he had experienced even as an eighteen-year-old kid in full hormonal rage. He seemed to be in a perpetual semi-aroused state when she was around.

With her, none of his anti-commitment internal warnings were going off the way they usually did. No burning stomach, no headaches, no panic. Just pure pleasure. But then, he'd always enjoyed the pursuit of a new woman, the give and take as they got to know each other, the enjoyment of coming together, the excitement of making love.

His usual girlfriends had been more worldly—or was the word "jaded"—than Daria and just as anti-commitment as he was. Well, that wasn't totally true. Kerrie had turned out to be flaky, and Susan wanted only her own brand of commitment. Now he was always clear with any woman, up front: he was only in town for a short time, and wasn't interested in anything long term.

He waved his hand in dismissal at the thought of the two exceptions to this pattern. He'd been young and stupid and let his hormones get the better of him. He was neither of those things now.

On the other hand, he'd made no such statements of "clarity" to Daria. Doing so had not crossed his mind. Now, the notion of saying such a thing, even touching on the subject with her, caused him to squirm, and he rubbed his chest harder as the itch increased in intensity.

What could be causing his reaction to Daria? Plain old human chemistry? Natural attraction? Something in his body telling him it was time to settle down and this one looked like a good mate? Mate? Where did that word come from? Sounded like a term out of Neanderthal times.

"Ugh. You, Daria. Me, Bent. Come to my cave," he grunted out loud as he poured himself a Scotch. Then he laughed. Man, wouldn't that go over well with his independent consultant? Grinning, he sat down and applied himself to his reports again. At least the damn itch had quit bugging him.

In Houston, the work went smoothly on Saturday and Daria and the security staff were finished by 2:30. Dan helped her run errands and go grocery shopping afterward, but refused her offer of supper.

About six, she was standing in front of the open refrigerator contemplating what to eat when the phone rang. She picked it up to hear Bent's baritone hello. Suppressing the shiver that zipped from her ears down her backbone, she returned the greeting. "Hi, you're earlier than I had expected."

"I'm going to dinner with some people from headquarters, and they want to go dancing at a club afterward. Knowing this bunch, I won't get back to the hotel until late, so here I am now. How did it go today at the office?"

"Fine. Dan and his people were very efficient. I'm going to go over all the data tomorrow and see if anything jumps out. I doubt it will, but you never know. How was your day?"

"Quiet. I spent it with some of the financial people trying to discover any accounting anomalies, but the books still look clean. Catching the security thieves only helped the bottom line so much. Our expenses are still too high."

"I'm talking with the HR people on Monday and Tuesday. Maybe I'll pick up some helpful gossip."

"You be careful, Daria."

"Don't worry, Bent. Dan has security all around me. You enjoy yourself tonight."

"I'll call tomorrow night." He paused, as if he were going to say something else, and finally said simply, "Good night."

"Good night," she replied and hung up the phone. A wave of loneliness hit her so hard she had to lean against the counter for support. It took her several deep breaths before she could stand straight.

"This will never do," she muttered as she reached into the freezer and pulled out a plastic container of her mother's chicken soup. The family always claimed the soup was "good for what ailed you"; she was about to prove that assertion.

The soup did help perk her up, and she was able to drive out of her mind the frustrating picture of Bent dancing with someone else. But her desire for human companionship did not lessen, so later Daria phoned her mother. They talked for a long time about love and soulmates, Daria going round and round over her old arguments, her mother offering support and encouragement.

"Tell me, dear, what do you really think of him?" Antonia finally asked.

Daria put her hand over the mouthpiece so her mother couldn't hear her sigh. Here it was, the direct question. She might as well admit it out loud. "I like him a lot. He's the most exciting, attractive man I've ever met," she said, but couldn't stop from adding a qualifier. "But I don't know if it's love."

"It will be," Antonia reassured her. "Everything you're going through—the attraction, the vacillation, the uncertainty—is typical for witches when they meet their soulmates. Love is the most important part of being soulmates. It's the glue holding everything else together. And it will come, dear. Just relax and enjoy the sensation. Falling in love is one of the most pleasurable experiences we can have."

Her voice assumed a more practical tone. "Besides,

practitioners don't have an exclusive claim on being soulmates. Non-practitioners find theirs all the time. Even if you weren't a practitioner, you and Bent would still be in love, soulmates, and friends. You two were meant to be together."

"I suppose," Daria said.

"Stop fighting it, Daria," Antonia counseled. "You're worried about nothing. It will all work out. Let me add some very practical advice: you know all the birth control spells; practice those."

"Mo-ther!" Daria was glad her mother could not see her blushing, although she did practice the spells before she went to bed.

Chapter Ten

Bent flew back to Houston late Tuesday night. He looked at his watch as he entered his hotel room. One in the morning, thanks to some weather that delayed the departure from Kennedy—too late to call Daria. They'd agreed he wouldn't call when he arrived, but he sure would like to hear her voice.

"Oh, what the hell," he muttered, dialing.

Her soft, sleepy "Hello?" rippled down his spine and lodged in his cock. It obviously wanted to say hello, too.

"Hi, it's me," he managed to say somehow in a normal voice. "I just wanted to let you know I'm here in Houston. Go back to sleep and I'll see you in the morning."

"I'm glad you're back," she murmured. He heard sheets moving and pictured her curled up in bed. The image caused his entire body to tense.

"Tomorrow," he said.

"Tomorrow," she repeated. "Good night." She hung up the phone.

He stood there willing his body to relax and listening to the dial tone until it started warbling at him. "Tomorrow, first thing," he promised as he put the phone down.

When Bent arrived at Glennell Wednesday morning at 7:30, he dropped off his briefcase and papers in his own office and went to Daria's. There he found Dan staring into his coffee cup and Daria leaning on one arm with her forehead cupped in her hand. Neither had a happy look. Bent stopped in his tracks. "What's the matter?" he demanded, coming into the office and closing the door behind him. This was not the way he planned on starting the morning.

"Dan has discovered a slight problem," Daria answered. She rose, poured Bent a cup of coffee, and gave it to him as he leaned against the shut door.

"One of my people called me at home last night to report that the order in which Daria was going to interview the departments was widely known," Dan stated. "Now the fact that people know the order is not so important. But the only people who are supposed to know the order are you, me, and Daria. She hasn't told anyone else yet. It therefore appears we have a leak or perhaps a spy somewhere. Did you let something drop at headquarters?"

"No, I told no one," Bent said.

"That's what we thought," Daria said. "Once you told me Joe Glennell was coming, I wasn't going to put out a schedule until we saw how much commotion his visit caused. We have been backtracking all my steps over the past few days to see if I let something slip. Dan has one of his computer people checking to see if anyone cracked my password to look into my network files. It wouldn't do anyone any good to see the files. There's nothing crucial in them, but if someone is hacking, it wouldn't hurt to know it either."

"We have come up with one possibility for where the leak occurred," Dan said, grimacing. "As I understand it, Daria wrote down the order of interviews only once and gave the piece of paper to you right after the staff meeting last Thursday."

"Yes, that's right," Bent said, remembering the action. "I put the paper into the file on my desk." He thought about the event as he sipped his coffee. Visualizing the moment with his desk and its stack of files, he closed his eyes and held out his hand as though he had the piece of paper in it. "No, wait. I took the paper from you . . ." He mimicked receiving the note. ". . . and put it . . ." He stretched out his hand toward his imaginary desk. ". . . put it on top of the Morgan file on my desk."

He opened his eyes and looked at Dan. "The file was on my desk when I returned from lunch and I stuck it into my briefcase and took it with me to New York, but I didn't need to refer to it after all. It should still be there." He swallowed the last of his coffee and put the cup down. "Let's go look."

The three of them trooped over to Bent's office where he retrieved the briefcase, pulled out the file, and located the piece of paper with the list on it. "Here it is." He handed it to Daria.

Dan and Daria looked at each other, clearly puzzled.

"There's another possibility," Daria said after a long moment. "Where was the paper when you returned from lunch?"

Bent closed his eyes again, matching his thoughts with arm movements. "I came in, came around the desk, picked up the file, and put it into my briefcase." He opened his eyes and glanced from Daria to Dan. "The paper must have been *in* the file because I didn't put it in there myself."

"How much do you trust Janet Adams?" Dan asked.

"She was my predecessor's executive assistant and has done well keeping the office running. I've formed the impression she was relieved *not* to be working for the former president. I've had no reason to distrust her up to now, and she's been dealing with some highly confidential information. There have been no leaks to my knowledge."

"Was there anything new on your desk when you came in from lunch?"

"Some letters and papers to sign." He looked at the desk ruefully. Damn, he hoped their suspicion wasn't true. He didn't want to bring in a new assistant at this point. "She must have seen the paper and put it into the file. But what makes you think she told someone?"

"She's sleeping with Phil Casey, the Public Relations manager, who's one of the biggest gossips in the company," Dan said. "And Jane Rutherford on my staff heard the information from a PR secretary."

"Oh hell," Bent muttered. "Isn't there anybody in this company I can trust?"

Daria spoke up. "It might not be so bad. The question then becomes, was it just something she told him in pillow talk, or did he pump her for it, or are they in cahoots for something else? This doesn't have the feel of a malicious act, just gossip. Is Casey trying to make himself look like the man who's in the know, who's smarter than he actually is? Finally, what are we going to do about him and especially her?"

"I haven't come in contact much with Casey," Bent said,

trying to recall the occasions they had been in the same room. "He's a good-looking California beach-boy type with blond hair and broad shoulders, but he's going a little soft around the middle. Always struck me as a ladies' man, you know the type. The way he does his job hasn't impressed me very favorably. When he has spoken in meetings, he hasn't contributed much of substance. He mostly just backed up his boss, Tom Evans, who does know what he is doing. When Tom and I discussed his department, Tom said he was going to let Casey go as part of the company-wide effort to streamline his staff. We've been concentrating on other departments first, those more crucial to the bottom line."

Disgusted, Bent ran his fingers through his hair. "What a company to run, where the non-essential positions are full of incompetent SOBs like Casey and Grady. God only knows how much they're dragging down morale. Firing the former Distribution VP obviously wasn't enough to convince anyone I meant business. Well, that will soon change."

He brought his attention back to the issue at hand and stared out the window for a moment. "Janet, on the other hand, has been efficient, helpful, and knowledgeable in her work, and I would have had a much harder time at the beginning without her. Okay, let's get her in here and see what she has to say for herself," he said.

Daria watched Bent turn toward his intercom button. She had to control this interview if they hoped to learn the truth. "Wait," she said and, eyebrows raised, Bent looked at her. "Let me handle this," she requested. "I've established enough rapport with her to set her at ease. I think she'll answer me truthfully as long as you two don't jump on her immediately. Okay?"

"Okay," Bent nodded, and hit the intercom button.

Daria threw several spells on herself: an I-am-trustworthy, an I-am-not-a-threat, and an I-will-hear-only-the-truth, along with a small power spell to reinforce the others. "Let's all sit down," she said as Janet walked in. Bent sat behind his desk, and the others took chairs around it.

"Janet," Daria said, "we need your help. Last week, just before Mr. Benthausen left for New York, I gave him this information." She handed Janet the paper with the interview order on it. "Did you see it then?"

Janet read the information and handed it back. "Yes, I remember it was lying loose on the desk, and I put it into the Morgan folder so it wouldn't get lost. Was that wrong? Should it have gone somewhere else?"

"No, Janet," Bent replied. "It was the proper place."

"Janet, did you tell anyone about what you read on this piece of paper?" Daria asked, concentrating on catching the woman's gaze so her attention was solely on Daria. She gave the spells a boost. "Anyone at all?"

"Only Phil," Janet answered, responding to the spells. Then her eyes widened and her hand flew to her mouth as if to stop the words from getting out, but it was too late. "Oh, Mr. Benthausen," she gasped. Her eyes darted from Daria to Bent to Dan and back to Daria. "It was just . . . I didn't think . . . He told somebody, didn't he?" She blanched as she realized the answer to her question. "I'm sorry. I know I shouldn't have done that," she concluded and dropped her gaze to her hands, now clenched in her lap.

"Janet, did he ask or did you just volunteer the information?" Daria asked quietly, leaning toward the woman and kicking the spells up another notch.

The spells pulled Janet's eyes up to Daria. The assistant answered in a whisper. "We were just lying there talking, and he asked what was going on with the new consultant and what I thought of the staff meeting. And I told him I thought you'd be a big help to Mr. Benthausen. Then he asked if I knew the interview order so he could prepare for it. And I told him. I didn't think about it, I just told him." She took a deep breath. "But I didn't tell anyone else. I swear. I never would." She shifted her focus to Bent. "I've *never* told him anything else about what goes on in this office, Mr. Benthausen, even when he asked. Who did he tell?"

"Just about everyone," Bent said.

Janet was silent for a moment, then she spoke. "You'll have my resignation as soon as I can type it, Mr. Benthausen." She blinked, obviously trying to hold back tears, but she managed to keep her composure.

Daria held up her hand before Bent could say anything. "What are you going to do about Phil Casey, Janet?"

Janet looked back at her hands in her lap. "When we . . ." came out in a croak. She cleared her throat and started again, her voice firmer, her eyes raised to Daria's. "When we first started dating, we talked about the company and the changes Mr. Benthausen was making. You know how people talk when there's a change in management. I told him then I couldn't speak about what went on in the executive offices, and he wasn't to repeat even the inconsequential things I might say. He promised not to."

She paused, a contemplative look on her face. "You know, now that I think about it, he never showed any interest in me until you, Mr. Benthausen, took over." She straightened her spine and stuck out her chin. "Now to find out he's been using me . . . that no-good . . . What am I going to do about him? Throw the snake out of my life," she said through gritted teeth. "I only wish I could do him damage."

"I'll take care of it, Janet." Bent leaned back in his chair and scrutinized his assistant. "Look, I know gossip is inevitable in any company, and it's easy to let something slip to someone you're close to and who's supposed to be trustworthy. I don't blame you for Casey being a jackass. You've done a fine job for me and been a big help. Your resignation won't be necessary if you'll give me your word that you won't do this sort of thing again."

He glanced at Daria who nodded agreement and swallowed a sigh of relief. Neither Casey nor Janet were the threat makers, she was certain. Casey was obviously a jackass, and Janet . . . Janet was a woman in the throes of an infatuation. Not unlike herself. She tucked the thought away for later consideration and listened to what else Janet was saying.

"Rest assured I won't tell anyone anything, Mr. Benthausen. Thank you." Janet's voice shook with obvious relief. Then her anger at Casey resurfaced. "What are you going to do about Phil?" The expression on her face indicated she clearly hoped he'd be boiled in oil and she'd be happy to stir the pot.

"Have a talk with his boss about doing some housecleaning on an accelerated schedule," Bent said with an ominous smile. He turned to Dan. "Alert your people so one of them is available when Evans talks to Casey. Put someone here in the outer office, too. I don't want Casey to come crying to Janet. Janet, call all the vice presidents and ask them the status of the reports I requested for Joe Glennell's visit. All except Tom Evans, Phil's boss. I'll call him myself. Let's get back to work." He punched in a phone number as Dan and Janet went into the outer office, closing the door behind them. "Tom? Bent. Could you come over here right away and tell no one where you're going? Good. I'll expect you in five minutes."

He hung up the phone, then walked around the desk to Daria, who had risen from her chair. "You, come here." He enveloped her in a large hug, lifting her off the ground as he squeezed her tight. Looking down into her eyes as he put her back on her feet, he said, "I've wanted to do that from the moment I walked in your office. And I want to do much more, but if I start, I won't want to stop, and we don't have any time right now."

Daria returned his hug—oh, it felt so good—and agreed. "I know. It looks like the weekend before we'll have any time to ourselves, doesn't it?" When Bent nodded, she continued, "Well, I'm going to keep on with Administrative Services and then reshuffle the interview order. I think I'll move Manufacturing up and then take on Finance."

"Whatever you think is best," Bent said, releasing her. The intercom buzzed. "That will be Tom," he said. "Remind me later to ask you how you convinced Janet to open up so quickly. I expected much more difficulty."

"Magic," was all she said as she opened the office door for the Public Relations VP, leaving after he walked in.

During the afternoon one of the PR administrative assistants stuck her head into Daria's office, asking if she'd heard the news. When Daria said no, Mavis Lawson, an overweight woman in her fifties, looked around conspiratorially and stepped in. "Phil Casey got fired this morning!" she informed Daria in a loud whisper.

"Is that good or bad?" Daria asked. She'd been curious about the employees' reaction to the situation.

"Oh, honey, that's good. The man thought he was God's gift to women and chased anything in a skirt. Couldn't keep his hands off anyone. Even me! I told him my Homer would flatten him if he touched me again and that stopped him, but I really felt for our young women, no matter what their title." She shivered in sympathy. "You know, we administrators see things, and that's not all Casey did. He sucked up to Mr. Evans something awful and badmouthed everybody's ideas but his own, or stole the good ones and didn't give his people any credit. Very few of them liked the man. Good riddance is what I say."

Daria thanked Mavis for the information and tactfully maneuvered the woman out of her office.

The remainder of the week went smoothly for Daria despite the fact she had to reschedule some interviews because of Joe Glennell's visit. She succeeded in meeting with the head of Administrative Services, but had to put off her managers until the next week. Outside of noting some understandable feelings by the woman that her department was unjustly put upon by people complaining about the copiers or the lack of their preferred ballpoint pen or some such foolishness, Daria detected nothing indicating a problem.

She tried not to think about Bent, but after his nightly calls, she was filled with longing and a new sensation—frustration. Damn, but she couldn't wait for his touch, his kiss.

Bent met with Joe Glennell and his management staff, toured the plants, and supplied the reams of information the man requested. All in all, he thought the visit was going well. If nothing else, the vice presidents and managers were witnessing first hand that Joe backed him completely in his plans for Glennell-Houston. If anyone was contemplating running to Corporate to protest Bent's actions, they would clearly receive a cold reception.

For himself, Bent was especially looking forward to taking Daria home Friday night after the dinner with the Glennells, but when Friday came, he and Joe were running late, trying to finish all their business before the Glennells returned to New York early Saturday morning. Their delay meant he had to ask Daria to meet them at the posh restaurant in the Galleria area, so there would be no taking her home. A security staff member dropped her off and would return at a pre-arranged time to escort her to her house.

Dinner with the Glennells turned out to be a great success, and Bent relaxed for the first time that week. Joe, a self-made billionaire, was as down-to-earth as they come, and his wife Lydia matched him well. They made an interesting couple, he of medium height, great energy, and a booming laugh, she slender and short, extremely chic, with a dry wit. Bent had loved them both for years, Joe having taken over as Bent's mentor when Ben Kasinsky died in an auto accident shortly after Bent had turned around his second acquisition for the company. Joe also knew Daria's father, having used Alaric's services several times in the past, so a Glennell-Morgan link existed already.

It was clear to Bent the Glennells were almost as taken with Daria as he was. Both were equally as appalled by the threat made against her. "Nothing like this has ever happened before at one of my companies," Joe said. "Dan Roth is the best in the business at providing security, and I want you to know, we'll do everything to keep you safe and get to the bottom of this, Daria."

"I appreciate it, Joe," she replied.

"Have you discovered anything that might help us find the letter writer?" Joe asked.

"Nothing yet. All I've found so far are petty problems that wouldn't cause such vehemence. I never expected much trouble with HR or Administrative Services, by the way. When I come into a company, I usually start with one or both of those departments to get everyone acclimated to my presence. Because their staffs work with the entire company, they're usually a good source of information and gossip. If there are larger problems, they're usually with the manufacturing, distribution, and finance departments."

"How's Bent doing?" Joe asked with a sly smile.

"I wasn't hired to report on his work," Daria said with a perfectly straight face. "That would require another contract, which I would have to decline."

"Why?"

"Conflict of interest," Daria said with a twinkle in her eye before she turned to Joe's wife. "Lydia, Bent told me you collect antiques. Did you get an opportunity to tour Bayou Bend?"

Bent watched Joe and Lydia absorb the information Daria's answer conveyed as they both shot a glance at him and then at each other. Lydia had been dropping hints he should settle down for years and a smug smile crossed her face before she went along with Daria's change of subject. After a discussion about the stately home and gardens that had been bequeathed to the city as a museum by the daughter of a Texas governor, the conversation moved elsewhere. Bent, however, was certain the subject of Daria would come up later and he planned how to tell them—pleasantly, of course—to butt out.

After dinner, Bent walked Daria to the car and her security staff chauffeur. "Let's spend tomorrow together, Daria," he said, taking her in his arms and kissing her lightly. God, she felt so good and he didn't want to let her go. He almost groaned at the effect holding her was having on his body. "I'd ask to come over later tonight, but I know how Joe works and he will want to have a nightcap and go over everything one more time." And if he did go over to Daria's, he wouldn't let her get any sleep, or not much anyway.

"Come for breakfast," she suggested. "Eight o'clock."

"I'll be there." He kissed her again and saw her off quickly, before temptation got the better of him.

Chapter Eleven

Zorro and Lolita woke Daria just before the perimeter alarm buzzed in the security control panel by her bed. The big black cat growled and leapt off the bed, up to the window seat overlooking the garden. Tilting the louvered shutter open with his paw, he stared down and laid his ears back. Lolita jumped down and scooted under the bed.

Her heart pounding from the abrupt awakening, Daria glanced at the glowing face of her alarm clock: four in the morning, still pitch dark. She shut off the alarm and listened for a moment. The house was silent and the other buttons in the panel were green. Nobody had breached the house defenses. She rose, took a deep breath for calm, crept over to the window, and peeked carefully through the shutters. She couldn't see anyone lurking on the patio. Zorro growled again. "Is someone in the side yard?" she asked the cat.

"Yah!" Zorro said as he jumped off the seat and trotted out the bedroom door toward the stairs.

Daria threw on a robe and tiptoed downstairs. Nothing moved outside, but she spotted Zorro heading for the back of the house. When she reached the kitchen, she could see two men skulking across the side lawn, headed toward the patio. His fur bristling and sharp teeth gleaming in the low light, Zorro stood in the sink, glared at the intruders, and hissed.

"It's okay, Zorro," Daria whispered to the angry feline.

"We'll get them." Pleased to see her hands were steady, even though she could feel the adrenaline streaking through her, she reached for the cordless phone and dialed 911. When the dispatcher answered, she identified herself and her address. "There are two men in my yard," she said softly. "They are looking at the upstairs windows and have some objects in their hands that look like rocks."

"Where are you, ma'am?"

"I'm in the kitchen with a cordless phone."

"Just a second. Don't hang up." There was a pause, then the dispatcher came back on the phone. "Officers are on their way and will be there in minutes. Please go to the front door, as far away from the men outside as you can."

Instead of following directions, Daria moved closer to a window. She could feel the spells shimmering around the house and knew the men would have a hard time actually getting in. She also doubted they could see her in her dark robe. She took a deep breath. All her rational thoughts had no effect on her rapid breathing or accelerated heartbeat. "They're pointing up to my bedroom window now and walking toward it," she whispered cautiously into the phone.

"Ma'am, please go to the front door," the dispatcher requested insistently.

"Now they're winding up . . . and throwing something at my window!" Daria watched the missiles arc into the air, bounce off the house spells and land back at the men's feet. A bright green flash of light preceded a loud BANG! BANG! The windows rattled, but no glass broke.

Zorro jumped about a foot and yowled, then leapt out of the sink and ran toward the front of the house.

"Ma'am! Are you all right?" The dispatcher sounded worried.

"Yes, I'm fine. Whatever they threw bounced back at them and blew up. There's a green cloud surrounding the men now and they're staggering around out of it. I think it was stink bombs . . . Yuck! One of them is throwing up on my petunias! Now they're both running for the front fence."

Whatever apprehension she had been feeling vanished in light of the farce playing out in front of her. Fascinated, she moved through the dining room and into the front hall to get a better view. "Oh, ouch! I bet that stings!"

"What's happening, ma'am?" The dispatcher sounded intrigued now.

"They're trying to climb the fence straight through the bougainvillea vine with all those nasty thorns. One of them is on top of the fence. Whoops! He slipped and it looks like he skewered his leg on one of the spikes." She could hear them hollering now. "The other one pulled him off and is practically carrying him to a pickup truck by the curb . . . Oh, my goodness!" She started laughing.

"Ma'am? What happened?" The dispatcher's voice rose. "The officers are only a couple of blocks away."

"They jumped in the cab, but the driver pushed them out again." Daria gasped through her laughter. "They must stink something awful. They're climbing into the truck bed. It's an old pickup. I can't tell the color, but it's a dark truck.

That's all I could see. The truck took off down the street, and here's the police car."

"Zorro, stay inside," she ordered the cat as she released the security alarm. She ran out the front door to the gate just as the police car pulled up with its lights flashing. "They just drove away in a pickup truck. See those lights turning the corner!" She yelled at the police and pointed toward the disappearing lights. With siren howling, the cops drove off in pursuit.

Daria unlocked the gate and turned to go back inside. She started coughing as the rotten-egg smell from the stink bombs wafted around the corner of the house. Then she saw a piece of paper stuck on the front door under the door knocker.

"Ma'am? Ma'am!" The dispatcher sounded perturbed, and Daria realized she still had the phone in her hands.

"I'm here. The cops just went after the truck, and I've found a note on the front door." She closed the door behind her and took a deep breath of the clean inside air.

"There's another car on the way, ma'am. Please go back inside."

"I'm already there. Thanks for your help. Would you please let Lieutenant Bill Childress know about this? I've had a previous problem here he's been helping with. Thanks. I'm going to hang up now."

She punched the disconnect button and leaned back against the door. Her breathing had slowed, but her hands were beginning to shake as she came down from the adrenaline rush. She could feel her heart decreasing its triphammer beat. For a moment, she concentrated on calming her body, and when she felt more stable, she immediately dialed Clay.

His sleepy voice grated in her ear. "This had better be important."

"Clay, it's me. Some guys just tried to stink-bomb the house and the police are in pursuit. There's some kind of note on the front door," she told him as she walked toward the kitchen for her tongs.

"Are you all right?" He no longer sounded sleepy.

"Yes, the spells held. The stink bombs bounced back and detonated right at their feet. Mother's repel-evil spell worked really well. You should have seen it." She couldn't help laughing as she related the tale. "They were so disoriented from the bombs exploding and probably also from Mother's curses that they climbed out of the yard straight over the bougainvillea. One of them caught his leg on the fence spikes. I don't think they're in very good shape at the moment." She took the tongs out of the drawer and headed for the front door again.

Clay laughed. "That'll teach them to mess with a Morgan. I'll be right there. Call Bent." He hung up.

Standing in the front hall, Daria called Bent. It seemed to take him a moment to wake up because his voice was a wonderful low rasp. "Daria, I was just dreaming about you. What time is it?" There was a pause as he must have looked at a clock and jumped to a conclusion. "What's the matter!"

She told him about the attempted vandalism. "And, yes, I'm fine, and here comes the second police car."

"I'll be right there."

The second set of officers helped her take the paper from the door and lay it out on the hall table. In big black letters, it screamed:

STAY AWAY FROM GLENNELL.
YOU HAVE BEEN WARNED.

Zorro stalked silently into the hall as the officers looked at the note. He caught a whiff of the paper and hissed, causing one of the policemen to jump and reach for his gun before realizing the source of the noise.

"It's all right, officer," Daria said. "It's just my cat." She tried not to smile.

"Yes, ma'am," the officer said faintly, while the other man grinned until he turned around and saw Zorro for himself. "Holy . . . That's some cat. We'll take a look out back, ma'am," he said as he pulled his comrade out the front door.

While the police officers investigated outside, Daria called her parents and reported the incident. "We'll be there between nine and ten," Alaric informed her. "Yes, and I want to renew those spells and add a couple," Antonia said. "We love you."

"Love you, too," Daria murmured as she turned to the police coming in the front door with her brother right behind them.

Bent was certain he broke every traffic law on the books getting to Daria's house. He parked across the street and hurried over to Clay and a police officer who stood watching another officer on a ladder scrape something from one of the iron fence spikes and put it into an evidence bag. The smell of the stink bomb permeated the neighborhood, and other officers were talking to a group of Daria's neighbors who had been drawn from their beds by the commotion.

"Hi, Bent," Clay said, just as though it were the middle of the afternoon. Then he turned to the police officer next to him. "The reason the points glow in the dark is because two smart-ass neighbor kids were giving me trouble when I was painting them with rust inhibitor. So, to keep them off the fence, I added some phosphorescent paint to the mix and told them it was curare."

The officer chuckled.

"Did the police capture the bastards?" Bent asked.

"No, but we have notified the hospitals. One of them left a lot of blood here," the officer said and looked pointedly at Bent. "And you are?"

"Bent's a good friend of the family," Clay answered for him. "Daria's inside, Bent. She's fine."

"I think I'll see for myself." As he entered the house, he took a deep breath, inhaling the surprisingly sweet air that held no taint of the acrid smell of the bomb. He found Daria in the kitchen, pouring coffee for Bill Childress and another officer. She looked adorable in her dark red robe and bare feet, but he noticed she jerked nervously when he stepped unexpectedly into the room. He waited until she put the coffeepot down before taking her in his arms. "Are you really all right?"

"I'm still a little jittery, but yes, I really am all right," she answered, returning his hug with a fierceness that told him she really wasn't. He held on to her until she pulled back with a grin. "You should have seen it. The whole episode was actually a comedy of errors." She repeated the tale and had all the men laughing when she finished. "Now, if you gentlemen will excuse me, I'm going to get dressed."

Bent poured himself a cup of coffee and sat down at the table. Clay came in and did the same. By the time Daria came down, only Bill Childress was left of the police force. "I, for one, am hungry. I assume everyone would like some breakfast?" Daria announced as she pulled eggs out of the refrigerator and a coffee cake from the freezer. "Lieutenant, you're perfectly welcome to eat with us."

"Thank you, ma'am. I'd appreciate it." The detective smiled at her. "Did you think of anything else to tell us about the incident?"

"No, nothing," Daria said, shaking her head for emphasis.

Childress' cell phone beeped. He answered, listened for a few minutes, and then said, "Good work . . . Yes, do it . . . I'll be along in a little while." He punched the phone button to end the call and stuck the device back in his pocket. "You'll be happy to know we've already apprehended one of the vandals, the one the fence bit. His buddies threw him out of the truck at the Ben Taub Hospital emergency room and took off. A couple of officers were just coming out of the hospital as they heard the radio call and figured he must be one of the perps because of the way he stank."

His audience laughed, as Childress continued, "He's being stitched up and will be taken to the station afterward as soon as he can travel. All he's said so far is someone hired the driver and the driver roped him and the other guy into the scheme. He doesn't know who the mastermind is. They were just supposed to stick the paper on your door, throw the bombs into a window, and run. They picked a back window to give them more time to climb out over the gate. I guess they forgot about that route when the bombs blew up at their feet. He was mad enough at the driver and the other man for dumping him to give us their names, and we're putting out an APB."

"Clay, put the coffee cake in the microwave and nuke it, will you?" Daria asked as she scrambled eggs. "Will I need to testify? I don't know if I could identify either one of them."

"If it comes to trial you might, but the one we caught is a petty criminal and will probably bargain for a more lenient sentence. The thing is, no one was hurt, no real damage was done, other than to the one vandal, and it's a misdemeanor as it stands. He'll probably get a fine and probation." Childress shrugged with a disgusted look on his face.

"And the police won't look too hard for his buddies for such an inconsequential crime, will they?" Bent asked as he gazed out the window, hands in his pockets, rocking back and forth on his feet. He frowned as he tried to pull all the facts and events together in his mind. What could they conclude from this latest threat to help them catch the bastard behind these threats? What were they—especially himself—going to do?

"Probably not," was Childress' answer.

"So, it means we're no closer to the man who originated the threats than when we started," Bent continued, "but the threats seem to be escalating, if this stink bomb and the note are any indication. We must be getting close to something or someone. That person is evidently afraid of Daria and what she might find. All the threats so far have been aimed at her, no one else."

"Where are you going with this?" Clay asked as he took the coffee cake from the microwave and Daria dished up the eggs.

Bent faced his audience, glancing first at Clay and then concentrating on Daria, who turned to him as she put the egg dish on the table. "Here's my plan. Glennell will supply all the security it can for Daria outside this house. Daria has already expressed her refusal to have staff stationed here inside or outside. But I don't like at all that she's alone at night, no matter how good the burglar alarms are. They're just not enough if someone is determined to break in. If these guys had broken into the house tonight, they could have done a lot of damage before the police arrived.

"That likelihood is not acceptable to me. Therefore, to provide at least a greater measure of security during the night, I'm going to move in to stay with her. With you, Daria." He was determined to do this, no matter what arguments she or her brother put up.

Daria said nothing, just stared at him with a frown on her face.

"It's either that, or we put security staff here in the house with you at night," Bent stated. "One or the other, take your pick."

Clay shot a glance at his sister and spoke up. "I think Bent's moving in is a good idea, Daria. I'd certainly feel better if you had someone here during the night, even with the alarms and locks and everything."

Daria pivoted to Clay. "You don't think the alarms and everything could keep them out?"

Bent heard the slight emphasis brother and sister put on the words, "and everything," but he ignored it. He had Clay's approval, now to secure Daria's. He'd let her brother make the argument.

Clay obligingly proceeded to do it. "Only up to a point. If they come en masse or with weapons, I don't know you could fend them off by yourself," he said.

"You realize, we'd have to . . ." She nodded slightly toward Bent.

"Yeah, but you were going to do it anyway, weren't you?"

"You know about this, uh, so—uh, thing?"

"Yeah. Dad talked to me and I've seen it happen a couple of times."

"What about . . . ?" She waved vaguely westward, toward the plant nursery and their parents.

"I think they'll agree and help with the other," Clay

stated. "I assume you called them."

"Yes, they'll be here this morning."

Bent and Childress watched the interchange as though they were at a tennis match, swinging from one to the other Morgan. Bent knew he had not understood all the nuances of their conversation, but it didn't matter.

He decided to focus on Daria. "Daria? What do you think?" He was determined to protect her and tried not to think about the added benefits to his plan. But he couldn't help it. Oh, God, to live with her here in the house, at night, in bed, in his arms. Because that was exactly where she would be, he was certain. A little itch started in the middle of his chest, and he rubbed it as he waited for her answer.

She gave a great sigh and drew herself up in a businesslike demeanor. "Yes, Bent. I agree with your analysis. I'd appreciate having someone here, you here, and there's plenty of room."

Bent didn't realize he was holding his breath until he exhaled at her answer. Utter contentment flashed through him and he grinned at her, noting her blush in reaction. She was probably thinking the same thing he was: whose bed would he be sleeping in? But he only said, "Good. I'll check out of the hotel today."

"Everybody eat before it gets cold," Daria said as the flush mounted in her face and she turned to pour more coffee.

Chapter Twelve

After breakfast, Clay showed Bent the intricacies of the security system; Childress went to question the vandal; and Daria tried to keep herself busy, first by cleaning up the kitchen. She knew she was still jittery from the excitement, and she tried to concentrate on her kitchen tasks.

Her mind, however, kept returning to the reality of having Bent stay with her. Oh, God, to have him here in the house, at night, in . . . She closed off that thought quickly. They'd have to explain about magic practitioners and all the rest this afternoon.

All the rest? She shook her head. She didn't want to think about *that* now.

She made up one of the two guest rooms to establish the fact—in her own mind, at least—that Bent *wouldn't* be sharing her bed. Then for a while, she sat in her bedroom with the still-agitated cats, petting them and talking soothingly. Since she herself was not exactly calm under the combined effects of the intruder incident and of apprehension about the coming confrontation, it didn't help any of the three of them very much, but it was better than nothing. Or so she tried to tell herself as she thought of what she had to say to Bent.

"I'm not really worried about explaining the practitioner part," she declared to Lolita after Zorro stalked off to patrol for intruders again. "Mother and Daddy will help there. But about us as soulmates? Oh, I'm such a coward."

Lolita stood up in Daria's lap and touched noses with her. "Rrowww," she said emphatically before turning around and settling down.

"You don't think so, huh? Well, thanks for the vote of confidence." Daria rubbed behind the elegant cat's ears and received a purr in return. Lolita's opinion notwithstanding, she still did not look forward to the discussion.

What would happen if Bent refused to believe them, or worse, thought they were all crazy and left her? Where would he and she be as soulmates? This soulmate attraction was getting stronger by the day and she was already more than half in love with the man.

No, to be honest, she was completely in love, just as her mother had predicted. She might as well admit it to herself. She couldn't wait to see him, she yearned for his touch, and she mooned over him when he wasn't with her. His mere presence excited her, both mentally and physically. And the feelings she had when she was in his arms . . .

She was bedazzled, enthralled, spellbound. If he'd been a practitioner, she'd have been certain he'd cast an enchantment. But he wasn't and he hadn't, and she had to do the honorable thing and give him his freedom if he wanted it. Oh, please, don't let him reject her, she prayed. A little pain shot through her breastbone at the thought.

Okay, she'd assume he wasn't going to reject her on the basis of her being a practitioner. No rejection led to the inexorable and the necessary: the mating act itself. Was she ready for that momentous step? Despite all her yearning for him, she was still nervous. After all, she'd never done *it*. What if she wasn't any good at *it*? Would she disappoint him? She couldn't just jump in bed with him to see, could she? Sort of on a trial basis? No, not feasible. Becoming soulmates was all or nothing. Mating set the soulmate bond in stone, according to her mother.

Bent wanted to take her to bed and soon; she knew it as surely as she knew every other practitioner used the *lux* spell to create light and *flamma* to set fire to a candle wick. With him living in the house, however, could she resist him?

A shiver ran down her back and she shuddered. She had to make the decision to mate for herself, make it actively, not passively. Not simply give in to passion, the heat of the moment, the force of the imperative. A witch had to come willingly, with no reservations, to the mating bed for the bond to work.

On the other hand, the revelations to come would surely give Bent pause and her some breathing room. Surely not even Bent could learn their secret and not take time to absorb its reality.

She grasped at the thin straw of that reasoning and wove it with another idea. She'd ask her parents to explain to Bent only about magic and practitioners and leave to her the task of telling him about soulmates. She could then delay both the soulmate explanation and the subsequent mating for a while. Give him a chance to come to terms with the idea of practitioners first. Give her more time to overcome her apprehension. Give them both the opportunity to know each other better. Tell him later when she was more certain of his reaction.

The plan perked her up and she sat up straight, thoroughly disturbing Lolita, who complained with a grunt. "Come on," she said. "We have things to do." She hugged the cat and rose to go downstairs. She had people coming over and hostess duties took precedence at the moment. Besides, making a grocery list would occupy her mind. The seesaw effect of her cogitations was making her dizzy.

Antonia and Alaric arrived earlier than they had originally planned, having decided after Daria's call not to even try to sleep longer, but simply to get in the car and go. Over coffee in the kitchen, they all discussed the situation.

Bent sat across the table from Daria's father and braced himself. If there was any opposition to his plan, he expected it to come from her father. Alaric Morgan was almost as tall as his six-foot-five son. As the daughters looked like their mother, so Clay inherited his father's square jaw and gray eyes. The paternal gray eyes were directly assessing Bent, who wondered if he himself looked as grim as the older man.

"Well, Bent," Alaric said, putting down his coffee cup, "what are you going to do to protect Daria?"

"I can take care of myself," Daria started to say, but she withdrew when her mother gave her one of those female looks that, even to Bent, said, "Let the men play their testosterone games."

Deciding to take the bull by the horns, so to speak, Bent stated firmly, "I'm going to move here from the hotel. Daria will have someone here at night and when she needs to go grocery shopping and the like, and we won't have to use quite so many of Glennell's security staff. You should know Joe Glennell ordered me to keep Daria safe."

"I know Joe," Alaric said, nodding. "That sounds like him. And I agree with you. I'll feel better knowing someone is here with her." He turned to his wife. "What do you think, Antonia?"

"I think it solves several problems at once," Antonia said with a smile. "And don't scowl so, dear, it only causes wrinkles," she added to Daria, patting her daughter's hand.

Bent breathed several sighs of relief. He hadn't known what to expect from Daria's parents, some opposition perhaps to his moving in since they were, after all, her parents, even if she was thirty years old. But they were both beaming at him in what looked like delight, and he wasn't sure he understood. Nothing mattered, however, as he would have Daria all to himself and very soon.

Antonia took charge. "Okay, here's the schedule. Bent, you check out of the hotel and bring your things over here. Clay, you take Daria grocery shopping. I know she's going to need some things for lunch with all of us here and with Bent in the house, she'll need to shop for the week. Alaric, you call Cassie and Gregor and ask them to come over. I could use some help. And I'll get going outside. Let's go, everybody." She clapped her hands for emphasis.

After Bent had left and Clay was showing Alaric the latest enhancements to the security system, Daria turned to Antonia. "You know, Mother, I really don't need Bent here. I *do* have defenses."

"Yes, but those only work up to a point. We can't put any lethal spells on the house. For one thing, it's too dangerous. That level of spell could harm innocent delivery people or a neighbor child coming into the yard for a lost ball. We'll cast protections against those with evil intent, but they'll activate only if the evil doers touch the house. As for your personal defenses, they will not halt a bullet. On the drive here, your father and I discussed the idea of Bent, or someone, being here with you. If he hadn't suggested it, we were going to. Those miscreants will think twice about tackling you with him in residence. Besides," she added with a twinkle, "it will further your soul-mating."

"Mother, we *must* tell him about practitioners, but *only* about practitioners, not the rest. Have you found out anything about how non-practitioners take this kind of news? You were going to talk to Mother Higgins, weren't you?"

"I know we must tell him, dear. We'll do it after lunch. And I agree, only about practitioners. You have to be the one to explain about soulmates and first mating. No to your other question. Mother Higgins is off visiting her grandchildren, so I haven't been able to talk with her or anybody in a mixed marriage." She smiled at her worried daughter and gave her a hug. "I really don't think you have any worries here, though. Bent is a wonderful man. Everything will come out all right, you'll see. Now, go to the grocery store. We have a bunch of people to feed."

When Bent returned from the hotel a couple of hours later, the first thing he noticed was the total absence of the cloying, nauseating smell of the stink bomb. Funny, he didn't think the slight breeze would dissipate it so quickly. He found Alaric in the kitchen.

"Daria's off grocery shopping," Alaric said. "Let me give you a hand taking your luggage upstairs."

"I called Dan Roth while I was at the hotel so he would know the arrangements," Bent reported as they walked out to his car.

"Roth? He's your security manager, isn't he?" Alaric asked.

"That's right. He's going to talk with the police, but neither of us thinks they'll find out who's behind this. Dan will alert his people so they'll be extra vigilant."

Alaric helped him move his things into the guest bedroom. As they carried the luggage from the car, the older man said, "I have to tell you, Bent, I'm glad Daria's going to have you in the house at night. I've been a little worried since the first note showed up in the mail."

"So have I," Bent replied, "but I couldn't talk her into on-site security."

"She's just like her mother at times," Alaric sighed, putting the suitcase down and hanging the garment bag in the closet. "Now, I won't say Antonia's stubborn . . ."

"I know what you mean," Bent agreed, thinking back to Daria's adamant arguments on why she should come to work for him after she found the first note in the mail. "Strong minded."

"Exactly. They can both be very . . . determined."

Bent looked Alaric in the eye. "I'll do my very best to keep her safe, sir."

"I know you will, Bent," Alaric stated, then added with a wink, "but don't call me 'sir.' The name's Alaric. Just watch out for my girl."

"Yes, uh, Alaric," Bent said with a grin. The two men shook hands in accord.

"Now, we'd better look at the garage," Alaric said. "The last time I saw it, she had half of it cluttered with boxes, and if you want to put your car in it, we'll need to rearrange things. Clay can help us. I just saw him drive up with Daria."

While the three men moved boxes, garden tools, and trashcans, Bent decided he must have passed Alaric's muster. He knew Alaric had been scrutinizing him in the conversations in the kitchen and bedroom, but it didn't surprise him. The man was her father, after all. He wondered how long the family would be staying.

Cassandra and Gregor had arrived while Bent was at the hotel and were engaged in something with Antonia outside, but he didn't know exactly what. Then it was time for lunch, where the conversation was freewheeling and covered a variety of topics, none of them having to do with the current problems. Bent relaxed, feeling quite at home, almost like a member of the family.

After lunch and subsequent cleanup, Antonia herded them all into the family room, saying, "Now, we need to talk." Everyone arranged themselves on the couch and chairs into a loose circle.

Bent looked around curiously as he followed the family. He hadn't paid much attention to the room previously. Like the other parts of Daria's house, this room with its long couch, easy chairs, fireplace, and generous-sized TV and entertainment center felt welcoming, comfortable, and homelike. It would be a great place to watch sports or to curl up with Daria on the couch on a rainy day. For a small woman, Daria certainly went in for furniture that fit a tall man, he thought, but it could be because of the tall men in her family.

Bent glanced at Daria and thought she looked particularly solemn. He had planned on sitting by her, but she walked over to the windows, almost avoiding him, and he didn't want to ask what was wrong in front of the family. Despite their acceptance of him, now wasn't the time for overt demonstrations of affection.

Daria sat down in a chair and Lolita immediately jumped into her lap. Zorro lounged at her feet, an arrogant look on his face as usual. It was almost as though the cats were protecting her. When Antonia asked Bent to sit by her on the couch, he had no choice but to do so, and when he looked around at the rest of the family, who were clearly focused on him, he began to feel some unease.

Antonia smiled and took his hand in hers. "Bent, if you are going to live here, especially under these trying circumstances, you are going to need to know some things we don't normally tell outsiders. There are several reasons why we're sharing this information, but before we do, we must have your word you will not repeat what we are about to say to anyone outside the Morgan family. Don't be alarmed, it's nothing illegal." She patted his hand for reassurance.

Bent glanced around the arc of the Morgan family. They were all watching him intently, waiting for his answer. Whatever it was, they were absolutely serious about it. What could it be? What could this fine, upstanding bunch of people be keeping secret? Was it political? Religious? Medical? Was it scandalous? Was there a crazy aunt in the attic? Well, he had learned the hard way not to theorize ahead of his data. There was only one way he would find out.

He looked back at Daria's mother. "You have my word," he answered, equally seriously.

"Thank you," Antonia said. "I'm not going to beat around the bush, Bent. Here's the situation in a nutshell. Our family line and those of many of our friends are ancient ones, going back hundreds of years. We have been able to trace some to the chaos of Europe after the Roman Empire fell and a very few even farther. But we're not just fervent genealogists. We need to know our lineage because we have inherited some of their talents. To put it succinctly, these ancestral lines trace the descent of 'magic practitioners.' We practitioners have the ability to cast spells and otherwise employ our skills, and we use our capabilities in making our livings. We practice magic in much the same way doctors practice medicine or lawyers practice law."

Bent blinked, completely flabbergasted. Of all the fantastic notions going through his mind about what the revelations would be, this was *definitely* not one of them. "Magic. Practitioners? Like witches?" he asked. "And warlocks? Sorcerers? Wizards?"

Oh, damn. He looked around the circle of faces. They were serious, completely serious. Come on, Bent, say something intelligent, he admonished himself. "Uh . . . What exactly are we talking about here? Spells? Bell, book, and candle? Halloween?" *Oh, that was brilliant.* They'd think Daria had gotten herself mixed up with an idiot for sure. *Get a grip, Benthausen.*

He glanced around at the group again and frowned, running a hand through his hair. Then he leaned back, crossed his arms, uncrossed them, and, extending his hand in a questioning gesture, asked in a definitely skeptical tone that he couldn't quite suppress, "What exactly do you people do?"

"Just go with us for a minute here, Bent," Alaric said, leaning forward in his chair to Bent's right. "First, let me assure you what we do is nothing like what you may have seen on television or in the movies. We don't wiggle our noses, or teleport all over the place, or evoke demons from hell, or change the weather.

"We *do* have certain abilities and talents and powers, developed by our ancestors and passed down over the centuries both genetically and by training and sometimes by the sheer luck of the draw, that's all. You know how one person can be gifted in one area, say with numbers, and another with music. We often call such a person a 'prodigy' or some type of genius. Some people have natural aptitudes for a certain kind of work—we say things like, 'he's a born engineer, or carpenter, or whatever.' Others may have what appears to be an inherent faculty for something else, and we say 'it's in the genes' or 'she takes after her mother.' "

"Okay," Bent said, in more of a keep-going tone than an agreeing one. Alaric's statements made sense—as far as they went. "I can follow that."

Antonia took up the narrative. "But it's more than just raw talent. Practitioners take their capabilities farther. To outsiders, or those uninitiated in the skill or discipline or craft, what we do can appear to be 'magic.' We call ourselves 'practitioners' because that is what we do—practice. We study and work at our art and craft just as non-practitioners do with theirs. Casting a spell is not easy, let me tell you. Using spells in your job is hard work. In the end, however, we're no different from anyone else. We live ordinary lives with ordinary lifespans. We simply use our abilities and talents to make our livings and to protect ourselves. And, I'll concede, sometimes to have fun." She smiled, then grew earnest once again.

"Let me give you some examples involving our family,"

she continued, waving her hand to encompass the group. "In fact, of everyone here, I'm the only one who is a 'witch' in the traditional sense of using plants and herbs and being close to nature. Gloriana, by the way, takes after me in this regard and has reached a very high level of practice. We use our abilities to grow marvelous plants and use them in cooking and, in a special program with several medical schools, in medicinal research."

She gestured toward her sister. "Cassie blends the ancient with the modern. I don't know if Daria told you, but Cassie's a psychiatrist and practices her gifts to help mentally disturbed children, using spells to start them talking and opening up about their troubles. She employs modern techniques to resolve those problems." She looked to her husband to pick up the explanation.

"The rest of us are definitely twentieth and twenty-first century magic practitioners," Alaric stated. "You know what Clay, Daria, and I do—on the surface. Gregor is in oil trading. The four of us use our talents to enhance our business dealings. I, in particular, use spells to bring out any discrepancies or inaccuracies in a company's financial accounts, make clear any patterns that disrupt the regular flow of money, or highlight any fraudulent dealings. Clay does something to those confounded computers, but I can't describe it."

Alaric stopped and looked around. "I'm sure I've forgotten something. Oh, by the way, we do use the terms 'witch' and 'warlock' as shorthand also, but only among ourselves. The terms are so misunderstood these days." He shook his head at the thought.

"What do you think so far, Bent?" Antonia asked. "Any questions?"

"Give me a moment." Bent finally persuaded his mind to begin working again as he ran his hands over his face. He rose and walked over to a window, where he stood staring out for a long minute, rocking back and forth with his hands in his pockets. What did he think? These people were definitely not stringing him along. They obviously believed everything they had told him.

What did he know about them? Certain facts and events bolstered their claims. He had seen Daria's garden bloom almost overnight. He knew Alaric's reputation for solving financial problems, and Joe Glennell vouched for the accountant, both personally and professionally. He himself had seen Clay walk into a computer room, stand there for a little while with his hand on the machine, and pinpoint five problems with hardware and software without looking at a line of code or inspecting a cable connection. There had to be a method behind what they did. Could it be magic? Was there any reason that it *couldn't* be magic?

He returned to the circle and sat down on the couch. "All right, let's say I go along with you for the time being. I'm not saying I believe you yet or even understand, only I'm keeping an open mind and I need more information. What about you, Daria? Where do you fit in here? How do you do what you do?" He looked at her as he said this because he really wanted, absolutely needed to hear something from her.

She smiled with grim determination and studied him for a moment. A little spark of hope flared in her middle. So far, so good. He hadn't run. He didn't look like he had concluded they were all crazy. He was still asking questions. In fact, he seemed to be treating the situation as he would a problem brought to him at Glennell—he was gathering all the available data before coming to a conclusion. Now it was her turn.

She sat a little straighter in her chair and looked him straight in the eyes. "Almost all practitioners can cast spells both on themselves and on others—people, animals, inanimate objects. They can often cause things to happen, like a candle to light, or a ball of light to appear, or in Clay's case for a computer to give up its secrets. I'm different from most. I can spell *only myself*. When I'm interviewing, I cast spells *on myself* so the person I'm with reacts to the spells and perceives me *as if I had spelled him*."

She placed Lolita on the floor and rose to stand by her father's chair. She laid a hand on Alaric's shoulder. "For example, if I was interviewing Daddy, and he was hostile to me or to the process, as employees so often are, I'd spell myself to be seen as unthreatening, as trustworthy, as someone he could and must confide in. Remember when I questioned Janet Adams? That's how we heard so much from her so quickly. She didn't mean to tell us about Phil Casey, but she couldn't help herself because of the spells."

"But in the interview, I perceived nothing out of the ordinary," Bent said. "I don't remember you as particularly anything. You were just you."

"We'll get to it later," Alaric interjected.

"The spells aren't supposed to show," Daria said, with a frown at her father. This was not the time to go into *that*. Luckily, Bent had gone onto another idea.

"Look, is there anything you *can* demonstrate to me? I'd feel a little better if I had something to take this on besides trust and faith," he said, opening his arms with his palms up in a supplicating gesture. He watched as all of them turned to Antonia again.

"Unfortunately, because of our particular, individual talents—we don't have a broken computer or a set of accounts handy—the only demonstrations we can make have the flavor of parlor tricks," Antonia responded. "Here's a ball of light."

A glowing blue ball about six inches wide appeared above her hand right in front of Bent, and he couldn't help jumping a little at the sight. When he poked it experimentally with a finger, the shimmering globe danced away like a helium-filled balloon would have. Its surface was hard, though, without the "give" of a balloon. It was also cold, and his fingertip tingled. "Ooookay," he responded, amused.

Antonia waved her hand and the ball of light vanished. "Then there's my favorite illusion, rose petals." She opened her hands and spread them apart and the room was immediately awash in pink rose petals. A layer several inches deep formed on the floor in no time. Sneezing, Zorro indignantly stood and glared at her. "Oh, I apologize, Zorro," Antonia laughed as she canceled the spell, and the petals disappeared.

Bent nodded and chuckled himself. This was more like it—just what he needed. If it wasn't magic, Antonia was a hell of an illusionist, better than any he'd ever seen.

"Come to the window, Bent." She drew him to the nearest window overlooking the garden. She waved at the floral display outside. "Pick a plant, any plant."

Bent pointed to a light green impatiens with small pink buds that was growing right below the window. "That one, second from the left."

Antonia concentrated on the plant and within seconds it grew visibly—not very much, but the stems were definitely larger and longer, the green darker, and the buds fatter. One bud even unfurled its petals. "Can you see the changes?" When he nodded, she said, "I'm stopping the spell there. It's not good for the plant to be forced any farther. Any comments, concerns? Do you think we're all crazy? Do you want to run screaming into the night?"

Bent smiled at the question. He wasn't about to run, not without Daria. "I won't say I'm absolutely convinced, but I do want to know why you're telling me this. What do your magical abilities have to do with me?" And with Daria. There had to be more than they were telling. He went back to the couch and sat.

Alaric answered. "In part because you will be living in this house. When those vandals threw the stink bombs at Daria's window, they didn't really miss. The bombs should have broken the window. Before they reached the glass, they bounced off the protective spells that surround the house.

Antonia, Cassie, and Gregor strengthened the spells today."

He glanced up at Daria, who was still standing by his chair, and took her hand in his. "If, heaven forbid, the vandals return, you must know how to act. For example, last night, it was imperative Daria stay in the house until those men cleared the fence in retreat. It doesn't feel good to walk into activated defensive spells, even when they're set up to defend you.

"After what we've added now, the next person who comes into the yard with the intent to do harm will find his plans backfiring. The spells aren't fatal, but they will certainly cause pain, perhaps incapacitate him, even knock him out, like that." He hit one fist into the other palm with a smack. "We can't have you needlessly running outside after someone, especially when you might get caught in the residual effects of a protective spell."

"That's understandable," Bent remarked. He still felt slightly confused. There had to be something else. He opened his mouth to ask a question, but didn't get the words out because Antonia spoke up.

"I know, Bent," she said, laying a hand on his arm. "I'm sure all these revelations come as something of a surprise and will take some getting used to. There's much more to being a practitioner than we have time to tell you at the moment. Our primary goals today were to tell you about ourselves and warn you about the house spells. Since you and Daria are obviously interested in each other, we would have had this talk later, but events have overtaken us.

"Just remember, basically, at heart, we're no different from anyone else. We're human, after all. Take some time to think about what we've told you. Talk to Daria. She can tell you more about being a practitioner, what it means and how it works." Antonia smiled at him and patted his arm. "And I can't tell you how glad I am you'll be staying here with her. Thank you." She kissed him lightly on the cheek.

"You're welcome," he replied, but couldn't think of anything to add. He definitely needed some time to absorb all these revelations—and to talk to Daria about them.

"We need to get going, Antonia," Alaric announced, "if we want to get home before dark."

Clay pushed himself off the mantel on which he had been leaning. "And I'm out of here." He kissed his mother, clapped his father on the back, and gave Daria a hug. "Bent," he said, shaking hands, "we'll talk later."

"We're leaving also." Cassie and Gregor said, gathering their things.

A general exodus ensued, until finally Daria and Bent waved them off and watched the cars drive away. Bent shut the front door and turned, intending to take Daria in his arms, but she backed away.

"I know you have questions," she said, searching his eyes for clues to his feelings.

"First things first," he answered, capturing her in a giant hug. "I feel deprived. I didn't have the opportunity to say hello properly." He gave her a long, thorough kiss, then nuzzled her neck as his hands rubbed her back.

After a few seconds of hugging, she took a deep breath and pushed on his shoulders to put some space between them. "We still need to talk," she said. "There's so much you don't know yet."

Chapter Thirteen

Daria led Bent into the kitchen and gestured at the table. She'd relaxed for the moments in his arms. He wasn't rejecting her—yet. She felt the anxiety return. "Have a seat. Would you like something to drink?"

"No, I'm fine." He sat down at the table.

She puttered around the sink for a moment, her movements quick and jerky. She was nervous, more nervous than she had been during her family's explanation about practitioners.

"Come sit down, honey, and talk to me," Bent said. He took a deep breath, let it out with a whoosh, and shook his head. "I must admit, all this threw me for quite a loop at first. Now my brain is working again, and I have a lot of questions. Tell me first, did I make much of a fool of myself?"

"What? A fool of yourself?" It was the last question she expected, and the absurdity of it caused a laugh and a slight relaxation. She sat down across from him. "Of course not. Wherever did you get that idea?"

"Well, your parents gave me a couple of odd looks when I started babbling about bell, book and candle. The idea of all of your being 'practitioners' was the last thing I expected. How do people usually react to the news?"

"I don't know," she replied with a shrug. "I don't think we've ever told anybody before. I never have. It's not exactly a subject you bring up in casual conversation, you know."

"I'll bet," he said with a smile.

"So, what do you think? Do you believe us?" She could hear the worry in her voice and hoped it wouldn't put him off. She clasped her hands together on the table and concentrated on *not* clenching them.

He ran a hand through his hair and leaned back in the chair. His expression was one of confusion. He thought about her question, then said, "I honestly don't know."

He held up one hand. "Part of me accepts everything. That part says, 'Of course, you're practitioners. What else could you be? How else could you do what you do?'"

He held up the other. "But another part still questions the whole idea. It says, 'C'mon? Magic? It's so fantastic.'"

He looked from one hand to the other, then clasped them in front of him. "I guess I'm trying to treat this dilemma like a problem somebody brings me at work. Look at both sides, gather data, and make a decision. I need some more information. Like *how* you do what you do. You have to tell me more about being a witch—excuse me, a practitioner."

"I'm not really sure where to start." She paused, tracing the grain of the wood in the tabletop with her fingers. "I guess the best place is at the beginning—my beginning. As long as I can remember, I've been doing magic. It's sort of like reading. I don't remember *not* being able to read, and I don't remember *not* being able to cast spells, at least on myself.

"When I was little and did something I wasn't supposed to, I'd put on an innocent face, you know, the way any child will do, but with me, it went farther. I was really spelling myself to look innocent to other people. Of course, my mother wasn't affected by my spells—family members aren't, you see—so she knew I wasn't as guiltless as I appeared." She gave a disgusted little sigh. "I couldn't get away with anything." They both chuckled.

"That I couldn't spell anything else caused some consternation among my family, but Clay couldn't spell people either, only things, then machinery, then computers, and Daddy has difficulty spelling people too so my inability wasn't wholly surprising. I think my mother despaired she had no one to inherit her mantle until Gloriana came along. I probably should mention that while the ability, the talent, to do magic is inherited, the particular skill set of the parents usually isn't. It works just like other genetic traits, you know, where a mathematically inclined person has a child who can barely do long division."

"How do you throw a spell, or, what do you say, spell something?" he asked.

"It's a matter of energy, concentration, some words—spoken or formed in the mind—and sometimes, gestures. Some spells may require physical catalysts or aids like herbs, crystals, and the like, but basically you focus your internal energy. You're born with a finite amount of magic energy, the ability to reach a certain level of spell-casting, and that's as high as you can go, except . . ." She stopped as she realized that if she wasn't careful, she'd get into soulmate territory, where the first mating could enhance powers.

"Anyway," she resumed quickly, "casting continuously or

casting higher-level spells really eats up your energy, which in the human body means calories. You can lose weight and become generally exhausted. When we met, I had just finished the third in a line of jobs requiring constant spells, and I was pretty debilitated."

"I remember." He looked at her warily. "Uh, this isn't black magic, is it?"

"No, no, not at all." She shook her head vigorously to emphasize the point. "There's nothing evil about us. This isn't necromancy or spiritualism or theosophy or religion. We don't communicate with the dead or worship strange idols. There are practitioners in the congregations of every major religion and most of the minor ones. You don't have to look so worried."

She raised a finger as she thought of something else. "Although—there are a very few practitioners who can cast fireballs and lightning bolts like the wizards in the movies, and Uncle Gregor does know some really nasty defensive spells and curses, and he applied them to the house. You don't want to be a man intending evil toward anyone in this house."

"Dare I ask?"

"Gregor laid on what he calls his 'D and B' curse. Any man intending evil who comes on the property and tries to get into the house—well . . ." She cleared her throat, felt herself blush, but continued. "Certain portions of his male anatomy will shrivel. I'll leave it to you to figure out what D and B mean."

"Ouch." Bent squirmed. "So you spell yourself, and

others react to the spells, do I have that right?"

"Yes, that's correct."

"Then why am I not affected by the spells? Why can't I see them? It sure would help my peace of mind to see or experience *something*."

Daria sighed. She didn't really want to get into the real reason—that soulmates were not affected by each other's spells, except for defense and healing—right now. She wanted more time to work on her explanation, and to prepare herself for its possible aftermath. Right now, she needed a diversion from answering his first question. So she seized on his last statement. "You know, there *might* be a way for you to see the *effects* of a spell."

"Great! What do we need to do?"

"Find a crowd. A mall would be ideal. I'll spell myself, and you can watch the people around us for their reactions."

"How about the Galleria, my home away from home? It should be full on a Saturday afternoon." He rose, pulled her around the table and gave her a quick hug and then a kiss when she returned the hug. "Let's go."

Walking in a crush of shoppers around the second level of the Galleria shopping mall above the skating rink, Daria pondered her spells. "All right, here we go. The first one will be an I-am-repulsive spell, but I won't make it too strong since I don't want anybody to vomit." Alarmed, Bent looked down at her. "No, watch the people, not me," she ordered. When he swung his eyes to the front, Daria spelled herself.

All of a sudden, distinct gasps sounded from both in front and in back of them. A few shoppers averted their eyes from Daria, while several others stared. "Look at that ugly lady, Mommy," cried one little boy, pointing at her, before his mother shushed him and dragged him away. A bubble of clear space formed around them as people backed off. Daria pulled Bent into a shop, dropping the spell as she did.

"Well?" she asked.

Bent's expression combined surprise and curiosity. "That was certainly impressive. People really reacted. Quite an effect for something I can't see at all. Do another."

They went back into the throng and stopped on one of the bridges over the ice rink. "I'm going to become the sexiest woman on earth. Watch the men, in particular." She spelled herself and every male over the age of fifteen jerked to attention and swiveled to look at her. The women assumed envious or disapproving expressions. Daria canceled the spell before any man actually moved toward her, and its cancellation left all the men with stupid looks on their faces as they tried to figure out what had just happened.

Bent laughed, then scowled, "Don't ever throw that spell again. I swear I saw some of the guys' ears actually come to points."

She grinned back at him. "Now for some of the best in my repertoire. Come on." She led him downstairs to an ice cream parlor. "With all this work, I need a hot fudge sundae to replenish my energy."

"You don't want it here," Bent told her. "I've been in here and the service is really slow."

"Not with me along," she replied, spelling herself with notice-me, I-will-be-obeyed, and a little power to boost the first two as they went through the door. Two waiters and the hostess came to them immediately and led them to a booth. Another waiter appeared with water glasses. "What can we get you today?" the latter asked, elbowing the other three away.

The order came within three minutes, by which time Bent was laughing heartily at the goings-on. "I give up, you've convinced me. I can't wait to take you to a couple of New York restaurants with this spell."

Daria looked around carefully before replying. No one was sitting close to them, but she canceled the active spells and cast I'm-not-worth-any-attention to be on the safe side. She spoke softly. "It's three spells, actually. I use them to get through receptionists and other gatekeepers. There's also an I-am-invisible spell when I don't want to be noticed, and I have a few nifty illusions."

"Like what?" Bent must have noticed Daria's inspection of their surroundings because he, too, lowered his voice.

She took a moment to take a bite of her sundae and savor the warm dark fudge against the cold creamy vanilla. "Like a tiger or a dragon. If the ceiling's suitably high, the dragon illusion can make me look like I'm twelve or fifteen feet tall. A strength spell gives me a 'dragon's muscle power,' to throw something heavy across a room. There is a physical limit to what I can throw, of course. I'm not bionic like in the movies. The laws of physics still apply."

She frowned and sighed. "But I can't seem to throw real fire out of the dragon's mouth, probably because I can't cast fire at all. I can't even light a puny little candle. I can, however, spell my voice and roar quite effectively. These illusions are really defensive spells, to be used in case of danger. I've been told they're quite frightening."

She paused. "Are you convinced? Do you need any more demonstrations? Do you have any questions?" Searching for a clue to his thoughts, she looked as deeply as she could into his blue eyes. Surely he hadn't even begun to assimilate the consequences and nuances of her being a practitioner. Finally she said, "You're taking all this rather calmly. I know you must have more questions."

He glanced around the room and back at her before saying, "Let me put it this way. I think I'm convinced. God knows, I don't have any better explanation for how you do what you do. Sure, I have more questions. You have to admit, this whole magic business takes some getting used to. You're certainly nothing like the witches of legend, or the ones on TV. I've been bewitched by you from the moment I met you, so . . ."

Alarm flashed through Daria. He mustn't think that! She reached across the table and put a hand on his. "Oh, no, Bent. You weren't bewitched. *Nobody* spelled you." The soulmate situation, the two being meant for each other without any say on their part, was bad enough. The last thing she needed was for him to think he had been artificially manipulated into doing something against his will.

"Okay, honey. No spells," he relented.

Relieved, she nodded and turned her attention to the ice cream again. Whew, that was a close one.

Bent scrutinized her for a long minute while she finished her sundae. He certainly felt bewitched. Or enchanted, charmed, fascinated, whatever you called it. He had never wanted a woman so badly as this one. Maybe he could chalk it up to plain old chemistry.

But 'something else' was nagging at him, an impression, a hunch, a suspicion she wasn't telling him everything. She still seemed wary and nervous. Did she have another secret?

As much as he wanted to take her home, strip them both naked, and bury himself in her until they didn't know where she ended and he began, whatever the 'something' was, it seemed to be telling him to wait and see, not to push her right now. Especially not into bed.

He had been part of too many negotiations not to recognize Daria wasn't ready to make such a . . . such a what? Commitment, that pesky word again? Sacrifice? He disliked the word even more. No, she just wasn't ready to take such a step. There, that terminology was better, more comfortable.

Their coming together, their "taking the step" would be more than the simple act of having sex; he'd recognized already by the effect that she had had on him. It would be making love—or maybe something greater still.

No, he wouldn't jump her bones. He'd take it nice and easy. Let her get used to having him around. After all, he was living in her house now. Let her come to him. Yeah, nudge her into being the instigator, the seducer. Get her used to his touch. Give her little samples of love-making—a kiss here, a caress there—until she was so wound up, she'd throw herself into his arms. Then he'd have her.

And the revelation struck him like a sledgehammer: *Once he had her, he would not want to let her go.*

Daria scraped the last little bit of fudge from her bowl and, licking the spoon, looked up straight into Bent's intent blue gaze. The sheer desire and determination on his face were plain to see, and his expression riveted her to the bench. A rush of heat flashed through her, and its passing left her breathless. "B-B-Bent?" she stuttered. "Is everything all right?"

He seemed to come back to himself and their surroundings with a blink and a sharp exhalation of breath. "It certainly is," he murmured. "Let's go back home."

Chapter Fourteen

It was late afternoon when they arrived at the house. As the car pulled into the garage, Daria could feel herself beginning to droop from lack of sleep and the excitement of the early morning. The wear and tear on her nervous system from anxiety over Bent's reaction to the practitioner declarations certainly hadn't helped her either, she thought, as she rubbed her aching temples.

Bent noticed, and after he turned off the ignition, put his hand on the back of her neck and massaged the tense muscles. "You okay?" he asked.

"I'm just tired, I guess," she replied, rotating her head on her shoulders to take better advantage of his ministrations.

"You should be, after the day you've had. Let's get inside so you can relax." He gave her a final pat and a quick little kiss.

"Did you unpack? Do you need anything?" she asked as they entered the house.

"Unpacking's not a problem. I do need some place with a phone line to plug into my laptop."

Daria thought for a moment. "Let's set you up in the study. There's a folding table in the back of the coat closet in the front hall, and there's room in the corner to the right of the door. When I moved in, I couldn't decide where to put my desk, so I had the study wired for computers and phone lines in two locations. You can plug your laptop into the same line I use for my computer."

"I remember the table. I'll get it first."

"And I'll clear out the corner."

They set about their appointed tasks, and in hardly any time at all, Bent had a working "desk" of his own, complete with a table lamp and a straight chair moved in from the kitchen.

Daria was yawning almost continuously as they finished the lunch leftovers for a quick, hassle-free dinner.

"Why don't you check me out on setting the alarms and go to bed, Daria?" Bent suggested as they finished cleaning up. "I want to dial into the office and collect my e-mail, and then I'll hit the sack too."

"Thanks, Bent," she replied around another yawn. "I'm not much of a hostess, but I can't keep my eyes open."

They activated the security system, and Bent walked her to the stairs. Taking her in his arms, he kissed her briefly and, smiling ruefully, said, "You know, when I wanted to spend the day together, this is not exactly what I had in mind."

Daria relaxed against him and gave him a hug. "Me either, but I'm glad you're here. I don't know how I would get any sleep if I were alone."

Bent held her close for a moment. Then he let go, turned her around, and gave her a little nudge toward the stairs. "Go to bed."

"Yes, sir," she grinned over her shoulder and climbed the stairs, the cats following in her wake.

Bent returned to the study and booted his computer. While he was waiting for it to make the connection with the office, he mused about his former plans for the evening. They had not entailed Daria's getting much sleep either.

His thoughts from the ice cream parlor came back to him. *Once he had her, he would not want to let her go.* He'd never in his life had such a thought, such a feeling of wanting her, needing her, of . . . damn it, commitment. How did he feel about that?

Scared to death, he admitted.

Would this time be like the others? Ulcer-producing, God-awful painful, sick-as-a-dog misery? Would she turn him down almost at the last minute like Kerrie? Or, like Susan, expect him to change? What had happened to his idea about having a fling with her, something short-term before he moved on to the next company? He'd learned the hard way to love 'em and leave 'em. It was best for his sanity—not to mention the wear and tear on his body.

What about now? What about Daria? The questions made a shiver run up his backbone. Then he yawned and decided he didn't have much more energy than Daria did, certainly not enough to ponder such enormous questions. After e-mailing Joe Glennell about his change of address and new phone number, he shut down his laptop and wearily climbed the stairs.

At the top, he noted Daria had left her door ajar just as Zorro stuck his head out from behind it. The large tomcat gave him a measuring look. "It's only me," he told Daria's guardian before going into his bedroom. Because he wanted to be able to hear any noise from downstairs, he copied Daria and left his own door open a few inches. He was asleep as soon as his head hit the pillow.

Bent woke up the next morning spread-eagled on his back with the sheet pulled up to his chest. He could hear water running, so he decided Daria must be awake. For a moment, he lay there, rubbing his chest, particularly the end of his itchy breastbone and wishing he were in the shower with her. When he decided to stretch, however, he realized he couldn't move. A hot brick seemed to be sitting on top of the sheet in the "V" of his crotch, and it pinned him to the bed. Then the brick began to vibrate.

He jerked his head up and raised his torso enough to look straight into Lolita's eyes. The tawny cat blinked lazily at him and purred harder. Bent sat up and scooped her into his hands. "You are a tease, lady," he said as he deposited her at his side and rose to head for his own bathroom.

Lolita ignored him as she scooted over to the warm spot where he had been lying and snuggled into the sheet. She was still there when he came back to dress.

"How do I rate you, instead of your mistress, in my bed?" he asked as he tied his shoes, but she did not reply, only rose, stretched at both ends, hopped off the bed, and led him down to the kitchen.

The alluring smell of fresh coffee and the equally enticing sight of Daria taking cinnamon rolls from the oven greeted him. "Good morning," he murmured as he grinned at her. "A man could get used to this, you know."

She placed the pan of rolls on an oven burner and turned to him, her eyebrows raised in confusion. "To what?"

He took her in his arms. "Finding you making breakfast in the morning."

She laughed up at him. "Don't get used to it. It's cold cereal and bananas during the week, unless . . ."

"Unless what?" He kissed her softly. "What do I have to do for a hot breakfast?" He nibbled on her ear until she squirmed.

"Fix it yourself." She poked him in the ribs to emphasize her point. When he jumped, she tickled him until he captured her hands and pulled her against him.

"You're sure?" Bent gave her a quick smooch.

"As sure as I am that if you don't let me go, the eggs will burn."

"Oh, all right," he pretend-pouted and released her. "I'll pour the coffee."

They idled away the morning over the newspapers and a leisurely breakfast. During the afternoon, they both prepared for the coming workweek while fielding calls from the various Morgans, Dan Roth, and Joe Glennell.

Daria took the call from her mother in the kitchen, ostensibly so as not to disturb Bent in the study.

"Well," Antonia asked, "have you told him?"

"No, Mother, I haven't," Daria rolled her eyes in exasperation. "We were both exhausted yesterday and the time just wasn't right. Please don't bug me about it, all right? I'll get to it. By the way, were you ever able to talk to Mother Higgins? About how non-practitioners might take the news?"

There was an ominous silence on the other end of the line.

"Mother?" Daria heard her own voice go up and her heart began to beat faster. "What happened, Mother. I need to know."

She heard her mother sigh and then Antonia spoke. "It's nothing to worry about, I'm sure, Daria. Mother Higgins had only anecdotal stories about . . ."

"What, Mother, what stories?" A shiver ran down Daria's back and she was certain she was leaving dents in the phone with her tight grip.

"Mother Higgins didn't know of any real research, only of some tales about non-practitioners refusing their soulmates."

"And what happened?"

"A great deal of unhappiness and heartbreak for everyone," Antonia concluded.

"Oh." A cold despair washed over Daria, and it was all she could do not to slump to the floor.

"Don't get discouraged, Daria." Her mother spoke briskly, just as she had when Daria was a little girl and couldn't cast a spell. "Those are stories from long ago, when people thought magic came from the devil and they were afraid of everything. There are no stories of any such happening in modern times."

"All right, Mother. I understand."

"Daria, you still have to tell him. You and Bent will be fine."

"I know, Mother." Certain she'd go stark raving crazy if she had to talk about "it" anymore with her mother and even more certain she needed to digest this new information, Daria decided to change the subject and asked about her sister. When the discussion of Gloriana's latest trials with new jungle plants ended, Daria pled the need to do laundry and persuaded her mother to say good-bye.

She had barely hung up on her end before the phone rang again. This time it was Dan Roth calling, so she was able to turn him over to Bent. Shaking her head over her mother's urgings, she climbed the stairs to collect the wash. At least she could accomplish one task, and she busied herself with housekeeping chores. It took an hour for her to calm down. Her mother was right: those tales from ancient history had no bearing on her situation—she hoped.

Before Daria knew it, however, evening was upon them. They ate dinner in front of the TV in the family room and after cleaning up the dishes settled down there to watch a movie, an old John Wayne cavalry western that was one of Bent's favorites. Bent put his arm around her and snuggled her to him, but made no other move. He seemed totally caught up in the film.

Daria didn't pay much attention to the action on the screen; her mind was definitely on the man by her side and what she had to tell him. But how to broach the subject? Possible scenarios flew through her head, each more ludicrous or bizarre than the last, all with the outcome in doubt. Various soulmate explanations repeated themselves until they finally became a monotonous chant. A commercial for a bankruptcy lawyer came on the TV, and Daria began to float mentally over the litany in her head and the fake drama on the screen.

Crack! Crack!

Suddenly, abruptly, the sound of a gavel striking a table brought her down to earth.

She stood in a darkly paneled courtroom and Bent sat on the high bench, looming over her, a stern look on his face, an enormous maul of a gavel in his hand. "It's judgment time," he intoned in a deep voice and peered down at her. "State your case."

"Well, Your Honor, I, I, uh . . ."

"Get on with it, woman! We don't have all day." His words reverberated in the large empty room.

Without any warning, her family filled the jury box. They all shouted, "Yes! Get on with it!"

Thoroughly disconcerted, Daria stumbled into an explanation, but the jury jeered at every sentence, claiming she could do better, taunting her that Bent would never believe her, cruelly ridiculing her attempts at coherence.

His Honor remained impassive above her.

Finally all she could do was stare up at Judge Bent and tremble in anticipation as he swung the huge hammer.

Crack! Crack! The unmistakable sound of wood whacking wood boomed around the courtroom.

"Here is my decision about this preposterous tale," Bent announced, frowning severely. "Daria."

"Yes?" She shook in every cell and closed her eyes, fearful of even looking at him. His rejection would devastate her, leave nothing of her but an empty shell, devoid of a heart.

"Daria."

"Yes?" Why didn't he get it over with? Her heart began to beat frantically. Say something, anything, Bent, except go away.

"Daria."

Bent was shaking her gently. Why was he doing that? *How* was he doing it from way up there on the judge's bench?

"Daria."

She opened her eyes to see him gazing down at her, smiling, holding her on the couch. "Oh, Bent," she breathed. She collapsed against him in relief as her heart pounded and her fingers clutched his arms. The trial had just been a dream.

"Daria, are you all right?" Bent asked, rubbing her back. "You must still be tired. You fell asleep during the movie. Just before I shook you, you started mumbling and twitching. Were you dreaming about the vandals?"

Dazed, she looked around the room. Everything was normal. They were still in the family room. The television was still on, the movie credits crawling across the screen. Bent still had his stocking feet on the coffee table. She didn't answer for a minute, but waited for her breathing to slow down and her nerves to settle.

Once relatively calm again and immensely grateful the

episode had only been a dream, Daria sat up. "No, it wasn't about them. It was more a garden-variety anxiety dream, I think. I can hardly remember what it was about now," she lied.

"You're still a little flushed," Bent said and pulled her down against him again. He rubbed her back for a minute.

Daria luxuriated in the gentle friction. This must be why Lolita gravitated to him—his sure touch made her want to purr. She raised her head to find his mouth right in front of her lips, and she couldn't help it, she had to kiss him. A small caress of the lips, then another, then a simultaneous meeting of tongues in a gentle tasting, then deeper . . . and deeper . . .

Daria felt herself melting as their tongues tangled. Oh, Lord, he was so irresistible. She wanted more. Her hands moved from his arms to his chest and then under his loose T-shirt to the hair-roughened skin beneath. She took a deep, sharp breath at the wonder of actually touching his skin without a barrier for the first time. She took a second breath at the pleasure of his scent as it permeated her body. A third when his hands found her breasts under her own shirt and his fondling almost sent her into hyperventilation. She was flying, carried away on a cloud of desire.

Crack! Crack! The bang of a gavel shattered her euphoria like a master wizard disintegrated a novice's spell gone wrong. She jerked away from Bent, and her head swung toward the TV. The station was replaying the same commercial extolling the virtues of the bankruptcy attorney.

Oh. My. God. Daria shakily leaned her forehead against his chest. She had almost forgotten herself, ignored her own resolve to explain everything to Bent *before* anything else happened between them. She took her hands out from under his shirt and felt his hands move to her back as she raised her eyes to his.

"I'm so sorry, Bent," Daria managed to croak out the words and her throat trembled with the effort. "I didn't mean to let . . . It happened so fast . . . It's not fair to you. Before we go any farther, you need to learn more about what getting involved with a practitioner entails. We haven't talked about it much, and there're still things I have to tell you. I'm sorry. I don't mean to be a tease. It's all my fault. I don't know what . . . I wouldn't blame you if you walked away right now. Oh, damn, I'm making a mess of everything." Hoping, praying, she searched his eyes for forgiveness.

Breathing heavily, his body hard, and primed, and *ready*, Bent stared back at her. It took a moment for the blood to stop pounding in his ears so that he could hear what she was saying.

Damn it! He almost had her where he wanted her, pliant and willing and eager. When she kissed him, he'd reveled. When she'd touched his skin—at her own instigation, too—he'd rejoiced. But then? *Bam!* She'd jumped like she'd been shot. Whatever had spooked her, he didn't know. But now she was apologizing to him and babbling about practitioners.

He moved his hands, still under her shirt, to her ribs and gave her a little shake. She stopped talking and just looked at him, a woeful, and at the same time fearful, expression on her face.

"Let's get one thing straight right now, Daria." He could hear his voice grating with the exertion of overcoming his system, still rampaging with desire. "I want you. I want you in bed, or on the floor, or on the desk in my office. I don't need to think about it. Whatever you have to tell me, it doesn't matter and won't change a thing. I promise you. Your being a practitioner, or a witch, or whatever, has nothing to do with it. I'd want you if you were a Martian. With antennae protruding from your head." He shook her gently to emphasize his words. "Do you understand that?"

"Yes," she answered in a very small voice, but she began to smile, a wondrous, incandescent smile that lit her face.

Maybe, from the looks of her smile, he was finally getting through to her. She just needed more reassurance. "Now, it appears you're not ready to take the leap to being lovers. Okay. It's up to you when we make love. But it will happen. I promise you that, too. You say you have more to tell me about the practitioner business. That's fine too." He took his hands out from under her shirt and smoothed the material over her back. "I'm not going anywhere. We have all the time in the world."

She opened her mouth to say something, but he interrupted. "But not right now. I'm in no shape to listen. Right now I need a cold shower, a very cold shower. It's getting late, and we both have an early day tomorrow. So, let's get to bed—our separate beds." He did not add the "before I explode" that he was thinking.

Daria just nodded, then said, "Thank you, Bent," and

she moved to put some distance between them.

He held her still. "Just a minute." He gave her a hard kiss that communicated a tiny bit of his frustration, then softened it to a sweet caress. "Good night, Daria."

She smiled back at him, the same bright look on her face. "Good night, Bent."

Together they turned off the TV and lights, set the alarm, and walked up the stairs. At the top, Bent hugged her and said, "I don't know what the problem is, or what you have to tell me, but everything will be all right, Daria."

"I'm beginning to think so too," she said, turning toward her door. "Good night."

"Good night," he replied and walked into his room. He looked at himself in his bathroom mirror. "Remember your plan," he told his reflection. "Let *her* come to *you*. Even if it kills you. It's working. She wants you. The little episode on the couch proves it. But she has this mysterious 'more' she has to tell you.

"Whatever she has to say, it must be important to put her into the state she's in. She's having a hell of a lot of trouble getting it out. It has to have a connection to this practitioner situation. Maybe it's because you're not one of them. Your being with her is sort of like a mixed marriage." A warm glow suffused his chest, but as he really heard that last word, his entire body tensed.

Marriage. Now there was a word—and a state—to contemplate. A much more loaded word than commitment. He shook his head. He didn't want to think about either one now. Didn't want to rehash the past. He needed to think of the future.

He reached for his toothbrush and toothpaste. He'd be in Houston at least six more months. No need to rush into such heavy subjects as commitment or, God help him, marriage. Between the company and its problems and getting Daria into bed, he had enough to think about.

First things first: Make Daria his.

He shook his head again. He could almost hear a little voice telling him the next few days could be some of the most difficult and most important of his life. He wished his chest would stop itching.

Chapter Fifteen

Despite her insides singing in arousal and in exultation—he hadn't rejected her after her monumentally stupid attempts at apologizing for leading him on, quite the opposite, in fact—Daria slept well and woke refreshed on Monday morning. She felt great, like everything was finally coming together. Bent wasn't put off by her practitioner abilities. He didn't care a flip about them. He wanted her, he'd said so in no uncertain terms, practitioner or not.

Her intuition, or maybe the imperative, was telling her the time was right for "the talk." Maybe that weird dream had gotten all her anxieties out of her system. Maybe his all-business declaration had cleared the way. Whatever it was, all of a sudden, she had known, way deep down in her bones, he wouldn't reject her. Everything would be all right. She replayed his words in her mind and giggled at the thought of having alien antennae.

Tonight, she pledged as she brushed her teeth, tonight she'd tell him about soulmates. She'd sit him down on the couch after supper and just spit it out. Her mother was right, she didn't have to worry. She was just thinking too much, running and rerunning scenarios, overanalyzing every statement or movement—succumbing to an occupational hazard for consultants. Soulmates were, after all, soulmates. They were supposed to be together.

"Just don't think about *it* during the day," she admonished herself, shaking her toothbrush at her reflection. "You're only making everything more difficult, the more you rehearse. Concentrate on your interviews, and put the other Out of Your Head." She felt calmer already, she assured herself as she rubbed the itchy bottom of her breastbone.

At breakfast and on the way to the office, Bent didn't mention the previous evening and neither did she. Instead, they discussed their schedules and her next target, Manufacturing and its vice president, Merle Wharton.

"I'm expecting some resistance from him," Daria remarked. "He seemed so contentious at the first big meeting when you introduced me."

"That's just his way," Bent replied. "I think he likes to test people, intimidate them if he can. Under his bluff exterior, he's very good at what he does. I'm surprised Triangle was able to keep him. He doesn't suffer fools gladly, and the former company president was definitely a jerk. I'd have expected Merle to get fed up and leave long before now." He reached over and patted her knee. "You can handle him, honey. Just jack up the spells, and he won't know what hit him."

She pictured Wharton in her mind's eye. His every fiber radiated challenge from his solid body and very square and granite-like jaw. For a man of average height, he came off as being much taller. But then, she'd handled men with even more of a sense of command than Merle. "I guess we'll see," she said, her thoughts reviewing possible approaches as they pulled into the parking garage.

Her interviews with Administrative Services went so smoothly during the morning and early afternoon Daria was certain she could finish with the department on Tuesday. Good, because then she'd be able to start with Manufacturing ahead of schedule on Wednesday. If she could speed her process up, she might be able to more quickly discover clues to the person behind the threats.

As she congratulated herself on her progress, she realized she was even beginning to look forward to the evening when she and Bent would have "the talk." She was reaching for the phone about three o'clock to call Wharton when it rang.

"Daria," Bent's harried voice came over the line, "there's been some sort of manufacturing accident at the plant in Baytown. Merle and I are headed over there right now. I don't know how long this will take, so Dan will take you home when you're ready. I'll be there when you see me."

"Is it serious?" she asked. "Did anybody get hurt?"

"It could be a real problem. A machine went haywire, and one of the workers was slightly injured. As we've been learning, Triangle wasn't too safety conscious and didn't always push preventive maintenance as they should. Merle said he fought constantly over the need for more budget, people, and attention but never got anywhere.

"Since Glennell took over, we've been able to catch most problems before they reached this stage, but this one slipped by our inspections—or the inspectors didn't do their jobs. I'm going along to show the corporate flag, back up Merle, reassure the employees we have safety and their interests at heart. Between you and me, I also want to observe him in action." Bent sighed loudly. "But I don't know when I'll get home tonight."

"Don't worry about me," Daria replied. "I have plenty to keep me occupied."

"Be sure whoever takes you home checks out the house," Bent ordered. "I'll see you later."

"Yes, sir," she answered before saying good-bye. "Well, phooey!" she exclaimed to the phone as she put the handset down. To have her plans, *all* her plans evaporate in the blink of an eye was more than frustrating. Figuring the accident and its resulting repercussions would take at least another day to resolve, and then he'd have to catch up with the work the emergency had postponed, Merle probably wouldn't be able to sit down with her until Thursday at the earliest. Oh well. So much for speeding up the timetable. It was a good thing she was used to rearranging schedules.

But, what about Bent and what she had planned for the evening. She couldn't have "the talk" with him tonight. Right when her courage and her determination were high, she had nothing to do with them, no use to put them to. She felt all dressed up with no place to go. She indulged herself with a Zorro-like growl, but it didn't alleviate her feeling of being thwarted. Thoroughly disgruntled, she returned to her work.

Bent finally arrived home at ten o'clock. Daria greeted

him at the door and he enfolded her in his arms with a sigh. "What a day."

She returned his hug and leaned back to see him more clearly. The man looked exhausted. "Is everything okay? Did you get anything to eat?"

"Merle and I grabbed some food on the way back. The worker wasn't badly hurt, thank goodness. The machine he was working on is another matter, however. It needs a major overhaul. Pour me a brandy, and I'll tell you all about it."

They sat in the family room while Bent related the details of the accident and machinery problems and Wharton's remedies for the situation. "I tell you, Daria, Merle's good, damn good. He just wades right into the problems and comes out the other side with workable plans to solve them. His workers respect him because they know he doesn't give them any bull. I'd be very surprised if he were involved in the threats against you. On the other hand, I think you can do him some good when you look at his managers. Somebody fell down on the job, and it resulted in the accident today, and he could use your help finding out who it was."

Bent stopped to take a sip of his brandy. "Besides the usual suspects, of course. It turns out some of the former president's relatives and cronies were foisted on Merle and every other department. Merle fired most of them when Glennell took over and we cut staff numbers, but there are still a couple around."

"What about sabotage?" Daria asked. "Could the accident have been not so accidental?"

"We investigated, but it appears to have been caused by shoddy maintenance. When we went back to the office, I sent Joe Glennell an e-mail to let him know the problem and how we were going to fix it."

"Does Joe micromanage that much?" She was astounded that the CEO and chairman of the board would be interested in a little accident.

"No, he doesn't, but he's a fanatic about safety and has issued standing orders to be informed about any injury-causing accidents. He's always been particularly sensitive to them when a new company comes under the Glennell umbrella." Bent finished his brandy and rose. "Let's turn in. Tomorrow will be extra full, catching up on the work I missed this afternoon and dealing with the repercussions of the accident."

At the top of the stairs, Daria turned into Bent's arms automatically. She tried to keep her side of the kiss light and sensed Bent wanted to do the same thing, but the slide of tongues and the rubbing of hands and the press of torsos combined in a powerful conflagration of the senses, leaving them clinging together, loath to separate.

Bent finally grasped her shoulders and put a little space between them. "Oh, Daria, it's getting harder every day to let you go to bed alone."

"For me, too," she whispered. "We'll talk tomorrow, I promise."

When tomorrow arrived, however, so did the corporate safety manager from New York. Explaining Joe Glennell personally had sent him, the man was apologetic to both

Bent and Merle Wharton, especially after he heard their comprehensive plans for bringing Glennell-Houston up to corporate standards.

Bent and Merle were angry over the intrusion, and Bent had an "interesting" phone call with Joe himself. Joe, of course, claimed he was just trying to show support and denied he had any thoughts of Bent not being able to do his job. After a discussion about possible sabotage—no, it wasn't that—and the lack of any progress in the matter of the threats—they had only just started the investigation—Bent concluded the chairman of the board was mostly frustrated at not being where the action was. The last thing he needed was for Joe to come down to Houston. So, he soothed his boss and thanked him for his support. Such was corporate life in the Glennell Companies.

Bent and Wharton took the safety manager to dinner, thanked him for coming and for his good suggestions, and sent him off to catch a late plane back to New York. Bent headed for home.

Once in the house, Bent practically draped himself around Daria and simply held her tight for a while. "I'm sorry, Daria," he murmured in her ear.

"What for? It was hardly your fault Joe sent the fellow down here and threw all of our schedules into a tizzy. You did what you had to do." She gave him an extra hug. "I can wait."

"We were going to talk about practitioners this evening, weren't we?"

"Tomorrow," Daria said firmly.

"Tomorrow," Bent promised. Then he kissed her, with the usual results. Aching, they went to their separate beds.

Chapter Sixteen

Wednesday, Daria woke absolutely resolved to have "the talk" that night, even if she had to kidnap Bent to get him alone. The last two nights she had felt like climbing the walls. Monday was bad enough, but Tuesday she had paced the floors until it became clear Bent would not be home in time to start any important discussion. She had tried reading her latest copy of W^2: *The Witches and Warlocks Journal*, but her attention soon wandered from the article about the esoteric argument between her traditionalist sister and some theoretical mathematician over the best way to cast spells.

Then she had fidgeted so much watching television, the cats had abandoned her. "Sorry," she had apologized to them. "I know, what good am I if I don't provide a stationary lap?" Neither Lolita nor Zorro had bothered to answer verbally, but the way they stalked from the room, tails held high with the tips twitching in disapproval, indicated their opinion.

Today was going to be different. She was absolutely determined. She ruthlessly squashed any tiny gremlins of doubt who had the temerity to raise their heads and repeated what was becoming a mantra: *It will be all right. He won't reject you. Soulmates are soulmates.*

Events conspired against them only marginally, and they were able to leave the office around six. Daria kept sneaking little peeks at Bent. He appeared perfectly calm. But he didn't know what was coming. Probably thought she'd tell him more about how to do magic or her training.

Boy, was he in for a surprise.

"How about something quick for supper? Pasta and a salad, maybe?" she asked as he pulled the car into the garage.

"Sounds fine. What do you have planned for the evening, now we're home at a reasonable hour?"

"Eat first, then talk."

"Great." He watched her as she unlocked the door. She was wound tight, even stiff in some of her normally graceful movements, so he tried to help her by maintaining a placid expression. He hadn't had any time over the past few days to think about what she could have to say to him, but he wasn't worried. After the bombshell about practitioners, he could take anything. He was just happy to be home at an early hour.

They greeted the cats, he went for the mail, and Daria started food preparation. Over pasta with mushrooms, pesto, and leftover grilled chicken, a green salad, and glasses of cabernet, they discussed their respective days.

Bent ate like he always did, cleaning his plate. Daria picked at her food at first, but he concentrated on engaging her attention in the details of the sales and marketing plans. He was pleased to see his diversion had worked: she had consumed most of what was on her plate. She still seemed nervous, but less so than before supper. After a quick and easy cleanup, he followed her into the family room.

"You sit on the couch," she told him, "and I'll take the

chair." She pulled a chair over so that she faced him from about two feet away. She placed the glass of wine she hadn't finished at supper on the table beside her.

"But I can't touch you over there," he complained as he followed her instructions.

"It will be better for clear thinking if we don't touch, Bent. Better for my thinking, at any rate."

He grinned at her. "I know what you mean." He leaned back into the cushions, stretched out his legs to either side of her chair, and spread his arms along the back of the sofa. He hoped his posture indicated his total openness to whatever she had to say. "All right, what do you have to tell me?"

Silently repeating her mantra, Daria took a sip of wine to moisten her suddenly dry mouth. She put the glass back on the table and clasped her hands. Taking a deep breath, she looked into his eyes. He appeared to be receptive to whatever she had to say, and his willingness bucked up her courage. "You know about practitioners now, a little about our abilities. You've had a chance to think about us. Do you believe us, that we are what we say we are?"

Bent returned her gaze. "I have been doing some thinking about what your family told me. Fantastic as it all seems, I do believe you can use spells and magic to do what you do. I can conceive of no other explanation. Your mother's making the plant grow and your demo at the Galleria convinced me. Seeing all those people reacting to you, it's hard to dispute the effect that you were having on them."

He started chuckling. "I thought one woman was about

to throw up with your repulsive spell, and then, when you did the 'sexiest woman' bit, I was certain I was going to have to defend you from hordes of horny guys." He paused, then grew serious. "What I don't understand is, if everyone else is affected, why can't I see you, how do you say it, as spelled?"

"That's part of what I wanted to talk about tonight," Daria replied. "This is somewhat complicated, and it's going to be a little long-winded, so please bear with me. You need to understand the totality of the situation, and I can't think of any other way to explain it."

"Okay," he smiled. "I'll try not to theorize ahead of your data."

She said a quick prayer for success and plunged ahead. "You see, besides the ability to do magic, practitioners have another aspect to their lives—a phenomenon known as 'soulmates.' This isn't very different from the way the term is used in the non-practitioner world. Soulmates are temperamentally suited to each other. They get along fantastically, often thinking alike, having the same interests, liking the same things. They are sexually attracted to each other."

"And you think you and I . . ."

"There's more," Daria said, holding up her hand to stop him. "In the practitioner concept, the two soulmates are bound together. The phenomenon is also called an *imperative* because it pushes the mates together. Emotions are heightened, and the attraction is irresistible, according to my mother. The feeling grows that one is not 'complete,' not 'whole' without the other, and the bond grows stronger over time. To give you some examples, my parents are soulmates, as are Aunt Cassie and Uncle Gregor."

"But I'm not a practitioner. Where does it leave me?" He was frowning, but appeared more confused than angry.

"Mother did some research. Over the past century, more and more of us have found our soulmates outside the practitioner community. No one knows why this is happening, but it doesn't appear to have a negative effect. The bonds have been just as strong as any two-practitioner combination."

She took a sip of her wine. She wasn't about to say anything about children inheriting magic abilities; that discussion was for much later. She could feel tension coiling inside her, increasing her anxiety more with each word she uttered, but Bent seemed to be accepting her explanation—so far.

He sat up and leaned toward her, resting his elbows on his knees. His eyes twinkled with dark blue lights as he said, "Irresistible, huh? I have to say I've felt a more powerful attraction to you than to any other woman I've ever known. I'm not surprised to find out a reason for it. How do we know if we really are soulmates?"

"The evidence is strong. To begin with, there's the attraction and what happens to us when we kiss." She could feel herself blushing but doggedly continued. "Then, as you've noticed, my spells don't affect you. In a practitioner family, the members can't spell each other, except for healing and defensive spells. That's just how magic works for us.

"If two people are soulmates, they can't spell each other

either, even before mating. If they can't, you know it's a true soul-mating, and not some false love enchantment causing you to feel attraction. This situation holds even in 'mixed' couples. In your case, even if I could spell others, I would not be able to spell you. As my soulmate, you aren't affected by my spells, so you can't see or feel them. My family is not affected either, but they can tell if I have a spell active."

"I still maintain I've been under a spell where you're concerned," he interjected. "Doesn't matter to me if it's yours or from this 'phenomenon.'"

"Then there's the final major point." Daria took another sip of wine, using the break to gauge Bent's reaction. He still looked receptive, almost eager, not at all horrified, and his smile encouraged her to keep going. "The first mating between soulmates can enhance practitioner powers and talents, or confer new ones, or it can do nothing at all to either one of them." She shrugged. "There's no guarantee what will happen. According to my mother's sources, however, no non-practitioner has ever become a practitioner from first mating."

He started to say something, but she raised a hand in supplication. "Just let me get through this, Bent, please, before you say anything."

Bent nodded and sat back.

Daria took another sip of wine and carefully replaced the glass on the table when she saw her hands were trembling faintly. She couldn't tell what he was thinking. He wasn't smiling, as he had been, but he did look thoughtful. Well, she had no choice except to go on.

"Mother first reminded me about the imperative the week before you and I met. Oh, I had heard Mother and Daddy refer to themselves as each other's soulmate all my life, and they told us about it when we were teenagers—sort of an addition to the 'facts of life' talk parents give their children. But I didn't pay much attention or realize all of the connotations, and certainly not in regard to *me*.

"Growing up, I was involved in school, and trying to cast spells, and riding horses, and I wasn't sure I even liked boys as people, much less as boyfriends. And later, when I was in college and then working, I forgot about what Mother had told me. Men just didn't interest me, except as friends." She clasped her hands together to have something physical to hold on to and spoke softly, dreading what she had to say next.

"At first when Mother told me I should be meeting my soulmate soon, I was, to put it mildly, outraged and horrified. The whole situation sounded so medieval, something arranged without my approval, and I had no say in the matter. This imperative would decide who was my mate. I had no free will. Some man would come into my life and I'd be hit with the soulmate thunderbolt and stuck with him, no matter who or what he was. I felt trapped. All of a sudden, I had no control of my life. Like I was going to be spelled; and you need to know that practitioners will fight to the death *not* to be spelled against their will by anybody or anything."

She paused and took another deep breath. This was harder than she thought it would be. She gazed down at her hands so she wouldn't have to look at him. "Now, you're not a warlock. I don't know how you feel at this moment, especially after hearing all this, but the last thing I want is for you to feel trapped or coerced in any way."

She paused to swallow and then said the hardest thing of all. "If you don't want to have anything to do with this whole situation or with me, then you're free to walk away. I won't blame you." How she'd live without him was another matter altogether.

He would have said something then, but she kept talking and somehow mustered the courage to look at him again. "I don't want you to think I'm using you, just in the hopes of enhancing my powers."

Her bones were hurting, she was clenching her hands so tightly. Just a few more words to say. "You see, Bent, this soulmate connection is very serious. It's more than simply being lovers. The bond created is enormously powerful, and soulmates seal it by making love. The feelings for each other, the desire to be together, they are compelling, undeniable. The impulse is imperative, dominant, practically omnipotent. Once sealed, it's a binding for life, a commitment to each other impossible to break."

Daria shut her mouth. She'd said what she had to say, or almost all of it. She needed now to hear from Bent. He looked pale, and his eyes were a little glassy. Seconds dragged by and she began to feel nibbles of panic. He wasn't saying anything—anything at all.

Bent sat there, staring into space, trying to think, to absorb what Daria had just told him. He'd been going along with her tale, imagining them in bed together after her comment about being irresistible to each other, then wondering what kind of enhancement he might get out of their 'mating,' and finally thinking about hauling her across the short distance between them, and kissing her.

Her last sentence brought him crashing back from the daydreams. Back to reality. What had she just said? That, according to this "phenomenon," he and she were soulmates. Bound together for life.

This was commitment—big time. He felt himself start to sweat as he anticipated a pain to start growing in his stomach. When nothing happened, he forced his brain to begin working.

A soulmate imperative? A magical force brought them together? Was this thing, this concept, this phenomenon real? Had she arrived at this conclusion or simply concocted the idea because he was attracted and just wanted to take her to bed? Because she was attracted and her mother had fed her a lot of mumbo jumbo about soulmates? Was all of what he had been feeling just a witchy spell? Was he caught in a practitioner web?

He couldn't deny the mutual attraction, he admitted. It had nearly blown him off his feet. Any, no, *all* of his experience with other women had paled into insignificance in comparison to what he felt with Daria.

He blinked, brought his eyes into focus and studied her more closely. She looked scared to death, but she believed what she had told him. He knew she was honest, had integrity, wouldn't lie to him. She was expecting an answer, at least an acknowledgment of the situation, but he had more questions.

"Wait a minute. Let me see if I have this straight." He ran a hand through his hair as he tried to sort out his feelings. "You people, you 'practitioners' have this, uh, condition you call 'soulmates' where you're bound to each other for life. It doesn't matter if you like each other or not, you're still stuck."

"Yes, that's essentially true," Daria answered, "but it's much more than a condition or a circumstance, and soulmates always like each other and get along very well, according to my parents. Look at the two of us, how we get along with each other."

"Yeah." He had to acknowledge, but only to himself for the time being, they did like many of the same things, like movies, books, leisure activities. They did have the same work habits, commitment to the job, and outlook on life. Hell, there was that "c" word again.

He crossed his arms over his chest. "Okay. And you say there's been no spell cast on me, by you or anybody else, what I've been feeling is not, oh, I don't know, artificial."

"There's nothing artificial here. No spell, not by me or anybody else. Bent, I couldn't cast a spell on you even if I wanted to. You saw the reaction of those people in the Galleria to my spells. Did you feel anything? Anything at all?"

"No." She had him there, so he tried another tack.

"But you mean to tell me, you never thought about this soulmate business before you met me? You must have gone out on dates. What about them? The thought one of them might be your soulmate never crossed your mind? What about Tom What's-his-name from the gala? I thought you had dated him." A flare of jealousy shot through him at the thought of Tom even touching her. He knew it was irrational; he couldn't have it both ways—have her, yet not have her—but he was past caring. He concentrated on her answer.

"I went out with Tom a few times, that's all. He's a nice man, but I never felt attracted." She shook her head. "No, I forgot about soulmates until Mother reminded me, and that was the week before I met you at the Scrowcrofts. I never had any reason to remember. Bent, I've never before felt attraction the way I do for you now. I never let a man get close to me. Never wanted one to."

"Never?" He saw her face change from puzzled to apprehensive as he said the word. She hadn't told him something. "What?"

Daria sighed. "There's the matter of the f-first ma-mating for a witch," she stammered, looking down again at her clasped hands.

"What's the problem? You might come out of it with enhanced powers. According to your parents, it doesn't look like I become a warlock, although the idea is intriguing." He mused for a moment on the ability to cast spells, then dragged his mind back to the matter at hand—figuring out what the hell this 'soulmate' business meant. Then words connected in his brain. "Wait a minute. When they said 'first mating,' they meant the first time we have sex, didn't they?"

She nodded affirmatively. "But it's a little more. Witches never make love with any man until with their soulmates." She glanced quickly up at him and than back down again.

Bent unfolded his arms and, leaning forward, used one hand to raise her head so he could see her eyes. Touching her made his fingers tingle. Her green eyes shimmered with her apprehension. "You're a v—, uh, you've never been with a man." It was a statement more than a question.

"No." She shook her head very slowly.

He felt a primitive flash deep inside and a satisfied smile cross his face. She'd be his, *only his*. Forever. He felt a warm glow in his middle. Committed to each other for life.

Damn, there was that word again. He took his fingers from her chin and rubbed them together. The prickling abated. He dismissed the sensation as he thought of another question. "Look, are you sure we're soulmates? What if it's just plain old lust? I haven't had a wo—, uh, companionship, uh, a relationship in a while. Maybe I'm just horny." God, did he sound lame, or what?

"Maybe if it were only *you* feeling attracted to *me*, but, Bent, *I'm* absolutely attracted to *you*, and in my case, it can't be anything else."

"Is there any way to prove this thing exists? That we are or we aren't?" He wanted some hard evidence—an empirical, straightforward, non-theoretical, non-fairy-tale confirmation, not this feeling business.

"There's only one way I know of, from what my parents said, to prove we're not. If, by some chance, we really aren't soulmates, we won't be able to . . . consummate the union. When we try to 'come together,' we just won't be able to, as I understand it. But if we aren't soulmates, we wouldn't be having this effect on each other," she concluded.

"I think that's circular reasoning—or skewed or some sort of self-fulfilling prophecy," he said. "The only way to prove or disprove the idea is to go to bed. If we aren't, then nothing will happen. If we are, then something will happen, and, boom, we're tied together for life. Do I have it straight?"

"Yes."

He rose from the couch and felt her gaze follow him to the window. He put his hands in his pockets and rocked back and forth as he gazed at his reflection in the glass.

Bent knew he was upsetting her. But he didn't quite feel on stable ground himself. All he had wanted to do was have sex, a little fling, to go to bed with a woman to whom he was attracted.

No, he had to confess those statements weren't quite right. He had to be honest: he wanted to make love to Daria. Badly. Overwhelmingly.

He'd thought tonight she'd tell him more details about practitioners and magic, and he'd take her to bed. He'd planned it all out. He'd been in a state of semi-arousal all day in anticipation. Then she laid all this on him. He never saw it coming. Now he couldn't seem to think straight and his . . . anticipation had certainly deflated.

He needed some time to sort all this out. Yeah, that was it. He needed to study this situation like he would any other.

Analyze it thoughtfully and carefully. He was a CEO, he should act like one. Take charge.

As he formulated those thoughts, a small pain pricked him, right in his middle. He grimaced and rubbed the spot. Just what he needed, a rerun from the past. It had sure taken long enough to show up.

He turned back to her and almost winced at the scared look on her face. He felt his heart twist. He had to be careful, no matter what; she was too precious to hurt. "Daria, I don't know what to say. You've knocked me for a loop."

"That's all right, Bent, I understand, believe me. It takes time to get used to the idea. I felt the same way after the talk with Mother." She gulped and he could almost see her gather herself before continuing. "If you want to leave, or don't want to have anything to do with all this, as I said, you're free to walk away."

"Hell, no, I'm not leaving." The words came out of his mouth before he could stop them, but he recognized the truth in them immediately. She wouldn't have been threatened if they hadn't met. No matter what, he wasn't going to walk out. He still had to protect her from the goons who were after her. As if in agreement, the discomfort in his chest subsided and was replaced by a warm glow.

"Daria, do you want me to go?" he asked. Acute, astonishing anguish gripped him as he waited for her answer. He did not want her to answer his question affirmatively.

For a long moment that almost terrified him, she locked his eyes. She finally shook her head with a jerk. "No. It's the last thing I want. But I don't want you to feel trapped or used either."

"I just need a little time, that's all, time to take it all in," he stated, thinking he sounded like a weasel. A sharp stab in his stomach confirmed his weaselness. "Maybe we need to talk more about this soulmate situation. You can tell me more about how it works. Do you feel trapped with me?"

"No. I've never felt trapped with you, once I came to know you. I think I was more ambushed by the idea than the reality in the beginning."

"I tell you what," he said, seeing a possible out for the conversation. He badly needed some space to come to terms with the jumble in his brain and the pain in his chest. "Let's sleep on it. There's too much going on in my head to make sense now. We'll get a fresh start tomorrow. Okay?"

She looked to him a little defeated, but she raised her chin and gave him a crooked smile. "Okay." She picked up her glass and took it to the kitchen.

Bent turned out the lights in the family room and followed her into the kitchen, then to the hall and up the stairs. Neither said a word until they reached their usual parting place between the bedrooms. Daria didn't look back at him to say good night, and for a reason he couldn't articulate right this second, it made him angry. Was she cutting him out before he'd had a chance to decide anything?

"Wait." He touched her shoulder and she stopped. He turned her around. "I didn't get my good-night kiss." He put his arms around her and lowered his lips to hers.

As usual, the touch of lips and tongues ignited a mutual conflagration that was not totally extinguished when they parted.

"Good night," Daria whispered with a shaky voice.

"Good night," he responded and heard his tone quiver as much as hers had.

They walked into their respective bedrooms and shut the doors.

Oh, God, she'd botched it. Utterly spent, Daria leaned against her closed door, her body still reacting to the goodnight kiss, her mind in turmoil. She'd finally mustered the courage to have "the talk" and what had it gotten her?

All her fears were coming true. He was going to leave, she just knew it. The look on his face said it when he was asking those questions about soulmates as if it were something she'd made up, some goofy idea dreamed up by crazy people who thought they could do magic. And that strange reference to Tom. What was going on in his mind?

She'd told him she was a virgin, and he'd looked stunned—or afraid, maybe. What had he been thinking? Didn't he believe her? For someone who made her living reading people and their thoughts by their words and reactions, she was doing a horrible job reading her own soulmate.

He'd seemed okay with the concept all through her explanation—until her last statement about a commitment for life. Was that the problem? Was he a man who couldn't make a commitment? Please, don't let it be that.

This situation was so confusing. Why couldn't she have found a nice practitioner who understood the concept, who wouldn't put her through this anguish?

Trying not to think at all, she heaved herself off the door and undressed, managing to hang up her suit and toss the rest in the hamper. She put on her nightshirt and walked into her bathroom.

Analyze your feelings, she told herself as she washed her face and used the washcloth to press cold water on her eyelids. She wanted to cry, and she almost had in the hall before he kissed her. But crying wouldn't do any good, and she'd be damned if she'd start the workday tomorrow with puffy lids advertising her . . . her defeat? No, defeat wasn't the right word. Dismay? No, she didn't like that one either.

What was she? Where was she? In limbo? In purgatory?

No, wait. Be realistic. He'd said he needed to think about the situation. Heaven knew, she had had the same reaction after the first talk with her mother. Just take his statement at face value. He hadn't walked out. He'd kissed her, with every evidence of passion. Was his passion a lie on his part? It couldn't have been, not with the soulmate imperative driving both of them.

Maybe she was in *hope*, if such a place existed. Hope the imperative would solve their problems, convince him they belonged together. Hope he wouldn't feel resentful or leave. Where would he go?

What did she know of his life previous to coming to Houston? He'd had little to no stability, going from new company to new company. He traveled a great deal, had no basic home of his own, just an condo in Chicago which he rarely saw. Quite an adjustment from rootlessness to the idea of a soulmate, a home, a commitment.

Would he even want to settle in one place? Or keep traveling? What would she do then? She was a person who needed roots, a home. Oh, these thoughts were getting her nowhere but into deeper confusion. She had to stop thinking.

Daria took the washcloth from her eyes, brushed her teeth, and went to bed. She tried to read the novel she had been working on, but gave up after she realized the page was a blur before her eyes. She turned out the light and composed herself, but it took forever to turn off the movie playing in her head, rerunning "the talk" with Bent over and over.

In his bedroom, Bent sat for long minutes on the bed, his head in his hands, his body finally calming down after their good-night embrace. Why had he kissed her? He hadn't meant to, he knew it would complicate things, then he couldn't stop himself. A manifestation of this soulmate force? Just how strong was this thing? How *imperative* was it?

As if in answer, a sharp tiny pain like a mosquito bite stabbed the end of his breastbone, then subsided into that persistent itching sensation. He rubbed the spot and hoped this business didn't set off an ulcer. True, the doctors had not been able to find anything wrong with him the last two times his stomach had ached, but those situations were nothing compared to this one. He forced himself to think.

What was he going to do about this situation, this . . . what? Relationship? Would it be a repeat of the past? Every time he'd gotten close enough to a woman to start thinking about the long term, a piercing, burning, physical agony in his gut had stopped him cold.

It had been bad enough with Kerrie, and he'd made the firm decision after Susan that he wanted nothing to do with commitment. He didn't need it. He enjoyed the traveling, the challenges of a new company and a new city. He'd gotten where he was by being able to move fast, no ties, no strings. What did he need a wife for?

But . . . he wanted this woman. He wanted Daria with every cell in his body. If this was magic, it was the sweetest, the most enticing enchantment he'd ever known. Then came her revelations about their being soulmates and what it meant—what a surprise! A definite shock to his system. Like an unexpected proposal of marriage . . . uh, better not go there. An unexpected job offer, the most wonderful job in the world. Yeah, those were better terms.

More, he needed to know more. He needed to understand all the ramifications. Don't theorize ahead of your data, he reminded himself as he took off his clothes. Talk to her, he thought as he brushed his teeth.

Maybe you aren't soulmates, he suggested as he climbed

into bed and turned out the light. A wave of dismay washed over him at his last thought, and the itch under his breastbone turned into a dull ache. He spent several hours staring at the ceiling, repeating their conversation in his head, massaging the ache, before he finally slept.

Outside in the hallway, Zorro and Lolita looked at the two closed doors and then at each other. The big black cat growled and pulled his right front paw across the carpet in a burying motion, and the dainty reddish female glowered, first in Bent's direction and then in Daria's. Together they trotted down the stairs, leaving the two humans to sleep as best they could without any companionship, human or feline.

Chapter Seventeen

Thursday morning Daria and Bent rose and went through their usual routines of eating breakfast, reading the paper, and going to the office. Neither said a word about the conversation the night before. Both kept their good-morning kiss almost perfunctory, although a little sizzle did tantalize their lips. Each thought the other looked a little the worse for wear, but did not mention it. They concentrated on business. They both felt like cowards, but rationalized the idea by thinking that now was not the time to broach the subject of soulmates. They had to go to work.

About ten o'clock, Daria had just concluded a call with Merle Wharton, arranging the time for their first interview, when the phone rang while her hand was still on the receiver.

"Daria Morgan," she said into the mouthpiece.

"Hi, Daria, it's me," Antonia replied.

"Oh, hi, Mother. How are you and Daddy?" Oh, great, she thought, rolling her eyes. Her parents. Just what she needed. She'd managed to work by ruthlessly banning any thoughts about Bent from her head. Now she had to think about the mess all over again.

"We're just fine, dear. Now, we don't want to pry, but you know your father. He's worried about you. So he 'suggested' I give you a call to find out how you and Bent were doing. How did he take learning about practitioners after he had some time to think about it? Have you told him about soulmates yet?"

Daria sighed. It wasn't just her father who was worried, but she let her mother give him the blame for "making her call." "Bent's just fine. He believes us, about being practitioners, I mean. I know he has some more questions, but he's been working late, and we haven't had much time to talk." She knew she was hedging, but she really didn't want to get into this.

Her mother obviously wasn't about to let Daria off the hook, however. "Daria, being soulmates is not as simple as it looks," she said with one of those motherly I-won't-take-any-excuses voices. "You must tell him. You yourself said it."

"Mother, I told him last night." Daria's words came out as a resigned sigh.

"And?"

"And? He's . . . thinking about it."

"And? What's he thinking? What's to think about? Is anything wrong?"

"Mother!" She had finally had enough, Daria decided. She was really terminally tired of her mother's nagging and interference. Besides, she absolutely did not want to tell her mother she'd failed, and Bent had not accepted or believed the truth of the matter. The last thing she wanted or needed was her parents' interference. What would Bent think then? They were trying to pressure him? He was facing a shotgun wedding?

She and Bent had to work it out for and by themselves.

It was time her mother butted out. Daria exerted all her willpower and garnered enough control not to yell, but it was a close thing. "Look, Mother. Whatever I told him, or he's thinking, or we're doing is none of your business," she enunciated precisely into the phone. "We're fine. We'll work it out. Now leave us alone. Please. Did your mother ask you such questions?"

There was a stark silence on the other end of the phone. Then Antonia spoke, chagrin clear in her voice. "Daria, I'm sorry. You're right. It is none of our business. My mother was nosy and drove me crazy too, so I guess it's in the genes. She did the same thing to me, and I had the same reaction then you're having now. I should have remembered. I apologize."

"It's all right, Mother," Daria replied, suddenly wondering if she would treat her own daughters the same way. *Her own daughters? Bent's children?* The idea stunned her. She'd never allowed herself to think that far ahead.

"Daria, you know we just want you to be happy."

Daria dragged herself back to the present. "I know, Mother. I appreciate it. Look, I have to go back to work." Anything to get out of this conversation.

"We love you, Daria," Antonia said. Daria could hear her smile through the phone lines.

"Love you too." Daria hung up and put her face in her hands for a moment, rubbing her temples. She had been doing just fine, thank you very much, *not* thinking about the previous night. Now her mother had brought it all back.

With a mental wrench that almost banged her brain

against her skull, she blanked her mind and turned to her computer and the list of questions she was creating for Manufacturing. She could do this, get through however long it took Bent to 'think,' if she just didn't dwell on disastrous possibilities. Eventually she managed to concentrate again. When Ellen Brill from HR stuck her head in and suggested lunch, Daria leaped at the chance for a diversion.

That afternoon in his office, Bent had just finished another getting-nowhere discussion of the company's financial situation with Theo Wall. He was standing in the doorway to his office as the Financial VP was leaving when Janet said, "Mr. Benthausen, there's an Alaric Morgan on the phone for you. Do you want to speak to him?"

"Yes, I do," Bent replied. "Tell him I'll be right with him." He turned to Wall. "And I'll get your report later today, you said?"

"Yes, I'll have it to you before five." Wall paused, then said, "I've heard of Alaric Morgan. Isn't he the auditing troubleshooter?" He pushed his glasses back up his nose and blinked rapidly.

"Yes, he's Daria's father," Bent answered offhandedly, noticing Wall seemed pale all of a sudden. The man looked okay otherwise, so Bent put Theo's lack of color down to the fluorescent lighting and promptly forgot about it. He turned and walked back into his office, closing the door behind him.

As he picked up the phone, he hoped Alaric wasn't going to pull a heavy-handed don't-touch-my-little-girl stunt. Or worse, get a shotgun. He hadn't seemed like that type of father. In light of the past evening, Bent wasn't entirely certain he wanted to talk to the man, but it had been a way to get Theo out of his office, and now he was stuck. Maybe he could learn something more about soulmates. "Hello, Alaric. What can I do for you?"

"Bent, how are you?" The older man's voice boomed over the phone.

"I'm fine. Better than fine, in fact. Excellent," Bent lied.

"Good." Alaric paused, then cleared his throat. "Antonia talked to Daria this morning. Now, I don't want you to get the idea we're checking up on the two of you or anything, and I'm working hard on accepting the fact she's all grown up and not my little girl anymore."

He paused again, then blurted, "Damn, this is harder than I thought it would be. Look, Bent. The reason I called is, since Daria has told you about practitioner soulmates, I felt there were a couple of things you needed to know from a man's perspective. From a *practitioner's* perspective. Sort of a father-to-son discussion about the soulmate imperative and first matings. I don't want to intrude, but there's nobody else who can tell you."

"Go on," Bent encouraged, smiling to himself. It had been a long time since his own father had sat him down to discuss the birds and the bees. He doubted he needed a refresher, but if it made Alaric happy, okay. At least the man wasn't yelling at him for his reaction to Daria's tale. Then the term "first matings" hit him between the eyes, and he snapped to attention. He wanted more data; well, here was a primary source. "What do I need to know?"

"I'll tell you what my father told me and what I told my own son. Take your time. Don't rush her. Everything will come out all right, but it won't be easy on you. I know how you feel about this time, like you're going to explode. Right?"

"Yes, sir." Man, was he ever right, Bent thought. "I've been trying—to give her however much time she needs, that is." He moved restlessly as it struck him he was talking to Daria's *father*, for crying out loud, about sex with the man's own daughter. But Alaric had information, and from his tone of voice, he probably found this discussion as embarrassing as Bent did.

"Good," Alaric kept talking doggedly on. "Warlocks seem to be preconditioned—it's in our genes or something—to let our women come to us. Maybe it works the same for non-practitioners. I don't know. My grandfather told me our patience comes from the way witches were mistreated in the past, when they were beaten or raped, or worse. They have to be sure we're not out to hurt them. They have to trust us. Probably has something to do with the virgin business too. But that's neither here nor there. You'll know when she's made up her mind."

Alaric paused and Bent could hear him take a drink of something. Like father, like daughter, Bent thought, remembering how Daria had sipped wine while explaining soulmates. He didn't mention Alaric's daughter had already made up her mind. The problem was *he* had not. That particular item, he decided, wasn't any of her father's business.

"Now, according to tradition and probably some old rules or maybe to make certain of a true and secure bonding, as it were, the first mating must be without barriers of any kind," Alaric continued. "No condoms, no diaphragms, no birth control pills."

"Uhhhh," Bent tried to form the words of objection to the rule, but the notion of being bare inside Daria demolished his reasoning capacity for a few seconds.

"You're healthy, aren't you?" Alaric asked in a sharp tone.

"Yes, sir, I'm fine. And I've always used condoms," Bent reassured the older man, but didn't add that it had been so long since he'd had sex, he didn't have a single piece of protection or if he did, it had crumbled to dust. Then he realized he hadn't even thought of buying condoms before now. Usually when attracted to a woman who reciprocated his advances, he procured a supply early on.

"Well, you won't need them. Witches have their own innate built-in health and birth controls, so you don't have to worry about it. Soulmates don't have children unless both want them."

"That's . . . good to know," Bent said. Children. He hadn't thought about children. But that wasn't a discussion for now. Back to the basics, his more important questions about the whole concept. "Look, can I ask you a question?"

"Certainly."

"Just how real is this soulmate business? I don't mean to disparage or minimize it or anything, but it is pretty fantastic. From a non-practitioner's point of view, anyway."

"Hit you pretty hard, didn't it?" Alaric's tone was now man-to-man, not fatherly at all.

"Yeah, it did." He absentmindedly rubbed the damn itch on his chest as he answered. It had started giving him little twinges of pain every so often.

"The soulmate imperative is as real as a hurricane, Bent. It's powerful, primeval, inexorable. It stops a man in his tracks and makes him concentrate on what's important in life. Focuses him on one woman, his mate. Being with her brings a sense of completeness that must be felt to be believed. Yes, it's magic. After all, what's between a man and a woman is the oldest kind of magic.

"Now, you may try to fight it, but you'll have about as much success as you would trying to turn back one of those storms. You may question it, and you should certainly understand what it does to you in creating a bond between you and your mate. But, in the end, it's got you, and each of us must each deal with it, accept it in our own way."

"I'm not sure that's much help," Bent said.

Alaric chuckled. "I guarantee, everything will be clear in the end. Bent, my boy, treasure my daughter. And let me tell you one more thing."

"Yes?"

"Being soulmates just gets better all the time." On that note, Alaric hung up.

Bent put the phone down and sat there for a moment. Some phone call, he mused. It must have been awkward as hell for Alaric. It hadn't been any the less for himself. He wouldn't be surprised if he were blushing like a schoolboy. He ran his fingers through his hair and considered what the older man had told him.

So, practitioners were predisposed to wait for their witches to come to them. He thought back over his plans for Daria, formed practically at the beginning, ever since the Saturday he helped with the garden. Something then had told him to take it easy, wait for her to come to him. Evidently this soulmate connection worked on non-practitioners and warlocks in the same, organic way.

No barriers, no condoms. Bent found the idea of making love without a condom highly erotic, and his cock stirred in anticipation. He grimaced in reaction. He had had enough trouble with that portion of his anatomy long before the "soulmate" talk, and he told himself to calm down. A constant state of horniness wouldn't help him think clearly. His body, however, paid scant attention to his mind's commands.

No condoms? Witches had their own internal control and soulmates had to agree on a child? Then there were no unwanted children. A vision appeared in his mind's eye of Daria pregnant with his child, and a wave of longing enveloped him. He had never wanted children before, but with Daria . . . ?

Children meant marriage, of course. There was that word again. Funny how it didn't seem as frightening as it once had, before he met Daria. In fact, he didn't feel anything like he had with Kerrie and Susan, none of the cold sweats, none of the burning deep in his gut, none of the stomach-churning fear and foreboding about committing himself to a woman. All he had was this damnable itch stabbing him in the chest every so often.

He had to acknowledge to himself the idea of matrimony and commitment had insinuated itself into his musings over and over lately. If he were being brutally honest with himself, he had to admit that, fight the idea as he might, it seemed more and more to be the natural outcome for the two of them.

A warm feeling of pleasure radiated out from his heart, then the itch returned.

Well, hell. "Something" seemed to be working on him, changing his views and deeply entrenched ideas. "The oldest kind of magic," indeed.

The ringing phone brought him out of his contemplations, and he firmly closed the Daria compartment in his mind to again concentrate on business.

Chapter Eighteen

On Thursday night, Daria and Bent went home, ate, and concentrated on work, a false concentration because each was waiting for the other to bring up the "subject." Daria mulled over her list of questions for Merle Wharton, and Bent perused the report Theo Wall had delivered just before five. The evening dragged by and both went to bed early.

Both worked hard to ignore the attraction pulling them together, but their determination dissolved—as usual—when they said good night in the upstairs hall. The kiss went on and on, hands stroked up and down and around, and only the need to breathe split them apart. Trembling like children standing before a pile of Christmas presents but forbidden to touch so much as a single one, they made their separate ways to their respective bedrooms. Adhering to their previous patterns, each left the door cracked open.

After the kiss, Daria wobbled into her room. She tingled all over as she relived Bent's kiss and caresses in her mind. Somehow she undressed, even neatly hung up her clothes, and washed her face. It wasn't until she finished brushing her teeth and looked into her own eyes in the mirror that she came back down to earth. Her center felt distinctly hollow, and her chest was tight. At least the itching had subsided.

What was he going to decide? Wednesday night he said he wanted to talk more. Tonight he didn't say a word. What was he thinking?

She had to imagine something else besides a bad outcome. What if he accepted the soulmate situation? What if they did make love?

For the first time in her life.

A small wave of panic washed over her. What if she didn't do *it* well? What if she disappointed him? What if she couldn't satisfy him? She tried to recall everything she had ever read about making love—not that she had read much, given the fact that she hardly thought about . . . sex. Well, she certainly was thinking about it now.

Technique? She had none.

Seduction? She didn't have the slightest idea where to begin.

Her reflection shrugged back at her, and as she stared into her own face, she suddenly felt like a fool. This sort of thinking would never do. Women had been making love for centuries; how hard could it be? Besides, Bent knew what he was doing. That was obvious from his kisses. He had enough technique for both of them. She had no reason to be scared. "You ninny," she scolded herself. "You idiot. Remember what Mother always says. 'Soulmates are soulmates. You have nothing to worry about.' " She gave a "so there" nod to her reflection, put her toothbrush away, and turned out the bathroom light.

She turned back the covers, dislodging Lolita, who waited for Daria to settle herself for their nightly ritual. Daria turned out the bedside lamp, and the dainty cat snuggled at her side. Idly petting her purring companion, Daria tried to compose herself for sleep. She had to quell a small repeat of her bathroom anxieties and then a replay of the good-night kiss that had her shifting all over the bed. The third time Daria turned over, Lolita complained, jumped off the bed, and left the room entirely.

Daria heard the shower in the other bathroom turned off, and she thought she heard Bent's voice, but she decided it was her imagination. Who was he talking to? Himself? And not her? She turned over again, punched the pillow, and tried to will her body to relax. Maybe everything would be better in the morning.

After the kiss, Bent walked into his bedroom and headed straight for the bathroom, shedding clothes as he moved. Standing under a cold shower, he braced himself with his hands on the walls as the water did nothing to lessen his lust. He was still stiff as a board.

After that incendiary kiss it had been all he could do to let her go. Damn, but he wanted this woman. He wanted to sink into her depths and never come out, and conversely, to absorb her into himself. If this was the soulmate "imperative" driving his libido, it had to be one of the most powerful forces in the universe.

Explode? Hell! He felt more like a star about to go nova.

Giving up on his attempt to control his body, he shut off

the water and reached for a towel. What was he going to do about Daria, about himself, about the situation? He had to decide; he couldn't put her or himself through more of this confusion. He was a decisive person. He knew how to make a choice.

But he had sure acted like a coward tonight. He hadn't brought up the soulmate subject, not a word. She was obviously waiting for him to initiate the discussion. He'd started to say something a couple of times, but couldn't think of a question to ask, not one single question.

What was to know? It wasn't the idea of the phenomenon holding him back.

Was it the idea of commitment? Being with one woman? If he had a wife, he'd want her to be with him, one hundred percent. He'd want the whole package—love, honor, trust, loyalty, joy, companionship, humor, friendship, hot sex. In a word, Daria.

He looked at his reflection in the mirror. "What is the matter with you?" he asked it. "You're a thirty-six-year-old man. A man. Not a boy. You're not a twenty-year-old jackass who thinks with your dick. You've found a woman who suits you exactly, to every specification. What are you afraid of?"

Only one possibility came to mind.

"That physical reaction and rejection like in the past?" Sure, Kerrie standing him up at their rehearsal dinner hadn't been pleasant, but he'd had those stomach pains before the event and they went away immediately afterward. He'd felt much worse with Susan, and had even checked with two doctors. He'd had to force himself to go to work. She hadn't liked his job, his traveling, his long hours, and she'd hated the fact that they wouldn't be living in New York City. When she'd given him an ultimatum, marry her and change jobs or "good-bye," and he'd hesitated as more pain wracked his body, she'd left. He'd been both relieved and suddenly free of pain, he remembered now.

What did he think would happen this time? He'd develop an ulcer? "Nah," he scoffed to the mirror, "it doesn't fly."

Besides, this time the pain was different. It came on differently, stabbed, not burned, itched . . . Wait a minute. *Itched.* He'd been itching ever since he met Daria. Was this a manifestation of the imperative? Could that damn phenomenon have been working on him all along? He put the idea aside to think about later. He had more important considerations.

He studied his face and ran his hand around his jaw. He looked like hell.

"What about Daria?" he asked his baggy-eyed self. What was he going to do about her? Maybe he was afraid she'd turn him down?

"Nah," he said again. Not if the soulmate imperative was driving her as strongly as it did him. What then?

"Are you going to leave her? Could you leave? What if she wasn't in your life? How would you feel then?" A tidal wave of longing rushed out from his heart, engulfed him, and weakened his knees so much he had to grab the towel rack for support. The very idea of not being with Daria made his whole chest ache; then a sharp stab of pain to his solar plexus took his breath away and bent him over in agony.

At least one of his questions was answered, he thought as he panted. It was the damned imperative behind this agony.

He hung up the towel, hobbled into the bedroom, and threw himself on the bed where he writhed on the sheets from the increasing torment in his torso. He could feel his heart being crushed by the mass of loneliness descending upon him.

He'd settle this tomorrow. Explain how he'd come to agree, tell her he was her soulmate. Then he'd take her to bed and bind her to him and they'd have each other forever. "All right, all right. I'm an idiot. I want her, I need her. I give up," he groaned. "We're soulmates."

No sooner had the words passed his lips and the thoughts gone through his mind than the pain disappeared, he could breathe again, and his erection finally subsided. He collapsed, exhausted, spread-eagle on the bed.

Just as he gained the energy to reach up and turn off the bedside light, Lolita pushed the door open another inch and leaped onto the bed. Bent was about to greet her, but she didn't give him a chance. The look she gave him would have fried a mouse. Then she growled and bit him on the toe.

"Ouch!" he yelped. "What was that for?"

"Rrrrrrgh," was all she answered before jumping off the bed and leaving the room.

"Crazy cat," he muttered as he inspected his toe. At least she hadn't punctured the skin. What was the matter with her? Or was she just putting her two cents in, telling him she thought he was an idiot, too? God Almighty! Even the cats knew what was going on.

He turned off the light, closed his eyes, and thought about his plans for the next day. "Tomorrow" repeated itself in his head like an incantation.

The next thing he knew, he and Daria were in bed together, naked in each other's arms. Sweet heaven, she was everything he had expected and more. Hot, wet, and wild. He ran his hands over her lush body, luxuriating in the satiny feel of her skin. She tasted as sweet as honey, even better than she felt, and he suckled at her breasts, then trailed his mouth down her stomach and lower.

Now, his body screamed at him as he raised himself over her, poised to take her in a fiery possession that both of them would remember forever. *Now, now, now!*

But as he forged forward, his cock, which had been stiff as titanium and throbbing to the point of pain, wilted.

Sagged.

Drooped.

Just about curled up and died.

Her feminine passage, which had been open and receptive, weeping for his entry, closed with the finality of a castle gate slamming shut before the invading Huns.

No. No, no, no! This couldn't be happening! They were soulmates, for crying out loud!

"No, no, no!" he shouted as Daria vanished before his eyes and he collapsed on the bed where she had lain.

"No!" he yelled again, thrashing around in the bed and fighting with the covers. This time he woke himself up. Coming to, he was sitting bold upright, tangled in the sheets, struggling for breath, and sweating like a pig. He ran his hands through his hair and looked around wildly. He saw only his normal bedroom.

It had just been a nightmare, he told himself. Just all his latent neuroses coming to the fore in his subconscious, or his unconscious, or whatever the hell it was. He didn't have anything to worry about. It would be all right. Soulmates were soulmates. They were destined to be together.

The bedroom door, slightly ajar from Lolita's exit, opened a little more. Had he awakened Daria? He almost groaned at the thought of telling her about the dream. He wouldn't tell her, he decided quickly. It was nothing she needed to know. He looked toward the hall. No one appeared in the doorway. What had caused the door to open?

He jumped as Zorro leaped onto the bed. "Rrrrrrow," the miniature black panther said, for once without his arrogant haughtiness. When Bent reached out to him, Zorro rubbed his head along Bent's hand and gave it a lick. Then he settled down at Bent's side and began to purr.

"Thanks, man," Bent said, smiling as he lay back down. The big cat had evidently changed his mind about him. If Zorro's change of attitude wasn't proof he and Daria were soulmates, he didn't know what was. He fell asleep, telling himself everything would be all right. Daria would be his tomorrow.

Daria woke up groggy and unsettled on Friday morning. She couldn't bring herself to offer her lips for their usual good-morning kiss. She didn't think she could take an embrace that escalated into an inferno; neither could she stand it if the kiss degenerated into a cold touch of the lips and nothing more.

Bent, on the other hand, seemed subdued at first, but a couple of cups of coffee perked him up; he spent the drive to the office telling her about the distribution plans his new vice president had concocted. She caught him sneaking odd looks at her, but couldn't interpret them. Only when they parted at the elevator did he lean down with a glint in his eye to whisper, "We're going to talk tonight. That's a promise." He kissed her quick and hard, gave her a wicked grin, and left for his office.

"Tonight," Daria whispered as she watched him walk down the hall. A surge of joy ran through her veins. He must have come to a positive decision. Oh God, it was going to be all right.

Eyes shut, hand on the magic center under her breastbone where fireworks were going off, she allowed herself a moment for exhilaration. Then she marched in the opposite direction, ruthlessly forcing herself to focus on the job she had to do.

As it turned out, she spent an interesting morning with

Merle Wharton who, once he found that he couldn't intimidate her and that she asked perceptive questions, relaxed and cooperated completely. Daria discovered Merle viewed his staff and their abilities clearly and objectively, and he made excellent additions to her list of questions.

During the afternoon, she kept relentlessly busy, arranging interviews at the plants for the next week and, with Merle's help, actually meeting with two of his managers who had come to headquarters on other matters. Proud of herself for being able to get through the day in one piece, she was tidying up her office at 4:30 when the phone rang. Oh, *please*, she prayed, don't let it be Bent saying he had to work late. She picked up the phone. "Daria Morgan."

"Hi, honey," his rich baritone flowed into her ear.

"Hi," she answered softly, squinching her eyes shut and crossing her fingers. Please . . .

"You about ready to leave?"

Her eyes popped open. "Already? Yes, certainly. I can be ready in five minutes. Isn't it early?" The words came out in a rush and she practically danced with lustful anticipation.

"I've been stuck in damn boring meetings all day," Bent said disgustedly. "If I don't get out now, I'll go crazy." His voice dropped low, full of sexy promise. "Besides, we have to talk."

Daria felt her heartbeat accelerate upon these words, and she shivered in anticipation. "I'll be right there."

"No, I'll come to you before the phone rings or somebody else walks in to ask me something. See you in a minute."

He held true to his word, and as they fled the building, they left one vice president and a couple of managers staring in their wake.

Within five minutes, they were climbing into the car. Both were silent as Bent navigated their way out of the parking garage and through the heavy Galleria traffic.

Daria sat still, hands clenched together, silently ordering her shoulders and back, her stomach, her whole body to relax. She knew if she looked at him, she wouldn't be able to keep her hands off, and she had absolutely no idea what to talk about.

So she surreptitiously watched him drive. He seemed totally concentrated on the task. Bent's hands on the steering wheel, long fingers grasping it lightly, letting the wheel slide through them as the car straightened out after a turn, fascinated her. She quelled a shiver when she imagined those hands on her, sliding down her back, up over her breasts. *Breathe*, she ordered herself. *Breathe*. By the time they reached the house, she felt almost lightheaded.

Chapter Nineteen

Bent followed Daria into the house, stripping off his tie as he went. He stopped at the security panel. "Check me out as I lock up," he said. She watched him hit the buttons. "Was that right? We're all locked in?"

"Yes, perfect. Would you like anything? Coffee, tea? Dinner?" she asked, turning into the kitchen.

He stopped her, putting his hands on her shoulders from behind. "Yes, I'd like something," he whispered, nuzzling her neck and kissing the spot just behind her ear.

Daria relaxed against him, slanting her head to give him better access as he moved her collar away and worked his way down her neck to her shoulder. She could feel the tingle of goose-bumps all down her spine. "Wh-what would you like?" came hoarsely out of a throat suddenly gone dry.

Bent turned her to face him and put his hands on her waist. "I'd like to explore the possibilities of this soulmate connection," he whispered with his lips half an inch above hers. He kissed her, a long, lingering, lollapalooza of a kiss. Then he hugged her, rubbing her back until their breathing approached normal.

Holding her by her shoulders so he could see her face, Bent looked her in the eyes. "Daria, I've been an idiot, and I have to tell you why," he said in a low tone, almost a whisper. "Twice in the past, I was serious or thought I was, about two women. The first one abandoned me at our rehearsal dinner and ran off with the guy she'd been dating before me. The second split because I'm a workaholic and she wanted to live in New York City."

"Oh, Bent, I'm so sorry." She said, then listened to her last words. What was she saying? "Or rather, I'm sorry you had to go through that, but I'm not sorry those stupid women left you for me to find," she corrected herself.

He smiled a little grimly. "Wait. There's more to this. Both times, with the second being the worst, I went through a helluva lot of pain—physical pain, not psychic. My insides hurt, especially right here"—he pointed to the spot between his ribs—"and I was sure I was getting an ulcer, but the doctors couldn't find any problems. Each time after the woman left, I felt instantly better."

"Do you think the imperative had already picked you out?"

"Yeah, I do. I've been thinking about it off and on all day. I think the damn phenomenon was warning me off those women. But the pain it caused me had some consequences I don't think it intended to. It convinced me there was no way in hell I was going to go through that agony again. I decided my body was letting me know that I was not cut out for commitment to a woman. Getting seriously involved with someone would kill me the next time for sure.

"When you started talking about how the soulmate bond was for life, I panicked. 'Here we go again,' I thought. Sure enough, when I balked, the pain came back. I didn't realize until last night that this time it was different from those other two. It went away when I thought of you and hit me hard when I thought about leaving."

He stood up a little straighter, took a deep breath, and said, "I believe you about the existence of the soulmate imperative. It's put me through two days of sheer agony. Can you forgive me for acting like a jackass?"

He slid his hands down her arms and took her hands in his. His blue eyes were the bluest she'd ever seen them. His voice came out in a rasp as he spoke again before she could answer his question.

"I want you, I need you. Just the thought of not having you in my life cuts through me like one of your carving knives. You're everything I've ever wanted in a woman. You don't have to worry. I don't feel trapped, I don't feel used. It doesn't matter if our being together comes from the soulmate business or from good, old-fashioned chemistry, but whatever it is, I'm yours. Are you mine?"

Daria tightened her grip on his fingers. "Oh, yes, Bent, I'm yours. But there's nothing to forgive."

"You're too generous, honey, but I'll make it up to you." He grinned, looking like a novice practitioner who'd just successfully cast his first upper-level spell. "Now, shall we prove we're soulmates?"

She put her arms around his neck, leaned back and looked up at him. All of her former anxieties had vanished as if they had never existed, and a warm glow took their place. He was right, it was time to do this thing, to find out what was between them, to claim each other as soulmates. She wanted to be his, in every way. "Yes," was all she said.

Bent saw the promise in her gaze, her green eyes enormous emeralds, hazed with passion, burning with fire in their depths. It would be all right, he thought as he banished memories of his nightmare to the lower reaches of hell. She was his.

"Good." He took his time kissing her, exploring, tasting, savoring. Or rather, he had planned to take his time, but his long-unfulfilled need and his hunger drove his actions, and he soon thrust his tongue in a rhythm he wanted to repeat with another part of his body, a part demanding its own release.

When Daria, her former inhibitions seemingly flown out the window, responded with her own forays into his mouth, he deepened the kiss, demanding and receiving more. By the time he finished, the blood was roaring in his ears, and she was plastered to him from thighs to shoulders, sex to sex, her feet almost off the floor, his hands cupping her derriere. He set her down and they rested, gulping air, until he managed to croak, "Oh, Lord, Daria. I want you so much."

"I want you, too," she whispered.

Exhilarated, he gave her a hug that forced the breath from her body. "Then let's find a bed. Your first time shouldn't be on the floor." He led her by the hand down the hall and up the stairs.

The two cats sat on the landing watching, and they moved out of the way as the humans came up the stairs. Both felines had smug looks on their faces and turned to each other as if to say, "It's about time."

Daria led him into her bedroom. Before he could stop her, she moved to the bed, stripped the spread and throw pillows off, and flipped back the top sheet. She was nervous, he knew, as he turned her to face him, tipping her chin up with his hand.

Smiling down at her, he massaged her shoulders and kissed her again, one of those long, mind-numbing, body-melting kisses that soon had her pliable in his hands. He coaxed her out of her suit coat and shed his own. He loved the little suits she wore; he'd been fantasizing for days about getting her out of them.

He backed away far enough to start unbuttoning her shirt. "Honey, do the same for me," he pleaded between small kisses. She awkwardly complied until she reached his belt. He yanked his shirttails out and she completed the unbuttoning job, dropping her hands just as he lifted off her shirt. Her bra was champagne lace, hardly there at all. He carefully unhooked the front clasp and slid the straps from her shoulders, letting the lacy scrap fall to the floor. Her breasts were small and firm, graced with light pink nipples and areolae. The nipples were darkening, already hardening with arousal.

"Oh, Daria, you are so beautiful," he breathed as his hands covered each inviting mound, lifting, weighing, flicking the peaks with his thumbs.

She whimpered, and her hands covered his to pull them against her as her back arched, pushing from the other way.

Her head went back in surrender to his touch.

"Touch me, Daria," he whispered, taking one of her hands and placing it on his bared chest.

From the look on her face, she seemed to find the texture and feel of his chest intriguing as she explored. When he arched a little under her hands, he realized he was trembling slightly himself. When her hands moved down to his belt, he stopped her. "Not too fast, honey," he murmured as he brought her hands to his shoulders and knelt before her.

Reaching behind her, he unhooked her skirt and gingerly opened the zipper. He lowered the skirt and her half slip at the same time. "Step out of them and your shoes, honey," he instructed as she clung to his shoulders for balance. Then he rose, picking her up at the same time, and lay her in the middle of the big bed.

Running his hands from her shoulders to her feet, taking her pantyhose and panties with them, Bent just stared at her for a long moment. She was delicately made, perfectly formed, with a flare to her hips that drew his hands up to her waist. He kissed her softly again. "Perfect, you're just perfect," he breathed against her lips. Then he straightened and removed the remainder of his clothes, looking at her body all the while.

His, just his. His satisfaction and his lust were both immense, and he as was hard as granite.

Daria watched him from under her eyelashes. A fleeting thought that she probably should have been embarrassed skittered in and out of her mind, but the look on his face during his perusal of her body had been one of such wonder and delight, it thrilled her to the core.

When he began to undress, the reality of it was she was curious and more than a little in awe of what his nudity revealed. She had known he was tall, of course, but had not recognized that he was smoothly muscled, hard and flat, long-boned and sleek. His chest was slightly smattered with reddish brown hair that arrowed down to his navel. From a thatch of reddish brown curls, his sex rose proudly, larger than she had expected with her limited knowledge, yet she felt no apprehension.

Hers, he was hers. She trembled in anticipation of him and held up her arms to him as he joined her on the bed.

He seemed larger somehow, as he lay by her side, sliding his bottom arm under her head and shoulder and pulling her to him with his other hand. He thrust his top leg through hers, and she could feel his hard shaft against her, smooth as velvet, rigid as steel.

Textures, Daria thought, it's all different textures, as their legs rubbed and her fingers combed through his curly chest hair and around to sample the smooth skin on his back, feeling the firm muscles flexing beneath. Then he was kissing her and thought fled, leaving only sensations, each briefly realized before another replaced it.

She had known she enjoyed his touch before, but it was nothing compared to this now, flesh to flesh, no barriers, a mixture of textures, smells, and tastes. And warmth. He was so warm. Her hands roamed his body as his explored hers. But when he turned her on her back and began moving down, kissing, laving, nipping her neck, collarbones, and shoulders, her hands stilled and she gave herself over to him.

When he suckled her breasts, she gripped his hair to keep him there a while. The slight necking and petting they had engaged in previously simply had not prepared her for the intense pleasure of being skin to skin, the hot electricity rocketing through her. Where she had been pliant before, now she became tense, a tension that arched her body, thrusting her breasts to him for succor, but instead of affording relief, the action only tightened her further. She heard him chuckle, or mumble, something she couldn't hear with the blood pounding in her ears, but it sounded encouraging in tone.

When his hand moved to the curly hair between her legs and cupped her mound, she arched into it, gasping as he pressed and rotated the heel of his hand in a circle. Lightning shot through her as his fingers parted her soft feminine folds, rubbing her most sensitive nub. Her body made no attempt to clasp her thighs together, but welcomed the intrusion of his finger into her tight, wet softness. She was aching and he promised relief. "Don't wait," she gasped, her fingers clutching at his shoulders as her hips arched again into his hand. She couldn't bear waiting, she had to resolve the tension building in her, had to find release now.

Bent seemed to read her mind because he rose over her and settled between her legs, urged them up around his hips. Braced on his straight arms, his rigid shaft at her gateway, he said, "Daria, look at me."

She gazed into his eyes, lost in the blue pools, as he thrust slowly, relentlessly, into her slick passage. She felt the pressure building, her body stretching to accommodate him. A sharp pain caused her to flinch, then it was no more, and when she arched her hips instinctively, she accepted him to the hilt. She blinked in surprise, then smiled in delight. Oh yes. This was the way it was supposed to be. She belonged to him now. Together.

Bent knew he couldn't wait much longer. Her satin skin called for his touch, her taste made him hungrier, her scent filled his nostrils. He would probably shatter into a million pieces if he didn't have her soon. She was ready, but so tight, so tight. So hot, so wet, so slick.

He answered her smile with his own, slightly frayed about the edges as he fought himself for control. Inside her at last. Oh, sweet mercy. He belonged there, to her. It was like coming home. They were one. Together.

"Hold on tight," he grated. He began to move, a slow rhythm at first, but as she rose to meet each thrust, gasping "faster, faster," he increased the pace until they were hammering at each other, his thrusts hard and deep. They stared into each other's eyes, every thrust a possession, a claiming, with each possessed, each claimed in the taking. It seemed to go on forever.

Suddenly a tidal wave of release hit her, scant seconds before it roared over him, and its power overcame them for what seemed like minutes. She convulsed, locking her legs around him, throwing her hips upward as his came down to meet her. Shuddering, he emptied himself into her as she milked him for every drop.

The suddenly calm aftermath left him stunned. Somehow before collapsing onto her, he managed to lift a leg over hers and roll to their original position, facing each other on their sides. He was still inside her as they clung to each other, lungs aching, bodies exhausted.

Eventually he regained what he thought was consciousness. Never had he felt so drained, and at the same time, so satisfied. "Are you all right?" came out with great effort; even his vocal cords had been affected by the experience.

At first Daria could only nod her head. "I didn't expect . . . I wasn't prepared for . . ." Her whisper trailed off. Words couldn't adequately describe the experience. She had never imagined the heat, the release, the thrill, the exhaustion. She had never expected to be able to feel his hot seed pulsing into her, warming her to the core.

"Neither was I," he answered. "Neither was I." He stroked her back from nape to buttock and back again.

She snuggled a little closer to him, then realized he was still within her. "I'm fine," she smiled up at him and squeezed some delicate muscles.

"So you are," Bent laughed softly and gave her a little hug and a kiss. He thought he could move now. "Let's get you cleaned up. I'll be right back." He gently withdrew from her, rose, and walked into her bathroom. He returned with a damp washcloth and a hand towel. Cleaning her carefully, he murmured, "You hardly bled at all. There's no blood on the sheets." He took the washcloth and towel back into the bathroom.

Daria watched him walk across the room and realized she liked his back view as much as his front. She was turning into a brazen hussy, she told herself, as she felt a wide grin spread across her face. She didn't even have the modesty to be embarrassed when a man was washing her off, and intimately at that. And she didn't care at all. In fact, she felt wonderful, absolutely wonderful.

She was no longer a virgin. She had to laugh at herself—all those anxieties, all her worry and torture she had put herself through. And now, the wonder of it all. She had finally made love with a man, with Bent, with her soulmate.

Bent returned from the bathroom, climbed into bed, and pulled up the sheet to cover them. He snuggled her close. "I think we answered that question," he murmured after a quick kiss.

"What question?"

"Whether or not we're soulmates."

"Oh, *that* question."

They looked at each other and started laughing in sheer contentment. "We did, indeed," Daria said.

After huge sighs of pleasure, they cuddled, relaxed so thoroughly that they fell asleep.

Daria was the first to awaken. She was on her back, and

Bent was on his side, facing her, one arm across her middle. Replaying the love making in her mind, she could only shake her head. She hadn't known—not even an inkling—what she had been missing before Bent. Which was probably a good thing, she admitted. It was circular reasoning—she couldn't know what she was missing because she couldn't learn because she wasn't supposed to be interested in just any man until she met her soulmate and that wouldn't happen, according to her mother, until she was "ready for it." How her readiness was determined or who or what determined it remained a mystery. Oh well. *It* had finally happened—boy, had it ever.

Bent opened his eyes and noted the big grin on her face. "You look like the proverbial cat," he claimed. "Am I the canary?"

"Mmrrrrow," she answered with a smirk on her face and laughter in her eyes.

"Oh, my God, I've created a monster. Are you going to turn me into a toad?"

Daria sat straight up, surprise on her face. "Oh. You know, I forgot all about it. My powers, I mean. And I can't spell you, even if I could spell others."

"What about that enhancement business? Wasn't there the possibility? Let's find out. Try something."

Encouraged by his curiosity and acceptance, Daria scooted away from him on the bed and sat with legs crossed and the sheet pulled up around her. "Don't touch me," she warned him when he reached to put his hand on her knee. "I have a hard enough time concentrating, just being near you. When you touch me, I can hardly think."

Bent grinned smugly at her small confession, pushed himself up on the pillows, and interlaced his hands over his chest. "Okay, have at."

"I'll try for the rose petals." She closed her eyes, took a deep breath, opened her eyes, and cast the spell.

Nothing. Not a single petal, not even a whiff of rose scent.

Daria slumped, then looked at an ivy plant in the window. "Mother worked with me for ages on plant growth. Maybe this will work." She concentrated again.

Nothing. Not even a wiggle from the stem closest to them.

"Well, perhaps I can use the *flamma* spell. Lighting a candle is one of the most basic spells, the one almost everybody can manage," she told him. She focused on the candle on her dresser.

Nothing. Not a spark of heat, not a puff of smoke, not a flicker of flame.

She looked dejectedly at Bent, who was frowning at her. "Nothing. I tried three and nothing happened. Why are you frowning?" she asked.

"Put on one of your regular spells."

She cast an I-am-trustworthy. "What?"

"I can see a shimmering in the air around you."

"What color is it?"

"Sort of bluish violet."

"Then you can see that I'm spelled just like my family can. Tell me what colors you see." She threw on a variety of spells, canceling each before casting the next.

"Red . . . Now blue . . . Now a putrid sort of green . . . Now a clear emerald green," he said as the spells went on and off. He absently rubbed the end of his breastbone, which had started itching like mad.

"What's the matter?" Daria asked, putting her hand on his atop his chest.

The itching stopped abruptly. "Nothing. I just have this itch every once in a while."

"How long have you had it?" She started smiling.

"Oh, I don't know, about as long as I've known you, I guess. When you put your hand on mine, it stopped. Why?"

She laughed. "If we had any doubts about being connected somehow, I think they would have just been dispelled." She pressed her fingers down on her own sternum. "That has to be what Mother meant."

"Has to be what?"

"You know how some meditation techniques and martial arts teach you to 'center yourself?' "

"Yeah, so?"

"To cast spells, a practitioner has to do the same thing: center, concentrate, pull energy for the spell from a focal point. The place in a practitioner's body is usually considered to be right under the end of the sternum, literally in the center of the body, close to the heart. Right here." She pointed to her chest. "My 'magic center' has been itching like crazy ever since Mother told me I would be finding my soulmate soon. She even warned me I'd feel it."

"Well, hell. That's the exact spot where all my pain originated. I never put the two together until now. This damn imperative has certainly scrambled my brain. I wish I'd told you earlier. It might have helped me accept the situation. But as for now," he touched a hand to her center and leered lecherously, "I'll scratch your itch if you scratch mine."

Daria groaned and swatted at his hand as it began to roam. She finally captured it in hers. They both laughed.

"Is my itch going to stop now that we're together?" Bent asked.

"I don't know. We'll just have to see. When did it start just now?"

"When you were trying your spells."

"Hmm. Maybe it's another manifestation of your being able to see my spell aura. I guess we'll have to keep track." She collapsed beside him and snuggled. "It seems you received the benefit of the mating. I didn't receive any new capabilities, and I'll have to be tested to determine if my general power increased. I wonder if you can see my family's spell auras, too."

"What do you mean, *I* received the benefit of the mating. It appeared to me you enjoyed it as much as I did," he teased.

"Yes, I did." She nodded her head emphatically, then realized what she had said. "You're turning me into a wanton woman." She plucked at a few of his chest hairs as a small punishment for the "crime."

"Ouch!" He stilled her hand by capturing it with his and

gave her a mock-stern frown. "I certainly hope so. Now let's get some rest. I have big plans for the rest of the night, but we've had a long day already."

"Big plans, huh? Dare I guess what they are?" she asked, coquettishly.

"No. Hush," Bent ordered, fitting her to his side more comfortably.

Daria kissed his arm, the nearest part of him she could reach, and relaxed against him. She felt euphoric, floating but secure with Bent. She was a little disappointed, she had to admit to herself, that the mating had not increased her powers, but it hadn't decreased them either, from what she could tell. Her center gave a twitch as if to say she was just fine. She kissed Bent's arm again and closed her eyes. Sleep took her before she knew it.

Bent felt her relax and heard her steady breathing as she fell asleep. He glanced around the bedroom, shadowed now as night began to fall. The décor was not frilly or overwhelmingly feminine as he might have expected. In fact, it was neutral, just right for a couple, for them, to share. The walls were light blue; the window coverings, white louvered shutters, and the bedspread dark blue. Pillows in jewel tones, now on the floor along with the spread, offered colorful accents, and the oak of the antique four-poster bedstead and chests of drawers shone, too. The big king-sized bed held the two of them perfectly—enough room to play and comfortable for cuddling.

Cuddling. Bent smiled to himself and pulled Daria a

little closer. Good God, what an experience, making love—no, mating—no, making love, definitely—with Daria. He wondered what the next time would be like. He wondered if he had another next time in him in the following twenty-four hours. If the next time was like the first time, he wondered if he'd survive. But Lord have mercy, what a way to go! The thought plastered a goofy grin across his face. He drifted off with the smirk still in place.

Chapter Twenty

They woke up together about eight that night and turned naturally to each other, as if they had been lovers for years. Bent discovered he did indeed have it in him; in fact, it was clamoring to get out. The feelings and responses they drew from and with each other were not as intense as the first time, but for him, the experience still outranked all previous times with any other woman. Afterward hunger of another sort claimed their attention, so they donned bathrobes, went downstairs, and made themselves ham-and-cheese sandwiches.

"I have to ask you about something I just realized," Bent said after he inhaled half of his first sandwich and looked around the cheery kitchen. Daria was busy chewing and only raised her eyebrows at him. "I've been in the homes of some women in which I could hardly move for all the furniture, or which had lady-sized furniture, the kind incapable of holding a man unless he sits very carefully. Yet here you are, a single woman, not more than five-foot-three, and your furniture could fit anyone. It certainly fits me, and so does the décor, even in your bedroom. I feel comfortable everywhere in this house. Why is that?"

After quelling a spear of jealousy that flew through her at the thought of Bent in some other woman's house, especially some other woman's arms, Daria thought for a moment about the question. "As for the size of the furniture, I grew up with tall men like Daddy and Uncle Gregor and now Clay. My parents' furniture is on the same scale. What I have here just seems natural and the larger pieces fit the room dimensions. I've never been one much for frills or frilly furniture.

"I looked for months before finding this house and knew the moment I walked in that it was perfect. I never considered it was too big for me as a single woman, and it hasn't been, what with family dropping in from time to time. In fact, I increased its size. I had the office and my bedroom above it built on right after I bought it." She munched on a pickle slice before continuing. "I'm glad you feel comfortable here. This could be part of the soulmate thing, you know, like tastes and all that."

"I thought about it. You know, we could use some more information, especially on what to expect."

"I'll ask Mother if she found out anything more about mixed couples, and maybe she can set up a meeting with Mother Higgins. She's as old as the hills and has been Mother's best source. There should be some other sources in the practitioners' libraries." She yawned delicately.

"Well, first things first," he said, rising to clear the table. "Back to bed. You obviously need some more sleep."

Bent woke up several hours later, his lust rising. With slow strokes down her body, he awakened Daria, who languidly returned the caresses. "Hmmmmm," was all she said as he mounted her and thrust slowly into her softness. Totally relaxed, they almost didn't move at all, just a slight rocking on his part and small clenches on hers. When they came, the sensation was sublime, the impression of fusing into one person, and they held each other for a long time thereafter. Then without a word, they cuddled and slept again.

At dawn, Daria's eyes popped open of their own accord, and she lay there staring at the ceiling. A nagging feeling was telling her there was still something in this mating that had to be done to authoritatively secure the bond. She sat up and looked down at Bent, who was lying on his back, one arm over his head, the other stretched out from where she had been lying on it. A faint, knowing smile curved his lips.

Oh, my goodness, he looked delicious. All that tanned skin, the tousled auburn hair, the long limbs. As she drank in the sight of him, she knew what she had to do.

Carefully she began to stroke his body, testing his muscle resiliency, acquainting herself with his textures, exploring and learning. Kneeling beside him, she stroked from his shoulders, down over his chest, separating her hands at his waist to his hips, down his thighs and calves to his feet. Then back up. She watched with fascination as his erection grew in response, and she knew the exact moment when he woke. The surface of his skin changed, his heartbeat increased, his eyes barely slitted open, and his hands clenched into fists. But he didn't move otherwise. She knew this was costing him because she could feel his muscles tense as her hands passed over them. She didn't look at his face, but concentrated on her task.

When she reached his shoulders again, she brought her head down for her mouth to follow her hands. Kissing, licking, nipping, she tasted and savored. His flat nipples tightened in response to her attentions. His rib muscles quivered as her lips passed over them. He sucked in his stomach when her tongue found his navel.

She didn't touch his now-throbbing arousal, but bypassed it to linger over his inner thighs. When she glanced up at him to check her effect, his hands were gripping the sheets and he was breathing hard, his eyes sapphire flames and his face hard with passion. When she took him in her hands, he gasped and thrust upward. When she took him in her mouth, he groaned, arching his back and thrusting again.

"Daria," he rasped.

She raised herself, then straddled his hips, positioning herself above him, leaning on her straight arms. He cupped her breasts, caressing, molding. "Bent," she breathed huskily, looking him straight in the eyes, as she lowered herself, taking him in until she held him completely, claiming him for her own. Then she began to move.

It was like the first time, only more so. Their vision locked. Wildly their tension and movements intensified until she convulsed, shattering. She felt him jetting hotly into her, shuddering as he held her hips to his. She collapsed on his chest.

Their bond was secure, she knew it. A feeling of contentment permeated her body from her center to the extremities, and she smiled as she lay there, stretched out on top of him, thoroughly replete.

Bent felt like he'd lived through every man's secret lovemaking fantasy. She'd almost killed him. He had thought he was going to detonate before she sheathed his straining sex inside her and then his climax hit like an atomic bomb. What was it Alaric had said about being soulmates getting better all the time? How was that possible? He'd just had the greatest night of his entire sex life; he couldn't imagine it getting any better than this. But if it would, well, God Almighty. It would only happen with Daria, of that he was certain. He hugged her possessively, then moved her to his favorite position, facing each other on their sides, his upper leg between hers.

"Daria," he whispered.

She opened her eyes, dark green now with spent passion, and smiled and stretched against him. "Mmmmm?"

"You're mine." He couldn't stop his hands from caressing her from shoulder to behind, down her leg wrapped around his hip all the way to her foot and back up. Satin and silk. He didn't want to stop. Keeping his hands off her had become impossible.

"Yes. And you're mine."

She pushed him back after another kiss. "You're sure you don't feel trapped by this soulmate situation?"

"No. I got over the idea." He chuckled. "Way over."

"I was so scared you would feel coerced or trapped by the soulmate imperative, you'd have nothing to do with me," she said.

He looked at her blankly, then spoke. "Woman, that has to be one of the—no, *the* most stupid idea you've ever had. Now, come here and let me show you how much I don't want to have anything to do with you."

"Yes, Bent," she answered in a mock-submissive voice and with a blatantly teasing grin.

They held on to each other for a while, kissing and hugging, rubbing and fondling. Then Bent groaned as he felt an important piece of his anatomy stir—again. "Daria, you're going to be the death of me."

"What are you talking about?" she asked perplexed. The light dawned as he pulled her hips to his. "Oh. Hellllloooo."

"Hello, indeed. I wasn't this horny even when I was eighteen," he growled. "What have you done to me, Daria?"

She grinned and wiggled her hips, and the curly hair on her mound tickled the head of his cock, teasing, exciting, inviting.

Growling again as he took her mouth with his own, Bent thrust into her warm, tight depths. He began a slow, languid advance and withdrawal and soon drove Daria crazy—until she was practically begging for deliverance. When release came, it swept over them both like a blue Norther, furious in its turbulence, calm in its aftermath, and it left them a tangled mass on the bed.

Daria stirred several hours later, wondering at first why she couldn't move, then discovering Bent's arm and leg anchoring her in place. She jiggled his arm and tried to squirm out from under. A scratchy chin rubbed her earlobe and a deep, gravelly voice murmured, "Where do you think you're going?"

When she turned her head, sleepy blue eyes smiled at her, and a pair of soft lips kissed her. She grinned, kissed the lips back, and said, "I thought I'd take a shower and do something about breakfast."

"Good. Your shower looked big enough for two."

"It is."

"Fine. Let's go."

The rest of the day was spent in an afterglow that astonished them both. They tried to do mundane things like the laundry and grocery shopping, but found that they couldn't keep their hands off each other. Shopping in the supermarket became one long contactless episode of foreplay. The worst spot was in the fruit and vegetable section, where every piece of produce assumed connotations of sex.

It was worse when they went home. Working in the study resulted in a tumultuous mating that ended with them lying—naked—side by side on the rug in front of the fireplace.

"We have to get control of this," Bent said, still breathing hard.

"I know," Daria replied, interlacing her fingers with his. "We can't do this sort of thing in the office."

"I can just see you stretched out on my ebony-and-mahogany desk," he said, then groaned. "No, that would never do, would it?"

She turned to feebly smack his chest with her free hand and flopped back down. "Bent! I don't want to even think about that! Just get it out of your mind!" *And out of yours, woman*, she told herself as her mind's eye imagined them tangled on his office floor, the plush, deep, blue carpet matching the azure of his eyes. It was her turn to groan. When he tried to turn on his side and prop himself up on his elbow, she pushed him down again. "It's easier to think if I'm not looking at you. And don't do that either!" she ordered as his hand wandered up her torso.

"Yes, ma'am." He lay there for a couple of minutes, then sat up. "You're right, of course. Why don't we try putting on our clothes again and working separately. I *must* look over these reports today in case I need to go into the office tomorrow to be ready for Monday morning. I'll set up in the kitchen or living room or upstairs. You work on your reports or whatever here."

"Sounds like a plan to me," she answered as she rose and started looking for her underwear. "We'll meet in the kitchen at six to fix dinner."

The separation helped—as did the thorough exhaustion that claimed both of them. After dinner and some TV watching—limiting their kisses to commercial breaks only— they fell into bed and slept intertwined. Their sleep was only interrupted twice as one or the other woke and couldn't help a small fondle or a tiny kiss that ignited passion again; and, of course, they lingered over rising—from bed, that is.

Late Sunday morning, over French toast and scrambled eggs, Bent looked up from the business section of the newspaper. "I don't need to visit the office today, so why don't we take advantage of the nice weather and get out of the house? Maybe if we're around other people more, our libidos will calm down. Sort of like a test run for tomorrow."

"That's a good idea. How about the zoo?"

"Sounds fine. You know," he mused, "I don't think either

THE OLDEST KIND OF MAGIC

one of us expected the reactions we've had."

"No," Daria agreed, "it must be the soulmate bonding—making the bond secure. Mother never warned me."

"Your father didn't exactly warn me either when he called."

"What? Daddy called you?"

"Yeah, he wanted to tell me about the no-barriers business and all."

"Oh, for pity's sake! If it's not one, it's the other calling to see 'how we are.' Well, I'm not going to put up with any more. I'll make it more emphatic that we're fine, thank you very much, and they are to stay out of our business and to stop interfering."

"I don't think Alaric was interfering, honey. I found his information useful and something that I would never have thought of. Besides, he said something very important."

She raised her eyebrows at him. "What?"

"He said being soulmates just gets better all the time, and if the past two nights are any indication, I'd say we have a lot to look forward to."

"Oh. Yes. We do." She looked both mollified and a little guilty at her outburst. She rose and started clearing the dishes. "Be that as it may, let's get out of here before they call again."

Bent grinned and pulled her into a kiss. "I agree."

It was a glorious April day, just right for a trip to the Hermann Park Zoo. They spent a carefree afternoon, first at the zoo and then at the nearby Museum of Fine Arts. Daria did call her parents that evening, just to tell them that everything was fine. Neither Antonia nor Alaric asked any intrusive questions. They didn't have to; Daria was certain they could hear the joy in their voices with no difficulty. She hung up, satisfied they'd leave her and Bent alone now. She'd forgotten to tell her mother about the itching but she could do that later. Neither she nor Bent had itched all day. Or rather, what itched hadn't been their breastbones.

Chapter Twenty-One

Monday morning Daria woke refreshed, energized, and happy—unreservedly happy. Just looking at him brought a smile to her face, a feeling of contentment to her body, and a giddiness to her soul. The excesses of the previous two days seemed to have tamped down the wild desire that had driven them so relentlessly—a good thing, Daria decided, or they would be absolutely useless.

Being separated at work helped also. She found herself able to concentrate as usual, blocking out everything but the job. Dan drove her out to the Sugarland plant where she met with the plant manager, the assistant manager in charge of preventive maintenance, and a couple of the foremen. The meetings went well, and she returned late in the day.

Bent was also pleased he could immerse himself in his job without being distracted, and he worked on the marketing and advertising plan with Sales, Distribution, and Public Relations during the morning. That afternoon he mulled over the first quarter's financial reports and discussed possible reorganization of his department with Theo Wall. The Financial VP was on his way out of Bent's office when he stopped and said, "Excuse my curiosity, but you know Alaric Morgan. Is he as good as his reputation suggests? I've heard the man's a wizard with an audit."

Bent smiled to himself at Wall's unknowing use of the

term, "wizard," but answered with a straight face. "I only know him through Daria, but Joe Glennell has used his services in the past and swears by his abilities."

"Are you considering using him here?"

"No, I don't see the need . . . unless there's something you're not telling me," Bent finished in a teasing voice.

"No, no, of course not," Wall said rapidly, but his face grew pale. He pushed his glasses up on his nose. "I was just interested. It never hurts to know who can help you," he finished quickly, then turned and walked out the door.

That was strange, Bent thought to himself. Wall seemed nervous about something. Accounting types could be so conservative. He probably didn't like the coming changes.

The phone rang, and the call removed Wall's question and reaction from Bent's mind as he turned his attention to Merle Wharton.

On Tuesday afternoon, Daria was writing up her notes from the previous day's meetings and the one she had just concluded with another manufacturing manager when there was a knock on her office door. "Come in," she called out, and Dennis from the mail room opened the door.

"Here's some mail for you, Ms. Morgan," the young man said as he placed some envelopes in her in-box.

"Thanks, Dennis," she replied, reaching for the envelopes. With luck, this would be the information she had asked for and she could finish this report today. When she picked up the third one, an internal-mail manila envelope, however, the reek of evil struck her like a slap in the face. She dropped the thing on the desk and studied it for a moment. It appeared to have only one piece of paper in it, visible through the holes in the envelope. Fragments of black printed letters showed through.

Daria carefully unwound the tie securing the envelope flap, grasped the corners, and shook the contents out on her desk. The single sheet slid out, writing side up. The block printing was stark on the page.

GET OUT!
THIS IS YOUR LAST WARNING!

Daria reached for the phone and punched in Bent's number. Janet Adams told her Bent was out at the Baytown plant and was expected back around four o'clock. Daria thanked her, told her it was nothing important and depressed the button, then called Dan Roth.

"Dan, it's Daria. I just received a threatening letter in the office mail."

"I'll be right there."

The security manager was in her office within two minutes. He looked at the paper and then at Daria. "Hell," he said slowly, "it looks like the person behind this hasn't given up." He picked up the envelope by the string tie. "I doubt we'll find any fingerprints that will do us any good—in fact, there'll be too many fingerprints. This envelope has been all over the place." He looked at the list of recipients covering one side and most of the other. The last entry named a "J.

Emerson" in Distribution.

"I've seen envelopes like this in stacks next to copiers and office administrators and in the mail room," Daria commented.

"Exactly. If you have a folder I can use for the note, we can try to lift some prints off the paper, but it looks like regular copier paper, so it could have come from anywhere." She handed him a folder and he put the note in it. "Did you call Bent?"

"Yes, but he's in Baytown and isn't due back until four."

"I'll let Childress at the police know of this, and I'll meet you in Bent's office when he gets back. Okay?"

"Fine, although I don't think there is much to discuss. I don't intend to quit." She lifted her chin and clenched her teeth with gritty determination.

Dan looked at her for a moment. "I know," he said softly.

Lieutenant Childress joined them in the meeting at four. It was a somber gathering, but Dan had nothing to report: no fingerprints, no luck tracking down the envelope or tracing its path through the company to Daria's desk. They agreed it would not be productive to post security in the mailroom trying to pinpoint the source, as anyone could drop an envelope into any number of pickup stations. One of Dan's people would stop by the mailroom periodically and look at Daria's mail as a precaution before it was delivered.

"You've been unable to discover anything about who's behind these threats?" Childress asked Daria.

"No. I haven't picked up a whiff of any real problems so far in my interviews—none that would cause such threats.

Nothing has been out of the ordinary. I've met a few executives who seemed extra nervous, like David Grady in HR, but I've concluded that they're worried about getting fired, not about getting caught for any crime."

"So, does anybody have any ideas about what might be the next point of attack?" Bent asked, as he reclined in his chair and stretched.

"Where will you be over the next few days, Daria?" Dan asked her.

"Baytown tomorrow, then here in the building through the rest of this week and into the next," she replied. "I'm looking at Manufacturing now and have an appointment with Theo Wall on Friday to start Finance."

"Good," Dan nodded. "It will be easier to keep track of you then. Instead of your calling your escort when you finish an interview ahead of schedule, I'm going to have someone outside your interviews all the time." He turned to Bent. "And of course, we'll continue to drive her to the plants."

"I agree with that," Bent interjected.

Daria sighed and looked from Dan to Bent. "All right. I'm not going to fight a battle I can't win."

Bent thanked Childress for coming, and the meeting broke up.

On the way home, Daria said, "Merle Wharton has been very helpful. I think I may have found his incompetent safety inspector, and tomorrow I'm going to hone in on a senior foreman who's come to my attention. I'll meet with Merle on Thursday. Do you want me to tell him my conclusions? I usually save those for the CEO I'm reporting to, but in this case . . ."

"Yeah, tell me first, but tell him on Thursday. We don't need any more accidents." He paused while making a turn. "Finance is next?"

"Yes. I expect to spend most of Friday morning with Theo, and I'll interview his accounting managers next week. I'm curious about the group dynamics there. Theo strikes me as a worry wart."

Bent grimaced. "My sentiments exactly. He's competent enough, but I haven't decided about his abilities to accept all the changes I have in mind for that department, especially with regard to the extent of computerization and electronic commerce we're planning. Theo is something of a bean counter, guarding his pile of beans vigilantly, but with no real vision of the future or of the company as a whole. From all accounts, he doesn't like to spend money unless the return will be almost immediate and he can't seem to understand that the computer infrastructure is indispensable to the company's future success."

He paused as he took the car around a corner. "Or, rather, he doesn't like accepting the cost for all the computer upgrades we need. I've already decided to cut Information Technology loose from Finance, set up with its own Vice President. As for Theo, I don't expect him to be here a year from now. His type usually heads for calmer waters rather than stay and fight it out or change."

Daria nodded. "I'll file the information in the back of

my brain for now. But, you know something? For some reason, I'm not looking forward to the Finance interviews."

The Wednesday meetings at the Baytown plant went smoothly, and she was able to determine who had been responsible for the lax maintenance. That night she had just finished discussing her report to Wharton with Bent when the phone rang. It was her father.

"Hi, Daddy. What's up?" she asked when she recognized his voice.

"I'm going to be in Houston tomorrow and would like to take you and Bent to lunch. My business lunch was canceled, but I need to be in your area in the afternoon, so I thought you might like to see your poor old father."

"Right, Daddy," she chided sarcastically. "Poor old father, indeed. But I'd love to see you. I'm free for lunch. Hold on while I check with Bent." She turned to Bent across the room. "Daddy's going to be in town tomorrow and wants to take us to lunch. Can you come with us?"

"Sure. Let me check on the time." He punched some buttons on his laptop to call up his schedule. "I can be free at noon, if that's all right."

"Fine. It will work for me also. I'm meeting with Merle at two." Daria relayed the information and told Alaric to come to Bent's office just before noon.

As they were leaving for lunch the next day, they ran

into Theo Wall at the elevator. Bent introduced Alaric to the vice president.

Wall shook Alaric's hand. "I'm pleased to meet you, Mr. Morgan. I've heard about your auditing capabilities from several of my counterparts at other companies. Any chance you'll be auditing us in the future?"

"You never know, in the present business climate," Alaric answered blandly. "But today I'm checking up on Daria. Her mother asked me to see how y'all are treating her little girl."

Daria just shook her head. She and her father were going to have to have another one of those treat-me-like-a-professional talks.

The elevator arrived, and the three separated from Wall. On the way down, Daria said, "Bent, did Theo look a little strange to you?"

"I didn't notice anything. Why?"

"He just seemed a little pale at the end of our conversation."

"He had a limp handshake, and his hands were sweaty, too," Alaric added.

"I hope he's not coming down with something," Daria said. "Our first meeting is tomorrow."

The next day on the way home, Bent asked how the meeting with Wall had gone.

"It turned out to be somewhat anticlimactic," Daria replied. "I don't know what I was expecting, but he gave me the impression of being on top of his department, cognizant of all its workings, and precise in his explanations. We discussed only the accounting side, by the way, not

Information Technology."

"Did you use any spells?"

"No . . . well, hardly any. Just a couple to see me as trustworthy and having his best interests at heart, that sort of thing. I usually don't push it too much in the first interview unless the subject is clearly hostile. I also didn't ask his opinions of his own senior staff yet. Theo, his managers, and I will meet next week. I want to see them in action, relating to each other, without any prejudicial comments in my mind."

"I haven't worked with them directly, so I'll be looking forward to your impressions. How was Theo? Still pale? Was he sick?"

"No, he seemed fine." The statement put an end to discussion of work and their talk veered off to more pleasant topics, like what they were going to do over the weekend.

Early Saturday afternoon, Daria gazed around her patio and let herself enjoy the feeling of contentment that flooded her body. They had risen a bit later than they had originally planned—what with one thing or another and a long double shower—but they managed to finish the usual weekend chores, grocery shopping, going to the cleaners and drugstore, and other small tasks without attacking each other. Now they sat in the chaises reading the papers, drinking iced tea, and admiring the garden. Zorro was spread out like a black rug on the brick pavement, and Lolita was slinking in and out of the flowering plants, wending her way toward some sparrows on the grass near the feeder.

Bent looked up from his perusal of a newspaper insert for office equipment. "You know, I'm thinking of getting a proper desk and chair for my corner of the study. I've never been one for piles of files sitting around, so I could use some storage space. What do you think?"

"Fine with me," Daria replied. She hid a smile behind the newspaper as she realized Bent was moving right in, seemingly taking for granted that they were living together in every sense of the term. What with all the happenings lately, they hadn't talked about their future yet. It was all right with her also. Once they had gotten to the bottom of the threats, they'd have time to decide what to do.

True, he hadn't yet told her that he loved her. And his not saying the words didn't bother her too much. She knew deep down she and Bent were together forever now, so she wasn't worried. What a difference in her attitude and thoughts succumbing to the imperative had wrought. She had not realized how much she wanted or needed him. She was still learning how big a difference he made in her life. And the mating itself . . .

That thought brought up another, and she voiced it out loud. "I'm relieved, you know, we discovered that we could work together in the same room without . . ."

"Without . . . ?" Bent's eyebrows went up, and a smirk decorated his lips.

"Without, uh, distracting each other," Daria finished

primly and felt her face warming. She rattled the paper to straighten it out and ducked behind it.

Bent laughed out loud. He couldn't help feeling smug—not to mention satiated. Putting the advertisement down, he looked around the pleasant garden for a moment before reality intruded. He put his thoughts into words. "It's such a beautiful day. I could almost forget about those bastards making the threats. I hope we can find out soon who our culprits are."

"So do I. I'm very tired of being on the receiving end of those nasty messages."

"Honey, we have to talk about the security situation. Promise me you won't go anywhere by yourself until this mess is resolved. I don't want you to be unprotected for a minute."

"I promise," she said soberly. "But I'm not without certain defenses, you know."

"I know you've mentioned you can cast defensive spells on yourself, but I haven't seen you do so. Can you show me?"

"We can try. It might be interesting to find out what you can actually see. These defense spells are the only true illusions I can cast, incidentally. My other spells . . ." she shrugged. "None of the master sorcerers has ever been able to figure out exactly how they work since my face doesn't change or it looks like I have a mask on. People merely perceive me as I have spelled myself." She stood up and stepped several feet away from the chaise lounges.

"We're out of others' sight here behind the house, so I'll cast where we have some space. Most of my defensive spells involve a combination of illusion and strength or power spells. For example, I can turn myself into a big cat . . ." She cast the spell and crouched down in a catlike pose. "What do you see?"

"I see a shimmering aura around you." He rose, squinted his eyes, and moved a few steps back. "With your other spells, the aura sort of fades out at its boundaries, but this one has definite edges in a sort of cat shape."

"Wait, I'll kick the power up." She did so.

Bent stepped backward abruptly. "I see, *I really see*, a solid panther, a black one with green eyes and big teeth." He jumped another step back when she took a swipe at him with a paw bristling with long, sharp claws. He laughed nervously. "Be careful, Daria."

The big cat smiled and said, "Look as closely as you can. Can you see through the illusion?"

Bent concentrated on where he knew her body had to be. "Yeah . . . Now I can see *you* with sharp edges outlining the cat. It's not amorphous or diffused like it had been before."

"Okay. Now I can make my cat bigger . . ." She suited the action to the words and the cat image became larger than life.

Bent stood his ground, even when the animal swished its tail and licked its chops. He shot a glance at Zorro and Lolita, who had come onto the patio and was lying next to her mate. They were watching Daria closely, but seemed unconcerned, so he assumed that either they could not see the illusion or they could see through it. He pointed at the two lounging felines. "The cats don't seem perturbed. What do they see?"

"I don't know. They never react to one of my spells, although they do to Mother's. Remember the rose petals?"

"Oh, yeah. Zorro sneezed." Bent looked again at the cats and thought of a question he had been meaning to ask. "Uh, are the cats magic? You know, like your 'familiars?' Like witches are supposed to have?"

The cat illusion stood up on its hind legs, put its front paws on its hips, and looked distinctly disgusted. "Bent, I told you I wasn't that kind of a witch. As to their being magic, well, I guess they're as magic as any other cat is. They do seem to understand when you talk to them, and they definitely picked up on the evil in those threatening notes. As to anything else, I guess we'll just have to wait for them to tell us." Her large panther shape shrugged.

When she moved, Bent noticed something else. "Daria, it looks like the little table there goes right into the body of your cat."

"This is only an illusion spell, Bent. There's no substance. You dodged back when I swiped at you with my 'paw,' but I could not have hurt you with it like a real panther. To hit you, I have to actually smack you with my hand or a stick or something." She showed him how reaching out with the illusory paw now several feet from the end of her actual hand had no effect on the furniture or him.

"I can also become a dragon and add some sound . . ." A blue dragon appeared suddenly and grew until its head reached eight or nine feet off the ground. It extended its razor-clawed "hands," threw back its head, and *roared*.

Bent jumped about a foot as the force of the bellow hit him. "Holy—" He put his hand on his rapidly beating heart. "That was effective," he gasped.

"It was only a little roar," she laughed. "No sense in disturbing the neighbors. I told you I could roar, remember?"

"Yeah, but hearing you is something else. I'd hate to be on the receiving end of that in an enclosed space."

Daria returned to normal. "Come here." She sat down at the patio table. "Sit across from me. I can also cast strength and speed spells. Give me your hand." She assumed the traditional arm-wrestling pose. "This is the quickest way I can think of to show you strength."

Bent sat down and clasped her hand, his elbow on the table.

"First with no spell," Daria said. "Ready? Set. Go."

She was stronger than she looked, Bent realized, but it did not take him long to press her hand down to the smooth tabletop.

"Now with a spell."

He saw the spell aura, a dark blue one, surround her.

"Ready, set, go," she said.

Thud! His hand hit the table before he knew it. "Let's do it again," he growled. "I'll say 'go' this time." They clasped hands and he set himself carefully. "Ready, set, go."

Whap! Same result.

"Want to do it again? Or shall I pick you up and carry you up the stairs?" she asked in a falsely earnest tone as he wiggled his hand to restore circulation.

"Oh, I believe you," he sighed, leaning back in his chair. "What else can you do?"

"Variations on a theme, mostly. I can use speed and strength to attack or flee. I can hum or roar at a sonic frequency known to cause fright and even terror in people. I threw a little of that into my roar just now. The dragon is most effective, especially with the roar, but as I told you, I can't throw real fire, only the illusion of it. Since there's no heat, the fire really wouldn't work in close quarters."

"This is all well and good," Bent commented, "but do these spells really work? What if a thug really grabbed you?"

"I know the spells work because I've used them." She grinned smugly.

"Wait a minute," Bent interjected. "You've used them? When? What happened?" My God, if anything had happened to her, he'd find the guy who did it and kill him.

"It was several years ago," Daria related matter-of-factly. "Trudi, another practitioner, and I were walking into her apartment complex after a late party and a man jumped out in front of us. He had a knife and told us to hand over our purses. I cast a dragon and Trudi did a tiger. She swatted the knife out of his hand with her purse, and I grabbed his other arm and flung him into the bushes. Trudi cast 'fright' upon him. Trying to get away from us, he ran into a tree and knocked himself out. The police hauled him away. He was babbling about monsters when he regained consciousness."

"What did you tell the police about subduing him?" he

asked as fear for her settled like a chill ball of ice in his stomach.

"Just that we both took karate."

"What if he had had a gun?" he protested.

"First, run and scream. If we can't do that, we're taught it's better to cast a very large and tall monster and threaten with the head. People tend to watch and aim at the head, where the teeth are. That way you can attack them from below." She held up one hand, simulating a head, and gestured with the other to indicate a lower attack. "You were looking up at the dragon's head, not down at the body," she added.

Bent rubbed his hands over his face as if to scrub off the thoughts his imagination was conjuring in his brain. The idea of her facing down any criminal, even with spells like those she had just shown him, sent the ice ball out of his stomach and up and down his spine. He rose, came around the table, and pulled Daria to her feet. His hands on her shoulders, he gazed into her eyes. "Daria, promise me you won't do anything reckless. I don't expect you will be put in a position like the one with that mugger again. Dan, your brother and father, the whole damn Houston police force, and I will do everything we can to make sure. But the thought of you wading into a fight, spells or not, scares me to death."

The look in her green eyes was sincere as she absorbed his words. "I'll be careful, Bent. I promise."

He hugged her and sighed.

"What?" she whispered in his ear.

"I just wish you could cast one of those spells on me." Then, certainly he could protect her. He kissed her quickly and composed himself. He didn't want to think about this mess anymore. "C'mon. Enough of this conversation. Let's go look for my desk and chair."

Chapter Twenty-Two

The group dynamics among the Finance senior staff turned out to be more enlightening than she had expected, Daria thought late Monday afternoon, as she watched and listened to the men—she couldn't picture a woman working with this group—discuss the future for the department. She had spelled herself with only I-am-not-a-threat and I-can-be-ignored, the better to let the group act in their normal manner—or as normal as it could be with her present. She followed her usual methodology for initial meetings: let the participants set the tone and topics while she observed and asked questions.

Theo Wall only nominally presided over the meeting. His manner had taken a 180-degree turn from the one he exhibited in their one-on-one the previous week. Now the vice president played with his pen nervously, glancing at Daria periodically whenever he thought she wasn't looking. He had made a few introductory remarks about the meeting's purpose, as she had suggested, but then he had let Accounting Manager Virgil McAffee effectively take over.

McAffee was a large man in his late forties, over six feet, graying at the temples of his short, dark hair, good-looking in an aging-athlete sort of way. He clearly still worked out regularly, and his clothes, while accountant-conservative, were of excellent quality. His approach to Daria had been professional, but she could tell he was used to affecting women favorably when he wanted to.

Almost ignoring his vice president, McAffee directed the discussion, calling on his assistant managers in turn: Hank Billings in Payroll, John Forrest in Payables, and Steve Howarth in Receivables. They discussed their accounting practices and safeguards in excruciating detail, so much so that Daria began to wonder why they were placing so much emphasis on them—extreme even by high accounting standards.

She asked some questions to lead the subject to the competency of each department's staff, but McAffee managed to cast the ensuing answers into a statement of belief in the honesty and abilities of the people—and in his safeguard system that would certainly catch any accounting shenanigans. "I know everything happening with our accounts," he claimed proudly.

That evening she discussed the meeting with Bent over supper. She related the discussion about accounting practices, thought for a moment and said, "They were protesting too much, declaring too often how strict their methods were, stating too forcefully precisely how honest they all were. Especially claiming that no accounting mistake, however trivial, could possibly occur with their staffs."

"You and I know perfection is impossible," Bent put in as he reached for the salad dressing. "If they're so good, why can't one of them tell me why expenses are not coming down?"

"My intuition is telling me something isn't quite right here, but it's not being specific." She gave herself another helping of broccoli. "I felt a vague sense of hostility toward me from the group as a whole. It wasn't pinpointed from one individual. But then, it's often the case when I begin meetings with a new group. They could just be resenting me for even thinking about criticizing their methods. Also, they're accountants, and accountants, in my experience, usually don't like upsets."

"So, what's next?"

"Tomorrow I start the individual meetings, first with Theo again for his opinions about his managers, then McAffee." She wasn't entirely certain she wanted to be alone in a room with the Accounting Manager, as something in the man's manner was beginning to grate, but she decided she could always throw on a defensive spell if she needed one. She didn't mention this thought to Bent.

The next morning at 9:30 after a frustrating meeting with Wall, Daria wearily walked off the elevator and headed down the hall toward her office, accompanied by Nate, her security escort. The vice president had made not one critical observation, not even a tiny one, about any member of his staff, but asserted they were all sterling, competent employees full of valor and integrity. She'd meet next with the individual managers and then return to Wall, this time with a strong I-will-hear-nothing-but-the-truth spell. It was her own fault for not spelling herself during the meeting, she reflected. She had been fascinated by Wall's refusal to speak ill of anyone. But was he being truthful or was he hiding something?

She turned the corner and almost ran into Dennis, who was delivering the mail.

"You have some mail, Ms. Morgan," he said, "and look, someone's left you a package."

A small brown-paper-wrapped box about the size of a thick paperback book lay in front of her door, and Dennis picked it up while she unlocked the office. He followed her in and lay the mail and package in her in-box.

"I'm not going anywhere for a while, Nate," Daria told the escort, and he sat down in the chair in the hall. She breathed a sigh of relief. At least she was allowed privacy in her own office.

"Thank you, Dennis," Daria said distractedly as she dropped her briefcase on the desk and sat down.

"You're welcome," Dennis answered and left to push his mail cart in the direction of Public Relations. He bumped the desk on his way out, and the envelopes he had balanced on top of the package slid off onto the desktop.

Daria was reaching for the phone to check her voice mail when an overwhelming sense of evil and danger struck her, and she jerked around in her chair. A malevolent stench was coming from the small package. She looked at it closely. Her name was printed in black letters on the outside—all-too-familiar black letters.

"Calm, be calm," she told herself as she felt her heartbeat accelerate and her muscles tense. Gingerly she slid her chair back, rose, picked up her purse and briefcase, and vacated the room without touching the desk or the package.

"Come with me," she ordered Nate, who had risen when she walked out the door. She locked the door behind her and walked swiftly down to the president's office, casting a calming spell so nobody would notice how exceptionally agitated she was. The spell also acted to soothe herself. When she reached Janet Adams's office, she crossed to Janet's desk.

"Hello, Daria," Janet smiled. "What can I do for you?"

"Is Bent around?"

"No, he's out at the Sugarland plant."

"I need to use the phone in his office, if that's okay."

Janet shrugged and said, "Sure, help yourself."

"Just have a seat, Nate," she told the man, who was looking puzzled, but she wasn't going to try to explain the situation to him. Daria walked into Bent's office, closed the door behind her, went immediately to the phone and dialed Dan.

"Dan, it's Daria. I think a package bomb was just delivered to my office."

"What!? Where are you?" the security manager exclaimed.

"I'm in Bent's office."

"Where's Nate?"

"Sitting outside in Janet's office. I didn't tell him anything, just got the two of us out of there."

"I'll be right up."

Dan appeared within two minutes. "Tell me what happened."

Daria related the events from the time she met Dennis

until her phone call to Dan.

"How do you know it's a bomb?" he asked skeptically.

"Dan, I know this is not going to make much sense to you, but the thing just radiates evil. There's no postage, the block printing looks like the printing on the envelopes from the threatening letters, and I'm expecting nothing in a package."

"I'm going to look at it. You stay here."

He returned in a few minutes. "I don't know if it's a bomb or not, but we aren't going to take any chances." He picked up the phone and called Bill Childress.

While he was waiting for Childress to answer, Daria told him, "Let's keep this as quiet as we can, if possible. We don't need a media frenzy."

"I don't think so either," Dan replied. "I have an idea about that." Childress came on the line and the two men spoke for a few minutes. Dan hung up and turned to Daria. "Here's what we're going to do. We want to keep it quiet and not panic anybody. Bill agrees with us. Suppressing this is in our best interest. We know this isn't some crazy foreign terrorist, just our own homegrown kind who's only after you."

"Thanks, I think," Daria replied, "but I know what you mean."

"I'm going to order a fire drill to clear the offices and get everyone outside. We'll direct them to the side away from the parking ramp and the loading dock," Dan continued. "Bill's going to alert the fire department to stand by. He'll bring the bomb squad to the dock and they'll enter the building where nobody can see them. He's going to see that nothing goes out over the police band airwaves where any listening reporters can hear it. My people will make sure nobody's around when the police go up to your office."

"Fine. I'll call Bent."

Bent took it more calmly than she had, or at least his voice was calmer than she felt. "I'll be there as soon as I can, Daria. You get out of that building immediately! Tell Dan he has my backing for anything he needs to do."

The resulting controlled chaos did not resolve itself until early afternoon, although the entire office remained unsettled from the abrupt change in routine. On the other hand, it looked like they had come through the crisis without a leak to the media—in these days, a miracle. Bent, Daria, Dan, Childress, Hugh Peterson from the bomb squad, and Steve Guthrie, Dan's second-in-command, met in Bent's office.

Peterson, a small man with thick sandy hair and long-fingered hands a surgeon or pianist would envy, took the floor. "You were right, Ms. Morgan. It was a bomb, and if you had opened it, it would have gone off in your face."

"How powerful was it?" Childress asked.

"Not very. The blast would have taken out her office and damaged the adjoining rooms. Anyone in those rooms would certainly have been injured. But she would have been seriously injured, perhaps killed."

"Any clue as to who made it?" Dan asked.

"We found no fingerprints after we disabled it. It was a simple construction job and well done. It wouldn't have gone off by accident. You had to slide the box out of its case to complete the circuit. The thing is, you can find the instructions for these devices on the Internet, so anyone could make them," Peterson said disgustedly. "How did it get at Ms. Morgan's door?"

Steve Guthrie spoke up. "Our security camera showed one of the PR secretaries, Mavis Lawson, putting it there about half an hour before Daria returned from her meeting. Mavis said she took some press kits to the mail room for special wrapping about 8:45 and the package was on her desk when she returned. She brought it to Daria's office and left it by the door when Daria wasn't there."

The bomb squad captain glanced at his watch and stood. "I have to get back to my office. Childress, I'll let you know if we discover anything about the bomb parts, but they could have been easily purchased in hardware stores or on the streets." He walked to Daria and shook her hand. "You did fine, realizing package was a bomb, ma'am. How did you come to that conclusion?"

Daria smiled somewhat disingenuously. "It must have been magic, Captain."

Dan saw the officer out and returned. "Steve, I want you to talk to Nate and all the other escorts for Daria. She should never have come that close to the package."

"I already said something to him. He swears he'll do better from now on, but I'm transferring him to one of the plants for a while. I'm meeting with the escorts at four this afternoon," Steve answered.

"Dan," Daria said quickly, "it wasn't Nate's fault. He did everything he was supposed to do."

"He should have at least looked at the package, Daria. Don't worry, I'm not going to fire him." Dan turned to Bent. "We did learn something else from this episode—we need more fire drills. God! What a mess."

"Did everyone get out okay?" Bent asked.

"Yes, but not in good order by any means. And we discovered some places where the alarm can't be heard at all." Dan turned to Guthrie. "Steve, have our people make a run through all the offices to see how the staff is taking this. Use the pretense of wanting to know about the fire drill and how to improve it. Let people talk! I'm curious what the rumor mill is saying."

"So am I," Childress said. "Somebody's got to be worried since the device has not exploded as planned, especially since there's been no word about a bomb."

"I'll get right on it," Steve said and left.

The remaining four looked at each other. "All right," Daria said, "I'll say it. What next? How can we find out who's doing this? They just proved they can get close with little effort. What can we do to smoke them out?"

"We're not putting you on the firing line, Daria," Bent stated, frowning at her. "The first thing we're doing is moving you into this set of offices and putting a security person out front at all times."

"I agree," Dan said and moved to the phone to start the process. "There's the vacant office next door where the former president's executive assistant sat but did nothing. We'll move you into it."

"But, we're not giving up, Bent," Daria stated. "I'm obviously getting too close for someone, and they're getting desperate. I'm working on Finance now, and Distribution is next. Could it be someone in those places?"

"You know," Bent said, "According to my experience with other turnarounds, Finance and often Information Technology have always been ripe places for inside, white-collar theft. The opportunities for embezzlement practically jump out of the woodwork." He rose, paced to the window, and stood rocking back and forth on his feet, his hands in his pockets, his eyes focused on the middle distance.

"Where are you going with this, Bent?" Dan asked as he finished his call and replaced the phone receiver in its cradle.

"When Glennell took over Triangle, we did the usual audit. The books appeared to be in order—for a company losing money, that is. The reasons for the loss were the usual: low sales, a product line needing overhaul, inefficient manufacturing and distribution processes, and high overhead. These executive offices and an overstaffed workforce were the prime examples of the last."

He turned back into the room. "When we discovered the theft by the security department, we thought we had the culprits for the losses not explained by those I just listed. Now, we're in the middle of fixing our product line, sales are already picking up, we've almost worked out the bugs in our processes, and we've pared down our staff to get rid of the deadwood and featherbedding.

"But when I was looking at the preliminary financials for last month, the reports didn't reflect the savings or the increase to cash flow that I thought they should have. We haven't rebounded as fast as I expected, but I couldn't put my finger on the location of the problem. We're still spending too much, but where isn't obvious."

Bent came back to his desk and sat down. "What if we do have embezzlers in Finance somewhere? Right where Daria's concentrating now."

"These attacks are coming fast and furious all of a sudden," Dan said. "Daria, when did you inform Theo Wall that Finance would be next on your list?"

"Last Tuesday so I could set up the appointments," she replied. "I called Theo in the morning."

"That would work from a timing basis for these attacks," Bent said, picking up his scheduling calendar from his desk and pointing to each date in turn. "Tuesday morning Finance found out they're next, Tuesday afternoon the second threatening letter arrived saying it was your last warning. You start the interviews, seemingly ignoring the threat, and today the bomb is delivered. It looks like somebody really doesn't want to talk to you."

He put the calendar down and looked at her. "Now the question becomes, how do we discover who without putting you in any further danger?" He turned to Childress who had been sitting quietly watching. "What do you think, Bill?"

The detective ran his hand over his chin. "What you're

conjecturing is certainly plausible. But I need some hard facts and strong evidence before I can arrest anyone—or even question them intelligently."

"All right, let's do a hypothetical situation," Daria offered. She was beginning to feel ragged and cast another self-calming spell and one to help her concentration. It wouldn't do to fall apart now. "Let's say McAffee is the culprit. The way the system is configured now—contrary to good practice, by the way—he has the clearances to get into any accounting computer application he wants to. In fact, he told me he ordered the clearances in the first place so he could monitor details and productivity. He said he had to get the former president's approval, over the objections of the I.T. people. Seemed proud of that 'coup.' "

"Well, that's going to change," Bent interrupted.

"From what I saw and heard in the group meeting," Daria continued, "he's certainly on top of his department, he understands his accounting applications, and Wall won't take action without him. Talking to one of his assistant managers, putting pressure on, say, Billings in Payroll or Forrest in Payables, might even give us some hard data to work with, but if there's more than one of them in it or McAffee has them all under his thumb, we're just tipping our hand."

"How did your first meeting go with them yesterday?" Dan asked.

"Strangely. McAffee especially kept talking about how secure his systems and safeguards are and what an honest and competent staff he had assembled. Nobody seemed willing to say a critical word about any person, either."

She thought for a moment. "Except John Forrest in Payables. Somehow he didn't seem to be part of the group with McAffee, Billings, and Howarth—more nervous, too. I didn't try to, uh, 'direct' the conversation," she glanced significantly at Bent as she said this, "or to push it except for a few leading questions from time to time. I usually don't do that sort of thing at the initial meeting because I'm watching group dynamics as much as anything else. I did wonder afterward why they had emphasized security, honesty, and competence so much, even for accountants, and I sensed a feeling of hostility toward me, but I couldn't localize it." She shrugged. "And groups are often slightly hostile on the first meeting, until they get to know me."

"We need more," Bent said. "We need an in-depth look at the financials to see if they 'cooked' the books to get it. But we don't want to tip them off. Daria, was Matt Schultz at your meeting?"

"No, this was only accounting managers. Since Matt's Manager of Information Technologies, and his department is the other half of Wall's department, I thought it best to concentrate on one part at a time because the two are not usually managed the same way. Wall didn't have much to say about I.T. at our initial meeting, except he thinks they spend too much money. I agree with you that it's doubtful if Wall understands what it takes to make all the upgrades necessary to the computer system, and that he probably just doesn't like to spend the money."

"Good," he replied. "I'm going to hope Schultz is not part of the pack in Finance. We need to see the accounting books and it will be simpler if Matt's people can get us to them. It's not going to be easy to find what they've done. The corporate computer guys found nothing when they went over everything before the purchase."

"Shall I call Daddy and Clay?" Daria asked. "If he has kept to the schedule he told us about, Daddy should still be in town. They can find any problems quickly, and Clay has some, uh, search programs that can pinpoint computer entries by the same person."

"Will they want to help?"

"After we tell them about the bomb, you won't be able to keep them away."

"I know Clay's a computer whiz," Childress commented. "What does Mr. Morgan do?"

"He's the best auditor at finding discrepancies you'll ever meet," Bent replied. "Okay, Daria. Call them now and ask them to be here by six o'clock. We'll see if we can come up with something tonight after the office closes down."

Bent turned to Dan. "You discover what you can about the personal financials of the Accounting staff. Who might be living beyond his means, that sort of thing."

"I'll get right on it," Dan replied. "Oh, and I'm going to schedule fire drills at the plants. If Triangle was lax at one place, they've probably been equally lax at others." The security manager walked toward the door.

"I'll go with you, Roth," Childress said. "I'll check on them with my sources. And I'd like to be here this evening, too."

"Good," Bent said. "I'll talk to Matt right now, and, Dan, let me know when our suspects are out of the building."

Dan nodded, and the two men left.

"Now, what I've been needing since your phone call," Bent said, traversing the office and pulling Daria into his arms. "The quick hug we had when I came back from Sugarland wasn't enough."

"Me too," she whispered as she began to tremble. "Look at me, I'm shaking. I thought I was doing a good job holding myself together, but now, when it's over . . ."

"Shhhh. I've got you."

They just held each other tightly for a while.

"You scared the daylights out of me, honey," Bent finally murmured in her ear. "I needed this as much as you did."

"I thought you took it very calmly," Daria said, burrowing into his warmth.

"I broke every traffic law on the books getting here." He pulled back so he could see her face. "We're going to find these bastards, Daria. Nothing's going to happen to you."

"I know." She took a deep breath and smiled.

He kissed her softly, a kiss to reassure both of them they still had each other. "Now, let's get to work, but do me a favor and stay where I can see you. My imagination's on overload whenever you're out of my sight."

She kissed him back. "That's fine with me." She didn't want to be out of his sight either.

Bent called Matt Schultz in and Daria cast some spells

to make sure the I.T. manager was truthful about not knowing what the Finance managers were up to. When Schultz answered Bent's leading questions and proved to be honest, Bent told him their conclusions and plans.

Schultz ordered his computer operators to immediately begin running a printout of the financials and vendor, payroll, and customer lists. He was understandably disgusted. "I told Wall and the former president they were begging for trouble, letting anyone have the kind of access McAffee had," the manager complained, "but nobody listened to me."

Daria called Alaric and Clay. News of the bomb incensed both men, and they quickly agreed to help, stating they would be at the office by six.

A couple of Dan's staff members moved Daria's things into the office next to Bent's, but she remained with him. Upping her calming spells just a notch, she reset her appointments with the accounting managers for the next day, as though the fire drill were nothing more than an unwelcome interruption in her schedule.

At six, a group of people sat around the large conference room table making plans while they ate poor-boy sandwiches and potato salad ordered in from a nearby deli. Clay and Alaric joined Bent, Daria, Bill Childress and Dan, and Matt Schultz had brought his assistant manager for software development, Trish Biando, a brassy blonde who, according to Matt, knew her stuff and "took nothing off nobody."

Bill and Dan had not been able to discover any new or damaging information about the finance managers. They all had impeccable credit ratings and none had made any recent purchases outside their income brackets. Based mainly on their experience with crooks, however, both the police officer and the security manager were suffering "funny hunches" about their subjects. The managers were too perfect to be true. Daria agreed with them.

After a general discussion, Alaric and Bent carried the financial printouts into Bent's office while Matt and Trish took Clay on a tour of the computer. In the conference room, Bill and Dan called their contacts again and traded war stories. Daria worked on her reports on her laptop in a corner of Bent's office.

After about two hours, Bent and Alaric called the others into Bent's office. "I think we have something," Bent announced. If he had harbored any lingering doubts about the Morgan family's ability to practice magic, they had vanished in the demonstration Alaric had given him. Numbers and letters glowed in multicolored patterns, revealing the extent of the embezzlement. The auditor had spelled the books with exceptional thoroughness, highlighting and cross-referencing anomalies across Payables, Receivables, Payroll, and the employee, customer, and vendor lists.

Alaric took the floor. "From all appearances, McAffee and his cohorts had been skimming the company for a great deal of money by both substantial amounts as well by pennies at a time. You may not be aware of it, but FICA and sales taxes are calculated to three or four digits on the right side of the decimal point. Since you can't pay someone fractions of a cent, these taxes are rounded to the nearest penny. The rounding can be finagled so that it always goes down instead of up, thus leaving bits of pennies in the system to accumulate into hidden accounts. Over time, these bits can amount to a substantial sum.

"Interest on customer accounts can also be placed in these hiding places. In addition, we found at least three phony vendors who are charging the company for goods and services not delivered, and five fake employees have been the recipients of the hidden payroll accounts.

"I think this is the tip of the iceberg," Alaric concluded after explaining in detail what he had found. "Once we attack these books with a team of auditors, we'll probably find more."

"Now, we need to tie these transactions to the people who entered them," Bent said, looking pointedly at Clay.

"There have been no unauthorized transactions, no hacking of the system," Clay said. "Now that I have some names to go on, it'll be easier. I'll call you when I have something. Dad, I'll need your help, but I'd appreciate it if no one else came with us. I hate having people hanging over me." That stopped Trish and Matt in their tracks, but they followed the two anyway, saying they'd be working in their offices if Clay needed them. Clay and Alaric gathered the printouts and left.

The remaining four headed for Accounting to check the paper files for the fraudulent vendors and spurious employees. Dan scouted the offices first, to make certain nobody was working late. Only two of the cleaning crew were going about their chores, and they were due to leave in five minutes. The investigators read and copied the files, discovering another possibly dubious vendor in the process. Dan searched the managers' desks also, but found nothing, not that anyone expected to after word had gotten out about what the former security manager had left behind. Nobody would keep incriminating evidence in their own desks with that object lesson staring them in the face.

It wasn't too long before everyone met again in the conference room. Clay had fresh printouts detailing transgressions, and the group had a pile of files for the phony companies and employees. "Here's what we have," he told the group. "One assistant manager or another has made most of the computer entries setting up the scam. Likewise approving the invoices and payroll checks for payment."

"Isn't this interesting?" Bill Childress remarked. "Virgil McAffee's name appears nowhere?"

"Except when he used his password to give the other access," Clay interjected.

"I need to turn this over to the fraud department," the police lieutenant stated. "If I'm reading this right, we may be able to make some arrests, but we need more hard evidence for a trial. If these guys stick together, am I correct that it will be very difficult to pin anything on McAffee?"

Several people answered affirmatively.

"What about the money?" Childress asked. "Any record of where it went?"

"We have a record of some wire transfers and direct

deposits, but I didn't look into that yet," Clay answered. "We have the account numbers."

"Daria, you've been studying these people," Bent said. "Who's the weak link here?"

Daria sat back in her chair, running impressions through her mind. "Probably John Forrest in Payables. He was the most nervous in the meeting, and he kept looking at McAffee—almost as if asking for approval. But I'm not certain. I haven't started the individual meetings yet."

"No," Dan commented. "The bomb was probably intended to stop you from meeting."

A small silence settled over the group at that pronouncement. Bent, sitting next to Daria, reached for her hand and gave it a squeeze of protective encouragement.

Childress stepped into the breach. "So I'll take this to Fraud. I'm sure they'll want to confer with you tomorrow. What's your next step, Bent?"

"Tell the fraud people to call me. It will take a few days to set up an audit with Corporate. I'll call Joe Glennell tonight, but I don't see how they can be down here until Sunday or Monday at the earliest." He ran his free hand over his jaw as he contemplated. "I assume we don't want to tip anybody off, so I guess we go along with business as usual until then. Anyone disagree?"

Nobody did.

"I'm supposed to see McAffee tomorrow afternoon and the others in the following days," Daria said. "Shall I go ahead with that?"

Bent and Dan immediately looked at each other with raised eyebrows. "Where?" Dan asked.

"In his office," Daria replied.

"No," Bent stated.

"Yes," Daria said just as firmly. "It will look strange if we treat him any differently from any of my other interviews." She gestured with her free hand imploringly as she glanced from one to the other. "I'll be careful about what I ask and how I phrase my questions. It will just be a routine interview."

Bent slumped back in his chair. "All right, honey." He shot a look at Dan. "But I want someone outside the door, covering all exits from Accounting."

"Unobtrusively," Daria interjected.

"You won't even know we're there," Dan assured them.

After a hug for Daria, Alaric left with Clay. Dan said he'd walk Bill Childress out. Their exits left the office to Bent and Daria. Bent called Joe Glennell to relate the story of the bomb and their findings. When he hung up the phone, he turned to Daria. "Joe hit the ceiling over the bomb, as I'm sure you heard."

"Yes, his voices carries, even through the phone lines. I'm glad you managed to talk him out of flying down here."

"The last thing we need is him running around, stirring things up. McAffee and company would certainly know something was going on then. But Joe did agree to send the auditors as quickly as possible." Bent gave Daria a long look. "C'mon, honey, it's late. We can't do anything else here. Let's go home."

Chapter Twenty-Three

Two anxious cats greeted them when they walked into the kitchen. Yowling loudly, Zorro and Lolita twined around their humans' legs and would hardly let them take a step.

"It's all right," Daria told the cats as she knelt down to pet them. Zorro sniffed her carefully before allowing himself to relax.

"How do they know something's wrong?" Bent leaned over to run his hand over Lolita's back.

"I haven't the foggiest. They've always been able to tell when I'm upset." She rose, closed her eyes and took a deep breath. She could feel the events of the day return to her, feel the descending weariness that she'd kept at bay by willpower and spells, feel an insidious cold slither through her bones. She exhaled and started to tremble.

Then Bent's arms were around her, his warmth engulfed her, and his smooth baritone murmured in her ear, "Shhhh. It's all right. I'm here and you're safe."

"Oh, Bent, I was so scared," Daria whispered, her arms tight around his waist, her cheek to his chest.

"I know, so was I." He rested his head on her hair and rubbed her back, his hands moving slowly, soothingly over her shoulders, down to her waist and back again.

Her trembling ceased, and she luxuriated in his support for a long moment. Then she leaned back and smiled up at him. "I'm okay. Really."

"I don't know how you held it together so long. I feel like a basket case."

"Spells, lots of calm-yourself spells."

"I could have used a few of those. I knew you had activated something. I could see the auras, mostly blues and greens. But I thought they were aimed at the others."

"No, these were on me."

"You're not spelling yourself now."

"No. I really am all right."

He looked at her skeptically.

"Or at least I don't need the spells anymore," she begrudgingly admitted.

"C'mon, honey. Let's go to bed. I'm not okay, and I need some reassurance." Bent set the alarm system, took her hand and led her upstairs.

Once in the bedroom, he put his hands on her shoulders and kissed her lightly. "I need some of your magic tonight, little witch."

"All you want."

They undressed each other slowly, taking time between pieces of clothing to kiss and caress. Daria sighed somewhere in the middle of the process.

"What?" Bent asked in a whisper.

"The miracle of touch," she answered, "you feel so good." She ran a hand around his rib cage and up his back to his shoulder. This brought her bare breasts to his unclothed chest, and they both caught their breath when she rubbed her nipples across him and went up on tiptoe to press herself more fully against him.

"Daria," he said, his voice a rasp, and he kissed her until she started trembling again, but not from fear. He picked her up and laid her on the bed. After removing what little clothing she still had on, he divested himself of his own and came down beside her. They lay facing each other, his top leg between hers, his top hand on her breast.

After another hug that felt to Daria like he was trying to absorb her into him, Bent kissed her lips, then her neck, then nudged her to her back and started working his way down her body.

The miracle of touch, indeed, Daria thought as each kiss at a new place sent shivers through her—shivers of heat. Where she had been cold before, now she was burning. She held his head to keep his mouth first at her neck, then at her breast. His suckling, first at one nipple, then at the other, increased the blaze, and she felt herself begin to melt.

Given her own way, she would have been content to let him suck and nip and lick right where he was for a very long time, but it became clear he had other plans. Kissing his way from the tender underside of her breasts, he pressed his mouth to the end of her breastbone. His kiss on her magic center ignited a torch that arched her back and fisted her hands in his hair. She could feel power sizzle within her.

He raised his head and she looked down into his eyes, deep blue pools of fiery desire. He flashed a grin, as if he knew exactly what he'd done, and continued on his journey down to her navel and beyond.

She shuddered as he turned his attention to her inner thighs with long strokes of his tongue. She arched again as he nuzzled her nest of hair and darted his tongue through her folds to the little nub of nerve endings. He flicked it and her hips jerked as she gasped. She could feel tension building inside her. He flicked it again and she couldn't stop herself from beginning to writhe. He reached one hand up to press it on her magic center while he sucked on the nub.

The combination sent energy rocketing between the two spots—energy that burst when it reached each end of the line. With fireballs exploding in two parts of her body at once, Daria shattered with a gasp.

When she had put herself back together from the million pieces she had been flung into, she opened her eyes to gaze straight into Bent's. His face was stark with desire as he moved up to cover her body and brace himself on his arms above her.

"Put your legs around me," he grated and she grasped his hips between her thighs. She put her hands on his ribs. His aroused sex nudged her folds. He leaned down to kiss her lips and she could taste herself, smell herself on him.

"Yours and mine, Daria."

"Yours and mine, Bent."

Eyes locked with hers, he thrust himself into her body, and she rose to accept him. Slowly at first, then with increasing speed, they came together and retreated, came together and retreated.

Daria felt herself tensing and his body growing harder. Without conscious volition, she pulled her hands around and pressed both to his breastbone. Her fingers tingled, her body quivered, her own center blazed again as magic power burst from her and flowed into him.

Bent froze as the energy poured from her hands through his body to his sex. He felt himself growing impossibly larger and harder. Lightning bolts coursed along his spine. Sparks seemed to fly from her green eyes to his blue ones.

Then the energy flow reached their joined flesh. Power hummed between them, around them, and through them. It increased in magnitude with each stroke until they were both gasping for breath, reaching for the same goal.

Reaching . . . reaching . . . Climax!

She convulsed with a cry, hammering her hips upward against him. He stroked like a madman once, twice, three times before following her over the edge with his own shout. Their frenzy seemed to last forever before they collapsed into each other's arms.

She held on him as if he were her life raft in a turbulent sea. She could still feel the remnants of power shimmering inside her, a reaction she had felt before only when casting a spell at the top of her level. This love-making had been much stronger, more intense than their first mating. Something had happened to her, she knew deep down, but she hadn't a clue as to what it was. Maybe it was simply that their bodies were attuned to one another now. The more they made love, the better it became.

Eventually she loosened her grip and he did the same. He rolled to his side and pulled her with him.

She opened her eyes to look at him, but his were still closed. "Bent," she whispered. "Are you all right?"

"Yeah," he breathed and opened his own eyes about half way. "What the hell happened? I thought I'd been hit by a rocket. Whoa, what a ride." He'd thought they'd experienced mind-boggling love-making before, but now he knew better. His mind and body were still reeling from the aftereffects.

"You touched my magic center and I touched yours."

"Magic center, what magic center? I don't have one, I just itch, remember?" He glanced down at the spot. It didn't look any different from usual.

"No, I think there's more to it now." Daria pushed him back a few inches from her torso. "Put your fingers right at the end of my breastbone, and I'll do the same to you."

He did as instructed. "My fingers are, I don't know, itching."

"Now, me." She touched his chest.

Both gasped from the small shock that zapped between them.

"I can feel power, magical power, flowing between us," Daria said. "What do you feel?"

"Like I stuck my finger in a light socket and the current is coursing through me." He couldn't be imagining this sensation. Heat and a sort of sizzle were running up his nerves from the exact place where her fingers were resting. He moved his hand away from her. The sensation lessened by half. He put his hand back on its original position. Full power restored. "The current is still there."

His hand still on her, Bent moved farther back and glanced up and down their bodies. Somehow he was not surprised. "There's an aura too, but it's around both of us, not just you alone, like when you have cast a spell."

"I can't see it," Daria said. "What color?"

"Deep red. Let's try not touching each other."

They pulled back their hands. "The aura's still there."

"We're still touching," Daria pointed out. "Our legs and other arms are."

They unwrapped themselves from each other. Daria sat up and Bent sprawled on his back.

"It's gone," he announced. "Give me your hand." She did so. "Nothing," he said, "no aura."

She shifted, put his fingers on her center, and laid hers on his. "Anything? I don't feel the power moving as it was before."

"No zap. No aura either. What do you suppose is going on? Another manifestation of being soulmates?"

"Probably. For that magic power flow, it appears that we need to be, uh, more, uh . . ."

He grinned as he watched her blush. "More intimately involved? More tightly connected? Inside each other? Plugged in?" he rapidly suggested.

"Something like that," she said and shrugged, a shoulder movement that drew his gaze down to her breasts.

He pulled her down onto his chest and kissed her lightly. "When I said I needed some of your magic tonight, I had no idea I was speaking literally."

She shook her head. "Neither did I." She sighed.

The sigh made him recall the day's events. "How do you feel, Daria? Are you still shaken up from what happened today?"

"Not now," she said, after considering the question. Then she grinned. "Your magic touch fixed everything."

He grinned back. "Yours did incredible things to me."

She smiled and kissed him, then yawned. "Excuse me, I guess I'm a little tired."

Her yawn precipitated one from him. "Me, too. Somehow I don't think we'll have any trouble sleeping tonight."

They kissed again, cuddled, and slept dreamlessly in each other's arms.

Chapter Twenty-Four

Daria, revitalized and determined, met with Virgil McAffee Wednesday afternoon. In preparation she had spelled herself with only mild I-am-no-threat and I-can-be-told-anything spells. During her casting, she noted no obvious changes brought about by the tumultuous love-making of the night before, except for a nebulous feeling of a deeper reservoir of energy.

But she couldn't think about that now. Her first visit with any interviewee was ordinarily too early for any strong I-must-be-told-the-truth enchantments, and the plan was to obtain evidence first, then confront the miscreants. In any event, she needed to assess McAffee before she tried stronger sorcery, having learned in the past that very determined individuals could fight off all but the most powerful spells if they had the will power. If the accounting manager was anything, he was determined.

Sure enough, when she strengthened the weak spells and threw in I-am-sympathetic-to-you and I-am-very-understanding ones, McAffee narrowed his eyes at her, opened his mouth and shut it again, and almost lost the thread of his narrative about the worth and competence of Hank Billings. But he offered no incriminating statements, and the implacable look on his face said he would make no mistakes.

The only nervous gesture she observed was his tendency

to play with his pinkie ring, a thick gold band that broadened to a flat top with a crest on it. His hands were immaculately groomed and exceedingly clean. But then, it appeared the big man certainly did not like to get his hands dirty, either with actual grime or with subterranean dealings in the accounts.

He was slightly patronizing, but such was not unusual or unexpected. Senior staff members, even honest ones, often had that attitude toward her in her consulting role. Daria asked her usual questions and managed to lead McAffee into a fairly comprehensive and in-depth discussion of his department in its present state. He had little to say, however, about any visions for the future, falling back instead on the present need to assimilate into Glennell, the parent company.

In closing, as was courteous, she informed him of her interview schedule with his subordinates: Billings in Payroll on Thursday morning, Howarth in Receivables that afternoon, and Forrest in Payables Friday morning. McAffee expressed his desire to see her report on his department, but suggested neither an approach to, nor questions for, his assistant managers.

They finally said a cordial good-bye, and Daria left the office feeling frustrated. She was never happy when her spells didn't work, but she knew it would have been dangerous to push them any further than she had. Well, maybe she could get more out of the other men.

That evening Bent, Daria, Clay, Alaric, and Dan sat around the kitchen table finishing Chinese take-out and plotting their next moves.

"You got nowhere with McAffee?" Dan asked.

"He's very sly," Daria replied. "I tried a number of tricks, but he gave away practically nothing. The most I could get out of him was all impressionistic on my part, such as a few shrewd or satisfied or suspicious looks or comments or tone of voice. He made no straightforward comments that gave anything away. As for his statements about his assistant managers, the only derogatory comments he made were that John Forrest should have fired a lazy clerk faster than he did, and Steve Howarth needed to watch one particular customer's payment schedule more closely." She shrugged her shoulders. "Not exactly any actionable comments."

"No, but indicative of an enormous tendency to micromanage," Bent commented.

"Shall I push the others to see if they're easier to deal with or might make a slip? I am going ahead with the interviews, after all." Her last sentence was a firm statement.

Bent rose and strolled to a window overlooking the lush garden. He stuck his hands in his pockets and rocked back and forth on his heels, thinking the situation through. The others were silent. After a few minutes Bent turned. "I see no alternative except to go on with the interviews."

Clay, Alaric, and Dan nodded agreement while Daria said, "Okay."

"But, Daria," Bent continued, "keep them normal. There's no need to raise suspicions until we're ready to move."

"All right," she said, frowning at her iced tea. He was right, she knew, but she'd really like to do something instead of waiting. She raised her head to meet his eyes. "I'll keep it routine."

Bent relaxed with Daria's acquiescence.

"When do you expect the auditors from Corporate, Bent?" Alaric asked.

"I'll know for sure on Friday, but probably not before Saturday. They'll hit the Accounting department on Sunday when no one's there. Joe Glennell complimented us on what we're doing and said we have his blessing for whatever course we want to take. I talked with the head of the police fraud division, and we decided to hold off on any action until the auditors arrive."

"Well, then, I think I'll head home," Alaric said. "I can't do more with the books without raising suspicion. I'll be back Monday if that's all right."

Daria reached across the table to take her father's hand. "You know you're welcome any time, Daddy."

"I'll plan on being in the I.T. offices Monday morning, unless you tell me differently," Clay spoke up. "I agree with Dad that you don't need us on the premises until then."

"I'll let Bill Childress know so the Fraud people can be there also," Dan interjected. "We have someone in the mail room, checking everything addressed to you and Daria, Bent, but after some discussion, we in Security will not change any of the escorts we've been giving you around the building. There are some rumors to the effect there was more to the fire drill than met the eye, but nobody has said anything about my people being in strange places—yet. We've managed to keep our presence low key and seemingly coincidental."

"Fine, Dan," Bent stated. "I'm going to be in my office all week. Don't you have some plant meetings scheduled?"

"Yeah," the security manager groaned. "One of the results of our impromptu fire drill was that it showed us how derelict Triangle had been in safety procedures. It looks like all their drills and procedures were only on paper. Spot inspections along those lines at the plants yesterday have raised numerous questions and issues. We have drills scheduled at the plants next week, and I need to visit both Baytown and Sugarland on Friday. I think I'm going to fire one or both of the security managers and/or safety officers. I've scheduled Sugarland for the morning and Baytown for the afternoon."

"You do what you think best there, Dan," Bent commented. He glanced around the circle of faces. "Anything else?"

All shook their heads negatively, and the group broke up, Alaric to drive back to the plant nursery and Clay and Dan to head off on their own business. Bent and Daria cleaned up and went to bed and each other's arms.

Thursday morning Daria met with Hank Billings in Payroll. Billings was a big heavyset man with a florid face, a seemingly sure candidate for high blood pressure. He could have been mistaken for a good-ol'-boy redneck except for his conservative, well-cut suit, unmistakably a copy of the clothes McAffee favored. Rumor said he ran his area like a martinet, demanding perfection and absolute adherence to the chain of command. In keeping with his complexion, his temper was legendary. Billings himself said the only reason his area worked so well was because he kept abreast of everybody. His office had the highest turnover among those in entry-level positions, a fact of which he claimed to be proud. He did not want anyone working for him who could not do a proper job, he emphatically maintained.

Billings was a carbon copy of McAffee in more than just style of dress. He had the same determination to admit to no wrongdoing or even slight weakness, either on his part or on that of any of his staff. Daria doubted his subordinates had any idea what he was up to. Clay had traced the original entry of non-existent employees and subsequent entries transferring funds to Billings' user-name and password.

Daria made no attempt to force more from Billings by means of her spells. She certainly did not want to raise their suspicions as to the extent of her or Bent's knowledge of their nefarious deeds. It was clear from her observations so far that McAffee and Billings were the most forceful of the four men, with McAffee the leader and Billings the fervent second in command. She conducted her usual interview, thanked the payroll manager for his time and attention, and returned to her own office.

Anxious for a report, Bent took her to lunch, but she had little to tell him. She was hoping for more from the remaining two assistant managers.

Steve Howarth in Receivables was a short man built along

the lines of a fireplug, and he had a short man's pugnacity, designed to overcome any challenge set forth by taller men. Daria surmised that, while it clearly had its origins in his youth, Howarth's demeanor meant that he was determined to hold his own against the larger McAffee and Billings. His dress echoed that of the other two, but he carried it to a superior meticulousness. He was the only senior staff member she had met who wore shirts with French cuffs and cufflinks, and he kept his coat on, the better to shoot his cuffs and show off the heavy gold links. This fastidiousness was also evident in his surroundings, especially his immaculate desk, and Daria had heard of his complaints about the cleaning crew's inability to keep his office the way he wanted it.

Because of McAffee's statement that Howarth did not pay sufficient attention to one particular customer's timely payments, Daria raised the general question of the need for prompt receipt of payments. He threw a barrage of numbers at her, citing percentages of current accounts and past due amounts that "proved" his department was better at collections than Glennell Companies as a whole. His indignation at even the hint of being thought of as subpar in the way he or his staff carried out their duties was convincing—or would have been if Daria had not seen his deceit in the accounts with her own eyes.

Howarth being no more forthcoming than the other two, that left John Forrest in Payables for Friday morning. Based on nothing more substantial than intuition, Daria had moderately high hopes for the interview.

When Daria arrived at Forrest's office that morning, McAffee was just leaving it. "Now, remember, John," the big man was saying, "I'm counting on you to handle the matter." Then he turned and saw Daria. "Good morning," he said in a jovial tone. "How are you getting along with my people?"

Daria personally thought butter wouldn't melt in his mouth, but she smiled and answered brightly, "Very well, thanks. I should be able to start the general surveys among the staff by the beginning of next week."

"Good, good." McAffee smiled like a shark eyeing a particularly choice piece of swimmer. "I'll leave you to it then." He strode out of the office.

"Ready, John?" Daria asked as she came into Forrest's office and sat down.

Forrest was of medium height and thin to the point that it appeared only a puff from McAffee's lips would blow the man away. Extremely nervous, he bit his nails to the quick and was always fidgeting—playing with a pen or pencil, straightening the papers on his cluttered desk, or shifting position in his chair. His sparse graying hair looked like he had been continually running his fingers through it in agitation. He tried to emulate the others in dress, but couldn't pull it off somehow; and his clothes didn't fit correctly, as though he had recently lost weight. This morning he looked like he'd rather jump off the top tier of the Galleria and hope he'd spontaneously learn to fly before he hit the ice rink than take part in the interview. He smiled with a grimace and nodded.

The interview jerked to a start, with Forrest answering at first in single syllables. It took Daria at least twenty minutes to get the man relaxed enough to answer first in sentences and finally in short paragraphs, and she had to use her mildest, friendliest, most nonthreatening spells to do it. Several times she thought the assistant payables manager was about to say more, or even something of importance, but he backed out each time. He became most anxious in discussions about his system of checks and balances and own internal audit procedures. He was most comfortable discussing his subordinates and their abilities, exhibiting what appeared to be a genuine concern for them personally. Word around the company was that his employees liked him, a situation not found among the other Accounting senior staff.

After almost three hours, three times as long as any of the other interviews had taken (thanks to Forrest's hesitancy, reticence, and difficulty formulating answers), Daria was able to end the session. "There now, John," she couldn't help trying to get a smile out of him, "that wasn't so bad, was it?"

Forrest gave a short bark of nervous laughter, heavily laced with relief. "I guess not," he said, taking out a handkerchief to wipe his brow.

"It will be easier the next time," she assured him.

"The, the n-next time?" His face was a mask of alarm. "There's more?" he squeaked.

"We need to discuss the results of the survey of your staff, at least. Often a number of questions arise from that. And after I formulate my preliminary report, I usually find I have some more questions, just to clarify a few points." She spoke in the most normal voice she could muster. "I'm sure you will have nothing to worry about. Your people clearly like you and think you're doing a good job."

"Oh. Of, of course." He smiled weakly.

"I'll give you a call when the survey is completed." With that, she took her leave.

Bent and Dan were waiting for her in Bent's office. They had been discussing Dan's morning inspection and meetings at the Sugarland plant, and both looked expectantly at Daria as she entered.

"Nothing," she shook her head as she plopped herself in a chair. "Getting even the simplest information out of him was excruciatingly difficult." She gave them some examples. "I thought he was going to come clean a couple of times, but he backed off. McAffee was either bucking him up or threatening him—I couldn't tell which—when I came to his office this morning, and whatever he said must have worked."

"Would Forrest hold up under more intense questioning?" Dan asked.

"I think he'd cave in," she answered. "The man is obviously terrified."

"We'll tackle Forrest when we have some hard auditor's information. Let's get some lunch," Bent interjected. "I have a conference call with Joe Glennell and some corporate people about this situation at one o'clock. Join us, Dan?"

"I have to get out to Baytown," the security manager said with a disgruntled sigh. "The mess there is greater than what we found at Sugarland."

"Give me a call tonight," Bent said.

"Will do," came the reply.

Chapter Twenty-Five

About five in the afternoon, Daria was still working on her reports from the accounting department meetings when the phone rang.

"Daria Morgan," she answered.

"Daria," a hoarse voice said.

"Who is this?"

"John Forrest. I have to talk to you." His voice croaked and broke.

"What's the matter, John? You don't sound well. Are you all right? I can be at your office in just a minute." He sounded terrified. Wishing her spells could work through telephone lines, she tried to sound reassuring, even with excitement stirring her blood. She just knew Forrest had cracked under the pressure.

"No, no. I'm not at the office." There was a pause and some noise on his end and it sounded like he had put his hand over the receiver.

"John? Are you there?"

"Somebody just walked by," he whispered in explanation.

"Where are you? What's wrong, John? I can hardly hear you."

He spoke a little louder. "I'm at the Sugarland plant. I have to talk to you. It's about those threats you've been getting and that bomb."

"John! Do you know who's behind it?"

"Yes. But I'll tell only you and Benthausen. Nobody else! Come out here and meet me in the loading dock, door number three. Honk and I'll open the door."

"Why don't you come back here, John? Security can protect you, if that's what's worrying you."

"No! I can't come there. They'll see me! You have to come here!" He was almost shrieking. He stopped again and Daria could hear him gulping air. "Please come here," came out in a pitiful groan of supplication.

He sounded like he was about to disintegrate right there on the phone. She tried to speak calmly. "Okay, John, okay. We'll get there, but it's rush hour, and it will take us some time."

"You have an hour. If you're not here by six, I'm gone. And just you and Benthausen! Nobody else! Don't alert security or the police! If I see anybody looking for me or searching the warehouse, I'm taking off."

"All right, John. We'll be there as soon as we can. Door number three, right? John, you take care of yourself. John? John?" She was speaking to dead air, then the dial tone wailed in her ear.

Daria grabbed her purse and ran into Bent's office. She quickly explained the call.

"Damn!" Bent exclaimed. "Come on. It'll take almost till six to get there in rush hour traffic. We'll phone Dan from the car."

They commandeered an elevator and shot down to the

garage, where they jumped into Bent's car and headed for the Southwest Freeway. While Bent fought the traffic, Daria called Dan on his cell phone and explained the situation. "Forrest was scared to death, Dan. If he sees any of your people or anybody else, he'll run, I'm sure," she said.

"I'm already on the way back and should be only fifteen or twenty minutes behind you," Dan replied. "I'll call security in Sugarland and tell them not to do anything unusual, but to keep their eyes open and stay out of the warehouse. I'll get in touch with Bill Childress too. I'd hate to bring the Sugarland police in right now without explanation. There's too much chance they'd blunder around and spook Forrest. Maybe Bill can call the Sugarland Police for us."

Daria relayed Dan's comments to Bent, who said only, "Tell him to get here as soon as he can."

"I heard that, Daria. You two be careful."

"We'll call you as soon as we have Forrest with us." She ended the call.

For once, freeway traffic moved well and they made good time. The guard at the gate allowed them onto the grounds at the truck entrance with no words other than, "Hello, Mr. Benthausen." The place was quiet in the late afternoon sunlight. No trucks moved on the blacktop driveways, and no employees were in sight. The parking lot over on the office side of the sprawling building was almost empty.

"Where is everybody?" Daria asked.

"We're running only one shift here at the moment, from eight to five. We won't go to a second shift until next month.

There should be no one here except security unless somebody's working late in the office," Bent answered as he drove toward the loading dock, a huge enclosed space with large truck-sized doors, all closed.

"I've been out here, but to the office, never to the warehouse or loading dock," Daria said. "How is the dock constructed?"

"Normally eighteen-wheelers back their trailers into the building, leaving their cabs sticking out of the doors," he explained. "This enclosed configuration is an unusual one for this climate. Usually a dock in the South will have only a roof to protect from the rain since there's no real extreme cold or snow. This design costs more to build, of course. It's another example of the previous president's disregard for overhead costs, I assume. Which door did Forrest say to come to?"

"Go to door number three and honk."

Bent drove up to the green metal door in the middle of the line of truck entrances and honked. Just as he stopped the car, the door began to slide upward, revealing a dark cavern beyond. Since the sun was setting on the other side of the building, no light penetrated very far into the interior. Bent switched on the car's headlights and drove halfway into the dock area.

As their eyes adjusted to the darkness, they saw John Forrest, illuminated by the car's beams, standing on the elevated dock directly ahead of them. He motioned them forward.

Bent moved the car slowly inside the building. No lamps lit the vast space except for one directly above the person-sized door into the warehouse behind Forrest. Behind the

Payables manager, all the ramp doors into the warehouse were also closed. Bent stopped the car just inside the space. "It's like a cave in here. Daria, do you see anybody else?" he asked, peering into the gloom on the left side of the vehicle.

Daria looked to the right. "No, but there's a car over by the far wall. Something doesn't feel right, Bent."

"I agree. Get out on your side and let's walk toward him. I'm going to try to talk him down here with us and into the car." Bent turned off the car's engine but left the headlights on. He and Daria climbed out and walked around their open doors.

"Forrest!" Bent called. "Come down here so we can talk." He held out his hand in appeal and continued to walk toward the dock as he said it. He could feel Daria about six feet to his right and about a foot behind him.

Stumbling, Forrest moved toward the stairs leading down from the dock and slowly descended them. He glanced from side to side nervously, his face pale, his movements jerky.

Bent and Daria had traversed about half the distance from their car to the dock when the personnel door behind Forrest opened. Billings, Howarth, and McAffee came through it quickly, the first two with revolvers in their hands pointed directly at Bent and Daria. McAffee punched a button on the wall and the open bay door behind Bent's car descended, imprisoning all of them.

Bent and Daria froze. Bent swore and muttered, "We're sitting ducks here. When I give the word, run for the car."

"Wait a minute," she whispered. "If I get the chance, I'm

going to cast my defensive spells. When I distract them, see if you can get a gun."

"Daria? No!"

"We have no choice!" she hissed through her teeth.

"I'm sorry, Daria, they made me call you," Forrest cried as he staggered toward them. He was shaking so much he could hardly put one foot in front of the other.

"Shut up, John!" McAffee snarled. "It's your fault we're all here now." He pointed at Daria and Bent. "You two just stay where you are. Hank and Steve, get down there."

Billings and Howarth walked down the stairs and stepped on either side of Forrest, who just stood there wringing his hands. Virgil McAffee followed them, but stayed behind the gunmen when they stopped about fifteen feet from Daria and Bent.

"You two have been causing enough trouble," McAffee said. "We're going to put you out of the way for a while until we can get out of the country."

"You promised me you wouldn't kill them." Forrest grasped McAffee's upper arm, but the big man shrugged him off.

"We're not, John. Just shut up." McAffee motioned toward the car Daria had observed parked against the far wall. "Benthausen, you and Daria get over there by the car. John, you drive their car. We'll meet at my beach house in Galveston like we planned."

"No! I'm not going anywhere by myself," Forrest stated. "You're just trying to get rid of me." He grabbed McAffee's arm again, this time swinging him halfway around. "I won't let you kill them."

"John! I told you what we're going to do. Get hold of yourself!" McAffee twisted out of Forrest's hold and was turning back toward the captives when Forrest yelled "No!" and reached out for the manager once more.

"You idiot!" McAffee roared as he swiveled, seized Forrest by his jacket lapels, and threw him to the ground behind the group. Yelling in pain, Forrest fell and began to cry. Billings and Howarth turned to look at the cringing, sobbing man.

That was all the diversion Daria needed. Putting every bit of energy and power she possessed into the spells, she cast dragon, strength, speed, and sound.

Bright multicolored flashes lit up the dark dock as bolts of brilliant red, blue, green, and silver power burst forth from her. The spells coalesced with a sharp crack of thunder, and a rumbling tremor shook the ground. When the flashes died, not one beast, but two rose in the dim cavern!

Two huge dragons, one red and the other blue, slick scales gleaming, powerful wings unfurling, razor-sharp talons clawing, reared up, their heads almost fifteen feet above the floor.

Bent looked at her and then himself. Her dragon looked confused and he was certain his did too. He could see the aura of the spells and the outline of the red dragon around him, and he felt his body take on strength and speed. He grinned and watched his beast's thoroughly toothy grin mimic his expression, only in ghastly proportions. Daria smiled back, flicked her tongue out, and shrugged. Then they both turned to the stunned quartet in front of them and *roared*.

The thunderous bellow had barely stopped reverberating off the metal walls before Billings and Howarth started shooting. The two aimed high, at the dragons' heads now swinging in their directions. Great dagger-like silver fangs shone in the dim light, and long forked blood-red tongues slithered as the monsters prepared to take the first bites of their prey.

McAffee screamed and scurried to take cover behind the shooters. His mouth was moving, but any sound he was making was lost in the dragons' roars and the gunfire. For his part, Forrest fainted dead away.

Billings and Howarth continued to pull the triggers until nothing could be heard except the click, click of hammers falling on empty chambers. They threw their guns at the dragons and turned to run for the stairs. McAffee made a break toward the car parked against the far wall.

Bent covered the ground between himself and the two evildoers in a stride and, using his augmented strength to advantage, threw first one, then the other into the wall of the dock. Daria caught McAffee by his arm before he took three steps and, pivoting, swung him around across the floor to collapse in a heap on top of the other two. Nobody moved.

When silence descended, Bent looked at Daria and said, "I thought . . ." He stopped when his words came out too loudly, almost at roar level. He cleared his throat and tried again, this time in a whisper. "I thought you couldn't spell me!"

Daria laughed at him. "So did I," she said. "Practitioners—

everybody except me, that is—can spell family members for healing and defense. It looks like our mating gave me the ability to cast defensive spells on you."

Throwing the two criminals across the room had exhilarated Bent so much he felt ready to take on an army. "This is great!" He experimented flexing his muscles and watched the red dragon surrounding him move likewise. A twist of his shoulders moved the wings, but he couldn't quite figure out how to control his tail. It didn't seem to want to curl around his body. He took a swipe at the air with a red arm tipped with black claws, then stalked across the cement and picked up the guns Howarth and Billings had thrown.

"You make a great dragon," Daria said, smiling as she watched him play at being the beast. "He has your blue eyes."

"You make an enchanting one and her eyes are green. Great smile too." He grinned, then looked closely at her within her spell aura and walked over to her. "Are you all right?" He leaned toward her and kissed her delicately.

"Fine," she replied and returned his kiss, but she took her time about it. Above their heads, the two dragons were also kissing.

She heard a moan and a following squeal and pulled back just in time to see John Forrest stare up at the monsters above him and keel over anew.

Bent looked at Forrest, then up at the dragons' heads, and started laughing. "I guess the sight of two dragons in love was too much for him," he said when he regained control of himself.

"I'd better negate these spells," Daria replied. "When I do, be prepared to feel a little weak at first when the strength spell cancels. Ready? One, two, three."

When the aura abruptly faded, Bent almost stumbled, but righted himself quickly. "I see what you mean." He stilled, listening. "I think I hear sirens."

Just then, someone started beating on the door into the warehouse. "Open up in there! This is Glennell Security!" a man shouted. The sounds of cars pulling up outside and doors slamming were succeeded by more people pounding on the truck doors.

Bent ran up the stairs and unlocked the door, hitting the outside truck door button at the same time. Guns drawn, Dan and two Sugarland policemen ran in, and a security guard did the same from the warehouse.

The security manager quickly took in the tableau of unconscious crooks, Bent with a gun in each hand, and Daria just standing there. "Well, hell." Dan shook his head. "What do you need us for, Two-Gun Bent?"

Chapter Twenty-Six

It was some time before the crooks were revived, babbling incoherently about some sort of demons and dragons, and then were hauled away. Bill Childress arrived, as did a Sugarland detective, Carl Nelson.

Bent and Daria explained somewhat vaguely about how they had overpowered the gunmen. "I just was so angry," Bent stated, "that they would threaten Daria. I think I went berserk. When McAffee threw Forrest down and the other two looked away from us, I punched Billings and grabbed his gun. I must have hit Howarth with it. I don't really remember."

"McAffee was cowering behind the other two," Daria added. "I ran up behind him and kicked him as hard as I could. I guess he was off balance to begin with because he sort of rolled into the wall and hit his head."

The policemen laughed. "Lady, that was one good kick in the butt," Nelson said in admiration.

Neither Dan, Childress, nor Nelson asked for more information. It didn't really matter to them how Bent and Daria had subdued their assailants. What counted was that there was enough evidence to hold them for assault until the other charges for fraud could be brought.

At the Sugarland police station, Childress and Nelson called Daria and Bent into an interrogation room where John Forrest sat slumped in a chair behind a table. Two officers stood by the door.

"Forrest here requested to see you," Nelson said. "Says he wants to confess, especially to you, Ms. Morgan. Says he owes it to you. We've read him his rights, and he's offered to testify against the others."

Daria, Bent, and Childress sat down at the table. Nelson activated the recorder on the table and established the time, date, and names of the participants. He read Forrest his rights again and had the man state for the record that he didn't want a lawyer present. "Okay, Mr. Forrest," the detective said, "the floor is yours."

Forrest fidgeted, wrung his hands, and raised his eyes to Daria's. "I'm really sorry, Daria. I didn't mean for you to be involved in this mess. I didn't know about the bomb, honest."

"I believe you, John," she answered.

He nodded and rubbed his face with his hands. "It was all Virgil McAffee's idea to begin with. He and Hank Billings and Steve Howarth wanted to take Triangle for all it was worth. He was so contemptuous of the president and his cronies. They started about two years ago. I got involved because my wife had been sick and the Triangle insurance didn't cover all our expenses. Virgil knew that and I guess he saw me as easy pickings for the scheme. And I was.

"When Glennell bought the company, I became worried and tried to get out, but McAffee said he'd turn me in as an embezzler if I did. Virgil saw Glennell as the chance to steal more because Glennell had much deeper pockets."

"Where's the money?" Nelson asked.

"It's in offshore accounts. Virgil was very strict about that. He said we couldn't spend any of it until we left the country. We were planning on getting out in three months." Forrest paused to clear his throat. "Could I have some water, please?"

Nelson sent one of the officers for water. "Go on," he told Forrest.

"Greedy, they were all so greedy," Forrest said, shaking his head. "Virgil used to fight with the old president about spending too much on overhead, all those paintings and the fancy offices. But he was only complaining because he wanted more money available to steal.

"McAffee and the rest laid low while the purchase deal was being made with Glennell. We didn't know how much housecleaning the new regime would do. We wanted to make sure our jobs were secure. We were really surprised when Glennell sent just you, Mr. Benthausen. We expected a whole team of people. McAffee thought you'd be too busy to check up on the details of accounting, although he did get a little nervous when you started asking about why expenses hadn't gone down like they should have."

"I never could get a detailed answer out of him," Bent said. "He always laid the blame on Manufacturing and Distribution. When exactly were you going to skip town?"

"Just before the end of the fiscal year." Forrest took a swallow of water from the cup the officer placed in front of him. "Then you showed up, Daria. Virgil had heard about you from the accounting people and some of your clients. Especially when you caught those embezzlers over at Rydecker's. All they talked about was how you questioned everybody and discovered everything. It was like you were some sort of witch or something, your ability to find them out. People told you things they would never have told anybody." The last sentence came out in a wail.

"Word went around the company when you and Benthausen were seen together. At first, when it was only that idiot Grady telling the tale, nobody cared. But Theo Wall saw the two of you at that dance, and he told Virgil. Theo's such a nervous Nellie. He was sure you'd be coming to work at Glennell next."

"Is Wall part of the scheme?" Bent asked.

"No. Virgil would never trust him. Said Theo was too weak and would confess everything if you looked at him cross-eyed," Forrest responded. "When we heard about Daria, I wanted to take what we had and run, but McAffee, well, he doesn't think much of women anyway, he came up with the bright idea of frightening you away. He kept telling us all we had to do was keep our mouths shut and run our areas with no mistakes. We had all been very careful with our computer entries, and we knew it would take a thorough, detailed audit to discover what we had done."

"Did you know," Bent asked, "that McAffee never made one computer entry? He would have looked clean, but the rest of you were clearly messing with the accounts."

Forrest looked shocked. "No, I didn't know that. I assumed, well, that we were all making entries. That bastard!"

"What happened that caused you to try the bomb?" Childress interjected.

"Oh, Theo started it. We were having a managers meeting with McAffee and Wall came in, almost having a nervous breakdown. He had met Daria's father in the hall, I think."

"Yes, that must have been when Alaric came to take us to lunch," Bent said to Daria, who nodded.

"I don't know about that, but Theo said Morgan said something about 'never knowing' when he might be auditing a company. Theo was certain you were looking for a reason to fire him. Everybody in Accounting has heard about Alaric Morgan and his ability to find the smallest discrepancies in a company's financials. The idea of him looking at our books really scared Virgil."

He held up his hand as if taking an oath. "I swear to God, Daria, I didn't know about the bomb. I thought the fire drill was just a real drill. I almost had a heart attack when Virgil told me about it on Friday, and then I had to sit there and talk to you in our meeting like nothing was wrong."

"John, I knew something was bothering you. Why didn't you say something then?" Daria asked.

"Virgil threatened to kill me, that's why," Forrest wailed. "I tried to run right after our meeting, but I couldn't even get out of the parking ramp. Hank was coming back from a meeting and caught me there. He called McAffee and Howarth on his cell phone. They came down and we all climbed into Steve's big Cadillac and drove around while the three of them argued about what to do.

"McAffee was real angry the bomb had not gone off, but nobody knew why it hadn't. Virgil finally came up with the idea to get the two of you out of the way for a while to give us time to get out of the country. He figured the cops would be looking for you, but not us. Nobody would listen to me when I tried to say something. McAffee and Billings didn't listen to Steve either, when he got rattled and wanted to run.

"I thought the idea was just to kidnap you, stick you in Virgil's beach house on Galveston Island, but I think Virgil really had other plans. I think he was going to kill you. He was so mad you were thwarting his scheme." Forrest looked from Daria to Bent and back again. "I tried to stop him, you saw me grab him. I tried to stop him."

"Yes, you did, John," Daria agreed.

"Virgil is just so greedy," Forrest repeated, "and look what happened to him. I'm just glad it's over."

Eventually, Bent and Daria were allowed to go home. On the way they called Alaric and Clay to let them know what had happened.

"You were both dragons?" Alaric asked. "Wait a minute. Antonia has to hear this!"

When her mother came on the line, Daria had to tell the story all over again. "Well, that's one for the history books," Antonia finally stated. "And you're both fine? No injuries or anything?" After being assured all was well, the parents affirmed they would come to Houston on Monday as originally planned.

After Daria ended the call, Bent glanced over at her. "I don't know about you, but I'm still on an incredible high. I know I'm driving too fast, but I can hardly wait to get you in my arms and make absolutely certain that you're all right and I have you all to myself."

Daria felt the familiar rush of desire that almost overcame her every time she looked at him. This onslaught washed through her, leaving her tingling. "Me too," was all she said, but she clasped her hands tightly in her lap to keep herself from reaching for him.

"Being a dragon can do it to you, I guess. However you explain it, I just want us home and then I want you."

"Yes," was all she answered.

They reached the house and wasted no time garaging the car, entering the kitchen, and setting the alarms. The next moment they were holding on to each other for dear life and shaking like leaves being buffeted by a tornado. After a deep, cleansing, hungry kiss, Bent groaned, "Let's go upstairs."

In the bedroom, the cats looked up from their tangled pile of fur on the bed and meowed in greeting. When ignored by the two humans who were intent only on removing each other's clothes, Zorro and Lolita shared a look of boredom, rose, and left the room.

Bent stripped the last of Daria's underwear from her, threw the bedcovers on the floor, picked her up and laid her on the bed. She was so beautiful, he thought as he removed his shorts and joined her, pulling her into his favorite position on their sides facing each other. "I was so afraid I was going to lose you today," he murmured between kisses on her lips, neck, and shoulder. "Facing those assholes with nothing but a spell—it was like a nightmare come true."

She arched against him as his lips found a particularly sensitive point behind her ear and his thumb rubbed her nipple into a hard point. "I had the same thought," she whispered, and she hugged him fiercely. "But we make a pretty good team, don't we?"

"A team of dragons!" he chuckled. "My own dragon queen!"

Daria rolled her eyes at that, and they grinned at each other. "How do dragons make love?" she asked.

"Let me show you," Bent answered. He kissed her long and deep before moving over her and between her legs.

They locked hands and gazes.

"Yours and mine."

"Yours and mine."

Raised on his arms, Bent thrust into her moist, silky depths, drawing a sigh of pleasure from her and a grunt of satisfaction from him. He began to move. What started slowly gained in speed and strength as she lifted to meet him, urging him on. Each placed a hand on the other's magic center and power arced between them. Their simultaneous orgasms arched their backs, fused their hips, and threw them together into oblivious ecstasy.

Spent, he collapsed into her tight embrace, and they simply

held each other tight until breath and awareness returned.

Returning reluctantly to reality, Bent rolled to his side, taking her with him, holding her close, exchanging small kisses and languid caresses while they recovered.

Sweet Heaven, Bent thought. Alaric said being soulmates gets better all the time, and he was right. Then memories of the afternoon surfaced. He had been so frightened for her when those idiots showed up with guns and the possibility of losing her had been excruciatingly real. His arms tightened around her as he remembered the fear. He had not known what to do and probably would have tried some foolhardy stunt that would have gotten them both killed. But for Daria and her ability. She had turned him into a dragon! True, it was only the illusion of one, but the strength and speed she imbued him with had been real. He grinned fiercely at the satisfaction he still felt from throwing those bastards across the room.

Soulmates, he reflected, thinking back over the past weeks. The loving, the companionship, the laughter, the primal pleasure of sharing lives, the mountain-moving sex, the soul-searing certainty of completion both in and with her. There was not a doubt in his mind: they were meant for each other, meant to be with each other, forever.

What about his job? Could he stand being separated from her by his job? How would he handle all the travel he did, all the long stays in cold towns? The answer was, hell no, he refused to be separated. He'd talk to Joe tomorrow; he had some rearranging of his life to do.

He drew back so he could see her face. "Daria, open your eyes." When she did so, he murmured, "Soulmates. We've been well and truly mated." Then he frowned. Something was still missing between them. He hadn't told her everything.

"Well and truly," Daria replied, her own hands wandering down his back, then around and up to his shoulders. How much she loved this man, she thought; she could almost burst with happiness. She had been so downright stupid, so colossally fatuous, so absurdly arrogant, to think she could ignore the soulmate imperative. What would she have lost had refused she to have anything to do with him? If she had continued to deny the soulmate concept? Her heart and soul, that was all. What had her father told him? Being soulmates just gets better all the time? Oh, yes.

"I love you, you know."

She tilted her head back so her eyes could focus on his. She paused and could feel him holding his breath. "Oh Bent, I love you too."

Bent expelled the breath he was holding, and hugging her tightly, kissed her hard.

She hugged him back. She hadn't realized how much she needed to hear those words until he said them, and a feeling of utter joy washed through her. She was certain her entire body was glowing with happiness.

Bent suddenly looked somber, then a big grin crossed his face, and he started chuckling.

"What?" she asked.

"Oh, I just thought of something your father told me.

About how what's between a man and a woman is the oldest kind of magic."

"He's right, you know."

"Yes, indeed. You make me feel downright magical. Who knows? I may become a wizard after all." He paused to kiss her again. After a few more kisses, he said, "I've been thinking. What if I settled down at one company, quit this running around the country?"

"Is it what you really want to do? I don't want you to give up what you love to do." She hadn't thought about how they'd manage if he traveled all the time or if she traveled with him. Or what would happen with her career. She tried not to show her sudden apprehension at his answer.

"Even before I met you, I was having second thoughts about playing the turnaround game. I caught myself a couple of times getting tired of the travel and not having a place of my own—to come home to."

"Do you think the imperative could have had something to do with it? Sort of softening you up?" she asked.

"Hell if I know, but living here with you, well, the thought of being apart for any length of time makes my stomach hurt, with or without the imperative. I'm going to tell Joe Glennell I'm unavailable for turnarounds. I want to be permanent CEO of Glennell-Houston. I want to stay here with you. When are we getting married?" he asked, punctuating his question with another kiss.

She smiled again at his assumption. It wasn't a romantic proposal, but he was certainly clear about what he wanted.

She made some rapid calculations in her head. "In two or three months?"

"How about next Saturday?" he countered.

"My mother will kill us both if we deprive her of the opportunity to throw a wedding. Besides, we have family and friends who will certainly want to be there. We need to give them some sort of notice. And most importantly, I haven't even met your brother and sisters," she added, poking him in the chest for emphasis. "Don't worry, the time will fly and you won't have to do much," she assured him.

He had envisioned—well, he didn't know what he had envisioned—standing up before a judge, flying to Las Vegas? Then it didn't matter how big the shindig was and he began to look forward to showing her off, claiming her before God and witnesses. "Whatever you want, honey, just as long as we're together. Now kiss me, little witch. I love you so much."

"I love you, too," she replied and complied with his demand.

Some time later Zorro and Lolita walked into the darkened bedroom and glanced at the two sleeping humans and then at each other. They smiled in feline approval and settled into the rumpled bedspread on the floor. Zorro gave Lolita a lick on the ear, she nuzzled his head, and both sets of soulmates slept.

For more information

about other great titles from

Medallion Press, visit

www.medallionpress.com